About the Author

Robb Heckel is a writer, aspiring songwriter and lifestyle consultant, with over 40 years experience in healthy living practices. Robb has been an editor, published several academic pieces in the Honors Department at the University of Colorado at Colorado Springs, written a humor column, and several technical white papers. *Beneath It All* is Robb's debut novel, and he is busy writing more novels and short stories, as well as nonfiction books on living life well.

After earning his Bachelor of Science degree in Business Administration, Robb worked in nonprofit and information technology fields before following a life path in alternative health. He also holds a Master of Library Science degree. A Colorado native, Robb currently resides in the Sangre de Cristo Mountains near Santa Fe, New Mexico and his soul's home is Tofino, British Columbia, Canada.

Robb can be contacted at RobbHeckel@yahoo.com

Beneath It All

Robb Heckel

First Paperback Edition: February 2017

Published by Applied Holistics

ISBN 978-1-946736-05-5 (pbk.)

Acknowledgements

Thank you deeply and warmly to all who contributed to the great success of *Beneath It All*:

For enduring and endearing personal support and feedback: my sweetheart Liz, Cheryl Conklin, and many others so heartwarmingly numerous.

For technical assistance: Swiss-German language, Mucca Thümena and Maria Huber, Adliswil, Switzerland; aeronautical accuracy, Mike Lee and Bob Warren, Colorado Springs, Colorado; Spanish language, Maria Goñi, University of Colorado at Colorado Springs, and Robert Romero, Pecos, New Mexico.

For permission: Larry Norman, British Columbia, Canada; Albert Foote and friends, relations and acquaintances, Fort Peck Indian Reservation, Montana; Tom Clark Jr, Clark's Market, Aspen, Colorado; Jeremy Martin, Eldorado Natural Spring Water, Louisville, Colorado; Justin Todd and Sally Spaulding, The Little Nell, Aspen, Colorado; Chris "Dancer" Curran, Salon Tullio, Aspen, Colorado; Ryan Slabaugh, *The Aspen Times*; Donald M. Schusten, The Snowmass Club, Aspen, Colorado; Phillipe Gudin, Le Rosey, Rolle, Switzerland; William Jay Blackburn, Colorado Springs, Colorado; Vicki Nash, Glenwood Hot Springs, Glenwood Springs, Colorado; Jennifer Hobson, Ojo Calienté, New Mexico; Kiko Peña, Mi Casita, Carbondale, Colorado; Frederick Thomas, MHz Networks, Falls Church, Virginia; Robert Martin and Aggie Damron-Garner, The Lensic Performing Arts Center, Santa Fe, New Mexico; Cheryl Pick Sommer, Kaune's Neighborhood Market, Santa Fe, New Mexico; Gordon Hawkins, Colorado Springs, Colorado; Isabelle Koomoa, Guadalupé Cafe, Santa Fe, New Mexico; Joe Hoback, Pink Adobe,

Santa Fe, New Mexico; Daryll Stevens, Colorado College Music Library, Colorado Springs, Colorado; Charles Miner, Tesuque Glassworks, Tesuque, New Mexico; T. Kern Hicks, Shidoni Foundry and Galleries, Tesuque, New Mexico; Becky Elder and Michael Galvin, Manitou Springs, Colorado; Bryant Jones, Manitou Springs, Colorado; William Goldsmith, Radio Paradise, Paradise, California; Jan Garvernick, Manitou Springs, Colorado; Lydia Vallejo Martinez, Vallejo's Restaurant, Colorado Springs, Colorado; Farley McDonough, Adam's Mountain Café, Manitou Springs, Colorado; Thomas R. Warren, Mount Princeton Hot Springs Resort, Nathrop, Colorado.

Beneath It All

Chapter One: Up the Mountain

I was instantly attracted to that soft, sexy voice.

In my line of work, that is not a good thing.

I teach people to breathe underwater.

I've learned to be very happy underwater, but there's still one piece missing.

For now, I'm a life coach getting underway to meet my new client. The journey will take me over the Continental Divide, atop the Rocky Mountains, to a small town in one of the most beautiful high mountain valleys in all Colorado. A town where a dilapidated, two-room cabin on a six thousand square foot lot will sell for over four million. Dollars. But, that has little to do with breathing underwater. The rest is up to you.

~~~

On another gorgeous, overcast, late August Colorado mountain morning, 'Toids Café is quiet at 9:00. Lots of Manitoids don't exactly rise with the crack of dawn, and if they do, it's to paint or sculpt or run or levitate or something until a little later in the morning, before venturing out into the world.

Gazing out the window into downtown Manitou Springs from my golden, handmade black walnut table, I slowly sip maté and devour a couple of steam-poached, farm fresh eggs. Breakfast includes locally grown organic tomato slices, fresh goat feta cheese, and crushed, homegrown organic basil and thyme. Oh, and just-out-of-the-oven, sweet spelt bread. The bell on the door jingles.

"Matt! What's happenin', my man?"

"Hey, Josh. I'm just enjoying breakfast on my way out of town." After our old-school hand-shake-palm-glide-fist-bump-explosion, I sweep an open hand toward the other booth seat. "Join me for a
~~~

while?”

"Sure. Can't stay long, though. Let me refill my maté." Maté and coffee are self-serve here at 'Toids. He plops down with distinctly athletic grace, and reaches for a slice of my toast. "Where you headed?"

"Aspen."

"Dude, Aspen?"

"Yep. New client."

"Awesome. Why Aspen?"

"She lives in Snowmass. I'm going up to meet her."

"Snowmass is one of the ski resorts, right?"

"Well, yes, but Wynne lives in Old Snowmass."

"Where's that?"

"It's maybe ten miles west of Aspen, down valley toward Basalt."

"Didn't you do that library gig up there somewhere?" He brushes a tiny toast crumb from a deftly trimmed, short beard.

"Yep. Executive Director of the Roaring Fork Library District. I really miss that valley—especially the rivers, the water. Hey, how do you guys know you have crumbs in your beard?"

"Intuition, my man, intuition. Except for heavy chunks, of course."

Laughing, I barely manage to avoid losing a mouthful of egg and feta. With grand drama, Josh leans back and rests his head on the high-back booth seat, closes his eyes, paints himself into a satisfied smile, and strokes that auburn facial fur, as though petting a favored soft hamster. He slowly opens his eyes and sits up again. "Gotta take off bro'. Headed to Denver to stage a show at the Center for Performing Arts." He slides out, maté cup in the left hand, his right fist and mine colliding in a farewell bump. "Be there four days."

"Cool. I'll be in Aspen a week and a half."

"Nice. Have some fun, okay?"

"That's the plan. See you when I get back."

"Later."

"Later."

With breakfast done, I take my time, savoring not just another spectacular mountain monsoon morning, but also the prospect of meeting Wynne. Part of living a good life, from this life coach's viewpoint, involves enjoying opportunities to experience and re-experience those things that bring gratitude. Like a family dog doing what comes naturally, I roll often in the joyful stuff of life: energetic, smiling, and grateful.

<center>~~~</center>

Maroonbaru is waiting patiently under shady, ancient willows next to Fountain Creek. After giving thanks to *Mde Wakan* (Dakota Sioux: sacred water), I swing open the driver side door, slide over the felt velour seat, settle in as though melting into my own skin, belt up, and start the engine. 'Bu purrs, surely aware we're beginning a favorite journey, west into the Rocky Mountains via Highway 24. Ute Pass begins at the end of Manitou Springs, not more than a half-mile from 'Toids.

Maroonbaru and I speed by hundreds-strong herds of bison grazing in expansive South Park—probably not the indigenous genetic strain preserved, thanks to Lieut. Col. A. G. Brackett, in Yellowstone, but still, buffaloes. My fantasy Ferrari and I cruise effortlessly, passing below massive, roll down your window and touch 'em, Collegiate Peaks Range fourteeners: Yale, Oxford, and Harvard; a modest sampling of the great Continental Divide. Heading north out of Buena Vista, I risk a speeding ticket on this often-patrolled, smoothly engineered, curving, four-lane mountain highway. Cruising just under 80 miles an hour, my inner ear senses little more than a gentle, musical swinging from side to side. A lazy left wrist dangles loose across the top of the steering wheel while my right wrist holds strong and steady at 2:00. It's a comfortable 70-mile-an-hour limit spanning this soft, sixteen-mile stretch of US 24 West.

I encounter zero state troopers and almost no traffic. Turning west onto Colorado 82, toward Twin Lakes, I see both reservoirs still at least thirty feet low, not replenished by blessed and voluminous rains of a glorious, but nowadays rare, monsoon season. With another chunk of organic German dark chocolate sensually, slowly, melting across my tongue, I slow to fifty-five in the forty zone as four lanes of Highway 82 narrow to two, beginning serpentine curves that continue for forty-three miles up, over, and down Independence Pass into Aspen.

Having lived for a few years down valley from Aspen, I know this pavement intimately, and often drive 'Bu like he's a 1995 F50 Barchetta; not the traditional Rosso Corsa Red but transformed especially for this trip into another traditional Ferrari color, Argento Nurburgring metallic gray, much like today's billows overhead. What a fun, narrow mountain pass this is: tight, twisting curves, and stomach-wrenching cliffs—right there outside your car door, vertigo compelling

3

you over the edge—and all the while you inhale brilliantly clean, chill alpine air sweeping up or down sheer mountainsides, a mere stomach knot away.

In a couple thousand-foot-long stretches, Independence is one lane. Seriously, only one skinny, nine-foot-wide lane; extremely tight turns, zero visibility around those heart-bouncing corners—a solid rock south face to one side, the other side a steep tumble a thousand feet and more, all the way down to giant, jagged rocks opposing bursting water at the bottom, christening the Roaring Fork River. Did I mention no road shoulders? In my sure-footed Ferrari, I tiptoe through those playgrounds.

Pushing to pop my bladder are this morning's twenty-two ounce maté with coconut milk and stevia, and the downing of a full liter of home-filtered, bicarb-added, Colorado tap water. It's time for a pit stop during this delicate-scented, moisture-laden, cloudy, high mountain morning—a ten-minute break on the awesome drive to Aspen—where I'm looking forward to meeting my new client, whose silk telephone voice still captivates my always-agile imagination.

This year, like too many years for more than a decade now, there isn't a single dusty snowdrift remaining in August up here at 12,095 feet. Not even in numerous usual places where seventy-foot drifts live most of the rest of the year: This pass is only open Memorial Day through Labor Day. The small summit parking lot is filled with SUVs, an occasional vintage Subaru, and a platoon of RVs of all body types and personalities. The perm-a-potties call my name. They know me well.

~~~

Most happily relieved, I take a short stroll to the summit, and there stand in yoga mountain pose, unhurriedly emptying and refilling grateful lungs and blood with scant above-timberline oxygen, enveloped in the thick, clinging fog that is clouds. After something like seven minutes of that meditation, with just a whisper of lightheadedness, I slide back inside comfy old Maroonbaru and head down the west side, windows wide open, toward the Roaring Fork Valley.

The aspen trees aren't beginning to turn yet, though colder temperatures accompanying monsoon rains have tinged some leaves with golden-black trim, and whole slopes glow noticeably orange-green—especially where sunlight pokes a hole through flowing cotton balls to spotlight an occasional mountainside glen. And below, the
~~~

Roaring Fork is truly a River, even here at its headwaters—pounding like spring thaw.

'Bu and I delight in the descent, pretending four wheel drifts through tight curves and wild acceleration down short straights, until settling in behind a six member peleton, grudgingly drafting a giant RV—longer than the posted legal limit for this perilous pass—even without its hybrid car in tow. Our last eleven miles are tediously pedestrian.

After refilling Maroonbaru's gas tank with resort-priced fuel, my second stop is Clark's Market. I purchase simple necessities: Eldorado Natural Spring Water bottled just outside Boulder; organic Honey Crisp apples, Bing cherries, and heavenly peaches, from lush Colorado orchards around Paonia; plus non-native oranges and grapefruits to keep my pH balanced. To help feed a lightning-quick metabolism, my trusty big-black-librarian's-book-bag is packed already with four pounds of organic nuts, seeds, and dried mangoes, pineapples, and dates; all stuffed in front of my journal, drawing pad, mobile office, and camera. It's a load.

Also in my book bag are an unopened box of Certified Organic Maté and twenty-five, German 85% dark chocolate bars. As a lifestyle consultant, setting a well-rounded example is imperative.

Chapter Two: The Little Nell

The moment he notices me strolling in, Steffan bursts into a smile brighter than this gleaming, five-star hotel lobby. We endured a difficult hour arranging a room for me here at the Little Nell, during my last Colorado Public Library Directors annual conference—seven years ago. He and I were truly gentle and gracious with each other at a tense moment. People remember things like that. Even after thriving here in Aspen for more than a decade, Steffan's buoyant, Swiss-German accent remains. "Mr. Hale! How are you, sir?"

"I'm really well, Steffan. Thank you for asking. How are you, my friend?"

"Sir, I am living in Aspen, Colorado, and happy as can be!" He's not being superficial, or simply saying what a guest might want to hear—Steffan is genuinely happy. He turns to a pretty, middle-aged desk clerk with ruddy, curlish hair. Nell hospitality staff speak to each other in Swiss-German when not addressing guests. *"Bitte, kümmern Sie sich um das Gepäck und das Auto von Herr Hale, und bringen sie ihn zu Zimmer 403. Danke, Renate."*

My keys, of course, are in the car. Steffan doesn't even ask. A discernibly mischievous glint in his eyes, he extends a key card, room number not visible, lodged between his left index and middle fingers. "Ms. Worner let us know you would be arriving today, and has arranged your entire stay, Mr. Hale. We are informed to provide you with anything you might request. Have you any questions or instructions, sir?"

"Not at the moment, Steffan. Thank you."

"Renate will show you the way. Please let me know if you require anything at all, sir." Renate was already around the front desk, walking up to me, her head slightly bowed but eyes trained on mine. After offering a hearty smile and gentle nod, my head swivels back to Steffan.

"Thank you, Steffan, as always, for your kindness."

"Mr. Hale, it is purely my honor."

Hands in prayer—*anjali mudra*—I bow my head and turn to Renate. We head for the brass and oak elevator. Her darting eyes hint that Renate is nervous, probably because I insisted on carrying my own bags: gym bag, black book bag, and paper grocery sack.

"On second thought, Renate, I wonder if you might carry the grocery sack. I don't want it to tear."

She beams. "Of course, sir."

Turning my head side-to-side in the all-mirror elevator car, I notice my disheveled ponytail. Oh, well.

She stands aside while I insert and remove the key card. My computer bag and two pieces of old, airport beltway-soiled luggage are already in my room. I mean, these babies are so old they never even had wheels. Renate sets the groceries down on a marble kitchen countertop.

"Would you like me to help you unpack, Mr. Hale?"

"Oh, thank you Renate, but I can do that."

Backing out the door, she refuses a tip by raising her white-gloved left hand, palm toward me, like a traffic cop. In perfectly enunciated English, she says, "That has been taken care of, sir." I shove the bills in my pants pocket. Putting my hands together in prayer posture, I bow again, while our eyes touch.

Strolling through my temporary home, I'm struck by how much nicer 403 is than other rooms I've stayed in here at the Nell. I don't need a suite, but this *is* nice. The parlor has a half bath, small kitchen with a gas stove, and a maple dining table with eight high-backed chairs. A tastefully subtle, camelback woolen sofa and two matching Queen Anne armchairs are arranged in a semicircle in front of a gorgeous, floor-to-ceiling, moss rock fireplace. Next to that lives a not-mini-bar in a huge entertainment center. Too bad I'm not a television person. Well, there are public broadcasting and good cinema.

Discretely segregated from the parlor is a master bedroom. Its water closet sports a copious whirlpool tub, separate glazed-in shower, and two well-lighted vanities. Hemingway would like this room. Throughout the suite walls are dark wood, and elegant red on gold, raised fleur-de-lis wallpaper. I draw open heavy burgundy curtains to a spectacular view northwest over Aspen and the Roaring Fork Valley. I could live here. I'll need a substantial increase in income, however. Right away, I hop into the shower. Well, after undressing.

~~~

Time to unpack. Chocolate bars in the dinky refrigerator, alongside the fresh fruits, premium coconut milk, and organic maple syrup. I like my maté sweet and rich. I did also bring a shaker of Stevia to supplant the maple syrup. Business attire, more casual than dress, and a little outdoors gear is all I brought. No tie. Come on, this is Aspen after all. I'm prepared to be overdressed as it is, thinking a crisp, professional first impression might be best.

Up onto a polished pine fireplace mantle goes my life coach traveling library, arranged neatly in a bell curve: tallest pieces just off-center and to the right—away from the door. Life is art—and *Feng Shui*. I connect my ancient portable computer to an Internet jack above the writing desk, open it and tenderly press the power button. The Little Nell, for security, is optionally wired rather than wireless—as is my home, for that matter. Peeling an afternoon grapefruit, I check email, and then surf over to *The Aspen Times* website.

Even though this compact town is a well-known playground of the wealthy and famous, when reading *The Aspen Times* one rarely recognizes anything other than ordinary-seeming local news. There are mostly normal, small-town-sounding letters to the editor—well, okay, maybe quite a few better-constructed thoughts than many newspapers I've seen. A bull mastiff bit someone. This wasn't the fault of all bull mastiffs. Traffic backups at the roundabout are way out of control.

Sitting at the writing desk, in one of two heavy, white, Little Nell-emblazoned terry robes hanging in the cedar-lined, walk-in master closet, I add a few thoughts to my spiral-bound notebook-slash-journal before dressing for the evening.

> *The trip over the pass was damp, and totally awesome. The rains are such a blessing. As always, Maroonbaru handled like an F50. Steffan's still head clerk—recognized me like I was here just last week. Clark's is exactly the same. I'm in a freakin' suite—and it's incredible. I feel a little guilty. It's huge, and finely appointed. It's like the Presidential Suite or something. A toast—to providing clients your very best.*

I raise my water glass, no ice, to the guy in the mirror over the
~~~

desk.

After trying numerous ensembles, I decide on a pale pastel yellow, athletic fit, button down, professionally pressed shirt, lightweight gabardine slacks, and my favorite Harris Tweed. Even though it's August in Aspen, nighttime temperatures still get down into the fifties and forties. Plus, the jacket has discreet purple, orange, and green vertical pinstripes to color coordinate with my shirt. I'm doing okay maintaining a relaxed state, but as six o'clock approaches I meditate on centering with deep breathing. I'm really looking forward to this project—and to meeting Wynne.

~~~

At five minutes before six the Little Nell lobby is bustling. My book bag and I retreat to the seating lounge. I pull out my sketchbook, and pencil a sketch of Hemingway, sitting over there in a well-lighted corner, reading the paper, sipping a julep, cigar resting in the ashtray.

Every time those heavy main doors open, I look up. Thus far, no one clicking across the white marble lobby floor is looking for her life coach. Coming in the door are so many sturdy, double-handled shopping bags that it seems nothing might be left to purchase in Aspen. It is true that some shops in Aspen purvey unique, tasteful, high quality treasures.

Then my heart stops—so hard I feet a twinge of pain: a sharp, slicing cramp from upper left to lower right.
~~~

Chapter Three: Wynne and I

Into the foyer saunters a slender, sandy-blonde beauty, with wrap-around sunglasses pushed up on top of slightly tussled, naturally wavy, shoulder blade length hair. She's wearing a pomegranate-colored shirtwaist summer dress—the dress dancing perfectly in step with a gait so serene, she seems to be gliding. Almost certainly silk, the dress is hemmed three or four inches above the knee in front, and drips longer behind. It's strapless, with smocking gathered above firm, unfettered breasts; leaving smooth neck and shoulders exposed for every male animal to ache to kiss. Sucking in air, I stand up, raising a shaky arm.

She smiles affectionately, and waves vigorously, like we're ancient friends. I stop breathing again. Floating elegantly up to me, her hand extended, she says, "You *must* be Matt."

"Hello, Wynne."

Even without oxygen, my brain fires a gazillion synaptic connections a second. Do I take this elegant hand with a firm, business shake? Or use the genteel, fingers-in-the-palm greeting a gentleman offers to a Lady?

Hazel Jennings taught me that—how to gently, discretely, kiss the back of a Lady's hand. Hazel watched over me when I was three and four and Mom was working. I offer that greeting infrequently, and usually only in higher social settings. Well, Aspen *is* at almost 8,000 feet. High enough—I go for it.

She gives the greeting no particular notice. Relieved, I don't presume to kiss her hand. I *do* happily notice my own hand isn't trembling—too badly. I look into kind, playful, gray-green eyes. Her smile is so welcoming, so alluring, that my anxieties ooze away.

Softly, she asks, "Should we sit for a minute?"

"Oh—yes, of course." Shaking my head briskly to clear dense fog, I realize I'm behaving like an inexperienced teenager on his first date. My face flashes into a first-degree fireball.

She sets her large, hand woven shoulder bag on the floor. Distinctly Native American, certainly Southwestern, it's probably Navajo, but possibly from one of the New Mexico Pueblos. She spirals down into the chair next to mine. The back of that sleek summer dress is open all the way down to a slender waist. She gently lifts her dress, slowly crossing long, creamy legs. I try, somewhat unsuccessfully, to not watch. The hem lightly and innocently crawls up strong, lightly bronzed thighs. Firmly grabbing each chair arm, I let my strength ease me down, slowly. Falling over won't exactly make a good first impression. Of course, neither will blatant infatuation.

"I must say, Matt, you're just what I expected from your telephone voice."

That statement falls heavy, with a resounding thunk, into the irony column in my already crammed, long-term memory banks. Her voice keeps me mesmerized.

"It's a pleasure to meet you. Have you been to Aspen before?"

Despite a driving impulse to dive right into what she expected from my telephone voice, I manage a response. "Yes. Actually, I've been a local. Some years ago I was executive director of the Roaring Fork Library District. I spent as much time in Aspen as elsewhere in the Roaring Fork Valley. I miss it tremendously: especially the rivers."

"Excellent. Then, unless you say otherwise, I'll dispense with the usual tour."

"Yes, thank you. I do know my way around well enough to stay out of trouble."

"I see you have a notebook. Shall we get started?"

"Oh—no, let's just chat." Slapping the red notebook closed, I stack it onto the sketchbook, and stash both back in my humble, cotton duck, manufactured, black book bag; nestled there on the floor next to her handmade work of art.

She nods, smiling. "Are you pleased with your room?"

"You mean, *suite*? Wildly enthusiastic would be more like it. I apologize for forgetting to mention it. In fact, I'm happy to accept far more modest accommodations."

Again with that alluring smile—and a dismissive hand wave. "Nonsense! I want you to thoroughly enjoy your stay. I thought perhaps we might need a private place to meet. If you're concerned about cost, don't be. The owners are old family friends, so my rates are reasonable."

Smiling, I acknowledge her generosity with a respectful nod. "Thank you."

"Have you thought about where you might like to have dinner?"

Dipping my head in deference, maybe even feeling a little coy, I smile. "Your choice—please—if that's okay with you."

"Shall we go, then? My car is out front." In my experience, the Nell never allows anyone to leave a vehicle in its tiny driveway. But already, I know this isn't just anyone.

We rise from our comfy, not-too-deep armchairs. To my amazement, Wynne takes a light step my way, and leans over, laying a well-toned arm around my back and shoulder. She squeezes me close. She's wearing no perfume. Neither am I. Faintly though, I can smell her hair. Is that lavender and thyme? Maybe jasmine? I inhale delicately. She turns her head directly toward me, inviting eyes searching into mine.

"Matt, I'm so pleased you've come—and on such short notice. Thank you."

"You're quite welcome, though the pleasure is all mine."

She smiles big, releasing my shoulder with a last, strong squeeze. We reach down for our bags. Simultaneously lifting them to our shoulders, hers on her left, mine on my right, we stroll side by side into the lobby. This lovely creature is a little taller than I. And me without my heels.

Chapter Four: Knowing to Get You

"Wynne, I've never driven Owl Creek Road. Where does it go?" We had already passed through the troublesome roundabout at the west edge of Aspen. She was turning south, off Highway 82.

"It serves as access to The Snowmass Club, and of course Snowmass Village. Most people take Brush Creek Road."

"That's the next road down valley, right?"

"You do know your way around."

"Pretty well, except for Owl Creek, I guess."

We curve behind Sardy Field airport, passing kennels stocked with private and corporate jets, and a couple of turboprops.

"Does this road make its way to Old Snowmass?"

"It's a long, slow drive, and the last leg is essentially a four-wheel-drive road, but yes. We nearly always take Wagon Divide."

"One of my library trustees lived in Old Snowmass. It's a beautiful valley."

"A treasure, really. It's mostly larger parcels purchased decades ago, and since kept within families."

"Have you been there that long?"

"Seven years ago we purchased a one hundred and sixty acre ranch. We're still there."

"We?"

"Cassandra, my seventeen-year-old daughter, and myself."

"You're a single mom, then?"

She nods. "I don't mind. Cassie is intelligent, beautiful, and understanding. I have friends who complain about their kids driving them to distraction, or worse. Cassie and I are best buddies. I'm fortunate. How about you, Matt?"

"Never married—no children."

"Really?"

"Well, I didn't want children until I knew, with absolute certainty, that I would be a far better parent than mine. I'm only now getting there. And I've never had a lasting relationship."

"I'm surprised."

"Why?"

"Well, you're handsome, intelligent, and, I suspect, fun. Men like that are usually off the market. Surely you're in a relationship now."

"Nope."

She turns onto the smooth, black-paved drive into The Snowmass Club.

Maybe she didn't hear me. I break the silence. "You know, I've never been here."

"I believe you'll enjoy the Club."

"I believe you're right."

With lowering evening sunlight still available to drive and chase brilliant white golf balls, dapper dudes dot the manicured landscape. A red-vested, red-haired valet runs in front of the Lexus before we even slow to a stop. Following a brief internal debate, before climbing down from the SUV, I actually leave behind my book bag. It's almost never out of my reach. Wynne leads the way through the clubhouse to the restaurant: a spectacular setting, overlooking Brush Creek and the golf course.

"Your table is ready, Ms. Worner." We follow the maitre d' to a not-too-small table for two on the deck, commanding a breathtaking vista to the south.

"What a gorgeous view."

She smiles. "And the food is terrific."

The maitre d' pulls out Wynne's chair. Absolved of responsibility, I sit down, after first fumbling for my missing shoulder bag. Habit is habit, life coach or not.

~~~

Taking her first sip, Wynne looks over a St. Émilion into my eyes. These are happy eyes as far as I can see. "Are you a teetotaler, Matt?"

"No, not entirely. I do imbibe, but infrequently." I tip a water glass to my parched lips.

"May I ask why? You're missing an exquisite wine—my favorite here."

"Of course. Please ask anything you want. We need to establish understanding and trust. That comes with knowledge and
~~~

experience."

She nods, setting her wine glass down. "You have yet to damage my trust in you."

I smile. "Good. You need to feel completely comfortable asking me any question at all—knowing I'll respond honestly—and hopefully without judgment. But keep in mind, I need to feel okay asking you questions, too."

"Please do."

"The moment you feel uncomfortable in any way, for any reason, will you please let me know immediately?"

"Yes, of course. On the phone you talked about authenticity. You do follow through with that, don't you?"

"I try. It's just that, if we don't say what we're feeling when we feel it, communication can easily go astray. When we hold on to thoughts or feelings instead of expressing them, they build up inside. Eventually emotions have to be released—often as illness or anger or depression or any number of cathartic waterfalls."

Wynne leans forward, both elbows on the table.

A knot the size and weight of a bowling ball suddenly twists my solar plexus. "I'm sorry. I'm preaching."

"I don't think so. In fact, what you're saying makes perfect sense." She grins. "I think I need to take notes."

Effortlessly as it arose, the knot dissipates. "Probably not." I grin. "I'll badger you with this stuff until you're ready to have me assassinated. It's my job."

She laughs gleefully, eyes closed and head tilting back, breasts bouncing behind soft, pomegranate drapery. "If you're to help me improve my happiness and health, I'm more than willing to be badgered."

"Badgers are feisty critters, though."

She watches my eyes, grinning. "Perhaps you could just hound me?"

It's my turn to chuckle. "You bet. Getting back to the alcohol thing, when I was younger, I drank plenty—mostly aged scotch and dark ales. I'd love to have back those choices."

She nods in acknowledgment, raising her wine glass. "To our health!"

I lift my water glass. Following a wispy tinkling of fine crystal on fine crystal, I reach in for the lemon wedge, squeeze out juice and pulp, drop the wedge onto a saucer, and then savor a sweet-sour, alkaline-generating mouthful. "On the Fourth of July, I drank three beers. Actually, they were superb Colorado microbrew ales. For a short while it was fun being giddy and slightly out of control. With alcohol, though, one always seems to need more and more, to avoid the disorienting crash that always follows. All I drank, Wynne, over five hours and with constant buffet browsing, were those three ales. I felt toxic for four days—just not worth it in my book."

"A little red wine seems to work for me, though I know what you mean. I've often wondered how booze is legal when other options aren't; especially given the documented violence, automobile accidents and horrid health problems that result from alcohol consumption."

Gold pen in hand, up to our table strides a starched, black bow-tied, all-business waiter. I request local trout, caramelized and lightly braised, with steamed vegetables and Northern Minnesota wild rice. Wynne decides on a gargantuan Asian chicken shitake salad, with miso vegetable soup.

"Wynne, will you tell me a little about your background? Details, broad strokes, whatever you feel comfortable with. Take your time."

"Okay. I'll summarize. Please ask if you need to hear more."

"Deal."

"The de Gracias are originally from Spain, and of course I still have family there. We've been in New Mexico for two hundred and fifty years."

My head jerks and eyebrows reach for the sky, as I stop in mid-chew. "*Yiminee!* Two hundred and fifty years? I've known few people, other than Native Americans, whose family has been on this continent *that* long. That's incredible." Covering my mouth after the fact, I resume chewing.

She just smiles sweetly. "To be specific, as of last May, de Gracias have been here for 259 years. A Mexican midwife on the Las Cruces ranch brought me into this world. Our home is still there, although we maintain residences in Santa Fe, San Francisco, coastal Maine, and Zurich. And now, of course, here in Aspen."

"Las Cruces is nice." *Wow!* I'm dining with a beautiful woman many of us meet only in movies.

"You've been, then?"

"An artist buddy and his cultural anthropologist wife moved there several years ago. I've visited twice. Typically I don't go farther south than Santa Fe."

She nods. "I was educated at home until I turned thirteen. Then, in unfaltering family tradition, it was off to boarding school at Le Rosey, at Rolle on Lake Geneva in Switzerland. I earned a Master of Arts in Economics from Yale."

I smile affectionately. "With honors, I presume." I do already know the answer.

She smiles back, also affectionately. "Summa cum laude."

I keep hoping for the alluring smile she gave me when she first saw me. That's *the smile*. I feel deep stirrings when I get *the smile*.

"Boarding school? You said you have a residence in Zurich."

"Le Rosey is strictly residential. Traditional school curriculum includes emotional and developmental training. That's accomplished especially through peer relationships."

"There's an education I could have used."

"Your website indicated you might be self-taught."

"My curriculum was only as thorough as I was able to discover on my own, and with astute recommendations from librarians. However, there remain holes to this day."

"As in us all." After a sip of St. Émilion, she continues. "After my thesis defense, I took a position as Operations Director for the Boston Ballet."

"Awesome!"

"Am I boring you?"

"Are you kidding? This is the heroine's story in my next novel."

She smiles *the smile*. "Flatterer. I don't want to go on too much."

"Wynne, a coach needs to know—besides, we *all* have interesting stories—the least as well as the greatest of us."

She doesn't even blink. "My four-year marriage, to a college sweetheart turned Wall Street pirate, terminated for want of togetherness and love—and a perky little twenty-four-year-old administrative aide. Cassie and I moved from Cambridge to Aspen. We've been here fourteen years." She takes a bite of her salad.

"Shall I start my story, so you actually have time to eat?"

She takes her time to chew carefully, swallowing gently. "Thank you, but you really should enjoy your trout while it's still warm."

I nod, another mouthful already in the food processor.

"Now I manage family holdings and finances, so Mom and Dad are free to travel and smell the orchids. I travel, too, largely on family business. Cassie and I also raise Tobiano Paints."

"Tobiano Paints?"

"Horses."

"A friend of mine raises Appaloosas. And I know Paints, but not Tobiano specifically."

"Tobiano Paints are distinguished by quite large, dark patches on white, as opposed to small patches."

"Nice."

Without warning, Wynne's expression grows dark. She lets out an indelicate nasal snort—it turns out to be an utterance of unbridled disgust. "At the moment, I find myself embroiled in a legal duel with a two-year-departed ex-boyfriend. The son of a bitch is suing me for palimony." She sucks in a little air and covers her mouth.

I conjure a calm voice. "That's the first I've seen you irritated."

Those high cheekbones gradually turn an eensy-weensy bit crimson.

"Wynne, not to worry. You'll undoubtedly hear me say worse. I'm just on my best behavior right now, until you get to know me better."

Another sweet smile flows back into her countenance, returning brilliance to those gray-green eyes. "Then what?"

"Then, you'll hear me say worse."

She laughs. "Well, thank you, but that was uncalled for."

"Remember what I said about holding onto anger or emotions? It's best to let it out, trust me. I tell you what. Let me finish my last bite. Then I'll spin my story, okay?"

Without waiting for an answer, I swim the last fishy forkful around in my plate; rolling it in a pool of trout oil and hollandaise, with a hint of cayenne and fresh dill.

It's my turn to spill the brief-life beans.

Chapter Five: *Cadenza*

Settling back into my dining chair, eyes closed, I cross my hands on my belly. "Mmmm. Thank you for such a fine dinner. That was *muy rico*."

"You're most welcome. Would you like dessert?"

"Thank you, but I'll pass. I rarely have dessert. Instead, I take dark chocolate at midmorning."

Raised eyebrows ask an obvious question.

"Caffeine or sugars are best for me in the morning. At night, I prefer sleep to self-indulgence."

She nods. "That sounds like a good practice." Shifting in her chair, she says, "You seem to know Spanish."

"Not really. *Muy poquito, amiga*—barely enough to order a meal."

"You sound fluent." She grins my way. "I have heard the language before, you know."

"*Gracias, Señora Weene*." We both giggle. My giggle *is* macho, of course. "Well, where do I start?"

"From the beginning?"

"Well, I guess, but I'll do my best to tell a shortened version. Which, by the way, is something I don't do well."

Inquiring eyes, again.

"That is, doing anything condensed."

After a good chuckle, she adds, "Or abridged, from what I've seen so far."

Pursed lips twist in chagrin, as I tilt my head up and to the side, nodding. "Guilty as charged." With face afire, I forge on. "I was born in Colorado Springs. I've done a bazillion jobs, and didn't settle on a career until life coaching."

Wynne is busy choosing crisp salad morsels, so I story on. "After graduating, with a mere cum laude, from the College of Business at the University of Colorado, I had brief work experiences in a museum and a couple other non-profits, sold insurance for a year—yuck—and then studied alternative health care. For seven years I was in private practice as a neuromuscular therapist and registered unlicensed psychotherapist."

She chews carefully, listening, observing my face and eyes.

"When my spine was hurt in a car-train accident, I fell back on computer skills."

Her head snaps to attention. "A car-train accident?"

I nod. "I was a passenger in a car that was hit by a freight train."

"You're joking."

"No, dead serious."

"Seriously?"

"Seriously."

"How did it happen?"

"It was January, after *inipi*—a Sioux sweat lodge ceremony—over in Routt County, near Steamboat Springs. We slid to an icy stop, right in the middle of the tracks. Alan couldn't get the car to move. The tires just spun on the ice. He finally put the accelerator to the floor, in reverse. The car was filling with acrid smoke from burning rubber as we gradually moved backwards—at about an inch an hour."

I pause. Silence. Some who hear this story are incredulous that tires get hot on ice. My guess is they've never been stuck—especially with giant locomotives bearing down on them.

"I took off my seat belt to get out. We actually had plenty of time before we were hit. But it was a brand new Volvo with childproof locks, and a totally black night. I couldn't figure out how to get the door open."

She stops chewing, just watching my eyes.

"When the train was about eighty feet or so away, the horns vibrated my entire body. I simply sat back, in a sort of surreal cognizance: a peaceful acceptance of whatever my fate was to be. From that moment, everything moved in slow motion. Sticky, foul rubber smoke filled the car—it was like trying to see through black fog at midnight in Lubbock. Sparks like hordes of Yellow Swallowtail butterflies illuminated huge wheels shrieking across shiny slick rails, bathing the locomotives' jaws and bodies in an eerie, sickening, golden glow—while a single headlight waved back and forth like a Cyclops' lazy eye—slowly growing bigger and bigger. When the Volvo was finally hit, it was like being inside an explosion. A violent punch rocketed us off the tracks. I was thrown inside the car, and slammed into the driver's seat in front of me."

"That's incredible! Are you okay now?"

"That was nearly twenty years ago. I can still have problems, but most of the time I'm good." Making air quotes with my fingers, I continue. " 'Conventional' physical therapy didn't help much, and insurance would only allow a set number of PT sessions. Eventually I created my own successful rehabilitation. Yoga and Pilates were, and remain, a big part of that."

"Matt, I don't imagine many people live to tell such a story."

"Probably not. I'm grateful. I'm still careful, even though all my adult life, I've continually learned how to protect and use my body. I keep myself in great shape."

"So I've noticed."

Flaming rubescent yet again, I feign not noticing that last comment. "No longer able to employ my back, I gave up my private practice."

"Private practice?"

"Sorry—I provided soft tissue therapy and personal development consulting."

Extending a supine left palm in my direction, she asks, "Didn't you get a lawyer?" Glancing at the salad, she expertly selects and impales a smallish, black, flattop mushroom.

"Yes, and was promptly talked into a diminutive settlement. The lost income actually amounts to hundreds of thousands."

She nods. "I'm sorry. You mentioned a sweat lodge?" Wynne was now comfortable speaking with a small bite in her mouth. She was gracious of course, covering her mouth with her hand.

"I have Dakota Sioux friends and relations. They're on the Fort Peck Indian Reservation in northeastern Montana. I walk the Red Road, to a small degree."

"The Red Road?"

"The traditional *Oceti Sakowin* or Sioux spiritual path. I'm really not qualified to talk much about it. I'm just an infant in those ways— out of abiding respect, I say only what is mine to say."

She nods, gathering another bite on her fork. "I completely understand. Relations? Are you Native American?"

"Not that I know, other than in spirit. We refer often to *friends, relations, and acquaintances.*"

"How did you become a life coach?"

"Life coaching is a natural extension of many years of experience and education. Most of my life—well—yes, my entire life, has been about learning and self-healing. These days I might call it self-sustenance."

"Like after your accident? Doing it yourself, I mean?"

"Yes, but across a full spectrum of living: physical, emotional, intellectual, and spiritual."

"It's important to learn from the best sources, wouldn't you agree?"

"Absolutely. And I hold zero doubts that among those sources is oneself. I think I started in earnest to formally seek the meaning of life in the seventh grade."

"Seventh grade? You were what, thirteen?"

"Twelve. My parents put me in school just after I turned four. It was too early, especially given the emotional abyss I was lost in."

"Emotional abyss?"

I pause. This part of my story always worries me. Will people hear and understand? Will I convey it clearly? Or will I be judged as a self-indulgent victim? "Yes. As a child, I was severely abused. From all my experiences I've learned to empathize with others and to develop a proclivity for profound insight." I feel my upper lip curl in a grimace. "I hope that doesn't sound too egoistic."

Her eyes widen. "Can you say more?"

"About insight?"

Her head tilts. She might be thinking. Her eyes console the child in mine as she quietly says, "The abuse."

"Maybe another time. My childhood doesn't make for pleasant dinner conversation."

"Fair enough. Another time, then."

"So, vivid nightmares drove me to my parochial school library in search of meanings. I discovered Freud and Jung."

"Parochial school?"

"Yes. Fortunately, a public school fourth grade teacher convinced my parents that mine was an intellect needing private education. Lutheran school was where I landed. My parents were Lutheran."

"Good for you. I assume it was good?"

"Absolutely. It meant small classes and individual attention. From seventh grade on, I've read widely in psychology and philosophy. I read Nietzsche and Kierkegaard, Alfred North Whitehead and Bertrand Russell, Carl Jung and Gestalt psychologists, among other thinkers."

Wynne sets her fork down, lifts her wine glass to her lips, peering over the rim. After a tiny sip, she starts twirling the nearly empty goblet in her fingers. "Did you comprehend those authors?"

"I believe so. At the least, I gathered what I needed to help myself survive."

"Survive the abuse?"

I nod. "And more importantly, mollify my detrimental childhood development. Not that I'm perfect, by any definition."

"Matt, I'm so sorry."

"Thank you, Wynne."

She reaches over to lay her hand on mine, for a moment too brief, like an adoring mother, smoothing her treasured child's forehead.

"Nobody knew I was reading and studying—teaching myself. Not even my parents. They wouldn't have let me. In the manner of Louis L'Amour, I really have, over the course of my life, become a self-educated wanderer."

"But you also have formal education."

"Yes, Business and some Liberal Arts from the University of Colorado, and a Master of Library Science. I've studied accounting, business systems and strategy, fine art, comparative religious theory, philosophy, and other academic rigor, as well as neuromuscular and massage therapy, Oriental medicine and acupuncture, herbology, homeopathy—I could go on, but you get the point."

"You've been through a lot, haven't you, Matt?"

"I like to think I've journeyed much, and crossed mostly to greener shores. Sometimes it takes years following events in our lives, before realizations or knowledge are achieved—sometimes maybe a whole lifetime." I frown a bit: a self-deprecating habit. "My life continues to furnish a plethora of opportunities for growth."

"When you were little, wasn't there anything you could do?"

"I was just a child. I didn't know what existed outside my cage. Now, of course, I understand that I lived inside my head. To a greater extent than I want to admit, I definitely still do. That's how I survived—so it's a deeply habituated pattern."

Her eyes were sad. This time, those long, tanned fingers didn't depart from mine.

"There's still plenty of abuse going on today. Worse than what I lived through, I know. God help those kids—and the kids *they* bring into the world. I go out of my way to compliment people who treat children with love and respect. Well, people who treat *anyone* with respect."

"Were you an only child?"

"I have a brother seven years younger. He received similar treatment."

She squeezes my hand, and then gradually slides it away to lift her wine glass. "So, you were born quite far apart. I imagine you were always in explicitly different developmental stages." After another delicate sip, she slides the glass ever so gently back onto the table. Wynne dabs her lips with a white linen napkin.

I nod. "Excellent observation. We were raised in the same house, but we didn't grow up together."

"What about school? Did you try to talk to a counselor or teacher?"

"I did ask the pastor for help at school. He would quote biblical passages about respecting your parents. I think when I was in Confirmation classes I might have tried to broach the topic with Pastor Shell at our church, but that's all really hazy. I've no clear recollection."

"So—you were completely alone, weren't you, Matt."

"Yes."

Wynne reaches across the table with her napkin, and dabs away my tears, my own *Mde Wakan*. She's not telling me to stop crying, though. Her eyes water, too. I'm at the podium now, speaking on an intimately familiar topic. Once I start talking, often it seems I won't stop. "Should I go on?"

"Only if you care to. Please don't continue on my behalf. I certainly understand what you've described, though I have no personal experience with which to relate. No one in my entire family has ever been touched, so far as I know, except by love."

"You're so fortunate."

A slow smile spreads as she nods. "More, it seems, than I know."

"I did have two neighbor ladies who comforted me. Louise Blackburn was a trusted confidant throughout my childhood and teen years—and a friend all her life. I told her things no one else would ever know. The other was my nanny."

"You had a *nanny*?"

I don't think Wynne is being condescending. I know I don't always comport myself like someone who had nannies. All the same, I'm no sycophant; just maybe not your average guy. "Well, okay, technically not a nanny."

"Please, tell me more. Maybe this explains how you sometimes speak very formally."

Only slightly reddened, I continue. "One of my truly God-sent graces in life was Hazel Jennings. She took care of me days while Mom worked. Mrs. Jennings was English, proper indeed, and grandmotherly, gentle, and wise. She fed me delicious lunches and snacks, taught me etiquette, elocution, and spent lifetimes with me playing learning games—developing my intellect and persona."

I stop to gulp *Mde Wakan*. I can't remember anyone refilling my glass. A fresh lemon wedge is in there, too. I reach in, again with my fingers, to retrieve and squeeze it. That's one sort of action I do with prayer. I try to live every moment as prayer.

"She sounds wonderful."

"Mrs. Jennings was beyond wonderful. I loved her, I'm sure."

"She *was* a nanny, Matt."

Choking up now, waters of both joy and regret eddy near the top of my emotional dam. I lean forward, both elbows supported by the table. I cover my forehead and eyes with my hands. "I still wish I had tried to find her," water's over the top of the dam now, "after she and Mr. Jennings moved to Arizona, before she passed on—to thank her—for so very gracefully—saving my life." That's it. The dam breaks.

Wynne's hands firmly grasp the forearms hiding my eyes. I look up, feeling unprofessional, eyelids soaked, rivers running down my nose and cheeks. "Thank you, Wynne. Let your feelings happen when they're happening, right?"

She nods. Even sad smiles can be exquisitely alluring.

Suddenly, a cell phone plays twelve bars of the Sixth Brandenburg Concerto—startling me, heart instantaneously pounding, into realizing a world outside the two of us still exists.

Chapter Six: *Coachus Interruptus*

"I am so sorry, Matt. I left instructions to not be contacted tonight, so I'm afraid this may be important. Do you mind if I answer?"

"No, of course not! Please take the call. I can't have you entirely to myself, after all." Darn it.

Thrusting a hand into her bag, Wynne is not smiling. "I'll be as quick as possible. I promise."

She gets up and strides briskly to the foyer, phone at her ear. Following a hasty, animated conversation, she says something to the maitre d' before rushing back to our table.

I stand—ready to toss my napkin on the table and go. "What's wrong?"

"One of the Paints has been hurt. I need to get home. I'll see you tomorrow. Is it okay if the Club car takes you back to the hotel?"

"Absolutely! Is there anything I can do to help?"

A brief twinkle flickers under darkened brows. "Not unless you feel your veterinary skills are up to date."

"No, of course. I'd be in the way. Please, go quickly. I'll be fine."

Obviously needing to leave, Wynne is still gracious. "May I call you in the morning? About nine would be good, if that works for you."

My head bobs emphatically. "I'll expect your call at nine. Please don't hesitate to call at any time—for any reason."

She extends her hand. This time I bow, and kiss it, earning her most alluring smile.

"Thank you for a most interesting evening. And now I really must go. *Ciao.*"

Hands together at my heart, I bow. When I look up again, she's already twenty feet away.

I call after her. "Oh, wait. My bag's in the SUV."

Without looking, she waves the back of her hand. "I'll have the valet bring it in."

I pray aloud. "*Vaya con Dios, amiga. Hasta mañana.*" I don't know much Spanish, but the twenty-five words I know, I do pronounce and use pretty well.

Hers is now a fervent stride, rather than the elegant glide to which I've become accustomed. She hesitates at the foyer arch to look back, slowly raising her right hand, palm toward me, and waves it at waist height, from left to right—then turns and disappears. Some of my Dakota family do that, too.

~~~

Reclining in my solitary chair, at this table for two with a view, I pause for reflection. Thoughts, images, impressions, and feelings whirl around inside like a Pine Ridge dust devil. The maitre d' walks over. It's a welcome interruption. I sit up straight as he approaches.

"Are you finished, Mr. Hale?"

I don't remember mentioning my name to anyone here at the Snowmass Club. "Yes, thank you. The meal was excellent, and the service superb. My water glass was filled twice, with fresh lemon each time. I never even noticed who poured it. As I see it, or would provide it, that is exemplary service."

He smiles politely, though not perfunctorily. "Thank you, sir. I'll have the car brought around front for you, if you'll give me about five minutes. Unless you might care for a nightcap, sir?"

"You know, I'll have a glass of the St. Émilion."

He gives an approving nod and smile.

"Thank you. I'll just relax for a spell. Where can I find the valet?"

"I'll retrieve your—bag, is it, sir?" He follows the deadpan with a grin.

"Ah, a comedian."

"I didn't mean to offend."

"And you didn't. In fact, you'd better plan on getting paid back double, next time I'm here."

He grins. "Looking forward to it, sir. I'll get that most exquisite wine."

Once again I recline—okay, it's really a slump—but dignified, sort
~~~

of.   Looking out the bay window, it's near twilight now.   Over mountains less than two miles to the south, fair weather cumulus gather late evening pastels melting into rose.   I go foggy, fading into yesterday.

"Hello, this is Matt."

"Are you the life coach?"

"That would be me."

She has a creamy, literary voice.   "Do you help people who feel stuck?"

"I do my best.   How are you stuck?   Is it mud or cement?"

"I don't know.   If I did, I mightn't have called."

"You know you don't know.   That's good."   I like the way she said that.   Mightn't.   It reminds me of someone.   "What can I do for you?"

"I'd better think about this.   I apologize for bothering you."   Click.   Well, it wasn't really a click.   It was more like a solid, decisive, but not necessarily angry, receiver to cradle—a jab at the stop button.

Her voice—mellifluous, unaffected, and sexy—explores my....

"Your wine, sir."   As consciousness groggily merges back into the present moment, I observe a nearly black bottle, cradled and collared in a white linen towel and two gloved hands, extended low enough for me to examine the label.   It turns out to be *Premiers grands crus classés.* He pours an ounce in a goblet, plucks it from a sterling tray, sets it in the open palm of his hand, and bows to allow me to take the glass from his hand.

"I'm sure it's excellent."

"I insist you try it first, sir: house policy, you know."   Another smile.

I swirl the burgundy clockwise, sniff and sip; counterclockwise, sniff and sip; then hold the goblet so I can peer through at a chandelier, following another set of slow, silky smooth, well toned legs. "Nah, take it back."

Ignoring me, he pours into the goblet—until I realize he's going to fill 'till I stop him.   "When!" He smiles a little more brazenly this time. There are easily eleven ounces in the glass.

"I'm going to need at least half an hour, thanks to you." We both grin.

"Please let me know if you need anything else, Mr. Hale," he says as he tenderly places the wrapped baby on the table.

"I'll holler across the room."

Suppressing mirth, he takes his dramatic time surveying a still-packed, formal dining room. "Excellent, sir." He bows, stands, turns, and strides away, straight as a lodgepole pine—white gloves standing out like a brilliant full moon, tray balanced on the extended five fingers of his left hand, right hand and forearm in parade rest, rigid behind his back. I clap quietly.

Gazing again through the goblet, I know I've been a redder red numerous times this evening. But, that's who I am—and where I still swim. I "recline" a third time, fill my desirous mouth with several ounces of St. Émilion, and let the dining room fade into a blur.

Her greeting is more musical acknowledgment than inquiry as she says, "Hello."

"Hi. This is Matt Hale, returning Wynne's call."

"Yes, Mr. Hale. Thank you so much for calling back."

"You're very welcome. If you like, please call me Matt."

She hesitates. "Okay—Matt."

"Wynne—may I call you Wynne?"

"Thank you, yes. I prefer that."

"Wynne, I'm sorry about earlier. Sometimes I kid around with people before getting to know them. Or worse—before they get to know me."

"That's fine, but please let me apologize for my impatience. I was rude."

"Not to worry. How may I help you?"

"I'm not handling things well."

"I see. Let me jot down a bit of information, if you don't mind."

Silence.

"Would you mind spelling your name so I don't damage it in the future?"

"Yes, thank you. That's very thoughtful. W-y-n-n-e ... d-e ... G-r-a-c-i-a ... B-r-o-c-k-m-a-n ... W-o-r-n-e-r."

"Is that capital D and space before capital G?"

"Actually, it's lower case d with a space. Very good. I'm impressed."

"It's a long and beautiful name."

"Long? Try Wynne Luis María Caveza de Gracia Brockman Worner."

"Wow. Even more beautiful in my book. What can I do for you?"

"I'm not sure. Yesterday I saw a magazine article about life coaching. It seemed an intriguing idea, so I searched the Internet and found your name."

"You saw my website?"

"Yes."

That calls for a celebratory sip of wine. Not quite so groggy when I exit a mental movie by my own choice, I pick up the glass. Its contents are nearly half gone. I've not been paying attention. The in-flight movie is captivating—even if it is a rerun.

"Wynne, how about we start with where you feel you need coaching."

"I've been under stress. I'm not sleeping well at all, and my thoughts seem muddled."

"I understand." These are symptoms. Maybe she's unsure where she needs help. *"Would it help if I describe my customary procedure?"*

"What a fine idea. Thank you."

"Typically, I meet with a prospective client for an hour or two. At our first meeting, we identify dietary, emotional, and other lifestyle habits. Then we create a preliminary concept for addressing the client's specific circumstances, and adjust it until

we feel committed to our plan. We negotiate each other's boundaries and needs, and decide whether to go forward."

"I like that, though your approach sounds rather personal."

"True. It is—and that applies to both of us—you learn about me, too. If this makes you too uncomfortable, I understand. That's okay. My methodology doesn't fit with every person who contacts me."

"I must admit to feeling a bit uneasy. What are your fees?"

"Sixty an hour, plus expenses."

"Frankly, that sounds ridiculously reasonable."

"I maintain a modest lifestyle."

"Alright, I'll give it a try. To be honest with you, I feel lost, as though I'm drifting. I only get through routine days. I'm not sure I've recognized that until just now. Just talking with you helps me feel better—you know what?"

"I give up."

She chuckles. "I want to meet you. Tomorrow, if you're available."

"I'd be honored."

"Wonderful! What comes next?"

"We set up a time to meet in person. Where are you?"

"I live just outside Aspen, in Old Snowmass."

My eyes pop wide. "I can do that. But I think I'd need a place to stay overnight. I probably can't get to Aspen until around three tomorrow afternoon."

"I'm happy to arrange that."

"I'll put together a preliminary plan after our first meeting. Next morning we can get together again and hash out details. After I return to Manitou Springs, we can work by email and telephone."

"Matt, let's say, hypothetically, that you were coaching only one client. How long would you initially need to work with that

client?"

"That answer really depends on the client."

"What I mean to say, I suppose, is—if you focus on my situation exclusively, how much time or how many days would we need in order to get things moving as quickly as possible?"

"With most clients, I try to reach agreement on contact at least once a day for seven days. That way we can focus on habits and patterns over a full week. Then we confer as frequently as each client prefers."

"Then, is it reasonable for you to plan on staying in Aspen for a week?"

"Well, yes…."

"That is, of course, after we decide to go forward. Though, I must say I'm feeling confident that will be the case."

"You're suggesting a week in Aspen, expenses paid?"

"I realize this is short notice."

"I'd be happy to come for a week."

"I'll see about a room at the Little Nell Hotel, if that's acceptable. Can we meet over dinner? What do you think? Matt?"

I snap out of it. "It's a deal." The Little Nell is Five Star and Five Diamond.

"Where would you like to meet?"

"I'll pick you up at the hotel about six?"

"Ms. de Gracia, I look forward to meeting you."

"Likewise. And please, do continue to call me Wynne."

~~~

"Yes, sir, Mr. Hale?"

"Will you please bring the bill?"

"That won't be necessary, sir. Miss Worner has an account here at the club. I'll have Martin get the car." Bowing, he backs up a couple of steps, turns and heads for the phone at his kiosk. Our waiter *is* the maitre d'.
~~~

Several minutes later he reappears. "Martin is ready, sir, if you are as well."

"I am indeed. May I have your name, so I can thank you for your kindness?"

"My name is Donald, sir. I'm honored that you ask, so long as it's not to lodge a complaint."

Several tables look over to see who's laughing. It's just me. "Not at all, Donald. It seems only a common courtesy." I know I'm speaking formally. It's not a pretense or a false front at all—merely a way to show respect. I drain the last few drops from my goblet, wait a few seconds, and then finish my water as well.

"Please follow me, sir." Silently, I get out of my recliner and hoist my book bag, following Donald Lodgepole through the club. Donald steps aside and bows, gloved hand sweeping me out the front door. Holding open the windowless, wide, heavy wooden door is the same red-vested valet. A black Lincoln Towncar with black-tinted windows is waiting under the portico, engine running, with the rear door open.

Exhausted, I toss my bag on the seat, fall in with a big exhale, as the car door thumps snugly behind me. A dark, raspy voice, like someone who has chain-smoked for a thousand years, asks, "To the Little Nell, Mr. Hale?"

I sink heavily into black, baby's butt leather. "Please. Thank you."

Martin says nothing more until we arrive at the hotel. I don't mind. The silence is relaxing. As a valet opens the Towncar door for me, looking only into the rear view mirror, Martin says, "Good night, sir."

"Good night, Martin. Thank you." I'm weary following a long day, and already anxious for Wynne's 9 a.m. call.

Chapter Seven: *Paraíso con Sangre*

Precisely at nine a.m., four times, the telephone in sunlit suite 403 elegantly beeps, and then winks its amber eye at me until I pick up. I notice a red eye there, too—and look around for a green one as I grab the handset. "Good morning, Wynne."

Her voice is quiet and deliberate. "Good morning, Matt. It's nice to hear your voice. Did you sleep well?"

"Yes, thank you. But I have been concerned about you."

"Thank you. I lost one of my Paints last night. The vet was unable to save him." Wynne's lyric cadence lags. "He was my most prized stud—and one of my very best friends." Her voice is cracking. "I feel a huge loss. I'm afraid I'm still more than a bit traumatized."

"Wynne, I'm so sorry. It wasn't because you were having dinner with me, I hope?"

"Oh, Matt, no—not at all. I don't believe anything could have been done. Life goes on."

"Is there anything I can do?"

"You're sweet. No, I've lived on and operated ranches all my life—death and birth come with that territory. Browner was very special, though, and I am having a tough time knowing he's gone." She pauses. I faintly hear the scrape of a tissue being pulled from a box. Her speech is more strained. "Our eyes will never greet again."

"Let it out, girl. Let it out." My gaze flows out the parlor window, over the Roaring Fork Valley. Titanium white thunderheads already mushroom in the far west—maybe over the Colorado–Utah border. Scattered, fair weather cumulus puffballs float above the valley, and with morning sunrays still streaming brilliant, there can be few, if any, clouds behind the Little Nell, over Independence Pass.

Silence still, except for the heart breaking in my ear. Finally, a quiet, hesitating voice says, "Okay, I think I'm able to talk again."

"May I tell you a story? It might make us both cry, though." Of course, I already am.

"I trust your judgment, Matt."

"Your loss brings to mind my Yorkshire canary, Choing."

"Choing?"

"That was his name: formally, Choingbird. He earned that appellation from a coda at the end of his songs. About fifteen years ago I was awfully sick, dying in fact, for nearly a year. Choing would fly from his house in the kitchen, and spend most of his day on a curtain rod in my bedroom. Except for a few trips back to his house for food or water, he just stayed there with me: pooping on the windowsill, occasionally napping, and singing his incredibly beautiful songs. I've not heard a canary since, or before, that can equal his repertoire and volume. He did fly back home for sunset, and his trustworthy sleeping spot."

"Your canary flew into the bedroom?"

"My birdie buddies all live with an open door, except when I'm not home—and even that depends on each bird's individuality."

"Matt, that's way cool."

Did I really hear her say "way cool"? "They definitely appreciate freedom, and yet without exception prefer the safety provided by their houses."

"Houses?"

"Everybody gets his own domicile." I pause for questions from the audience.

"Please continue."

"Anyway, less than a year following my recovery, Choing spent seven dying weeks on the floor of his house, struggling to love and live life, before fluttering his last flutter. He responded to my voice until the end. I did my very best to be there for him, as he was for me. What I hold most dear from my years with Choingbird is the honest and unconditional love, or at least respect and mutual acknowledgement of one another. During his last couple of years, he would fly through the house to buzz an inch above my head, wherever I might be, when he needed his bathtub, or for me to move his house so he could enjoy an afternoon sunbath—whenever he needed me for anything—even to just come sit in the kitchen with him while he sang. It's the times we veritably share each other's lives, that are among life's most precious gifts."

Wynne is crying again—me too. That's a story I rarely narrate without at least my own tears. "I'm sorry. I shouldn't have brought up that particular account."

With a faltering voice, she says, "Matt, it's okay, really. What a wonderful, sad story. Thank you very much for sharing it with me. I'm sorry to cry. I'm just grief stricken."

"Cry away. Express your feelings completely. It's okay. The way I see it, you have no responsibility to apologize for your sorrow." I hesitate, teetering on the knife-edge of a confidence cliff—then jump. "I want to be there with you."

"Have you had breakfast?"

It takes little imagination to watch her tears streaming down soft cheeks, while I'm wiping my own on my sleeve. I'm such a macho stud. "Yes, here at the hotel. Do you need time to take care of things?"

"No—other than bereavement. My ranchman, Clancy, buried Browner in the center of the training ring at daybreak. We all cried together. Well, Cassie and I cried. Clancy was a dear and held me while I wailed." Sobbing returns, but she still is able to clearly say, "I really would like to get together today, Matt, but may we put off our project for a day?"

"Of course! I totally understand." It takes only an instant for an idea to burst into my mouth—an idea prominent in my thoughts since the invitation to Aspen. "Well, how 'bout we go down to Glenwood and hop in the Hot Springs. I could really use hot water this morning. I woke up stiff."

"What an outstanding idea! I can pick you up in about an hour. Does that sound okay?"

"I'll be waiting outside the hotel."

"See you soon, then." She pauses. "Thank you, Matt."

"I just hope I've provided more help than provocation. See you whenever you get here." Emphasis on "whenever."

From native friends I learned to avoid saying goodbye. I like that a lot. There are some friends, acquaintances, and relations, to whom you never want to say goodbye. Prayer comes in many forms.

~~~

At 9:20, the temperature in this steep ski valley is a heavenly sixty-two degrees. Sunray-thickened forenoon air remains sticky with a misty cocktail of wet forest floor, moss, conifers, and oxygenated, swift river water. Sitting tall on a herringbone-wool cushioned, thick
~~~

pine bench under the portico, I watch people, and birds, and certain automotive preferences—or necessities. What a shame we're such a vehicle-dominated society—isolation of driving leaves so little time for community.

When the silver SUV pulls up, Wynne isn't in the driver's seat. Instead, a gorgeous teenage clone bounces around the driver's seat, smiling broadly and waving vigorously—as though we're old friends. A valet opens the passenger door for me, and I climb in.

"You *must* be Cassandra."

"That's me. But please call me Cassie. I'm not quite as formal as Mom. Though we both lighten up as we get to know you, right?"

"Excellent! Is everything okay with you and your Mom?"

"Yes, I think so, except for Browner of course. Mom got a call from the Santa Fe attorney just as she was leaving, so here I am with the carriage. Are you ready to go?"

"You bet. Are we heading to the ranch?"

"Unless you need to stop anywhere?"

I sure do like these women. "I could live for a week on what's here in my bag—and thanks for asking. I'm good to go."

She turns her head ever so slightly up and to the right, eyes peering down her nose, and with an affected air of old-world nobility, pointing to the west, says, "Then go, we shall." Cassie starts the SUV and heads out from under the portico, turning west on Spring Street.

"So, Cassie, this is sure a comfy ride. I looked at the Lexus website this morning, and it seems these babies are pretty expensive. But it *is* nice." I don't know why I said that. Making conversation, I feebly rationalize.

She just nods matter-of-factly. "I know, right? Outfitted with what Mom considered important features, it was probably, like, $70,000." Without a trace of affront, condescension or arrogance, she continues. "I'm against SUVs most of the time, Mr. Hale. Often though, all wheel drive and clearance come in handy, you know, especially during winter—and mud season." She glances my way, smiling honestly, just like Mom. "The ranch is five mountain miles from the highway." Just honest statement of fact from genuine, kind spirit. Authenticity. I like this girl.

"And it's a hybrid, Mr. Hale. It averages, like, 30 MPG. Mom insists on, you know, social consciousness, whenever alternatives exist. The de Gracia Foundation privately funds research toward sustainability and green engineering. The family trust invests similarly.

We try to do our part. That's how I've been brought up, right? The world needs help, and I hope to find ways to do what I can, too." Gray-green eyes smile into mine.

While spitting out short, needle-quill, rigid, black crow feathers, I pray my smile extends as much humility as it does humiliation. "Thank you, Cassie, for setting me straight in such a gentle way. And please, call me Matt. You know, my old Subaru manages only 25 or so, on average, unless I travel more highway miles. This SUV does better than my car."

"Okay—Matt." Grinning, she turns her head back to watch the road. "Have you been to Aspen before?"

"I was executive director for the Roaring Fork Library District, and lived in the Crystal Valley. The house was right on Crystal River, actually, about four miles south of Carbondale. Now I'm on the other side of the Continental Divide, in Colorado Springs. I hear you go to a Swiss school." Sure, I'm making polite conversation, but I am curious how an American girl feels about attending a Swiss boarding school. "Do you like it?"

"It's wonderful, Mr.—Matt. I'd, like, really rather be closer to home. There are decent private schools here in the valley, and in Colorado. But, every de Gracia has attended Le Rosey for more than a hundred years, and it's really awesome. European society is cordial, and I practice French, Italian and German all the time. That's way cool. Our academic programs are, like, individually tailored. You know, in art I get to look original European masterworks, while I prepare for law."

"Law?"

"I'm going to be an environmental lawyer."

"Cassie, that's outstanding."

"Dude, thanks." Her head twitches just a teensy.

Perhaps I could have dressed more casually than a tan, starched, pinpoint button down. "Dude, can you tell me what happened to Browner?"

She grins at my "dude," but instantly stiffens. Cassie sounds so much like Wynne. "Matt, Browner was shot."

"*What?* What happened?"

"I know, right? We have no idea what happened. Clancy found him in the summer pasture during the last nighttime patrol. The vet came, but she couldn't do anything. The bullet probably hit the spine, and Browner lost way too much blood.

"Mom was inconsolable for hours. I don't think she slept at all. We stayed up until two, just looking at photo albums. We've had Browner since, like, before I can remember. He came out here with us from Massachusetts.

"I love—loved him." Teardrops slide down the valleys beside her nose. "He had, like, the gentlest gait I've ever known. He and Mom were best buds. She went out to say good morning to him every day, no matter what. She'd ask Clancy or me to hold the phone up to Browner's ear when she was out of town. He'd, like, snort a good one and paw the ground with his front left hoof."

I brush my own tears from my nose onto my index finger, and then rub the salty water with my thumb.

Cassie's got the courage to keep telling me the story. "He was such a sweetheart." A thunderstorm's gathering. "I don't get why anyone would do this."

The storm broke. Cassie begins sobbing hard. My rivers are running, too. A good life coach is empathic, though I have been accused of being too soft, more than a few times. *"You care too much about what others say,"* I've been told. Okay by me. Guilty as charged. Right now, I can't say anything. Sometimes words aren't there—just feelings.

We're quiet for about five minutes, until Cassie turns south from 82 onto Watson Divide Road. She breaks our silence.

"Have you been to the ranch before, Matt?"

"No, but I imagine it to be beautiful." I definitely imagine that.

We veer left onto Snowmass Creek Road. She wipes tears away with the back of her hand. "It really is. Snowmass Creek winds through it, and it's, like, a broad, protected valley—below most of the winter wind. It's in sun all year long. The trees are totally ancient, and have seeded to replace themselves."

Cassie's head dips to each side as she wipes tears onto the shoulders of her top. "It's perfect for horses. We raise Tobiano Paints, but only six at a time. The stable has ten stalls. We aim for two foals each year. Browner, ..." She hesitates, choking on grief for a moment. "...Has sired many best of show winners, right, and more than a few movie stars." She takes a hand off the wheel to wipe more tears on her hand. "Four of the ponies in *Dances with Wolves* were foaled here on the ranch."

"Awesome."

"*Dude.*" She grins at me with tear-soaked lips. "We're not

famous or anything, right, but a lot of equestrians know de Gracia Paints."

Locating tissues in the glovey, I yank a few between my left thumb and fingers, and extend them next to Cassie's seventeen-soft hand—it's securely gripping the steering wheel. Meanwhile, my inventive brain conjures a clear image of immaculate white fences and Tudor architecture, with a modest but not small ranch house, and a four car detached garage; all surrounded by green fields, tall with native grasses, in a carefully managed pasture for year round grazing—when snow cover allows it. I'm not far off.

~~~

"Here we are."

The fence is green-apple green, like maybe a Granny Smith. The buildings aren't even a far-distant third cousin to Tudor—they're early Aspen. Original hand-craftsmanship remains, and all the buildings sport arrays of windows to utilize passive solar energy. The ranch house probably is the original homestead home—completely modernized, except for 160-year-old architecture. This is a long, wide two-story, with solar panels of many sizes covering every available south-facing aspect.

"Cassie, everything in sight is extremely well maintained."

"I know, right? Granddad always said, 'Take care of things and things will take care of you.' "

I nod emphatically. "I couldn't agree more."

A deep, at least hundred-foot long, southern facing shed did protect some things new. There was a shiny Kubota front-loader with a backhoe showing fresh, wet dirt, along with numerous other bright attachments for mowing and grass harvesting; and a grading blade. There's a dually pickup truck, alongside three trailers for stock: a single, a double, and a quadruple. No question this is a working ranch, well outfitted. I'd have expected nothing less.

Wynne is already in the paved and freshly seal-coated, gently winding drive, waving vigorously. These de Gracia women must have some serious biceps and deltoids. And really strong smile muscles, too. There's one of the biggest secrets to living a good life, right there. In spite of news about Browner, I smile back—steel cables in my gut go soft. Cassie has helped. Wynne cements the deal.
~~~

Chapter Eight: Life Must Go On

Through my still-open, passenger-side window, I speak softly. "Good morning, Wynne." Mine's a tenuous smile; I can feel restricting muscles just under the cheekbones.

"Good morning, Matt." Wynne strides tall across the blacktop to open the SUV door. Her lips are closed, but smiling. Signs of grief belie her smile: her eyes are puffy and tired, with a lingering, swollen red lining. I have yet to see her wearing any makeup at all, so there's definitely no mascara or eyeliner to run down her face. Still, that gorgeous wavy hair is luxuriant and nearly motionless in today's delicate mountain breeze.

This is familiar, Colorado high country ether, crammed full with crisp, morning sunshine-prompted scents of fresh mountain creek water, wildflowers, conifers, and grasses—air that you want to bottle and give away to people the world over, just so they could pop a top and breathe in the moment. Well, there are a few brownish ranch smells as well, but those just provide a tawny finish to the bouquet.

"Wynne, the ranch is absolutely lovely. What a gorgeous spot." This is not flattery. Gentle, tree covered hills lie all around; maybe a quarter-mile to our left, north, that is, but otherwise none closer than a half mile or so. A high-water Snowmass Creek meanders north and west, on its way to join the Roaring Fork River seven miles hence. Bottomland stretches into the distance, eventually blending into higher foothills.

Verdant fields produce grasses of differing heights and shades of green, except for one out in the distance, in what must be the summer pasture. A portable, metal-rail fence creates a largish section in that pasture—a section being gradually mown by five picture-perfect Paints, and two still-leggy spring foals grazing beside their moms. All the pastures are spotted with groves of trees: willows and maples in the flats; gamble oak, piñon pine, and Douglas fir densely cluster, clan-like, up the hillsides. Maybe seven miles to the east and south, alpine peaks guard this garden—like a perfect Thomas Moran landscape.

As I swivel to get out, the soft leather tenaciously grabs the seat of my khaki cargo pants, emitting a certain and suspicious rumble. I freeze. Sheepish and crimson-faced, I slowly look to Wynne, who now has her left arm around Cassie.

All three of us break into unrestrained laughter. Well, mother and daughter first, then I join. Laughter is good for the soul. Like a kid, I hop down from the seat, onto smooth black asphalt.

Puffy-eyed or not, Wynne is gracious and fun. "Would you like the standard or the deluxe tour, Mr. Hale?"

~~~

Wynne and I take off on a slow, bumpy ride around the ranch, starting from the north side, over by the long, south facing shed, and then follow the fence line eastward. We're in a long-wheelbase all-terrain-vehicle. It has four leather seats and a small pickup bed, with a toolbox bin on the back. It's no Lexus, but a safe and comfy ride nonetheless.

These pastures are touched by wheeled vehicle traffic only next to fences. We slow for a narrow, surprisingly high, stone bridge arching over the creek, close to the northeast pastures: home to the tallest grasses, and the blackest soil. She stops the ATV atop the bridge— Snowmass Creek mutters over smooth rocks underneath us.

"We move the herd through grazing sections by season, so they always eat fresh grass. The grasses are cool or warm season varieties, depending on sun exposure, and also are chosen to contain season-specific nutrition. Those fence sections over there are lightweight and mobile. Chickens, in their own portable sections, follow the herd by several weeks—they recycle the manure for quick uptake by the soil." She hesitates, looking deep into my eyes. "Those eggs are out of this world."

Smiling, she continues my education. "We avoid chemicals of any kind."

"That sounds like permaculture, or certainly very sustainable agricultural practices."

"The de Gracia Family Foundation supports research, education, and dissemination of sustainable living practices, across a wide spectrum of life support systems. We walk our talk, as some might
~~~

say. Our seasonal pasture process is easy on the Earth, produces those incredible eggs, …" she grins, looking my way out of the corner of her eye. "…And superhero horses."

I look to the herd, still well east of our bridge viewpoint. "Which one is Pegasus?"

That's when I notice an area, about two hundred square feet, trampled flat and dark, near the center of a pasture section. Oops. My stomach hurls into my diaphragm. These aren't butterflies, they're bats.

She doesn't respond—that I observe. Not even her expression morphs. She says nothing, only prodding the electric ATV eastward, still along the fence line. Dozens of tracks, human and vehicular, lead directly to that spot—but we're clearly not taking that fresh path.

I chance the topic now. We're there. It's fresh in memory, and starkly in view. "Wynne, I'm so sorry about Browner. Cassie told me what happened."

Another Roaring Fork River instantly gushes down those silken cheeks. I want to lean over and kiss them out of the way, one at a time, but of course that's completely out of the question. Wynne stops the ATV, looking over to the devastated spot, maybe a football field from where we now sit, next to the Granny Smith fence. Snowmass Creek Road lies now about a quarter mile due south of us. She turns the key off. Quietly and deliberately, that beautiful head and shoulders bend down, resting on her forearms laid across the ATV steering bar. Her head's turned to the west, looking past me to where Browner died.

Not much longer than a minute later, she says, "I simply don't want to believe it. I'm still in shock." Her head turns to speak to the rubber floor. "But, life must go on."

"Well, yes, life goes on. And at the same time, I maintain that, usually, it's best to grieve to the fullest extent possible, and to take time to experience the stages of grief. What are they? Shock, denial, anger, bargaining, and acceptance, or something like that—I don't remember exactly, but I can look it up in a book I have at the hotel. As I see it, and have experienced it myself, one should grieve absolutely and completely as heartache arises."

Her head, still lying on her arms, gradually turns so she can see the stained patch.

"Wynne, I suggest that you do not hold on and be brave, or any of that bull. Stuffing it away accomplishes nothing but storing emotions in your body and spirit. Eventually all that oozes out anyway, often through disease, personality disorder, relationship difficulties, or some other undesirable outcome."

She rises unhurriedly, and her head falls hard on my left shoulder. Turning my torso toward her so her head can rest on my left pectoral muscles, I wrap my left arm around her and squeeze her into me—not tight, but with strong support. She starts moaning deeply, choking on growls—taking air in gulps.

This grief wants out now. "Go ahead, let it out totally; get in there and feel it in your core." My voice is quiet, deliberate, and near her ear. "I'm sorry, Wynne, I'm preaching again."

She struggles to speak through sobs. "Don't be sorry, Matt. You're absolutely right. Thank you for helping me let go."

"With your permission, I'll apply gentle pressure to a few appropriate points on your torso—only around your shoulders."

"It'll help me let go of this?"

"Yes, in all of my experience."

She raises her head. Soaked, sad eyes gaze into mine, but fast as a finger snap, her eyebrows turn stern. "Okay. Let's go for it." Her head falls back into my chest. In a matter of minutes she starts heaving, with growling sobs between gasps. "Okay … want this … need to let go."

And let go she does. Again and again, when her guttural grief processing begins to wane, I use my thumbs to press into pressure points around the coracoid process—and Wynne dives right back to swim in unfathomable waters of despair, heartbreak, and loss.

~~~

After probably forty or so seemingly never-ending minutes, the crying slowly subsides, and pressure points no longer push her deeper. Maybe ten, maybe fifteen minutes later, the beautiful and tender Wynne Luis Maria Caveza de Gracia Brockman Worner lets go a weighty, lungs-emptying sigh.

"Take your time, Wynne. Stay with everything you're feeling—we still have all day, if we need it."

She's quiet, breathing without any labor, but deeply and purposefully, with her head still against my tear-soaked, no longer professionally pressed, pinpoint oxford shirt. I gently and agonizingly pull my totally numb left arm from around her shoulders. Careful not to disturb Wynne any more than necessary, I reach my right arm in front of my face to raise my other deadened arm by the shirtsleeve.
~~~

Her head lifts without looking at anything other than her forearms crossing over the steering bar again. She slowly lays her forehead down.

"Wynne, it's really important right now that you come back carefully and slowly. Do not try to analyze, rationalize, or remember anything that happened while you were grieving. None of that is important—what *is* important—critical, in fact, is to patiently give yourself time to integrate what you feel in your body, and your conscious and unconscious mind. Just be there. Let everything happen without paying any attention, other than to experience and feel fully. Do you understand?"

Her head twitches a nod.

I let her have some silence.

"Matt?"

"Yes?"

"My lips went numb and froze. I couldn't move them at all."

"That's called tetany. It's not harmful, but it sure is uncomfortable. Are they still numb?"

"Just a little bit—that was strange."

"The tetany?"

"Yes. I wasn't afraid, because I knew you were right here. But I've never had that happen before."

"And you didn't let it interfere with your process—you just kept going. You did really good, girl. *Really* good."

From on top of her forearms, her head nods. She lifts herself, looks through foggy eyes, and then plops her head onto my shoulder. My left arm still lies useless at my side.

"Wow. That was intense." She stops, fills her lungs, and then gradually exhales. "You do that often?"

"Often—not necessarily. But it's a handy tool for helping myself, as well as others, let go. It works unfailingly."

"I'll say. I can't believe how light I am. I mean, inside, you know?"

"I do know. We can head back whenever you feel up to it. Take all the time you need, though. I'm here as long as you need."

"I think I'm actually okay to go. I feel lightheaded, and a little sluggish, but better. Complete."

"Well, you might have other waves of grief, Wynne."

"I understand. But the difference between now and the blackness I was feeling earlier is remarkable."

"Remember to avoid analyzing—this is only about releasing emotion."

"I get that. I'm really just feeling so much better—but groggy." She sniffs. "In fact, I'm famished." Her head nods emphatically up and down on my chest. "I'm ready to go."

"Sounds good. We can continue any time—well, any moment. Just let me know."

Her head rubs my chest again.

"Would you like me to take the wheel?"

Her head stays heavy on my shoulder.

"It might be easier for you stay with your sorrow, if I might be so bold."

She nods, and then sits up, while I steady her with my good arm. I get out like I'm leaving a church pew in the middle of the sermon. She moves across to the passenger seat as I run around.

Driving the ATV is easy to figure out. The controls are pretty much the same as driving a car and a motorcycle simultaneously. I carefully keep the ATV in preexisting tracks to avoid any more harm to pristine pastures. I also keep a watchful eye just outside the fence. Maybe some clue still awaits—not that I'm a sleuth—just a concerned lifestyle consultant.

Doing a u-turn, I backtrack away from the ranch house, following the fence line for several hundred yards, before gently wheeling around again. I do notice, however, footprints in rain soaked soil next to the Granny Apple green fence, as well as tire tracks off the road. Wynne doesn't seem pay attention to my erratic driving. At least, she's still silent—keeping her eyes trained on that trodden, blackened spot. Tears still flow from her eyes; and drip from mine.

"I'm really going to miss him."

I almost don't hear her over the ATV whine. Taking her hand from her lap, I squeeze gently. She squeezes back, robustly, and abruptly turns her head—the corners of her mouth upturned ever so slightly.

"Thanks, Coach."

"Thank *you*—for trusting me." My eyes water again, as I put both hands back to work driving the ATV.

As we approach the ranch house, Cassie runs out, looking concerned. I put my finger to my lips, and she slows immediately, nodding. Slipping her arm inside Wynne's, Cassie helps her mom out of the ATV, and, entwined, mother and daughter shuffle to the front door. I turn off the ATV and run ahead, opening the door for the de Gracias.

In the foyer, Cassie looks back at me—questioning. I motion hand to mouth and pretend to chew. She nods and we all head for the kitchen. She seats Wynne on a booth seat in a sunny, canary yellow breakfast nook. She leans over and kisses her mom, a feather touch, on the cheek, before tiptoeing into the kitchen. Cassie comes back with a pitcher of water, no ice, and three tall, multicolored, softly formed blown glass drinking glasses—they're familiar to me—but, why? Well, back to business. I watch as Cassie pours her mom a large glass of water, and then does the same for me. Cassie points at the bench seat Wynne is on.

I sit next to Wynne in the leather booth seat. She alternates her hazy gaze from looking out to the pastures, to Cassie busy in the kitchen, and back to me; laying her forearms on the table and clasping upright hands together. Ingrés talented or not, I indulge in an intense, though insatiate urge to draw those hands, right here and now.

Quietly, but with a steady tone, Wynne inquires, "What time is it?"

"Its 12:15," sings Cassie out of the kitchen, from whence wondrous smells already emerge. "Lunch will be ready in just a few minutes."

It takes Cassie only about twenty minutes to place a robust, homemade, chicken vegetable egg-drop soup in front of us. Ten minutes before that, she brought out a small, simple plate, with a variety of crackers and cheeses. Cassie sits down with us, not saying a word—just smiling and watching.

Wynne enjoys her meal graciously, if ravenously. Suddenly stopping, she glances into my eyes. "Matt, we were going to Glenwood Hot Springs!"

"Wynne, the pools are still there. I really appreciate our time this morning—time very well taken in my not so humble opinion."

She hesitates, and then her entire face forms a smile; innocent gray-greens beaming at me. She reaches for my hand and says softly, "Thank you again, Matt."

"You're very welcome. I'm glad to help whenever I'm able."

After finishing my scrumptious lunch, I slide out and stand to clear the table. Cassie jumps up. "I'll take those. Please, you stay with Mom." Her eyes smile "thank you" into mine, before she heads to the kitchen with our spotless lunch dishes.

I call after her. "Cassie, could I trouble you for a large mug of hot water?"

"No trouble at all. Would you like coffee?"

"No thank you. I stopped drinking coffee a long time ago."

"No way, really? I've never liked it myself. Why did you stop?"

"It's too acidic for my system. And gives me bad breath."

She nods. "Can I make you some tea?"

"Actually I have tea in my book bag."

"Can I get it for you? Is it in the car?"

"Thank you, Cassie. But you're busy. I'll go get it."

Wynne reaches along the table, taking my hand. I sit next to her again.

Without even looking my way, Cassie says, "Really, I don't mind at all. I'll get the bag." She sashays back with my bag on her left shoulder, and sits it next to me on the bench.

Wynne doesn't let go my hand until Cassie brings steaming hot water, in a small porcelain pot shaped like a cabbage, and a huge, thick mug on a stout plate—my kind of mug. I have a tea bag of maté ready to go.

"Thank you, Cassie."

She smiles the de Gracia smile, with a curtsy. "My pleasure." She slides in across from Wynne and me.

The tea bag goes into the cup, and I slowly pour hot water on top of it until the cup is full. After the requisite four minutes, give or take, I pull out the bag and put it into the cabbage. I settle for half-and-half and honey.

Cassie's eager to learn. "What sort of tea is that?"

"It's maté, a South American green tea variant. It'll help perk up my energy."

"Awesome." She looks to Wynne. "Mom, I need to get online and register for classes. Will you be okay with that?" She smiles at her mother's hand still on mine. "It appears you're in good hands here."

Wynne is looking out the window, toward the summer pasture out at the far end of the property. She turns her head slowly, leans across the table as her daughter leans in, kisses Cassie on each cheek, and says, "You're such a sweetheart, *mi chica bonita*. I'm fine, thank you. Go. I love you."

Sun still streams through the tall bay window, illuminating Wynne's face and shoulders like a full bust halo, highlighting her with a bright, warm glow. As her head swivels slowly back to the meadow, in her eyes I can see Browner out there in the field, frolicking with a colt, teaching him how to live a good life. I also see Browner is no longer there. *Yin* and *yang*. Spirit and body. Knowing and unknowing. Breathing underwater and dancing on the surface.

Wynne's head jerks toward me. Her eyes are red and wet. "Matt, let's go to the hot springs!"

Chapter Nine: Water for the Soul

Getting back into the Lexus, I preserve respect for the seat. "Would you like me to drive?"

"Thank you, but I'm fine—really. In fact, I want to drive. It'll help me feel like I'm back to normal. You can take in the scenery."

This *is* scenery. I have experienced it a thousand times already, but not so much for a few years now. I sit back in that comfy, untrustworthy, tan leather seat and take in the changes, and not-so-changes, from Old Snowmass down Colorado 82 to Glenwood Springs. The highway follows the Roaring Fork River all the way into Glenwood. "The river's plenty swift, though not early June high. Have the rivers claimed any lives this year?"

"An elderly fisherman and his wife both drowned the first week of June, by the old stone bridge on Catherine Store Road. And one kayaker went missing two weeks ago in Glenwood Canyon. He's still not been found."

"While I was living here, a kayaker drowned right in front of the house I was leasing on the Crystal River. If I hadn't been working at the library, I might have seen him. My eyes and ears were always on the river when I was home."

Wynne just nods without looking my way. She's deep in thought—or deep in feeling. I opt to leave her to her process. I don't need to be entertained, and neither does she.

Today, as during any season in these gold medal waters of the Frying Pan and Roaring Fork rivers, fisherpersons dot the banks in public areas, which are not plentiful. Private interests continue to purchase any available, and some not-so-available, property along the river.

~~~
~~~

Glenwood Hot Springs is one privately owned *Mde Wakan* resource that, for a fee, provides a hospitable and comfortable resort for enjoying two geothermal-heated pools—one a hot, shallow pool for sitting and soaking, and the second a warm, full-sized lap pool with two diving boards. I still have a Health Club visit remaining on my old punch card, but once again Wynne's membership pays my way. Somehow I keep forgetting, or can't quite get used to the fact, that this is to be an expenses paid engagement. It's just that, so far, this trip sits in my gut more like a visit with old friends, than a consultant–client relationship.

I don't recognize anyone in the locker room, even though I got to know a number of people during my Roaring Fork Valley library director experience. After a hot shower, I pull on black Jammer swim trunks, and then brace into a cold shower before heading out to the pools. Except in sweat lodges, I've never felt comfortable in those odd, loose-fitting, giant swim trunk things that some men wear—the kind that balloon with air when you enter water. Hard to live a good life in those babies, I'll tell you what.

Wasting no time, I stride to the hottest end of the soaking pool. I set my towels down on a nearby bench, sit on the tile edge, and slide in. At its deepest, the soaking pool is only about 40 inches, with a wide-enough ledge around the sides to provide underwater seating. There are at least two reasons I'm relishing hot water on this mostly sunny, seventy-something degree afternoon—for stiff and aching muscles, a result of too much sitting in the last twenty-four hours— and for nourishing my soul.

Being a Tiger according to Chinese astrology, I need strong exercise regimens and lots of activities in life. For me, this is not just true, but a law—whether or not one buys stock in astrology. Perhaps astrology is just a coincidence.

But then, I decided many years ago that coincidence is something I don't invest in. Random occurrence: yes. Coincidence: not necessarily. Destiny: possibly. But that's all just mathematics. Or physics. Or semantics, some would argue.

Does destiny exist? Are we born with, or do we develop during our lifetime, some predestined path to walk on this Earth? If so, many of us might be being led away from that path. Our cultures, social patterns, and learned habits often don't seem to foster exploration and maximization of individual needs and abilities, let alone some path that might not fit *The Norm*.

Faintly, I hear a familiar name sneaking into my dreamy din.

"Matt!"

Her hair in a bun, Wynne stands atop the first of the seven wide steps down into the pool. Her modest one-piece swimsuit does little to deter my less-professional dreams. Hers is a perfectly proportioned frame, with not an ounce of excess body fat, and not a poorly toned muscle to be seen.

Not that I notice, of course. "Hey! The water's perfect!"

She waves a waist high hand, and toe-points down the steps, like an Olympian, perfectly approaching a dive. She dips down briefly into the pool to get warm, coming back up wet from the neck down. Again, I barely notice. She wades through waist-high, 104-degree water, and sidles next to me on the ledge.

"Isn't this just wonderful? Matt, this was such a good idea! Thank you for suggesting it!"

"Well, the suggestion wasn't completely selfless. I live for hot water to be honest. Back in Colorado Springs, I'm a member at the downtown Y, where I do my utmost to get in the whirlpool at least fifty times a day."

No response to my exaggeration. That, of course, I definitely notice. Is this lovely creature already becoming accustomed to the kidding-around Matt? I'm pleased—highly pleased actually, since I mostly can't keep myself from the kidding around thing anyway. "Thank you for allowing me to exaggerate. I know I tend to do it a lot. Are you growing accustomed to my idiosyncrasies?"

"Like what?"

"Like my just saying 'I try to get in the whirlpool at least fifty times a day.' "

She chuckles, turning her head to look in my eyes. "Perhaps you're right. I didn't even notice." She straightens her head and neck, and slides down so that her neck and shoulders submerge. Her eyes close. We're quiet for at least several minutes, letting hot water soothe our necks, shoulders, and souls. Mid-afternoon cumulus clouds are thickening and expanding, letting sunshine through in brilliant patches on mountainsides all around us.

It's rare for me to remain quiet for long—except in meditation or contemplation. At the moment, I'm doing neither. "You know, some folks who know me never understand that among the ways I allow myself to be creative are using hyperbole, simile, and word play. If it becomes annoying, please tell me?"

Eyes still closed and head resting on the pool edge, she says, "I'm not sure I understand."

"If I'm going to get to know a person, or vice versa, I've found that it's critical to clear communication that my habits or idiosyncrasies are recognized, and hopefully accepted. Otherwise I feel stiff and uncomfortable. Not myself. Not authentic. Not joyful. I've discovered, though it's almost always my own fault, I can be easily misinterpreted and misunderstood."

"I think I understand what you're saying."

"Please let me know if I need to explain more. Wordplay's a pivotal way for me to create fun. The problem is, being habitual, sometimes I play too hard—or wrongly assume others understand what I'm doing or saying. I try to watch for that, and fix misunderstandings right away."

"Fix misunderstandings?"

My neck and shoulders swiftly go cold as I sit straight. "When people don't understand that I'm just playing, they often misinterpret irony or satire. It's really only as I've grown older that I've grown wiser—that's cliché, I know, but for good reason. I nurture the wisdom to recognize and correct my failings—especially when words or actions result in misinterpretation."

She nods, not saying a word.

I, of course, keep right on pontificating—though I hope I'm not sounding pompous. "I'm sure I've been using wordplay all my life. I just didn't realize that it's not normal—or more importantly, that people might not be following along. And often I've not been aware of consequences."

Still in water up to her chin, she turns her head my way. "Well, I'm not sure *normal* is the right expression. It might be conventional to speak plainly or simply, but I should think normal depends upon one's intellect, personality, and environment."

"Exactly. Jeez—you're *great*." I pause, and slide my chilled neck and shoulders back into the water. "Still, I want to be more observant of environments—and more considerate of the unfortunate people who try to hear or understand what I might be saying. I have learned to usually recognize when I've said something problematic, but I still tend to do it."

She nods, smiling at the sun-patched mountainside south of us, then looks my way again. "I do understand, Matt. I was brought up on a ranch, it's true, but for generations my family has been old-world traditional about childhood development. I'm often not particularly colloquial."

I chuckle quietly.

Her smile turns upside down. "Did I say something wrong?"

Under the water, I take her hand. "Oh, no. No. I was just chuckling at your not being 'particularly colloquial.'" She doesn't pull her hand away. "That was a perfect example of my not being observant or considerate."

The smile returns as naturally as it disappeared. "What do you mean?"

"I intended only to recognize your obvious education and well-bred persona."

She pulls away her hand—gently, but away.

I feel my face go stern, darn it. "Wynne, if I may be so forthright, to me you are obviously a woman of fine breeding. I myself am not from such a background—quite the opposite, actually. But I have read widely. I'm self-educated, and also benefited by excellent, albeit public, higher education to support my self-development. And I'm fortunate to know many wealthy or elegantly-raised people."

She sits up, turning her whole body toward me, hands on her hips—under the water. She's not smiling, but not frowning.

On the spot, I try to writhe away from it. "By that, I mean to say I definitely recognize when someone has acquired the ability and proclivity to be genuine, to seek to understand, and to dialog with others. Those traits are often exhibited, in my experience, by those who have elegant backgrounds." She winces. "Wynne, I'm using the term *elegant* in the mathematical sense. As I'm sure you know, an elegant mathematical proof is clear, concise, and employs only the simplest and shortest steps to reach its conclusion."

Her hands fall from her hips, and smiling again, she slips down into the water. "Why, yes, I did know that." Her eyes turn my way—it's her turn to chuckle.

"Anyway, I believe that personal elegance implies interpersonal abilities that enable innate, intrinsically innocent understanding and compassion. Not everybody maintains those qualities. That's one of the reasons I do what I do."

"That reason being—Mr. Philosopher?"

"That reason being, that I have applied myself to learning personal elegance. Don't misunderstand—I've a long way to go to reach perfection—but I do my best to help others learn to be genuine, to listen and understand, and to carry on authentic dialog: first with themselves, then with others, and lastly, with their social environments. I suspect you're already there, Wynne."

"Oh—okay—thank you—I think."

I go silent.

We aren't quiet very long before Wynne adeptly, or rather, elegantly, changes the subject. "So you like hot water. I must admit I don't come here often at all. Perhaps since we don't have a hot tub or whirlpool at the ranch, I don't think about hot water that much. It certainly feels healing, though. Especially after last night." Her shoulders slump, and tears promptly pool in the corners of her eyes.

"Do you need to process again?"

"I'm fine, Matt. Really, I've been here before, many times— though Browner was truly special."

"I'll wager we could use one of the massage rooms, and help you release."

She splashes hot pool water on her face, and looks in my eyes. "Thank you, but really, I'm fine."

"Well, okay."

"And this water is perfect therapy. I feel nurtured; by the water—and by you."

My face blazes—time to change the subject. "I've been a hot water devotee for many years now. I've been to almost every natural hot spring, privately owned or still in the public domain, in the State of Colorado."

"Really? For instance?"

"There are quite a few, as I'm sure you know. Some of my favorites are Mount Princeton Hot Springs, between Buena Vista and Salida; Strawberry Hot Springs in Steamboat Springs; and Desert Reef Beach Club, east of Florence. And even I've visited the tiny, hot eddy on the Crystal River just off Highway 133."

"I'm embarrassed to say that I've never been to any of those, Matt. Have you been to Ojo Caliente in New Mexico?"

"Absolutely. I don't go nearly as often these days as I used to."

"I've been going to Ojo since I was a little girl. I totally remember the old place. It was rustic and homey. It was like visiting a historic site. I still enjoy it. I love all the pools with different mineral waters. The herbal wraps and massages are also very relaxing."

"I'm totally with you there. Ojo was an anachronism in its own time."

"An anachronism in its own time?"

"One of my friends said that of me one night many years ago. I took it as a compliment."

She cocks her head. "Well, Mr. Philosopher Anachronism, let's go to Ojo sometime soon. Would you like that?"

"Love to. I haven't been there for at least four years. These days when I head down to New Mexico, I usually take I-25 rather than Highway 285. In too much of a hurry, I suppose, and for little good reason other than habit most of the time. I have friends in Santa Fe who own an architectural firm."

"Really?" She slides back down, neck deep into the hot water, smiling broadly again, exposing those perfect teeth. "Ahhhhh."

Perfect teeth. I'm searching for flaws. Why the heck am I doing that? Well, because I'm so aware of my own.

"Matt, I need to go to Santa Fe to meet with our attorneys. Would you like to come along? I really need to be there almost right away, but I don't want to interrupt our work together. We could go down on Sunday, and visit Ojo Calienté while we're there. I can get business taken care of the first part of the week, and then we can head back here, or even stay for a few days if you like. Are you interested?"

"Wynne, Santa Fe would be great. I have to admit, though, that I feel like I might not be taking care of my responsibilities. We've not talked about your needs and how I can help you."

"Coach, it hasn't even been twenty-four hours yet. And what's more, you've already been more helpful than I ever expected. Just keep being you, and let's enjoy the ride."

"Thank you."

She puts a toasty hand on my shoulder, leans over and pecks me on the cheek. I'm already red, sitting here in the hot end of the pool—I just turned redder.

"Matt, I'm going for some laps in the swimming pool. The exercise will do me good. Do you care to join me?"

"Thank you, but no. I'm just going to hang out here and relax."

I perform my own Glenwood Hot Springs laps, consisting of slow, exaggerated frog strokes, followed by strenuously walking forty laps, both forward and backward, across the 80-foot length of the hot pool. Walking and crawling both directions help develop brain and body coordination. At one point I notice Wynne, chin resting on her forearms at the edge of the lap pool, watching. I wave. She smiles, waves back, and pushes off for more laps.

~~~

With the sun lowering behind clouds in the Northwest sky, we decide to head back up-valley. After nearly two hours, we're both prunes anyway. I don't bother drying my long hair after the shower, but that's nothing unusual. In the dark, oak-paneled Health Club lobby, I sink into an armchair.

As Wynne flows down the wooden staircase to meet me, I see her hair is still damp, too. Is there nothing I can teach her? I watch as she floats up to me.

"Matt, I hope I didn't rush you."

"Oh no, I've just been relaxing. My hair is wet because I rarely artificially dry it—to avoid damage. Just one of my many eccentricities, I suppose."

She plops into the armchair next to mine. "You do mean to say 'one of your endearing life coach qualities,' don't you?" I turn crimson. "Or, if I may be so bold Matt, are you too humble to point out that you do model healthy behaviors, without being boorishly pedantic?"

Wow! Caught. Red-handed. Red-faced. Exposed. Peeled like a banana. My cover broken, I 'fess up. "Well, I suppose I do try to live those qualities, lessons, and gifts I've received in life. Walking my talk, too, you know. I didn't know I was being so obvious. In fact, I think you're just way more perceptive and intelligent than the average Jane."

"I'm not sure 'obvious' is accurate, either. And thank you for the compliment. I must say that I find the modeling you display to be quite subtle, as well as honest and unpretentious." She grins, leaning closer to me on the arm of her chair. "Most professional, one might say."

Okay. Now my entire body is blushing. Trapping the thermal energy I'm emitting would easily supply Aspen with electricity for a week.

I look away. "Aw, *jeez.*" Then I boldly gaze right back into her gorgeous gray-greens. "Thank you."

"You're most welcome, Coach. So what are you feeling like having for dinner?"

"Have you any preference?"

"Matt, you've led my wounded spirit so gently and perfectly through an incredibly difficult day, and if you don't mind, I'd love for you to continue to take the lead. I feel safe, and totally comfortable
~~~

with you—sort of." She laughs.

I don't hesitate. I don't blush. "Well, how about Mexican? I love Mi Casita in Carbondale." I purposely mispronounce the town's name, as do so many locals: *car•bōne•da•lāy*. This is perhaps politically incorrect, although it is a well-intentioned and good-natured play on the fact that Carbondale is home to a growing Hispanic community. Hey, that means really great, family-style Mexican dining. Way better than anything in Aspen, in this not-so-humble lifestyle consultant's Roaring Fork Valley experience.

Wynne closes her eyes, her head tilting slightly as she laughs. "I've only heard that pronunciation while listening to KDNK. Let's go!"

Chapter Ten: Food for the Soul

"Matt, this meal is absolutely wonderful!"

"I'm so glad. I was a little worried you might not like it."

"Why would you think that?"

"Well—I guess I thought you might be more accustomed to finer dining, like the Snowmass Club. This is more—well, what I suppose I'd call a common restaurant."

Narrowed eyes pierce my heart—more than that fork pointing at me—but the inflection of her voice remains calm. "I am not now nor ever have been royalty. Just because the de Gracias have money does not mean we're condescending or arrogant. At least, we certainly make every effort to not hold any attitude or belief that might encourage us to feel or act that way." She pauses, looks away, but only for an instant. "Should you ever observe any behavior in me that might lead to such a conclusion, I insist you let me know immediately."

"I'm so sorry. I didn't mean to offend you. I would never do so intentionally." I pause to see if she needs to continue—apparently not. She goes back to her *enchiladas de pollo con mole*.

"Wynne, I really do apologize. I'm still getting to know you. To be honest, I'm having difficulty understanding how you feel a need for coaching."

Her eyes remain on her enchiladas.

In hot water already, I take a few more steps toward the deep end. "It's true that so far we've only spent one day together, and now a lovely dinner two nights in row. Though, also to be honest, it feels to me more like a week."

She glances up from her plate, quizzical, chewing.

"Rewarding experiences are often like that. It's so much more fun, and healthy, to let joyful times expand into one's consciousness, rather than focus on suffering. We all experience both for sure. And have focused on both. I never said I walked on water, just breathed underwater and occasionally danced on top."

"I don't remember you saying that."

"Right, sorry. I probably just thought it out loud to myself. Sometimes I suspect you can read my mind."

Finally, a little smile, but just a tiny one. Still, it's genuine, not superficial or patronizing.

"Okay, you have this palimony lawsuit going. You told me on the phone that you were under stress, and not thinking clearly. So far you seem pretty clear to me. Even with Browner. And what about Browner? I still can't even begin to understand that. You said you hadn't been sleeping well."

The smile disappears. No—it changes to a Mona Lisa smile. She picks up her wine glass, takes a rather voluminous drink, and then keeps the glass in her hand.

I'm driving her to drink. "Am I going on too much?"

"No. This is most interesting. Do continue." She settles into her chair.

I dive back in. "You said you were feeling lost. But one of your best friends has just been murdered."

She starts to say something. My right forearm jumps off the table four inches or so, and I point my index finger in the air. "And in spite of that, you seem to have a pretty strong sense of direction to me."

She goes back to the enchiladas, knife in her right hand and fork in her left.

"And what about 'stuck in a place where I feel like nothing is working, and I'm smiling very little'? Your smile is so sweet—so honest. And I've been the happy recipient of that smile a great deal."

Mona Lisa reaches for a blue corn chip, and dips it in homemade, fiery hot salsa.

"And 'nothing working'? Wynne, I realize that we all have our challenges no matter what our station in life." I get a warning look. My finger goes up again. "I also recognize I probably can't imagine the extent of the challenges you face; but look at it from my perspective."

She's at least still looking my way. My switchblade finger snaps back into its hand.

"I'm supposed to help an incredibly beautiful, intelligent woman who seems to me to have everything working: a paradise ranch near Aspen; a caring and seemingly unconditional relationship with an equally beautiful and intelligent daughter; a firm handle on comfortable family finances; expensive attorneys that one would think are therefore highly capable and competent; what else? Okay, you cried today...." Her face goes white—I continue, index finger in its holster this time. "...And justifiably so."

Tears pool in the corners of her eyes.

"But, those smiles of yours are to die for." I lean forward with both elbows on the table, and clasp my hands together under my chin. "I have a number of unanswered questions, and there seems work for me to do. But you know what? As you said earlier, 'Just keep being you, and let's simply enjoy the ride.' "

I sit back in my *non*-arm chair, after reaching for arms. Smooth. "I sure do prefer arms on my chairs." She giggles, wiping away tears with her napkin. I rejoice, and chase after the giggle. "I'm okay with that—enjoying the ride, that is. In fact, I like it tremendously. But I am trying to balance enjoying the ride, with performing my professional responsibilities."

After a long drink of water, I crunch a chip dipped in salsa. It's really hot—matching my seat. "Usually I'm one to push too far, too hard, too fast. I'm learning to back off. I usually push ahead; thinking I have to perform, have to do my duty, have to be perfect. Well, I'm finally really getting it—getting that often, doing my duty means letting others be themselves."

Pausing only a for moment, I add, "And letting *me* be *myself.*"

Next thing I know, I get a smile—a familiar one. "Matt, I like that a lot. Let's be ourselves."

"It's a deal."

<div align="center">~~~</div>

As we leave the restaurant, the sun is setting in the northwest horizon, ecstatic rays blasting golden around the fringes of fearless clouds. As we motor back up valley to Aspen, I want to continue exploring some of the questions I still have. At the same time, I also want to be myself—which can often be more difficult than it sounds—practice helps.

"Wynne, I need to say a few things. Mostly this is about me being myself." I look over for a response.

"That's fine. Be forewarned, however, that I'm really tired. It's been an eventful day, and I didn't sleep at all last night."

"I understand. Please stop me if I swim too far into the deep end."

She just nods and keeps driving up the divided highway to Aspen—82 is the only way in or out of this valley, other than by airplane. Or perhaps kayak.

"I know I can be too pushy. It's from my childhood. I had to be perfect or I was punished." I pause. She's still intent on driving, so I keep swimming. "For me, and I think for most people, there's almost always some measure of fear, or uneasiness, when allowing events and life to unfold naturally, or even chaotically, rather than marching forward as expected, or as planned."

Wynne's eyes remain on the road.

"In my experience, and I suspect I'm not alone in this thinking, expectations can be securely confining or comfortably oppressive. Goals, on the other hand, leave lots of room for innovation and achievement.   Setting and achieving goals is part of breathing underwater, while expectations seem to me to be drowning."

After glancing over to see if she could get in a word, a sleepy voice says, "I agree that goals are a good lifestyle choice, or something like that. I'm too tired to carefully choose my words. Please forgive me."

"Not a problem." I open my mouth to continue.

Wynne is faster on the draw, and a deadly accurate shot. "I don't think I really had any expectations regarding your coaching me. I honestly didn't have any idea what to expect. I have to say, though, that I don't understand what you mean by 'breathing underwater.' "

I squirm, and then turn my whole body to face her, bending my left knee into the seat back. "I'm more accustomed to sitting down with a client, discussing circumstances, and then coming to a firm agreement about how to proceed. In my experience, moving forward on any type of project, without first establishing a solid foundation has nearly always resulted in eventual problems, and the occasional disaster.

"I'm still learning to be more spontaneous. Often I experience spontaneity through creativity: art, music, or writing. I find myself wanting to be more organized, more by the book, when I'm coaching someone. I take this responsibility very seriously. What that means, I'm discovering, is that I've become a bit inflexible in my approach— another old pattern. Nonetheless, coaching is, by necessity, a creative process."

No response. I notice little bags have filled under her eyes, and now the sun is down, further encouraging slumber. Fortunately, we're already passing by Basalt.

"You're so tired. Are you positive you don't want me to drive?"

"No. Thank you, though. I realize you're being thoughtful, and driving still is helping me stay present."

"I get that."

"Please continue. I'm listening."

"I never doubt that, Wynne."

She glances. "Now, about breathing underwater…."

"Okay. I'll try to avoid putting you to sleep."

She nods, not taking her eyes off the nearly empty road. A smattering of cars flows down from Aspen, but we're mostly alone in the eastbound lanes.

"I've held regular jobs most of my life, working to establish a so-called career, or just to make money. None lasted a long time. My heart wasn't in those jobs, and where my heart was, opportunities never seemed to come my way."

She looks over. I hold up my index finger. She smiles.

"But probably few children, or adults, have ever really been taught to look for or grab opportunities."

Mona Lisa looks over again, but doesn't say a word. I snuggle around in my seat, melting into it even more. "I'm reminded of a single panel cartoon from many years ago. So, I cut it from the newspaper and saved it for my personal scrapbook slash photo album."

She grins. "I'd like to see *that*."

"Perhaps you shall. In this cartoon, a male character is standing on his front porch with a bag of groceries in his arms. A note tacked to his door reads, 'Knocked while you were out—Opportunity.' "

She smiles wryly, nodding.

"So, when golden chances have come my way, and in hindsight I realize a fair number actually have, I either didn't recognize them until too late, or was too fearful or too unaware to climb out of the…." I make finger quotes again: I love doing that, and Wynne does glance over to witness my act. "…*Normal* paper bag, and grab the horns of some risky, unknown beast. Of course, I've never really worked hard at being normal, either."

"Somehow I don't doubt that. Now, about breathing underwater…."

"Bear with me, I'm leading up to it."

She sighs. "Okay."

"Well, I've finally given up all pretense of even trying to be normal. I've heard for what seems like a lifetime now, that a person should 'do what you love and the money will follow.' Hasn't been my experience." She chuckles, I keep talking. "But like most people, I was never taught how to love life, or what of life to love. I've had to teach myself, and I'm still learning. Now I teach others, too, and *that* I do love."

No response.

"As best as I can describe it right now, that's breathing underwater—*unlearning* much of what we've been taught or told, so that we can learn to love life, and determine what to love—rather than drown in artificial, arbitrary customs and habitual ways of thinking that may not serve health and happiness—even though we're still swimming under all the outside pressures. I imagine the pressures of parents, family, peers, schools, society, television culture, corporate government—all the crap we've been forced, really, into accepting or believing—is like a watery ocean we have to live in, to swim in, constantly. Most of us sink below the surface, because all those pressures aren't suited to our souls, and at the same time we aren't taught to be aware of our souls."

I'm not stopping for a response this time. I'm on a roll. Well, maybe it's a spelt bagel.

"It's a murky sea we navigate. So now, as life coach and creative guy, I help people breathe under that water. I help others open their eyes to betterment, and, hopefully, to happiness. I got here by closing my eyes—and taking the plunge off a high cliff just beyond the well-trodden path, falling slowly through soft air like you do in dreams, way down below into deep, cold, clear, blue water where you can't see the bottom. You just have to trust that you can swim, that you won't drown, that you can learn to swim better. Or breathe underwater. Water can wash us clean and nourish our souls if we just let it. Or it can blur our vision until we adapt—forgetting our lives, our dreams, and our hearts—so that eventually we come to know no other way than struggling to tread water, fearful of drowning. I maintain that we have the option to go under, and learn to breathe, letting all the rest happen above, on the surface, but not letting it affect us."

Wynne reaches over and squeezes my hand. I jump—I was elsewhere at the time.

"Thank you, Matt. You truly are an exceptionally inspired and imaginative man. Rather a rare bird in my experience. I'd love to see your artwork, and read some of your writing. Have you published?"

"No."

"Well, you should." She lets go my hand, just before turning off Spring Street and under the Little Nell portico. To my surprise, she reaches for the key and turns off the engine. Taking my hand again, she has more to say.

"I apologize if I've been a bit irritable today. You've been a gentleman about it, and have explained yourself well beyond the call of duty. Thank you again. You've left me with a great deal to think about, and I'm grateful. I suspect I'll retain the image of diving off a cliff, into the water of life, for a long time. However, I may require a breathing underwater refresher course."

I turn red. It's nearly dark now, even under the portico lights—maybe she doesn't notice my crimson face. It's tough being embarrassed about being embarrassed. Am I breathing? She squeezes my hand. I squeeze back. "Right now, I'm absolutely exhausted. If you don't mind, I'd like to get back to the ranch and go to bed."

"Sleep's good."

"May I suggest we have breakfast in town tomorrow morning, fairly late?"

I start to answer, but she's not finished. A cute, curly blond, four-year-old is in the driver's seat, pleading. "Will you come to the farmers' market with me, too? Please?"

A valet opens my door. "You bet. I love the farmers' market. Call me whenever you want in the morning. I'll be waiting in 403. *Buenas noches, mi amiga.*" I swing out and hop down to the pavement—a jarring landing, after folding my entire body into that tan leather seat for the last twenty minutes. I look back to my chauffeur.

"Sweet dreams, Coach."

<center>~~~</center>

I head straight for the elevator, and up to my suite. It takes a minute to find my journal. I thought I'd left it on the mantle with my traveling library, but it's under *The Aspen Times* on the writing desk. Over the last decade, leaving the controlling, Type A, Matt Hale behind and learning to relax into life, I have come to respect that sometimes I experience memory lapses.

At the writing desk, I open my notebook and jot down a few notes: Cassie, Browner, the ranch, the grieving, the hot water, a sparsity of professional interaction—and breathing underwater—it's obvious I need to morph that metaphor into a more assimilable monologue. I seldom discuss it aloud. After slipping the journal back onto the mantle, next to my tall, fat, herbal pharmacopoeia, I draw the heavy burgundy curtains—in both parlor and bedroom. Maybe I can sleep a little later than first light and be well rested for an Aspen Saturday, and a trip to New Mexico on Sunday.

Chapter Eleven: Aspen Summer Saturday

Unsuccessful at getting back to sleep, I roll off the firm, plush-top mattress at 6:30—ready for morning *Pal Dan Gum* and yoga. Pulling curtains open to another partly sunny morning, the view before me is its usual awesome self—sunshine streaming down from the heights of Independence Pass behind Aspen, illuminating gray and white fair weather cumulus out over the Roaring Fork Valley—like an idyllic stage set. Breathing deeply, seven times, with fresh air flowing through the bedroom window, and my entire spine straight and tall, I stretch my arms to the sky—and then go for my xylitol and calcium carbonate toothpaste.

Reclining in the armchair that I moved in front of the parlor picture window on Thursday, I enjoy a glass of Eldorado Natural Spring water before my a.m. workout. The quarter-inch purple mat is still on the parlor floor, where I left it, following bedtime yoga. For optimal *Feng Shui*, I usually pick up after myself. Last night I was just really tired.

Relishing my familiar routine, I contemplate upon slow, lungs-filling breathing, synchronized with expansive flexibility and range of motion-improving yoga poses—integrating mind, emotion, and body. My yoga practice is about exploring dynamics of physical embodiment. I'm not sure whether what I experience physiologically during my routines is what has been termed *kundalini*, or if I'm simply increasing endorphins, dopamine, and endogenous cannabinoids—similar perhaps to the renowned runner's high. Or maybe both that high and *kundalini* are the same phenomena. I haven't performed that research. Regardless, the almost daily thrill is welcome and uplifting.

So are those four quiet, amber beeps that at eight o'clock, blink earlier than I expected. "Good morning, Wynne."

"Good morning, Matt. How are you?"

"I'm feeling pretty well, thanks. I slept okay, and I'm really looking forward to today."

"Me, too. I'm ready to come into town."

"Did we each sleep less this morning than we might have hoped? I really wanted to sleep in, but I rolled out by six-thirty."

"I awoke about five-fifteen, following a protracted dream about Browner—we were performing a collected canter during a dressage in Connecticut. I was unable to return to sleep. But I feel quite well today—in fact, I'm feeling energized—not what I expected, though I am relieved, in a kind of detached, or, or what—possibly surreal—way."

"Way? You mean, like a frame of mind?"

"That might be how to express it, yes. As I talk about it—you know, I can't help but think—it's almost as though I've had several glasses of wine, or something like that."

"Is this a problem? Do we need to address it?"

"Oh, thank you, Matt, but I really am feeling energetic and relaxed; just a touch odd, as well. I'm ready to have breakfast—actually I'm hungry."

"Me too, now that you mention it."

"Shall I pick you up?"

I hope aloud. "I'll be ready."

"We should make it to the Nell in about 40 minutes."

"We would be Cassie and you?"

"Is that okay?"

"Of course. Absolutely."

"We'll see you soon, then."

"Yay! In a bit, then."

I'm still wearing my nightshirt. Well, it's an overgrown t-shirt. Anyway, after a quick shower I select outdoorsy clothes and my distance walking shoes, then saunter down the hall to the stairs. Well, I did make a maté, with organic coconut milk and stevia. That hot beverage is in the 22-ounce, thermal mug in my left hand, and my black book bag, of course, hangs over my right shoulder. My hair is wet and down. Talk about timing—I walk out the front doors just as the de Gracias pull under the portico.

Wynne is behind the wheel of the Lexus this time. I'd have been happy either way. Cassie is in the back seat, waving the de Gracia wave. While a valet holds the door open for me, I cautiously slide across that leather seat. Wynne notices my careful process, while Cassie giggles. Purposely turning so the seat grabs my pants, I smile happily and say, "Well, once burned, no longer shy, right?" Laughter rolls from the back seat.

Wynne looks tired, though her hair is its usual wavy, shiny self, and her lips are familiar and inviting. "You continue to make me smile, Matt. Thank you."

As the valet closes the door behind me, Wynne starts the Lexus, looking my way. "So is Little Annie's okay for breakfast?"

"You bet." I turn to look behind me, with ostentatious drama—obviously picking myself up in the seat. Cassie giggles. With a deep breath and a big smile, I take in de Gracia the Younger. "Cassie, how are you this morning?"

"I'm fine, Matt. I hear you're quite the water-walker!"

I turn crimson, sending a humble glance at Wynne. "Yes, it's one of my peculiarities I suppose." Turning back to Cassie, I say, "But I do enjoy walking in water, and I'm convinced it's good for my brain and coordination."

Still giggling, and endearingly melodramatic, she pleads, "Next time you have to take me along, okay? Please?"

"You can count on it. I'll give you some water-walking lessons."

"Thanks, Matt!"

Wynne pulls into a parking place about a block away from Annie's, close to the farmers' market. Me? Curious? "Wynne, do you come to the market often?"

"One of the reasons I suggested Little Annie's is, of course, because it's so close to the market. I come regularly during the season. The organic produce is wonderful." How am I to help this creature? She already seems to know plenty *get and stay healthy* concepts.

~~~

One of those restaurants that locals frequent, in all Aspen seasons, Little Annie's is unpretentious and rustic, in an Aspen unpretentious way of course. I love the rough-hewn woodwork, inexpensive wooden tables and chairs—and walls hung with autographed photos and memorabilia of famous visitors and upscale lifestyles. I notice I'm not on the wall yet. Even though the clock hands are on 9 and 12, we wait less than five minutes for a table.

"Are you seeing anything you want for breakfast, Matt?"

"Definitely. I'm not always picky. Just almost always."

Nobody laughs. Cassie glances at the menu, lays it back down on
~~~

the table, and watches Wynne and me.

"There are great choices on the menu. Still, it won't be my own predictable fare: organic sausage, organic vegetables, sprouted grain toast with ghee, and hemp and egg white protein powder in hot water with organic blackstrap molasses and rice milk. I'd have to open my own restaurant to order that breakfast."

Wynne is listening. "That certainly sounds healthy, although vegetables for breakfast seems perhaps a bit out of the ordinary. That said, it becomes increasingly obvious that you're not a standard-issue, meat-and-potatoes guy."

I bow my head. "I'll take that as a compliment."

Wynne chuckles. "As you should." Cassie watches.

"For many years, back in what now truly feels like a former life, I pushed into each day after matter-of-factly having a small breakfast, consisting of some sort of granola or cereal, and milk—cow's milk. For those same years, I experienced gas and digestive problems. When I went without breakfast I felt better, and seemed to have more energy. So I began simply not eating breakfast at all."

Cassie chimes in this time. "I thought it was best to, like, have a good breakfast?"

"Exactly right. Well, in hindsight, maybe no breakfast at all is smarter than eating what's not good for you—for a while, anyway. At the time I mistakenly thought my improved energy level was due to having no breakfast. Years later, I started experiencing chronic fatigue symptoms."

Wynne has a frown. "What did you do?"

"I was lucky to be treated for a while by a superb acupuncturist. She was Vietnamese: an Oriental Medical Doctor, trained in China. Anyway, she lectured me, in a gently demanding manner, about the necessity of eating breakfast. I religiously followed her daily smoothie prescription and other dietary recommendations. She said I had been starving my body for years, was depleting my muscle and other vital tissues, and needed to get back in balance. 'Eat food,' she said. 'Eat food that's good for you.' She was right."

Wynne is interested in this story. "Matt, why did you emphasize cow's milk?"

"I discovered that the temporary energy improvement I had felt was due to avoiding cow's milk and processed cereal grains. It turns out I'm definitely lactose intolerant. Some people can eat grains, others of us shouldn't. Or need to be very selective. I don't digest grains well, at all. Actually, we all need to discover what different foods work for our own individual constitutions."

Wynne is smiling a lot this morning—a heartening sight. "How is your breakfast food working for you, Matt?"

"The sausage is tasty, and the eggs are poached just right. Thanks for asking. I was rambling again, wasn't I?"

"Sermonizing a bit, perhaps, but I don't mind at all. You're simply sharing knowledge."

I notice that Cassie is enjoying the exact custom breakfast I ordered. I hadn't paid the same attention to her order as I had Wynne's. She beams. "So can I have some of your maté, too, Coach?"

"Absolutely, Cassandra! Get the waitress' attention and order yourself a pot of hot water." I reach down to my ever-present book bag to pull out the baggie of health aids. Opening the bag away from where it rests against my chair leg, I lift out the faded, orange tea bag tin, pop it open, and hand Cassie a maté tea bag.

It seems that Cassie paid close attention yesterday, when I made maté in the breakfast nook. She steeps the tea in the pot for about four minutes, pulls out the bag, pours a cup, and adds a tiny bit of cream, and a teaspoon of honey.

"Cassie, let me know what you think. I like maté, and I'm sure it's healthy for me. It is a stimulant, but it contains minerals, and has antioxidant and cholesterol-lowering properties. Research also suggests anti-cancer potential, and possibly vascular regeneration. I always get sun or air-dried maté, instead of the traditional South American process of smoke drying. It's also best to use moderately hot water, rather than boiling water—to preserve beneficial properties, and to avoid thermal stress on mouth, throat, and esophageal tissues."

Mom Wynne is concerned for her daughter. "What do you mean by 'stimulant'?"

"Some people seem to believe maté offers energizing properties without caffeine, although careful librarian-guy research has confirmed that it contains caffeine, or what some sources call mateine. Mateine is chemically identical to caffeine. So, since it definitely is a stimulant, I enjoy maté very moderately." Wynne nods, satisfied that I'm not leading her daughter down a path of hyperactivity.

Cassie blows across the tea in her cup, watching steam fly away. "I'll let you know what I think, Matt. Thank you for sharing it with me. I've tried, you know, lots of teas, but never maté." She takes a sip to see if it's hot—then sets the cup down. "Librarian-guy—I remember you told me in the Lexus that you were, like, a librarian, or manager, or something."

"Right. I still enjoy performing detailed research. I prefer to gather a comprehensive understanding of a topic from authoritative sources. I guess I'm really just a geek at heart."

"I know, right? They make, like, the best husbands. That's what I've heard anyway."

"Well, I'm not sure about that." I grin. "I'll have to research it."

Both de Gracias laugh. I don't blush.

<div align="center">~~~</div>

After we finish breakfast, Wynne leaves three crisp twenties on top of the bill, and we slip out the side door to cut through the alley to the farmers' market. The morning temperature is rising, but here, high in the Rocky Mountains, with a partly cloudy sky, the temperature remains in the mid seventies. Of course, Colorado weather can change faster than, and be deceiving as, political spin.

Aspen's outdoor farmers' market normally is a big one, with numerous arts and crafts booths down Hyman, and tables of local produce and other farm products up Spring Street. I pick some organic, fresh California pistachios to add to my bag's nourishment stash. Wynne purchases organic green beans, squashes, kale, collard greens, new red potatoes, carrots, broccoli, and several varieties of apples—including my favorite—Honey Crisp, from Paonia, Colorado. Cassie runs up with a homemade straw broom. "For the stable floors," she says. She also found a tastefully tie-died, button front cotton top, designed with subtle, Renoir-imitating floral motifs.

We three smile often, laugh, and talk about food and cooking, life and living, and Cassie's impending departure for Europe. When I fish a chocolate bar out of my bag, Cassie's eyes grow big. "Dude, you're eating chocolate? In the morning? Weird."

"Sure. Morning's the perfect time in my opinion." I extend the open wrapper and foil lining—inviting the ladies to partake in small, rectangular pieces broken away from the bar. "Besides, it's already past eleven. Chocolate time's eleven 'till two, I tell 'ya."

They're still skeptical, but eyes and smiles betray true inclinations. This sale won't take much more coaxing. "It's *really* good. It's German, 85% dark, and there are only three ingredients: organic cocoa liquor, organic cocoa butter, and organic raw cane sugar." I melodramatically place a rectangle on my tongue. "Mmmm, heaven. I

72

just let it melt—never chew and swallow. What a waste that would be." I close my eyes. "Mmmmm." I swing my hand back to my chest, as though to avoid spilling any pieces.

Cassie breaks first. "Okay. I'll try some." I make her reach for it. She punches my arm.

Wynne says, "Well, I have no intention of being left out."

We three finish the entire bar inside sixteen minutes.

Chapter Twelve: Butts

Back in the Lexus, supplies in hand, breakfast in bellies, chocolate melted onto tongues, we're set to return to the ranch. Without dense, weekday commuter and business traffic, in no time at all we're through the roundabout and already passing by Owl Creek Road and the airport. I opt to scratch an itch—often not a good idea.

"Wynne, has the Sheriff come out?" All color leaves her face. "Oh, no. I'm so sorry. Wynne, I'm sorry. Crap. That was really stupid. No warning, no nothing. I didn't even ask whether you mind if we talk about what happened." Cassie slaps the back of my head, and we're not talking about a love tap.

Wynne regains composure, but not her color. "Your question does come as a surprise, especially after such a sweet morning."

I must look guilty. Sure do feel that way.

Forlorn eyes shrink my heart to walnut size. "Yes, I'm still heartbroken, but life goes on. We love, we lose, and we love again."

"Sure, and we need to take care of ourselves. I feel horrible. I've ruined this beautiful day."

"Matt, it's fine, really. You haven't ruined the day—it's just a bit of a shock. I've loved and lost plenty in life, and you've only been helpful—and sincere—since you arrived. I have complete faith that you have only our best interests in your heart. I was deep in shock that night. Cassie is more aware of what went on. Please, what would you like to know?"

"Promise me you'll stop me the instant that talking about Browner bothers you at all." Turning my gaze to Ms. Head-slapper in the back seat, "Will you do that, both of you?" Cassie barely nods, eyes scrunched.

Wynne says, "I promise. Thank you for being concerned—and

kind."

"Well, all right then. But please, please, stop me at any moment." All quiet on the de Gracia front. "Can you tell me what was found, or wasn't found? I just don't understand how this could happen."

Wynne answers first. "I remember when I ran out to the summer pasture, Clancy said he knew it was a gunshot wound, and that he called the Sheriff immediately. Clancy keeps his cell phone with him whenever he's on the property, or on duty—essentially twenty-four by seven. He called the vet—then me. Cassie said Clancy called her at the house—asked her to get spare blankets, old sheets we keep for rags, and the first aid kit from the supply closet in the barn. Did I forget anything, sweetheart?"

Cassie's voice is cracking. "That's it, Mom. Dude, Clancy was intense. He just gave, like, orders. I had no idea what was going on. I ran to the barn in my jammies. Clancy told me to bring the ATV. I didn't take, like, ten minutes to get to the pasture. It was cloudy, right, but I could see Clancy." In short breaths now, between sobs, "Saw Browner—on the ground…got scared…started screaming."

I nab the tissue box from the glovey. Cassie grabs a handful. So does Wynne. Me too.

"Clancy was awesome. Never yelled, you know, but, like, told me exactly what to do. Only raised his voice once. He said, like, 'For Browner's sake, Cassie, stop screaming.' He tore sheets, and like, packed pieces into Browner's neck. Lifted Browner's head to get both sides. Wrapped a whole sheet around his entire neck. He had me press more rags against the bleeding." Crying hard and choking for breath, she keeps going. "It was horrible. I was crying, but I knew we were, like, trying to save him, right?" She stops to blow her nose and reach for more tissues. "I didn't know Browner, like, got shot, until Clancy told the Sheriff's Deputy."

Cassie packs handfuls of tissues on both eyes. In peripheral vision, I see Wynne doing the same.

"Dr. Bittman came as soon as she could. It was, maybe, like, thirty minutes, I guess—I don't know. But Browner just kept bleeding. Everything was," her eyes close and her lips twist, "like, soaked." Her whole body quakes. "I squeezed hard as I could, wrapping my arms around his neck. Blood was everywhere. It just kept coming and coming and—I—I—I couldn't—make it stop." She gasps for air. "He never even moved—just kept looking at me and Clancy. One time—his eye looked right into my eyes—and then—it just stopped moving. Shit!" Cassie collapses into the car door, covers her head with her arms, and wails. I pretty much just want to die. I start using my sleeve for my rivers—the tissue box is empty. The one item I don't carry in my bag.

No one says another word until we arrive, but I lean my knees up into the passenger seat again, turning to watch over a self-processing Cassie the rest of the way.

~ ~ ~

As we turn from bumpy Snowmass Creek Road onto the paved drive, Cassie sits up, wiping tears. We're all using sleeves now. Tissues flood the floor—the litterbag overflows.

"I'm sorry I brought this up. It's just too soon and too hard."

With a determined voice, Cassie speaks right through tears. "Matt, it's okay. What happened happened, right? Not talking about it won't, like, change anything, or, like, bring Browner back, right? I'm okay, I just need to cry." Wise words from a seventeen-year-old, as her mother glances my way with a lip-soaked smile.

We pile out of the Lexus and run to each other for a giant hug. Emotional conversations in cars are rarely a great idea. There are too many distractions and too much separation. People need to touch each other, to comfort one another, to be there for each other, to share the energy of the situation and feel in harmony with each other. Like I've admitted, sometimes I tend to push things too soon, to move things too fast.

We gather groceries, the broom, Cassie's new blouse, and walk up those broad steps into a hundred-sixty-year-old ranch house. Cassie immediately starts making lunch.

I wonder if she needs to do something else—like cry, for instance. "I'll be glad to make lunch, Cassie."

"Thanks, but it'll help me, like, get it together, right? Why don't you and Mom hang while I whip it up."

Wynne is already seated in the nook; soaked, red eyes gazing past pale yellow curtains—out to the pastures. I sit down too, across the table. No way am I starting the conversation again. Curiosity killed that cat. Wynne, on the other hand, wants to talk about it.

"That night, by then it was close to midnight, the Deputy said he had looked around and couldn't see much in the dark. He took photographs around the fence by the road, and said he found some tracks there. He put up that yellow, crime scene tape. He was going to return in the morning. He did come early yesterday, but didn't stop by the house with any new information. He and Clancy again looked around by the fence, and in the pasture. He took more photographs and left without saying anything."

"Wynne, can you think of any reason, or anyone who might have done this? I just can't picture either of you having any enemies, and you seem to have few neighbors. I don't understand why any of them would think they could get away with something like this. This just doesn't make much sense. Hunters aren't usually out at night. Legal ones, anyway."

"I don't know, either. I simply don't believe Patrick—the ex-boyfriend—would have done this. He's smart enough to know it might hurt his lawsuit. Plus, he's now managing a restaurant in Silverthorne. All our neighbors are really good friends." She starts to cry. "We help each other out, and watch out for one another. I've agonized over this a great deal, and I just haven't come up with any ideas. Maybe I don't want to know."

Cassie is stern. "Well, I want to know." She's busy in the kitchen, dicing chicken to add to red onions she's sautéing in coconut oil. I can smell fresh basil and parsley. She has bakery-fresh bread, spelt, at my suggestion, sliced, and ready to be toasted. Three glasses of water, no ice, with lemon, already sit on the table, next to a full pitcher. The kitchen door opens.

I turn to look behind me, as in walks a grizzled-looking fellow wearing tan, military-looking khaki pants and a matching vest—sporting at least three times as many pockets as my cargo pants. I know instantly who this is. He's wearing a floppy Boonie hat, its strap circling loose under a salt-and-pepper-bearded chin. He looks like he's still in Vietnam. He's wearing a pistol. Undoubtedly semiautomatic. Possibly nine millimeter. I'm betting there are no blanks in that magazine.

Wynne's sweet voice returns, and little evidence of the tears of moments ago are visible. "Clancy, come and meet Matt!"

Clancy strides over to the breakfast nook, hand extended. He is not smiling. His voice is gruff, heavy, no nonsense. "No need to get up Mr. Hale." My halfway raised butt sits back down on the bench. "Clancy Sandstrom."

"Clancy, pleased to meet you. You can call me Matt." I shake his hand with my firmest, professional grip. He's strong, so am I. There's no competitiveness in this greeting, though, like sometimes occurs between males—where at least one needs to assert himself as the alpha dog—just a firm, strong, equal acknowledgement between two guys. I look at the pistol, then into his eyes. I'm relieved to note a tiny twinkle at my notice of the armament. The handle is that of a Glock.

With virtually no change of that stony-faced expression, he says, "Seems like might be huntin' season 'round here." Clancy Sandstrom speaks with a distinct, possibly rural, northern New England dialect.

I smile a knowing, guy-smile back at him, and let go his hand.

Cassie, of course, is as considerate as ever. "Will you join us for lunch, Clancy?"

"Thanks, Miss Worner, but I had a sandwich a little while ago." Clancy turns to Wynne. "Ma'am, found somethin' out by th' fence you might want t' see."

I jump in the water, since I've already filled the pool with so many tears. "Wynne, if you don't mind, I'd like to see what Clancy has found, too."

Furrows in her brow unknot. "Thank you, Matt. And thank you, Clancy. I really prefer staying here. Maybe I'll walk out to meet you two a little later. But let's do have something to eat before you go."

Cassie calls from the kitchen. "And lunch is ready as we speak."

"Clancy, I'll eat quickly and come along. Where should I meet you?"

He responds calmly, while turning to leave. "ATV'll be out front in twenty." I'm seeing what Cassie was saying in the Lexus earlier. Clancy doesn't mess around.

~~~

As we bounce away from the ranch house, I cordially say, "Thanks for taking me along, Clancy."

This is obviously a man of many words. "Yeup." It's kind of yee-up, but comes out fast, rather than a slow drawl: more like a Mainer than a Texan, for sure.

I, however, am undeterred. "Cassie said you were in 'Nam. I know guys who were there, over in Colorado Springs, where I'm from. Fort Carson, or Fort Cartoon they called it, was an end-time-in-service point—ETS."

"Yeup."

Still undeterred, I am nonetheless not going to push too far. He deserves his privacy.

"They've told stories about what they went through, and have seen and done. It was horrible." I stop, waiting for a response.
~~~

Nope. "Just like now in the Middle East, our military were just doing what they were ordered to do. Most were drafted into the war against their will."

"Yeup."

"Sorry, Clancy. Sometimes I don't know when to keep my trap shut. I'll keep quiet."

"S'okay Matt. Don't mean t' be rude. Just don't talk much."

I answer with a grin. "Yeup."

Clancy's serious facial lines don't even budge. His eyes remain straight ahead: steely, not cold, but steady and threatening, like the sharp eyes of a large hawk, or eagle. I look at the path ahead, and examine the ground and road on the other side of the fence. I'm here to look for clues, after all.

He maneuvers the ATV past that black spot in the summer pasture without even turning his head. I, on the other hand, am paying detailed attention to everything as we head back west, along the fence. There are numerous sets of footprints in the wet soil. Some prints create a new path, from the bloodstained spot to the fence. On the other side is a stand of three huge willows—and footprints covering the ground, and on top of crushed cheat grass. I stare at the ground as carefully as possible, given the fence and a jarring ATV ride. There is no question that three sets of footprints exist in the mud. I take a chance on talking.

"Clancy, it looks like three sets of footprints out there, and two inside the fence here."

The ATV smoothly, but abruptly, comes to a halt. A seat belt would have been nice.

"Yeup. Me 'n Conrad reconnoitered 'round here pretty darn thorough. We climbed th' fence there at the willows 'cause Conrad spotted footprints. Did our best to not step on 'em. 'Rad took Polaroids of 'em—and recent tire tracks. Never found anythin' inside th' fence. Looked all up and down. Never saw anythin' else."

He turns those eyes toward me. Hair on the back of my neck bristles. " 'Rad came back yesterday. We eyeballed more in th' daylight, but never found more. But this mornin' I spotted this over here."

Clancy climbs down from the driver's seat to march the fence line to the east. I hop out to follow. He stops about five feet from the willow stand, and leans onto the fence. He doesn't say anything, just points down—once I finally catch up to him. Dude can move. Under a clump of rough grass is a cigarette butt. It hasn't been rained on yet, so it has to be recent.

"Called Conrad. He'll come look. Real strong Turkish brand. Only one guy 'round here smokes 'em I know of."

I wait. Clancy apparently is done. I'm not.

"Who's that, Clancy?"

"Martin, from th' club."

My heart races as the memory of the ride back to the Little Nell in the club car floods my mind. I look around carefully for anything else to see. There are no more footprints around this spot, thick with clumps of rough grass, but it's definitely close to the willows—where all the other activity had been. Out in the road is another butt, flattened out and muddy, lying in well-worn ruts of a frequently used gravel road.

Putting a foot on the lowest fence strut to climb over, I ask, "Clancy, do you suppose that's another one out there in the road?"

By the time I step up to the middle strut, Clancy is already on the other side, stepping onto the dirt road. This veteran is nimble for a man in his sixties.

"Yeup."

Chapter Thirteen: Parting Ways

Wynne prances down the steps onto the driveway, as Clancy and I approach the ranch house. Once more she's radiant, modeling the pomegranate dress she wore Wednesday, when we first met. That dress is sexy: plain and simple. Of course, so is she. The combination is killer. And I'm evolving into a very easy target.

I've been acceptable, I think anyway, about maintaining a professional relationship with her, in spite of nearly unbearable temptations I feel so covertly. But that dress undoes me, again. As we pull up, Clancy turns off the ATV, and we roll to a stop right in front of her—standing there, legs apart, hands on hips, as if she's itching for a fight. I know I'm radiating crimson. And I know I can't hide the heat.

She smiles sweetly, eyes meeting mine with fondness. I don't think I'm imagining that. Intuitively I sense only tenderness from her. Sure, that might be what I want to feel, but I have learned to trust my intuition. Averting my eyes, I focus on climbing out of the ATV. Clancy breaks a spell I won't. "Ma'am, Conrad's comin' back t' look at cigarette butts out by th' fence. Don't know if it'll come to much. Looks like all we've found so far: butts n' footprints. Maybe tire tracks. I'll let ya' know soon's I do."

She responds gently, lovingly. "Thank you, Clancy." Maybe she's merely immersed in a tender mood after all. While a damp alpine breeze puffs at her hair, a grin rides today's sunlight and shade roller coaster—grief barely noticeable in glistening skin and gray-green eyes.

Not that I notice, of course.

"Matt and I are leaving this afternoon for Santa Fe. We might be back midweek sometime."

Mouth dangling, my head snaps to attention.

Her eyes explore mine. She's swaying back and forth—like a damask salmon swimming upstream in the Columbia River. "The Santa Fe Chamber Ensemble is performing Vivaldi, Bach, Telemann, and Purcell at the Lensic tonight. I hope you won't mind leaving today rather than tomorrow. Is that okay?"

My heart's pumping—it's a European Grand Prix and I'm behind the wheel of an F1 Ferrari, one meter behind the race leader at a hundred and seventy-five, approaching a hairpin curve. "Are you kidding? I love classical music, especially Baroque. That sounds totally awesome. But, as I recall, Aspen to Santa Fe is at least five hours, even in a Ferrari—in summer, on dry roads, with no state troopers—well, wait a minute." I squint my eyes, reading an imaginary Colorado–New Mexico map on the bottoms of the clouds. "If we take 82 to 24 to 285, and the 17 shunt, given previously stated conditions—okay, three-and-a-half to four-and-a-half hours— depending on local traffic through Hernandez, Espanola, and into Santa Fe."

I earn a vigorous, succinct laugh. "Are you a big fan of Ferraris?"

"Oh yeah. Someday I'd love to drive one. Oh, yeah!"

I'm the only person who knows I own a Ferrari. It's a secret. I suspect I need to keep it that way, too. No offense 'Bu.

"Well, we may not be driving a Ferrari, but the trip will take us about two hours, Matt. We'll be flying."

~~~

Cassie runs down the steps just as I open the door to climb into the SUV—Wynne's taking me to the Little Nell to pick up my things. For the remainder of my stay, I'll occupy one of the guesthouses. Clancy has permanent residence in the smaller one. These are cottages, nestled next to the creek, down a path through a tree grove behind the ranch house. I hadn't even noticed them, painted the same Granny Apple green as the fence, camouflaged by dense Gamble Oak undergrowth and stashed under immense willows. The Nell is Five Star nice, but I can't wait to stay a few days in this fabulous valley. Not only is the de Gracia ranch truly a thick, juicy slice of paradise pie, but also I can keep a closer eye on the Browner mystery. And probably widen the focus on coaching my client.

"Matt, I'm leaving for school. Tuesday morning. Thank you for being here. I really like you, and I'm, like, going to miss you." She points a finger, scowling. "Remember, you still owe me a water-walking lesson, right?"
~~~

"But Cassie, we're just going into town to pick up my things. We'll be right back."

Even though she's wearing a happy face, dismay glowers in her green-gray irises—that I now notice are interspaced by slivers of turquoise. "I know, right? Only, you and Mom will be leaving, like, right away. Clancy will take me later to drive the Lexus back to the ranch. When you get back from Santa Fe, right, your stuff'll be in the guesthouse. Right now, you and Mom really need to get going!"

"Cassie, I'm really disappointed." Opening my wallet, I pull out and hand my sweet new buddy a business card. "Listen, will you leave your contact information for me? I'd like to stay in touch with you." I look to Wynne. "If that's okay with your mom." She nods. "And I'll send you a maté supply, too, if you'd like."

"Cool. Thank you." Not surprisingly, Cassie is way ahead of me. She reaches into her blouse pocket and hands me an index card—both sides covered with all her contact information. "I'll email you, right, as soon as I get there." She wraps her arms around my shoulders, hugging me hard, close, and long, her blond head turned into my shoulder. I return the gesture with a bear hug, lifting her off the driveway. After easing her back down, I take her hand and kiss it. Angel the Younger. Life doesn't get much better than this. Her arms gather me again. She plants an affectionate peck on my cheek, and whispers, "You and mom *have* to go. Take good care of her, right? Your black bag's in the back seat."

I look over her head at Clancy. His head dips once. One forearm rests on the Glock, the other is folded behind his back; his legs are parade rest apart. I hop into the Lexus, closing the door behind me.

"I think my daughter has fallen in love with you."

"The feeling's mutual. Cassie's got a really good heart. I'm honored that she thinks so highly of me, in such a short time."

"I have complete confidence that sentiment, also, is mutual."

Although I can't even tell the Lexus is running, I push down the window button as we move away from the ranch house, hang my head and shoulders out, look back and wave the de Gracia wave. Cassie returns the gesture, jumping up and down—with, like, respectable seventeen-year-old decorum, right—and blows me a kiss—Clancy at her side. Expressionless. No wave from that guy. Yeup, she's in good hands. We head through the gate, turning west onto the gravel road.

~~~
~~~

Steffan turns to Renate. *"Renate, wollen Sie bitte Herr Hale biem packen helfen?"*

Wynne remains at the counter to arrange the bill, as Renate and I head for the mirrored elevator. "We thought you might be staying longer, Mr. Hale."

Instinctively, it feels appropriate to protect Wynne's privacy. "That was the original plan, Renate, but things have changed. I'll miss the Little Nell. Thank you for being so kind."

I use my keycard to open 403. Renate immediately pulls my bags from the cedar closet, and zips them open on the bed. "Mr. Hale, I'll fold your clothes, and if you'll let me know what goes where, I'm to pack your bags for you."

"Thank you, Renate. I'll put my toiletries in the gym bag, and take a few things in that smaller bag. Let me know when you're ready, and I'll come help. Right now, I need to gather odds and ends from the parlor."

Renate doesn't look up from meticulous handiwork. "Yes, sir."

I empty refrigerator contents back into the Clarks grocery bag, and stash four bars of dark chocolate into my book bag. The librarian in me squeezes my row of reference books together, lifting them all at once from the fireplace mantle. The entire stack dominoes gently, still in order of course, onto the bed. "These can go in the big bag, Renate."

This time she does look up. "Yes sir, Mr. Hale."

My heart races as I look at the bed. My journal is not there. I scurry back to the parlor, head frantically turning every direction. Once again it's on the writing desk. This time, I know without a doubt I left it with my books on the mantle last night. I purposely sandwiched it between *Nutrition and Healing for Everyone,* and *Fundamentals of Chinese Medicine in the Occident.* Not once has the "Privacy Please" sign been removed from the door.

"Renate, who might have been in the room today?"

"Oh, Mr. Hale, I'm certain no one has been in the room at all, sir. Staff are instructed to respect your privacy when the sign is on the door."

"You're sure no one has been in here?"

"Oh, yes sir."

I let it go. Well, with Renate I let it go. Inside, I try to not fume. Anger doesn't help matters. But I feel violated. I tuck the journal into my black bag—this baby will not leave my sight again. Somehow, this has to be related to Wynne. There can be no other reason for anyone in Aspen to care about my journal. Or me. What the heck is going on? Is somebody trying to see what I'm doing? That is the only reasonable explanation. Should I tell Wynne?

Okay Matt, slow down, cool off. This is weird, but let's go easy here. Wynne has just had her best friend murdered. I need to contemplate my viewpoint.

~~~

Renate and I elevate down to the lobby. "Shall I have your car brought around, sir?"

Whoops. I haven't even considered Maroonbaru. "Renate, will the hotel allow me to leave my car here for a while?" No way am I going to mention Santa Fe. Not that I don't trust Renate, I just need to be careful.

"Certainly, Mr. Hale, although I'm sure the daily rate will apply."

"That will be fine, Renate. Will you let Steffan know if I forget?"

"Yes, sir."

"Thank you for all your help."

"My pleasure, sir."

The elevator opens. Immediately I scan the lobby for Wynne. She's in the seating lounge, reading *The Aspen Times*. She looks the same instant I see her, and waves, smiling. I wave back and give her a stop sign palm. Renate and I stride ahead to the front desk.

"Renate, can you have all my things put into Ms. Worner's car for me?"

"Yes sir, Mr. Hale." Renate leaves to call a valet.

I look at Steffan, now alone behind the front desk. "Steffan, has anyone inquired about me while I've been here?"

"Not at all, Mr. Hale. Why do you ask, sir?"

"My friend, it's probably nothing at all. I thought maybe something had been moved in my room today, but perhaps I'm mistaken."

"Did you have the privacy sign on the door, Mr. Hale?"

"Yes, I did. It's all right, Steffan. Really, don't concern yourself."

"Sir, it's my responsibility to be concerned. I'll inquire with housekeeping and staff. Please check back with me at your convenience and I'll inform you of what I learn. Will that be acceptable, Mr. Hale?"

"Of course, Steffan. Thank you very much. Renate said it might be okay to leave my car here. Is that true?"
~~~

"For you, sir, absolutely. Have you an idea how long you might need to leave it"

"To be honest I'm not sure if it will be a few days or another week or more. Can I let you know?"

"Mr. Hale, please leave the car as long as you like."

"Thank you, Steffan, for your always superb service."

"You are most welcome, sir. It is entirely my pleasure, Mr. Hale."

At exactly the same moment that I turn to the sitting lounge, Wynne's head swivels toward me—her face radiating such delight, as to take the place of a sun now totally hidden behind altostratus clouds. She rises like a ballerina from the same armchair where, only two nights ago, I sat spellbound as she floated into the lobby. Pulling that awesome woven bag over her shoulder, she glides to my side as I perfectly match her gait—she deftly hooks her arm inside mine, and we step together toward the front doors. I smell her hair—and inhale deeply.   More emotions and thoughts roll around my head than innumerable noisy marbles in a gallon glass jar.

Leaving the Little Nell is a tall, absolutely gorgeous sandy-blonde angel, slender, with wrap-around sunglasses pushed up into slightly tussled, naturally wavy long hair.   A solid pomegranate-colored, shirtwaist summer dress, almost certainly silk, strapless and gathered softly above perfect breasts, elegantly exposing smooth and unbearably inviting neck and shoulders all the way to the bottom of a soft low back; hemmed sensually two or three inches above the knee and draping longer behind, dances perfectly in step with a gait so gentle and smooth that it seems its wearer is actually gliding.

The pony-tailed blond guy at her arm definitely *is* gliding.

Chapter Fourteen: Do You Know the Way to Santa Fe

Wynne turns right, before we even enter the Sardy Field parking lot—and instead pulls up to a gated ramp. She reaches into her woven bag to pull out a magnetic security card, and it dawns on a dawdling heartbeat that we aren't taking a commercial flight. She swipes the card, and the heavy iron gate slowly creaks open, then closes behind us as we drive toward a set of tee hangars. My heart's thumpin'. We pull in front of number 4; then back away and to the side. I can no longer contain my elation.

"You have an airplane? I know it's obvious, but I'm a twelve-year-old kid right now. One who's always wanted to fly."

"Well, technically the family trust owns the plane, but Cassie and I are the only de Gracias to fly it. You are okay with this, aren't you? I didn't think to ask if you'd mind with flying with me. I apologize for the oversight."

"Can't wait. This is awesome."

"Matt, I find myself feeling so much like we're old friends—perhaps I'm beginning to assume you know everything about me."

"I haven't wanted to appear presumptuous, Wynne, but to be honest, I've been feeling like old friends, too. Rest assured, I'm so enthused about flying with you, it's all I can do to avoid gushing like a child—which, of course, is precisely what I'm doing."

"I certainly don't see you as presumptuous. You seem genuine—without pretension."

"Thank you. I take that as a heartfelt compliment. Anyway, I can't wait for *this* trip to Santa Fe."

"Have you ever flown in a private plane before?"

"Once, for a few approaches with a friend, but I didn't get to operate the controls."

"Well, you can fly the plane some if you want. You will be the copilot on this flight, of course."

"You're kidding, right?"

"Not at all, Coach." She hasn't called me that in at least a few hours. I like it a lot.

"I'm totally out of my element, Wynne, so please tell me what you need from me. I'm a babe in the clouds for sure."

With a mischievous grin, she looks in my eyes. "Student will teach Master, eh' Matt? Hop out and come with me."

I laugh, and can't help but appreciate watching that pomegranate summer dress slip up Wynne's thigh as she turns to slide down the driver's seat, onto the pavement. Since the step bars under the doors are apparently for sissies, I slide down the passenger side—my khaki pants turn out to be not quite as accommodating as Wynne's dress.

"I called ahead to have the flight crew check out the plane— maintenance and crew service is included in the lease fee. They never phoned back, so it should be ready to go." She unlocks and swings the service door open. "We'll push out the Cessna. Then will you pull the car into the hangar for me? We can't leave it in the way of other planes."

Bowing, I say, "Yes, Master."

She grins, reaching across me to push the hangar door opener. I take an opportunity to discreetly, though not covertly, smell her neck, only inches away. I close my eyes. "You smell so wonderful. Like the wildflowers in your pastures."

She might be mildly surprised. I know I am—and, of course, flaming red. "Why, thank you." I imagine she lingers just for a moment. "I'll be right back."

As the giant garage door slowly lets in more and more daylight, I look over the brilliant white nose of a twin engine Cessna. The hatch opens itself and stairs descend. Wynne bounces up the steps, reappearing inside the cockpit. She waves, smiling. I salute, while her mouth says, "Ohhh," and she playfully dismisses me with a hand wave. She skips back down the steps. "Matt?"

"Yes, Captain, my Captain?"

She nods emphatically, with a cute, smug grin. "That's better." I remain at attention. "At ease, Airman." We're having fun, and it feels nice. She removes chocks from the front wheel, setting them against the wall between the hangar door and the service door. "We'll each take a side behind a wing and roll the plane out slowly. You take the right side. I'll jump back in and set the brake again once we get outside. We stop just short of the center of the Tarmac. Use that handle if you need, to help slow the plane down. But not to worry: It won't roll very far on its own."

"Does this beauty have a name, Wynne?"

"You know, it doesn't. I have thought about that though. Do you name things?"

"Usually, yes. My car is a wine colored Subaru Legacy that I call Maroonbaru."

"Oh, that's cute!"

My face grows hot.

"No, I really mean that, Matt. Maroonbaru. A maroon Subaru. It's just cute as can be! Help me name the Cessna, will you?"

"I'll do my best!"

~~~

We push the plane out of the hangar, and I carefully drive the Lexus in. Wynne floats over to get her bags out of the car, so I grab mine too. Tagging alongside, I find myself wishing she hadn't worn that dress—especially now that afternoon sun highlights the physique beneath that soft silk. I try imagining her in greasy, tattered old coveralls and a bulky flight jacket, but all I see is pomegranate ruffles. I follow her up bouncing steps.

The seats are leather. There are three seats, not counting the cockpit. All the leather is cream colored, and without blemish. The interior is carpet or leathers everywhere: floor, walls and ceiling. Toward the rear and just behind the hatch door, is a small but comfortable looking bench seat that could easily be lain upon. There's even a video monitor. Absolutely beautiful: I've seen expensive homes that aren't this elegantly appointed.

"Wow! This is incredible. I've always imagined what the interior of a plane like this might be like, but I've not even been close. This is absolutely gorgeous."

"Thank you. We bought it from friends of the family who rarely flew it. It sounds as though you are aware that to maintain a private pilot license, it's necessary to log a minimum number of miles and landing approaches each year to re-certify one's skills. Jonathan wasn't doing even that anymore, and decided to stop flying altogether. His wife had breast cancer. He was completely devoted to her." She
~~~

weaves herself into the pilot seat, pointing me to the copilot chair. "The de Gracia clan tends to travel on a regular basis, and we fly the Cessna when necessary. Even though it uses a lot of fuel, I believe it's better than commercial jet fuel exhaust in the troposphere, and we can take exact, direct routes."

"Did Jonathan's wife recover?"

Her head cocks to one side as she gives me *the smile*. "Thank you for asking. Yes, Constance completely recovered and the cancer hasn't returned. It's amazing what love can do."

"Yes, yes it is."

She proceeds to explain controls and gauges. I'm in awe of the instrument panel. Wynne is all business in this cockpit. No joking around, no tomfoolery; just the importance of safety and correct operation of the plane.

"Wynne, I can't see myself flying this beautiful machine. I'll be scared to death that something might go wrong."

"Let's not be scared to death. That's an image I'd rather not see come true. You'll do fine. I'll show you all you need to know. It's really quite simple once you become familiar with basic controls and instruments. You'll be fine, trust me."

"I do trust you. It's me I'm concerned about."

She just keeps preparing for our departure. "This is a Cessna 414 RAM Series VI."

I nod—like I know what she's talking about.

"I wanted a twin-engine plane. It comfortably carries me and Cassie, as well as Mom and Dad, plus a reasonable load. It's always nice to have two engines in case one fails."

My eyes grow big.

She laughs. "In the very unlikely event that both engines fail, modern airplanes can glide safely for considerable distances, enabling safe emergency landings on roadways or fields, even if electricity also fails or landing gear won't descend."

I roll my eyes. "Wow, that makes me feel better."

She laughs again, while flipping a toggle switch—all the gauge needles snap to life.

"I feel completely safe. I have total confidence in the pilot."

She looks over. "Are you the kind of person who might get a queasy stomach?"

"Well, it's been a really long time since I've been on a carnival ride or anything, but I'm pretty sure I'll be fine. My yoga practice provides constant emphasis on balance."

"See? I told you you'd be fine. Well, just in case, airsick bags are in that pocket to your right."

She starts the engines. "I'm adjusting manifold pressure. We need more pressure and a richer fuel mixture during startup, and takeoff, of course."

"These two engines are a lot quieter than my buddy's single engine was." I know about engines, but adjusting manifold pressure isn't really clear. Yet. Something about needing to reduce pressure when engine demand is less. I'll ask for details later. Trying to absorb volumes of new information, all at once, with requisite perfect Matt retention, is too much for now.

She continues describing everything she's doing. "I'm setting the global positioning system to KSFE in Santa Fe. We can set it to other GPS transponders as necessary. This is the ATIS—an acronym for Air Transfer Information System—that's in-flight communications. We set Comm. 1 to ground control and Comm. 2 to tower control. Nav. 1 gets set to a localizer frequency for each airport, found in FAA approach books." She hands me an Aspen approach map from the outside pocket on her black leather flight bag.

"There is also ILS: the Instrument Landing System. It receives transmissions from ground control to the primary ILS instrument, the GS, or Glide Slope." She points. "It's a directional gyro set according to instructions from tower air traffic control. Here we have the airspeed indicator, attitude indicator, and altimeter. These are turn coordinator and vertical speed indicators." She points to her feet, now in running shoes. I never noticed her take off the sandals. "This pedal controls nose attitude and this one the rudders."

"I'm getting a little overwhelmed with information. I hope it's okay if I ask questions as we go, so I can reinforce what you've told me."

She shows me an understanding smile, and with a captain's efficiency keeps preparing for takeoff. "Absolutely. I know it's a lot to take in. Shall we go?"

My heart knocks against my ribs. "Oh yeah." Finally, I remember to pull the 3x5 memo pad from my left cargo pants pocket, to take notes. For a kid who always wanted to fly, it has been distracting to contain my excitement, and be focused enough to document the lesson.

Captain de Gracia contacts ground control to request our squawk code. "A squawk code is the radio frequency assigned to specifically identify a single airplane for the entire flight duration." She reaches down to the center console, slowly sliding the two throttles, one for each engine, forward toward the instrument panel. The engines respond with a shuddering growl, and we roll forward.

"I'm switching to Comm. 2—to let the tower know our desire to take off. Put on those headphones so you can listen in. In fact, you should have them on at all times."

It takes a minute for me adjust them to the least uncomfortable possible position. A male voice is saying to standby. We wait while a turboprop commuter plane, probably originating from Denver International, lands and taxies off the strip. We get the go-ahead to proceed, and Wynne moves us slowly onto the runway.

"I'm enriching fuel mixture for takeoff." She points to another set of levers on the center console. "These adjust propeller speed by changing propeller angle. I'll increase manifold pressure to forty-one PSI for takeoff, then back it off to twenty-five once we're in the air."

"Sure, you'd want the air-fuel ratio richer during takeoff or acceleration. I get that. I know someday I can make perfect sense of all this."

She doesn't respond. With fluid grace, and speedily but not too fast, she pushes the throttle levers all the way forward. The Cessna roars through my headphones, and we shoot up the runway—140 MPH in 16 seconds. I shiver with a stomach thrill—the combination tickle and unstoppable rising of the gut, like you get on a mammoth roller coaster dip—as the plane lifts from the pavement. That's a gripping moment—feeling resistance of runway against the tires suddenly disappear at the same time the plane dips back toward the ground. But then the ground drops away. Fast. Very fast.

"Woo-hoo!" I glance at Wynne, who's totally concentrating, eyes straight ahead, focused on takeoff. After about four or five minutes, and eight or nine thousand feet, she pulls back the throttles and reduces manifold PSI. I watch and scribble completely illegible notes. Leaving the wealth and luscious beauty of Aspen rapidly behind and below, we've embarked on a thrilling journey to Santa Fe, and the Land of Enchantment.

Chapter Fifteen: Here's the Deal

We soar over Schofield Pass and cobalt blue Taylor Reservoir, and then climb again at nearly 35 feet per second over the Collegiate Peaks, passing between Mount Yale and Mount Princeton. Wynne wanted me to point out Mount Princeton Hot Springs. The Continental Divide is awesome from the ground, but from up here the view, and the ride, is nearly orgasmic. Wynne's velvet voice is a tad distorted through headphones, now nestled unnoticed against my ears. "Are you familiar with Mount Blanca?"

"Sure. Blanca's just east of Alamosa. It's one of the sacred mountains of the *Diné*, I'm told." I point ahead and to the left a teensy. "It's just ahead."

"What did you say? Dintay?" Wynne looks my way, pointing to her microphone position. "You need to keep the microphone right next to your cheek and mouth, practically touching, or I can't hear you."

"Sorry. The Navajo people."

"Oh—*Diné*. Well, if you look below us, can you see a wire fence that demarks the national forest boundary?" We're flying past the southern edge of Poncha Pass, with the flat expanse of the Upper San Luis Valley stretching out in front of us.

"I think so. With little white signs every so often?"

"That's it. The de Gracia family, that is now only Cassie, myself, and my father and mother, holds an Eighteenth Century Spanish-Mexican grant to land and water rights here. They extend from the Gunnison National Forest border down there, all the way to Blanca, and beyond the Colorado–New Mexico border to Carson National Forest. The only exceptions are eminent domain litigations over the last hundred and sixty years, and some private properties that acquired various rights since the Treaty of Guadalupe Hidalgo. After the Mexican-American war, most of the land grants were sold by my ancestors, or lost to Governor Gilpin and other conqueror interests. Nevertheless, a lot of the Valley still leases water or land from The de Gracia Company, part of the family trust." She stops—eyes distant. I haven't seen that look before. Not even in the breakfast nook.

"Holy crap!" I turn a little red. "I'm sorry. I shouldn't have cursed."

"You call that cursing? Don't worry about it in the least. I'm not offended, and have said far, far worse—yesterday morning, in fact. I'll share those language choices with you if you'd like." She goes silent. My eyes avert from the valley below—she's grinning, a four-year-old about to spring something on me for sure. A tremor courses throughout my body. She softly says, "Maybe Student could work at removing me from that pedestal?"

"Wow. It's that obvious?"

She chuckles shamelessly. "Only to we immortals. In fact, I'm flattered. I like you, and find you to be invitingly honest. Your admiration, therefore, is gratefully appreciated, and returned in kind. Nonetheless, I'm hardly worthy of being lionized."

My face is blazing, back of my neck crawling.

She reaches over, takes my left hand, and places it on the yoke in front of me. "You've no need to impress me, be on your best behavior, or anything along those lines." She points to my right hand, and then to the yoke. Without thinking, I simply lift my other hand to the yoke. She puts her hand back on her yoke. "I think I know whom you are by now, unless you're a highly skilled con man, and, trust me, I've plenty of experience with those. I think you're incapable of lying. Or, at the very least, you would be hard pressed to cover up any dishonesty."

Still a man-furnace, in a matter-of-fact voice I hear myself say, "Thank you. I'll take that as yet another generous compliment."

"You damn well should!"

I look back down to the sage-covered high desert below us. Wynne angles the plane to my side, the yoke turning to the right, and slightly closer, under my hands. My stomach rises and then recedes, like a wave from shore on a calm January night. "Well, anyway, wow! That's incredible—a Spanish Grant. This valley is probably the most hotly contested water rights geography in Colorado—maybe in the nation." The yoke turns left and away as she levels the plane. "But,

I'm guessing you're already aware of that. Well, duh—I'm stating the obvious. Well, to you it's obvious. For mere mortals, you're talking about personal issues that are almost unimaginable!"

"You're astute, Matt. One reason I need to be in Santa Fe to meet with our attorneys is because of the water under this valley. We're being sued, attacked, and pressured from many angles. I told you I was under stress, and, what else did I complain about when we talked that first time on the telephone? Not thinking clearly—I don't remember all that I said. Well, right now we're flying over a primary reason for all that."

"I can only imagine…." I sit in the copilot chair, not stunned, just dazed: nearly hallucinating. Soft, exquisite leather. Instruments everywhere. Pomegranate whispering next to me. Twin engines cruising effortlessly. The Upper San Luis Valley stretching out for another seventy miles to the south. Continental Divide receding to the west, and the Sangre de Cristo mountain range alongside to the east. Mesas of New Mexico faint in the distance. Huge aquifers underneath us. The awesome responsibility it must be to manage such an asset: financial implications, political implications, ethical implications, and spiritual implications. *Mde Wakan.* Sacred water. Suddenly I feel a little homesick for my simple Manitoid life, with Fountain Creek flowing through Soda Springs Park. Sitting on the bench seat at my golden table in 'Toids, sipping maté and….

"Are you okay?" Wynne's checking in—I had checked out, and was leaving with the room key.

"Oh, yes, yes, I'm okay. *Lo siento, mi amiga.* I've just been trying to absorb what seems to me to be—monumental—ramifications of what you've just told me."

She nods. "It really is complicated. We've got Denver and other cities around the entire southwest, California, developers, farmers and ranchers, multinational agribusinesses, the military, various government entities, you name it, all after the water. There are some very powerful names involved. It's a pain in the butt." Wynne is not smiling as she pushes a blue plastic button. Instantly it glows peacefully. "I'm just trying to figure out what really is the right thing to do."

~~~

In the ten minutes since the Mount Blanca question, at 200 nautical miles per hour, we're already almost across the long valley, with flat mesas of New Mexico no longer so faint. Stratocumulus are
~~~

gathering a few hundred miles south, probably brewing an Albuquerque low, but we're still winging through nearly windless altitude—over enough underground water to quench the thirsty lawns and golf courses of Denver and Phoenix for perhaps decades. But, what then? What happens when these aquifers are emptied faster than they can refill, if they ever do, like what is happening to so many other water resources of the Earth? Like the Dawson Aquifer in Colorado and Ogallala in Wyoming—aquifers with twenty thousand year old water—that will never, ever recover. Like Twin Lakes on the way to Aspen. What happens to Fountain Creek back home in Manitou? Holy buckets. Or rather, holy water. *Mde Wakan.*

"Will you take over for a couple of minutes, please?"

My jaw hits the thoughtfully carpeted floor. "What? Hey, I've been paying attention, but we haven't talked about my taking over." My ticker revs beyond red line. "Wynne, I'm not sure that's a good idea."

She just turns her head, winks, and grins. "The Cessna's on autopilot, Matt. Just sit there and look cool, okay? You already do that well."

I'm truly getting bored with turning red-faced. Maybe I can finally stop doing it. Maybe I can finally learn to take compliments in stride, and get in some work at returning appreciation. That's something I need to practice—in addition to flying an airplane.

"And guess what? You have no choice. I drank a liter of water today before we took off. My life coach has encouraged me to drink at least a liter or two every day, and more if I'm active. After following his instructions, I definitely need to use the powder room."

My head swivels to look behind us into the cabin. Over-dramatizing, in yet another attempt to be funny, I drawl, "Where is this powder room?"

Wynne laughs heartily. "Do you see that bucket behind the front port passenger seat?" She's still giggling. "That's a unisex powder room!"

"At least it's stainless steel."

She guffaws, tilting her head back and letting it rip. "Yes sir, very classy indeed!"

"But seriously Wynne, what do I do?"

"I don't mean to be glib, but you need do nothing unless something disastrous happens. In that case, I'll be back at the yoke before you can blink an eye. I promised you a flying lesson, and we'll do that yet. This isn't it, really. I'm not a big believer in sink or swim learning." She winks again as she snaps off the harness to slide out from the seat. She leans over, pulls my headphone away, and right next to my ear, very softly, slowly, seductively whispers, "Now, don't you peek."

I keep my eyes on the airspace ahead. After all, there are eagles in this valley, and the area is often used for National Guard flight practice, though we are of course steering clear of "no fly zones." I've been soaking in clothing-optional, private hot springs here in the Upper San Luis Valley as F-16s screamed overhead, less than a thousand feet above the pools. Charming.

I watch the altimeter and attitude gauges closely. Still, I'm unable to resist temptation. With a devilish grin, I gradually start turning my head. Wynne hadn't even ducked behind the half partition in the aft, by the bench seat, so in blurry peripheral vision I can just barely tell she's crouching in the center of the cabin.

She lets out a playful shriek. "Don't you dare." My gaze zips back to the bow as we both chuckle nervously. The altimeter needle says we're cruising at an altitude of 10,000 feet; 2,500 above ground level, over Rio Grande headwaters flowing down from Colorado's San Juan Mountains. Not a single river, creek, or spring flows into Colorado—all water flows out of my home state.

After the tink-tinkling on stainless steel subsides, I hear the subdued, delicate rustle of silk, followed by twanging of snaps as the lid is secured back on the powder room. It's amazing what ears can still catch while wearing headphones. Wynne pours back into the captain's chair, but not before almost knocking off my headphones with a solid thump on the back of my head.

"You devil!"

"Flattery will get you everywhere with me."

~~~

While we approach the Colorado–New Mexico border, Wynne reviews instrumentation, GPS, and ATIS settings. After suggesting we buzz Ojo Caliente before our approach to Santa Fe, she switches to manual control by pressing the blue autopilot button. It winks once, and then fades to gray.

Captain de Gracia again demonstrates pedal control of rudder and nose attitude, and how to use the yoke to adjust attitude, altitude, to turn, and to accelerate. We veer southwest, toward the foothills under Bennett Peak, to avoid worrying Alamosa or Taos air traffic control,
~~~

but still tune in ATIS 117.6, just in case Taos needs to ask what the devil we're up to. We climb over and between Summit and Conejos Peaks, again crossing the Continental Divide, and then sink down into Chama valley. A guy could get used to this—and love it, believe me.

Changing airspeed, simulating emergency dives and climbs, and practicing acceleration and deceleration, I also perform majestic, buoyant turns: not the least of which being a sweeping 90 degree arc to the northeast over Abiquiu and Georgia O'Keefe's stomping grounds, followed by a voluptuously tight 270 above Ojo Caliente.

"I see the Rio Grande is low again, like it has been for so many years now."

She frowns. "Sadly, yes. You can also see drought devastation in the vast numbers of dead piñons."

"Wow. I hadn't really noticed. At least half must have died."

"The actual statistic is higher than that."

"Wynne, I'm still a little nervous, but totally a kid in the candy store. Thank you for this—it really is a dream come true."

She has both hands on her yoke, too. "You're doing splendidly. But, go ahead, be nervous, if that makes Student feel better."

"Yes, Master." Who's coaching whom here? Oh, right, I'm flying her airplane. "Should I turn around? We're headed back to Colorado."

"Let's take a quick side trip. There's something I'd like you to see."

"What is it?"

"It's a surprise." There's that coy smile again: I love it. It feels so seductive. "Let's take a 115 to the right."

I turn the yoke, holding at 115 degrees, and reach down to push up the throttles. We speed through the turn. After leveling the plane, I bring airspeed back down to 200 nautical miles per hour. "We're heading toward Interstate 25."

"Right. You've an excellent sense of direction and perspective, Matt."

"Thank you."

"This flight path will take us over Wagon Mound. You know Wagon Mound?"

"I know where it is, yes."

"Have you seen Canadian River Canyon?"

"I don't think so. Where is it?"

"It's 20 miles east of Wagon Mound, and extends for about 20 miles north. It's like a miniature Rio Grande Gorge."

"Wait! Yes, I do know where that is. The Doughan family owned a big ranch there that included part of the Canadian River Canyon. It's beautiful. They harbored endangered equine species there. I think they sold it some years ago however."

"Let's fly over it, Matt."

"With pleasure. For a short time I was an officer in an environmental group that the Doughans flew there in a private plane for a tour. There were zebras and horses from all over the world. It was spectacular. I've often wondered what became of the animals."

"They're still there."

"Oh, good. I was worried they'd been rescued from dire circumstances, given a safe haven, and then had to find new homes again." I pull up on the yoke to climb high enough to safely pass over the New Mexico Sangre de Cristo mountain range, and level the plane again at 10,000 feet. Wagon Mound is such a distinctive geological landmark that I can easily aim us that direction. "Should I go over the town and then head for the canyon?"

"Please. You're flying like an experienced pilot you know."

"Well, I owe that to an excellent instructor. Are you going to tell me the surprise?"

"When we're there, Matt, when we're there."

<p style="text-align:center">~~~</p>

As the black canyon comes into sight, Wynne says, "Turn north and follow the canyon for a few miles. Will you recognize the Doughan ranch?"

"I think so. We circled the ranch house and outbuildings before landing, and the ranch is so huge that no other buildings are around for miles."

"Let's circle it again."

"Let me know if I'm steering us wrong?"

"Of course, Matt. But you're a natural at flying. I'm really proud of you."

Not even turning red, I reply, "Thanks, 'Teach." At the end of the canyon, I perform a gentle 270 back south. "We're here."

Wynne, looking down below, doesn't respond.

My heart starts racing. "What is going on down there?" I'm looking at a sea of shining—something. "What are those?"

"Those are solar panels, Matt."

"Really? Can I dip down to take a closer look?"

"You're driving."

"This is incredible! You're right, of course. Solar panels. And what looks like wind generators—little ones. There must be thousands of them!"

"15,416 panels and just over 7,000 wind generators."

"Really?"

"The de Gracia trust purchased the ranch. We still take care of the horses, of course. The ranch is available for alternative energy research and development."

"Wow! That's incredible. I want to hug you."

Those gray-green eyes are whispering yes. "A little later, okay?"

"Look at that wind turbine! It's the size of a locomotive."

"It powers what's called a collaborator. There are a series of collaborators. They're like tiny substations that collect electricity and send it to larger collectors. We're working with a number of companies on the cutting edge of emerging technologies." She points to the south. "Let's head that way."

I follow captain's orders.

"That's a functioning power substation. We're supplying 25 percent of the electrical demand for Santa Fe, and peak demand for every small town in Northeastern New Mexico."

My eyes are dry from not blinking for at least five minutes. "Wynne, I don't know what to say. This is awesome!"

She grins like a proud parent. "You're saying enough already. Let's go to Santa Fe. We need to approach from the south, okay?"

"You got it."

~~~

Wynne takes over just before we fly over San Juan Pueblo—but I keep my hands and feet on the yoke and pedals, feeling her precise, smooth operation of this magnificent machine. I'm speechless. Well, okay—that doesn't really happen very often. "You know I have to have a plane now. My life will never be the same."

"You've been so easily bitten by the flying bug?"

"Must've been a humongous mosquito." I scratch my entire head, mussing up my hair under the headphones. "Itches like crazy."

She laughs. "Will you dial in Santa Fe ATIS for us?"

Quiz time. I reach for the New Mexico flight map in the pocket by my chair. The Santa Fe approach map is over in Wynne's flight bag. After locating SAF Comm. 2 setting on the map, I dial in 119.5, and listen to Wynne request a ground identifier from Santa Fe tower.
~~~

Paying intense attention, I write precise notes, legible this time, as she sets autopilot headings relayed by SAF air traffic control.

"How nice to have two headphones so I can listen." Jeez, that was dumb. "Well, duh, obviously a copilot needs to be in touch. Ah, yes, that's me: master of the obvious."

"Well, that is better than being master of the oblivious." She turns a tight 180, over frightening hill and arroyo-filled terrain, as we also drop sharply toward that very terrain.

I watch everything, intent and silent, furiously scribbling notes as Wynne adjusts autopilot instrumentation for our final approach, increases fuel mixture, manifold pressure, and propeller attitude. She punches off the blue autopilot button just before touching down, simultaneously setting maximum down flaps. The tires chirp as the plane shudders and the nose dips toward the Tarmac. She smoothly presses the brake pedal, and maximizes propeller attitude to help slow the Cessna, safely turning onto a taxiway to private hangars. It all happened so fast I couldn't take very detailed notes. Or particularly readable ones.

"What a cute little adobe-style terminal building. Wynne, I'm having a ball. Here I am, watching how and learning to fly a really nice private plane. My flight instructor was everything I could have asked for, albeit distractingly sexy." Did I just say that? "Thank you again for inviting me along."

She doesn't even flinch. Maybe she didn't hear me. That would be fine with me. She points the Cessna away from hangar 12, as two flight crewpersons, one a very pretty raven-haired woman, pull up in an electric cart. There are a lot fewer hangars than I had expected in Santa Fe, but still, more than were in Aspen where most of the planes wait outside. Wynne adjusts manifold pressure a last time, leans the fuel mixture all the way, and after about 30 seconds of idling, turns off the engines. They whine down slowly and graciously, if not exactly quietly—more like two twelve-cylinder Ferrari F50s, winding down, side-by-side.

Wynne takes off her harness, leans forward in her seat, reaching under the instrument panel. She pulls a set of keys and quickly tosses them my way. I catch them with ease. "I suspected your reflexes were superb. Would you pull out the car? The hangar door opener is immediately to your left."

I'm still totally jazzed by the whole experience: flying the Cessna, the water rights, the solar ranch, landing, being in Santa Fe with

Wynne. I reach down, unbuckle, and turn to climb out of the comfy copilot's seat. Wynne delicately lays a hand on my shoulder. "Thank you for flying Air de Gracia. We hope you enjoyed your flight." She pauses. "And will fly with us again soon."

"As often as you'll have me. Though right now I really have to pee. Is there a loo in the hangar?"

"I'm sorry, no."

I jump to grab the powder room by the handle, and then wait for the hatch to ascend and steps to descend, bounce down, and stride briskly for the hangar service door. The pretty crewwoman holds it open for me. I look for the door opener, press the toggle upward, unzip, and nearly overflow the bucket as the long aluminum hangar door folds horizontally into itself and up. I set the somewhat heavier bucket down next to the wall, and open the driver's side door to a mica green Prius sedan. The Toyota starts right up, and I drive onto the Tarmac, out of the way.

An electric cart slowly pushes *Wambli Gleska* tail first into the hangar. I had been thinking of names. I'm not sure of that one, but try it out telepathically. It might be inappropriate to use Sioux, but the naming intention is honorable, and is in part a respectful memory of a true Dakota brother and spiritual leader. I did feel like an eagle, flying up there with the Creator, observing life below. And this time, only miniscule fragments of the flight were fantasy.

Chapter Sixteen: Judgment—Cynicism Notwithstanding

On a narrow, twisting, paved road leading away from Santa Fe Airport, a giant, black SUV blasts by, going the other direction, and moving so fast its big-ass tires kick up rocks as it leans way out onto the gravel shoulder.

Whack!! We both jump. "Shit!"

The direct hit cracks the Prius windshield, splitting it nearly in half, diagonally from upper left down through the middle of the glass to the lower right hand corner.

"Damned SUV drivers. Drive like jerks. And sure as hell without any consideration for others."

Wynne looks over.

"Oops. Lost my cool—sorry."

"I'm sure you don't think every SUV driver is a jerk, Matt. I do understand that many drivers are inconsiderate, and sometimes misjudge the capabilities of their vehicle—even to the point of endangering others and themselves. But I suspect those habits pertain to most drivers, not just those who own an SUV."

"You're right, of course."

Only several minutes later, Wynne deftly skips a smooth, flat stone across the communication pond. "That crack is pretty nasty. We'll call the Toyota dealer from the condo and arrange a new windshield. You know how to get to Canyon, don't you, Coach?"

"Yeup." My Clancy imitation doesn't produce a smile. "One of the main reasons I love Santa Fe is fondness for art—and the smell of fresh oil paint. Soft adobe architecture and winding streets of old Santa Fe create way-comfy *ch'i*. I've been here so often that I actually know Santa Fe pretty well."

"With your hair and casual style, you look like a native. *Ch'i* indeed."

I wave my hand around, close to my head. "Did my feather fall out? Tourists sometimes do ask me for information; usually I'm able to answer. Wynne, I'd like to apologize. I opened my mouth and screwed up back there. It's an outburst evolved from genetic and learned past."

"Wow. You say something like, 'evolved from my genetic and learned past,' and then drop the topic? Dude."

"Oh, sigh. Someday I'll learn to keep quiet."

She glances.

"About my internal workings."

She stares.

I flap my lips with heavy breath release. "There is no good place to start. As a child, I was punished for screwing up, even when I hadn't. Most of us who experience childhood abuse suffer our entire lifetime—maybe more, who knows? If we're fortunate, we learn to understand how we've come to be who we've become. But damage is done. Scar tissue remains."

"I suppose I've been fortunate. My parents are loving, and always have been. At the same time they instilled strict discipline and personal responsibility. My family has never been hurt, or hit, or even so much as spanked. Well, except for Patrick, but he certainly is not family."

"What?"

"It was a slap, but yes. It was the first—and had better be the last—ever."

"And this jerk is suing you?"

"Nobody saw him. It's his word against mine."

"You'll have no trouble making that incident understood."

"Thanks. I hope so, if and when it might come up."

"Sorry that I brought out a little of my childhood stuff there."

"I don't mind at all. I love listening to you. Much that you say helps me, in some way or another, to see into myself, or to understand how others might feel. Were you punished a lot as a child?"

"I only remember two times from childhood when I felt loved or appreciated. My memories are mental, emotional, and physical strife. Jury's out on sex abuse. If it happened, I don't remember. I do have certain recurring dreams, though."

"It's hard for me to imagine you being abused at all. You seem, so—well-adjusted—Coach."

"Thank you. Well, my life is a path of self-improvement, in the completely holistic sense. Walking that path involves reliving childhood emotions, learning all I can about what imprinted my little-boy, developmental brain. Experiences linger in my grown-up mind, altering my perceptions of, and reactions to, events in life."

I glance—she's in the passenger seat, facing me.

"I still say or do things I regret."

"We all do that."

"You're right, of course. I just feel I'm more apt to do so than most."

Silence holds court.

"My rageaholic father passed away a decade ago, but I still punish myself in his stead. I learned from him to be—well—easily irritated, angry, and, sadly, intensely judgmental.

"It has taken time to recognize these traits, among others, in myself. I'm still learning—please let me know when you see behavior I might want to look at. And I mean that totally seriously—please tell me. I've asked friends to do the same, but rarely does the request produce honest feedback. But I have made immense progress. Now, I'd say I'm at a place in life where I almost always recognize when I act out habits and patterns. They still pop up. These days, though, at least I don't beat myself up—too badly—unless the stakes are really high. Right now, I feel like the stakes are really high. You are, by far, the most interesting client I've ever worked with, and I've learned to have deep respect for you. I like you a great deal. I feel as though I'm walking on eggs."

This time as I look away from the road, she's Mona Lisa. "I like you a lot, too. *You're* laying those eggs there, Matt."

"Right. You've been completely kind and gracious. They're my eggs, all right. I can rationalize that embarrassing and habitual faux pas help me learn humility, and that one needs to experience similar moments to really gain self-understanding—and empathy with others. Still, I'd rather not fall headlong into a polluted holding pond of unhealthy habits and patterns. Really tough to breathe in that crap, trust me—"

Silent for a moment, I story onward. "I was—thinking—about being so honest with you. Often in life, I've found that honesty is indeed *not* the best policy, despite the colloquialism to the contrary.

Truthfulness has gotten me into a whole lot of trouble."

"I like that—that you're honest. I know I can trust you."

"Thank you. With clients, and particularly with you, that's my intent. Many people just aren't ready for honesty. Or don't grow the beans to understand it, relate to it, or react to it with a good heart or an open mind. More and more these days, it seems that many people get locked into some doctrine, some ideal, some way of thinking that won't allow for any other way. Or they're just plain unconscious." I gulp an eight-ounce, well deserved slush from my water bottle.

"I know what you mean. Even in Aspen, I've acquaintances who simply play dodge ball by slinging slogans, rather than dialog around ideas."

"I totally get that—and while I try not to dance to dogma drums, I totally know I'm not perfect. I still have a judgmental or cynical side."

"You don't say."

"In my own defense, I've had direct and irrefutable experiences: in jobs, friendships, and especially as a library director. Lots of folks are driven by a desire, conscious or un-, to control and manipulate. I know I'm not innocent, but at least I'm aware, and I toil incessantly toward constant improvement. I do something about it.

"All my life, I stubbornly held onto an ideal that all people are created equal, have the same potential, the same capabilities, mental or otherwise. That ideal has proven to have been, indeed, simply an ideal. Altruistic, yes. A reality, no."

I empty my water bottle, and plop the liter back in my book bag—the right side—right there, in its place. "Being too smart, having too great an ability for vision and strategic planning, being too intuitive, too often has led me to wrongly assume that everyone else saw even a similar vision, was on the same page as I was, or was understanding what I was saying, where I was coming from, and where I was going. The result has always been—I'll just say— negative."

Her fingertips brush my hand on the steering wheel. "Matt, I'm so sorry. You don't deserve what's happened to you. Be proud of whom you've become. I am."

I fight tears, with a smile welling from deeper than almost anyone can know—except those who feel a similar place. "I'm doing okay, Wynne. My past contributed to, but is not an excuse for, my flaws, angry outbursts, or categorical accusations and/or assumptions based on limited facts and/or understanding. Those are habit—clearly my own responsibility."

Also clearly, in the rear view mirror, maybe a thousand feet away, traveling at the identical nautical air speed as the Prius, is a giant, black SUV.

Chapter Seventeen: Black Scorpion

"Matt, what do you mean by 'flaws'?"

I take my eyes off the rear view mirror and glance at furrowed brows. "I was referring to my outburst back there—only one of many flaws. I'm embarrassed by it. I've worked on ridding myself of similar explosions for years, yet still they leap out of me. Never comes to any good, but I still have the tendency. I'm flawed."

"So you're not perfect. None of us are. You should have heard me on the phone Wednesday morning. Sometimes it seems anger is an appropriate response, other times perhaps not. I think that some level of assertiveness might be appropriate given specific circumstances. You shouldn't beat yourself up about it, Coach."

Both of my hands are on the steering wheel, at ten o'clock and two o'clock, and both eyes are on the rear view mirror. "I don't deserve you."

"Well, you've got me nonetheless."

The SUV stays just visible in the rear view mirror as we drive east into town. When we near Cerrillos, it closes in to several cars behind us. I can't see inside—the windows are tinted black.

"Wynne, I'd like to stop by Kaune's to get some beef jerky. Kaune's is one of the few places I can find a particular brand made here in New Mexico."

"What a great idea. I stop at Kaune's every so often myself. Let's go!" I notice her sexy dress has been sliding sexily a little higher, and she's wearing her sandals again. My eyes snap back to the road, then the rear view mirrors.

"May I take a roundabout route to Kaune's?"

"Of course. You're piloting this craft."

Rather than turn onto Cerrillos, I pass through the intersection and zip up Rodeo to Zia, through Californicated, newer Santa Fe developments, commercial or residential. Not many adobes here. Instead, it's just square box after square box, some sporting kitsch, adobe-style facades. I speed up to distance us from the SUV, and then take an abrupt right onto Siringo, left on Botulph, left on St Michaels and a quick right onto Galisteo—back into authentic Santa Fe. Wynne doesn't say a word about my errant driving. Judgmental or not, I'm convinced the black SUV is not only following, but is probably the same one that cracked our windshield. What do I do? Do I bring this up?

"Where is Manitou Springs? During dinner at the club you said your house is in Colorado Springs, but you talk about Manitou Springs."

"Right. Sorry. I'm assuming you know things you may not." The SUV didn't turn down Galisteo—perhaps I am overreacting again. "I do that a lot—make assumptions that is—another habit I'd like to break."

"I suspect we all make assumptions, Matt. If I need to know something or want an explanation, I'm not reluctant to ask."

"Thanks, Wynne. Well, Manitou is a town of about 5,500 people, in the foothills under Pikes Peak. It's adjacent to and west of Colorado Springs. I spend most of my time in Manitou, not Colorado Springs. Other than enjoying the downtown YMCA, or going for cultural and social events, I don't much care to be in Colorado Springs."

"Why do you live there? If you don't like it, that is."

"Aside from the fact that it's my birthplace, Colorado Springs used to be a paradise. There remain less than, I'd say, ten neighborhoods in town, like where I live, that are sweet. More and more people come all the time, and a little town that grew too big, too fast, now has almost no sense of community. There seems to be a plethora of extreme religious and political viewpoints. That is opinion of course. Though an exceptionally astute one, I'm sure."

She looks over, laughing. I smile. She gets me. Dude, that's rare.

"Even though there are burgeoning political motivations— anachronistic development mentality—successfully changing Manitou into another mere JustLikeEverywhereElseVille, it still is a tiny town that claims community. People care about each other, help each other, laugh together, cry together, and live together. Almost all my friends live in Manitou."

I take a large drink of water. Soapbox speeches are nearly always too long—and too one-sided. "But really, I can't afford to make a move, and Sleeping Bear Oasis is only a thousand feet from the Manitou city line."

"Sleeping Bear Oasis?"

"The name of my house and property. I live a half-mile from the Garden of the Gods. Have you been there?"

"No, but I have heard about it."

"It's a beautiful big park, filled with towering red sandstone formations. I have a smaller example of those formations in my back yard. It looks like it has a twenty-foot-long bear sleeping on top of a rock the size of a delivery truck. The trees, garden, bird feeders, and sheltered setting all feel like an oasis, at least to me. I like to believe the critters also think it's an oasis: deer, fox, coyote, mountain lion, bobcat, bear, and the usual skunk and raccoon populations. Even had a wild turkey once—a true blessing in my experience."

"Matt, that sounds wonderful. Maybe I can come visit?"

"You bet. It's no Aspen, but Manirado Springs is pretty sweet in my not so humble opinion."

She doesn't need to ask.

"Part Manitou Springs—part Colorado Springs." I point the Prius onto Cordova, pondering my simple little Seventies rancher, and Wynne's background of wealth. Then, as we glide silently on Old Pecos Trail and onto Old Santa Fe Trail, I point out my friends' business. Wynne is more interested in my monologue.

"Anachronistic development mentality?"

I slant my head and squint my eyes. "You sure you want me to keep going?" She nods. "Okay. I don't mean to imply all is lost— because I do see signs of positive change—I just pray it's not way too little, too late. The USA, and the entire world, needs to move in completely new directions: creating appropriately localized social, economic and political paradigms.

"Sustainability should be the new mantra for every culture, every country, and for every human being. Due to ever-growing human activity, we now have a planet with vastly overused, depleted critical resources and increasingly obvious devastation. In my opinion, as far as is humanly possible, we all need to grow our own food, collect our own water, and learn to live without absolute dependence on gigantic corporate systems to provide for us. Talk about putting all your eggs in one basket.

"I try to do my part. I grow and store my own vegetables, beans and squashes. I'd love to find a way to have bees and chickens, but all the aforementioned Sleeping Bear Oasis wildlife make that impractical at best. I reuse, recycle, restore, and buy only what I need—and whenever possible I purchase local, or US-made products. Water, for all living things, is a problem many magnitudes more severe than food. I understand the massive-scale change I'm talking about has to come gradually, but we need to begin now. This is for real—and not going away by itself. But you know all this already—I'm just rambling again." I turn into the parking lot at Kaune's.

After switching off the Toyota, I walk around to open Wynne's door. She swings both legs out together and stands—stretching her arms to the sky. "I'm stiff from sitting so much. Typically I'm very active." We stroll toward the little strip mall. She grins. "Too bad you have no opinions."

"I'll take that as yet another of your generous compliments." I'm totally serious, even if unsure. Once again, the impassioned Matt, at bat and verbose beyond words, has fouled a wild pitch with a big, open mouth.

On the sidewalk, Wynne stops abruptly, glaring at a lotion-tanned fellow limping into the coffee shop next to Kaune's. Obviously a man of tempered refinement, he's walking with bare heels atop flattened deck shoes, and wearing greased-back hair, gold plastic sunglasses, a striped polo shirt and plaid Bermuda shorts. This is one of those middle-aging jocks, hoisting along a bum hip with a swagger designed to look like he's walking that way intentionally, being cool—while pining away inside for his glory days as a high school football star. Thank goodness I'm not judgmental or cynical.

He notices us. Suddenly donning an inane, cocky grin, he gives Wynne a suitably demeaning nod. "Hi there, Wynne."

Wynne is not smiling. With just enough ice in her voice to be noticeable, she says, "Hello, Patrick."

"How are things?"

"About as well as can be expected, Patrick." She apparently isn't interested in how his things are.

The two just surreptitiously glare at one another for an instant, until Patrick excuses himself. "Well, I guess I'll get an iced coffee." He offers a dismissive wave as he turns into the shop. "See you later."

As abruptly as she had stopped, she strides toward Kaune's, muttering quietly. "Not if I see you first."

I had to skip to keep up. "The infamous and palimonious Patrick?"

"The very same."

"Quite the dweeb. And I mean that in the nicest way."

Wynne does not giggle. "If only I had been as astute."

Scratch one suspect. That guy is incapable of accurately shooting anything, let alone Wynne's horse Browner with a carefully placed neck shot.

<center>~~~</center>

We intuitively go our separate ways. Wynne takes a right; I go straight—for the wine section. I select a bottle of organic Oregon State pinot noir. Lest anyone get a wrong impression, the life coach also winds his way through the store for a balanced product selection. I find lovely lemons and fresh figs, and snatch four packages of that not-organic, but pretty-darn-good New Mexican beef jerky. Wynne stealthily nudges up behind me at the cash register—her cart filled with two cans of coconut milk, stevia extract, Vermont maple syrup, four gallons of bottled water, a box of artichoke lasagna noodles, and a bottle of lavender and wildflower hair conditioner.

She sets her items on the flowing rubber tread, and then reaches her arm around my shoulder. "We need maté fixin's, Coach." That grin and endearing affectation melt away all remaining fears of my having damaged our relationship this afternoon. Professionally, I mean.

I smile back, more than a little humbled. After all, I had unwaveringly flown through heretofore-uncharted, interpersonal airspace. "Thank you, Wynne."

As I pull out my debit card, Wynne stops the cashier from totaling my purchase. "Connie, I'll get Mr. Hale's items too, please."

"Okay, Ms. Worner. You look absolutely stunning today. Are you in town long?" See, it's not just me.

"I'm not really sure, Connie. We're here for business and pleasure, and don't really have a definite itinerary."

"We haven't seen you recently, Ms. Worner. The weather has been really wonderful, with lots of rain. We need it badly. Did you see all the dead piñons as you came in?"

"Yes. It was hard to miss. It looks like half the forests have died. I'm guessing it's the drought?"

"That's what *The New Mexican* says. Another article Sunday warned about forest fire dangers. It's been so dry for so long it seems

112

like years. Thank God for the rain."

I chime in. "Amen to that." When Connie smiles at me, I notice the ornate gold cross on her sienna chest. Of course, I don't notice ample breasts barely covered by a delicate lace blouse designed by the devil himself.

Wynne and I head back into the crammed-full parking lot, with me pushing a grocery cart of goodies. I look over cautiously. "Thanks again, Wynne." She just grins bigger, and puts her arm around my shoulder, squeezing me into her.

Accepting gifts has never been a strong suit, and I continue to labor at absorbing that grace. I still feel uncomfortable. Embarrassed. And appreciative. Honored. Another roller coaster ride. Thrills, chills, spills. And a fantastic voyage when one is diving deep water, spelunking black, submerged caves—caverns that spark with silvery flashes of aquatic emotional life—exploding in and out of sight like gunfire on a moonless night.

Chapter Eighteen: The Great Wall of Compound

Waiting for an Audi R8 Spyder ahead of us to turn right, out of the parking lot, and onto Old Santa Fe Trail, I don't see any black SUVs. I slip into the right turn lane, behind the Audi, at the traffic light on Paseo de Peralta. The light turns green, and the silver bullet bolts around the corner. My turn is considerably more cautious.

"Do you know The Compound, Matt?"

"Yes, I do. In fact, I know two families who own condos there. You do, too, I assume? Have a condo, I mean."

"The trust does, yes. May I ask whom you know with a place there?"

"John and Paulette Baker, and the Stevens. For a few hours most weeks, I enjoy landscaping and garden maintenance at both estates in Colorado Springs."

"I don't recall that I've met them. You're a gardener, too?"

"Yes. I love playing in the dirt—creating art and harmonious *ch'i* with a palette from nature."

"You continue to surprise and amaze me, Matt. You're a man of many talents."

I don't turn crimson as we turn right, onto Canyon Road. The Prius, at 5 MPH, doesn't make a sound as we creep, behind tourist traffic, up the gallery-lined slope. The private drive down into The Compound requires another left turn, then a right. I stop at the guardhouse that sits quietly under and away from Canyon.

Steadying her lithe form with a left hand on my thigh, Wynne leans across me toward the open driver side window. "Hello, Gary. This is Matt Hale. Mr. Hale and I will be here for a few days or more. I hope you will allow him unencumbered entry."

The guard's response is polite: military-like. "As you wish, Miss

Worner."

"Thank you, Gary." She looks up at me from halfway in my lap, smiles the de Gracia smile, then pushes back gently into her seat. The black metal gate whirs open.

"I presume Worner is your ex-husband's name?"

"Yes, it is. I had hoped that by keeping the Worner moniker, I could deflect some of the pressure that comes with having been born a de Gracia. I suspect that plan hasn't worked quite as well as I'd hoped."

No kidding I think to myself as, for the first time in my dozen or so visits here, I examine The Compound's security provisions. This is an exclusive enclave of similarly designed and constructed Santa Fe style condominium homes, surrounded by a simple, relatively decrepit six-foot picket fence. The fence does create an aesthetically pleasing, rustic ambience—but as a serious security barrier, it certainly is no deterrent.

Wynne points to the garage at her condo. "The opener is on the visor."

I park next to a Jeep in the two-car garage, and press the remote control button to close the door behind us. The groceries are in the back seat, our bags in the trunk. For now, Wynne grabs only groceries. I follow her lead—well, I hoist the one remaining paper sack, and my gym bag, after throwing the ever-present book bag over my right shoulder.

We set groceries on the kitchen table, and Wynne points down the hall. "The guest bedroom is the second door."

"Thanks. I'll retrieve our bags."

"Thank you. I need to visit the powder room."

The stainless bucket I forgot to empty floods into my mind, and then flows right back out. After bringing in lightly packed baggage, I indulge in the guest bathroom to freshen up before dressing for the concert. Out of the shower, wet and towel-less, I hear Wynne say something from down the hall. I stick only my head out the bedroom door. "Sorry, I didn't hear you."

It's nice to hear chipper buoyancy in her voice. "Where would you like to have dinner?"

"Well, I'm okay with George's if you are. We could park at the public garage across from the Lensic."

"Perfect. I'll be ready in about twenty minutes, after a quick shower."

I wander through the condo, taking in the Santa Fe lifestyle of Wynne Luis Maria Caveza de Gracia Brockman Worner. Furniture is mostly ancient New Mexican, but still plenty comfortable. There's a small library, stuffed into a built-in bookcase in the living room. The holdings include local and southwestern history and art; sociology and personal development; and a smattering of classic fiction and recent novels. Sculptures and hanging art are plentiful—representing a knowledgeable blend of historic and contemporary genres: mostly Native American and *Santa Fe School.* A few original Baumann prints that I don't recognize hang beside Fremont Ellis paintings. A stunning Navajo weaving drapes the entire north wall in the living room.

While I'm examining a sand painting, Wynne glides in wearing a modest, cream-colored woven linen dress, and a peach, turquoise and eggshell shawl sporting a fringe of cut-glass beads—number 13s, actually. I, by contrast, am a bore, in usual khaki cargos and a starched, light blue, pinpoint oxford, but what the hey: this is Santa Fe. No one but me is going to give a hoot. Besides, I'll be with *her.*

We turn left onto one-way Canyon, from the falling-apart-fence-enclosed Compound. I whisk the Prius down Palace and then left on Alameda. We wind through the web of downtown streets, and pull into the parking garage. Luckily, a well-lighted parking spot waits, visible to the lot attendant in her little kiosk. I turn off the Toyota, and we walk into the hotel. Wynne slips her arm inside mine. I pretend to not care.

After an excellent New Mexican dinner, we linger around the Plaza, admiring traditional jewelry and artwork of Native American vendors in front of Palace of the Governors.

"You're looking for something specific, Matt?"

"Not really. I keep my eyes open for a nice bolo, but I've never really found a piece that speaks to me."

"What speaks to you?"

"Well, I don't wear jewelry, but a bolo is perfectly appropriate for even some formal occasions here in the Southwest, and Colorado, of course. Given experience with my relations at Fort Peck and elsewhere, I choose carefully what symbols and materials have been used in Native art. I don't wish to offend anyone. So, what speaks to me is both appropriate and beautiful."

She chuckles. "That certainly narrows it down."

"Yes, I'm adept at being specific." I grin, too.

We each point out and comment on jewelry and artwork that catches our eye. Window-shopping as we pass galleries on the way to the Lensic, we continue to agree on likes and dislikes. It's sort of like going to the candy store: "Oo, there's one I like. And that's scrumptious, but too sweet."

She leans over to bump me playfully. "You know, we have good taste." We both laugh.

"Wynne, do you often attend classical concerts?"

"As often as I can. I was raised with music, mostly Baroque, alongside, I know you'll be surprised, a generous dose of Spanish folk and dance."

"I absolutely love Baroque. I'm not familiar with Spanish folk or dance, though. I'd love to learn from your experience."

She squeezes my arm. "Another lesson? You are an adventurous pupil Matt."

"I do try to continue learning all time."

"I like that you have a broad education, and a considered appreciation of art, or so it seems." She smiles broadly, squeezing my arm again, against her breast. "Otherwise, I'd have to admit to having less than wonderful taste myself."

I squeeze back, away from that body part. "You know, our shared appreciation of art, music, and creative expression in general, suggests to me that, as a life coach, maybe my best chance at contributing to your happiness might be related to dealing with your business problems. That's where serious issues seem to reside. It appears that, with the exception of legal help, you might be going it alone and trying to breathe underwater. I still don't see that you have a need for coaching on how to live a good life. You're healthy, wise, strong, compassionate, self-aware, and downright wonderful."

She lets go my arm while I hold open one of the glass doors into the Lensic. "Takes one to know one."

I lightly place my palm in the small of her back as ticket-takers simply wave us by. Our seats are seventh row center. During the long Ciaccona of Bach's Partita Number 2, performed on an early Seventeenth Century violin, Wynne's shoulder nuzzles up to mine. She lays her head on my shoulder for those sweet minutes at the finale of the Partita. We remain shoulder to shoulder following the intermission—easier to pass my water bottle to and fro.

~~~

"Wynne, that was spectacular. Haydn, Bach, Purcell, and Vivaldi:
~~~

most of my favorite Baroque composers. Thank you so much. What fun. The quality of artistic expression in this relatively small town almost always amazes me, in spite of the fact that I've come to unfailingly expect it."

"There is indeed a fine pool of talent here. I ran a New York caliber ballet troupe for a season here in Santa Fe." She adjusts the shawl to warm her neck and shoulders, slips her arm inside mine again, and we saunter back to the parking garage on a balmy New Mexico night. She squeezes my arm close. I don't pretend to not notice. Instead, I squeeze back. It sure seems like we each are savoring this time together. I'm not imagining this, right? Not indulging my overreacting habit, right?

"Ran a ballet troupe?"

"I couldn't do the troupe justice, since my heart and horse remained in Aspen. I handed management over to a protégé. Would you like a nightcap, or perhaps dessert?"

"Thank you, but I honestly do imbibe alcohol or sugar in moderation. As you know, I do prefer my treats in late morning or early afternoon. I love my dark chocolate at eleven, and a small glass or two of a good red from three to seven."

"An afternoon delight." Wynne's tone is soft, gentle, and just a touch seductive—at least to me—although I'm probably not overly objective any more. "Do you know one of things I most like about you?"

I reply as professionally as is still possible. I'm ready to stop, plant my feet, throw her backwards over my leg, bend down, hold the back of her head, and kiss her like new lovers do. "I can't say that I do." With a boyish, hormone induced grin, I add, "But I'd love to learn what it is."

"You really do live by what you offer to teach others. You walk your talk. I find that refreshing, not to mention admirable. Honesty, nutrition, emotional exploration, and solid personal development—these aren't ideals you pretend—or worse, usurp for personal gain or use to manipulate others. I've experienced that numerous times. Thank you for being here—for responding to my call for help." She squeezes my arm hard enough to cut off circulation. Thank goodness for that plush pillow.

Chapter Nineteen: Grandfather In Eden

I awake early, around five-thirty. After *Pal Dan Gum* and yoga in the guest room, I fall into a maroon, luxurious terry bathrobe hanging in the closet, and tread barefoot to the kitchen for those maté fixin's. On the counter, next to a water kettle atop the stove, sits a heavy, big ceramic mug—probably sixteen ounces. It has a hand painted water bird on one side and teepee on the other. I know these symbols, having held doorkeeper and fireman responsibilities during related ceremonies. While the green tea steeps, I pad quietly back to the guest room for the shower sandals in my gym bag, and carry them to the kitchen. It's not even a quarter till seven when, maté in hand, I slip out the back door into the ultra-petite backyard. It would be tough to bury even one adult body here.

The Compound is designed to maximize common use areas, so the condos themselves typically have smallish, intimate outdoor spaces. That does, of course, mean less ground to maintain, especially for owners who may not spend much time here. Wynne's is near the center of the condominium group. In Sunday morning quiet, I easily hear splashing from the fountain out in the main courtyard—even above the veritable roar of a few zillion birds that also make their homes in this oasis of trees, superb xeric landscaping, and secluded privacy. I stroll out the back gate and around to Wynne's arched, wooden front gate, built like so many in New Mexico, into a customary adobe wall.

She has xeriscape gardens aft and fore, with a venerable apple tree standing sentry in this small, maybe thirty-by-thirty front yard. New apples are shaped like Pippin, or maybe Fuji, although the latter is less likely given the tree's obvious advanced age. With morning sun just starting to brush bright its uppermost branch tops, gentle reflected light illuminates this Grandfather's still-shaded heart. It's maybe three feet broad at the trunk, and squat and round overall, probably due to the many arid Santa Fe decades of its life, and careful pruning. Nonetheless, like many very old apples I have known, it is prolifically producing fruit. Gnarled branches sag with green apples slightly larger than golf balls. I try one. It's mouth-puckering tart, but a hint of sweetness carries the distinct assurance of delicious rewards to come.

Under the laden apple are shade-loving, very-low-water ground covers, grasses, and dwarf evergreens, artfully interspersed with a perennial palette offering a complete range of blooming times. The result is constant color and changing textures during the entire growing season. I am impressed. Without warning, Wynne bursts out the screened front door.

She's still wearing her nightshirt. It's loose fitting; pale pastel violet, and probably combed cotton. It has a little purple bow at the center of the neckline. It sure looks soft. I try my best to not notice it is, well, none-too-long. Meanwhile my anatomy begins to exhibit other ideas.

Raising my mug, I grin. "Coconut milk, maple syrup, and a man-size maté mug. On a beautiful Santa Fe Sunday morning with Wynne de Gracia. Now, *this* is livin'."

She's cheerful, happy, smiling. "Good morning. What do you think of the garden?"

"I love it, and a good morning to you, too. Awesome use of ground covers and grasses, alongside careful perennial selection and perfect placement. Very sweet. Who designed this little paradise?"

"Well, as a matter of fact, I did," she croons, puffing up her chest and swaying back and forth like a proud little four year old. I readily envision her at that age, showing off to loving, approving parents.

"Wow. I'm impressed—really—it's very nice. We could go into the landscaping business."

She chuckles. "Let's keep that in mind. I'm always interested in successful partnerships. I'll take a fast shower. We'll need breakfast— let me know where you'd like to go, okay? We don't have proper ingredients for a Coach-breakfast."

Her expression changes like she's feeling a sudden, stitching pain. "I do have a ten o'clock appointment." Instantly, though, the smile returns. "But then we have the rest of the day together to do what we want. We can stay in Santa Fe as long as you like, or as long as the legal bears need, whichever is your pleasure. I'm off for that shower."

She executes a perfect 180-degree *fouetté*. The pastel nightshirt twirls out, up, and away—it's all she's wearing.

Chapter Twenty: *Wasicun* (The Fat Takers)

I hear my name being called from inside the condo. Before I'm able to move my two hundred pound chair, Wynne crosses the threshold, bag on shoulder. "So here you are. I'm hoping for plenty of time to enjoy breakfast with you—before I face the boys."

"I'd like to go the Guadalupe. Is that okay with you?" I'm sitting out front, in a heavy old chair, at a heavy old table, under a heavy old portico, having a heavy old brain session, doodling in my red, spiral bound journal.

"Absolutely. Another great choice, Coach." She's wearing a gray pinstripe pantsuit over an off-white, satin blouse, and no jewelry.

"Jeez, you look so professional. Should I change?" I'm wearing a gray Martin guitar t-shirt under a teal, organic cotton long sleeve shirt, with the cuffs rolled up; and walking shoes. And of course, khaki cargo pants.

"Definitely not. You don't need to come with me. Be comfortable. Be *you*, remember?"

"Right. It's just past seven-thirty. Do we have time to walk?"

"Another great idea. Donovan's office is on East Palace. I can easily walk there, too, from the Guadalupe. It's perfect. Shall we go?" I nod. She locks the heavy, hand carved, eighteenth century wooden door, and latches the wimpy screen door.

After stashing the notebook-slash-journal back inside my book bag, I hoist it from the chair next to me, sling it over my right shoulder, take both arms to put my chair back, and we walk through Wynne's compact, brimming with life garden; out the tall, thick, heavy New Mexican gate. Pretty much everything in New Mexico is old and heavy, or new and lightweight. Damp air still is thronged with birdsong, and infused with fragrances both sweet and pungent.

Wynne and I wave at the guard on our way past the booth. Gary isn't on this morning. Wynne calls into the guardhouse. "Good morning, Frank." He looks up, smiling superficially, waves half-heartedly, and quickly resumes reading a magazine.

We enjoy the scenic route, strolling down Canyon and Camino Escondido, to the river walk along Alameda. No water runs in the Santa Fe River. Non-cynical I have a few words to spill.

"The river's dry again. I haven't seen running water in here for more than five years. Granted, during that time I haven't been in Santa Fe during spring snowmelt; nonetheless, I distinctly remember at least a small stream flowing, no matter what time of year. Maybe my memory's not accurate."

"Your memory is fine, Matt. The river dries up more with each year. The city and county have been discussing releasing a trickle from the reservoir, just to have running water. I certainly hope that is the decision."

"I just realized today is Sunday; and you're meeting with legal counsel. I know it's really none of my business, but it seems unusual that one meets a lawyer on a weekend. And Sunday?"

"You're absolutely right. Things have gotten ugly around the San Luis water rights, and Donovan wanted to meet right away. So here we are."

Ours is a quiet walk after I brought up the meeting. She's still smiling, though subdued, and we both simply enjoy a lovely Santa Fe Sunday morning. It bangs around in my overstuffed brain cells to mention the black SUV, but intuition nudges me to, for now, leave the topic alone. Having learned, or rather, finally having it become ever more clear to me in life, that intuition is always correct, I usually do as I'm told. Like most good things in life, or like most things in a good life, there is much to learn and much to unlearn. Intuition, though, is simply just there: only it's not so easy to trust gut feelings sans unlearning.

~~~

We wait only about five minutes for a table at the Guadalupe Café, a rarity during any season but especially in August. After *huevos rancheros con chorizo y* maté, I walk Wynne back to East Palace and into the law offices. It's not that she can't make it on her own, and she did offer. I'm still on the lookout for trouble, even though there has been no sign of a menacing black anything. And I've been watchful. Wynne either hasn't noticed that fact, or hasn't mentioned it.
~~~

"Matt, thank you for walking with me this morning. I'd invite you to stay, but I suspect the rest of the morning here will be unpleasant or boring." She reaches into that beautiful bag, so much at home here in New Mexico, pulling out her cell phone. "May I suggest that you enjoy the morning, and I'll call you from Donovan's office phone when we're done?"

"Will you set it to not ring?"

"Sure. I'll set it to vibrate." She takes my open left hand in hers, lays her cell phone in my palm, and doesn't let go. She offers a faltering, wry smile, and a lingering, faintly sorrowful gaze. My heart sinks to the Persian rug covered, wooden floorboards.

I plead gently. "Please call if you need anything at all."

She leans over to kiss my left cheek, and lets go my hand. I shove the cell phone in my cargo pants pocket—one of the pockets made for actual cargo. I don't often carry my cell phone. Don't want to own one. Muddies the water in my ever so humble life coach opinion. Like a salmon in springtime, I'd rather my underwater life be without upstream dams. Or bears.

~~~

I saunter over for another stroll around the Plaza, and by Native vendors under the portico at the Palace of the Governors. I can look more closely without likelihood that Wynne insists I have that buffalo and golden eagle bolo. Not one for wearing jewelry, although I do protect a wolf bone choker, and have been known to wear beaded necklaces and jackets, I always look for that perfect bolo. The just-right ones I've found in times past are always a distance from the reach of my wallet. It has pretty short little arms.

Surprise, surprise, the eagle and buffalo bolo is still there—at sixteen hundred. These artists, as do all, deserve a good price for superb work. I can't afford this beautiful craftsmanship, but it doesn't hurt to admire the piece, and complement its creator. He explains his wife is Lakota, and he lives with her clan in Pine Ridge; but sales are outstanding here in the summer.

Buffalo images are somewhat unusual this far south. Southwestern Native designs generally don't borrow too much from peoples of the Plains, although some pieces are created to appeal to tourists. Not this one. Sort of representative-abstractly inlaid in sterling, are mother of pearl, smoky quartz, jet obsidian, and a gorgeous array of earth-tone agates—depicting a magpie riding a bull bison's rear haunch, as a golden eagle turns away and up in the
~~~

foreground; in the distance are the Black Hills with a turquoise and pearl sky. Dude.

My preferences require subtle symbolism and practical spirituality, rather than ornate trappings. Often the finest artwork is made expressly for you, with foreknowledge of who you are, where you are in life, and where you might be headed. I decide to spend an hour at the Georgia O'Keefe Museum, and then stroll over to the Institute for American Indian Arts, where I happen to be a member.

While studying in-your-face, bold, and nakedly allegorical exhibits at IAIA, Wynne's cell phone suddenly buzzes my left leg. I wear cargo pants almost exclusively, so I have plenty pockets to hold stunning devices. Just a big book bag, big pockets, carries lots of stuff around kind of guy—a regular librarian Boy Scout.

"Hey there, gorgeous." Whoops. Say, that was professional. Hot blood boils my face. No one notices. They're all watching the giant steel wheel I just set spinning—it's a sort of Indian wheel of fortune, with mostly bankruptcies on which to land. Every one else was afraid to touch it. It was art. They were tourists. I, however, am not normal. The wheel and I comprise a match made in Santa Fe.

Wynne, as usual, is gracious enough to overlook my ingratiation. Of course, I can't see whether a smile graces her as I call her gorgeous. I don't intuit it either. And her voice gives no clue. "I'm done here for now. Shall we meet for lunch?"

I haven't noticed the time approaching twelve forty-five. Art does that to me. Whether creating my own or enjoying others' work, ticking and tocking loses all relevance to me. Not that I make time a priority anyway. I haven't even worn a watch for more than sixteen years. Native and spiritual mentors, seen and unseen, known and unknown, have guided me for years to live by nature, not by mechanisms of man. Now that she mentions it, I am feeling a tad hungry—in the impertinent way that we spoiled Americans often don't notice.

"I'll come over to meet you," I say, trying not to sound concerned about her walking alone with nasty looking, black widow SUVs climbing all over the sticky spider web that is Old Santa Fe streets.

"That won't be necessary. Donovan will drop me off. Where would you like to meet?" Before I respond, and possibly because I hesitate while mulling over the surfeit of choices, she quickly asks, "How about Coyote Café, or maybe the Pink Adobe?"

"Wynne, I haven't been to the Pink ever, though Francesca and

Jerron, my friends who own that little architecture firm on Old Santa Fe Trail opposite of Kaune's, say it's great. I love the Coyote Café, but I'd like to try the Pink, if that's okay with you." Either is fine with me. I know the Coyote is superb, especially for an O blood type hunter-gatherer like me.

She sounds frustrated and tired. "It's a deal. A far better one than I've discussed today. Where are you now?"

"I'm at the IAIA. I should be able to get to the Pink in less than 15 minutes."

I don't recall hearing Wynne sound this abrupt. And I'm not imagining it, either. "Perfect. Whoever arrives first can get a table. See you shortly." Click. Well, it wasn't really a click. It was more like a solid, decisive, and possibly furious, receiver slam to cradle—a knife to the heart of the stop button.

Right arm tightly covering my bag, I jog south down Cathedral, open the weather-beaten wooden door, framed into an adobe wall that surrounds the Inn at Loretto, where I cut through the parking lot to Old Santa Fe Trail, and again traverse that dry riverbed.

~~~

"You're here to meet Ms. Worner, sir?" inquires a hostess as I open the front door to the Pink.

"Yes, thank you."

"Right this way, please," suggests the young, pretty, petite blonde.

Wynne is concentrating on two stacks of legal papers as I come toward the table. When she sees me, she sets pages down but not away. She does smile my direction. Manage a smile is more like it. This isn't the same spirit that burst through the screen door to greet me this morning, shining and light, buoyant and joyous.

While taking my seat, I ask, "Are you okay?"

We're at a small table for two, tucked into a private corner, next to a tiny fireplace built into soft pink adobe walls. Perfectly Santa Fe. At another time this is a cuddling, romantic spot. Doesn't seem that way just now. More like a secluded hideout. I know that need also. I have her cell phone out in my hand.

She takes the phone, and holding it three feet above her bag, just lets it drop. "I'm sorry. I'm disappointed by the conference. I'm being told to seriously consider selling out to commercial water developers. In an attempt to beat Denver or Arizona to the water, a private Texas consortium has made a huge financial offer, with residual rights and royalties. It's extremely lucrative, and in perpetuity.
~~~

That would, of course, be good for the trust." Wynne's wounded-child eyes dart quickly away from mine, gazing down at the piles of paper lying on the table. "Donovan and Julian made sure I understood that."

She stares intently at the tabletop for one of those half-minutes that seem like half an hour. Then she looks back—eyes swelling and tears starting to create tiny rivulets next to her nose. "But—it feels like selling God for profit."

I'm angry. "Don't do it. There are whole sects making that sale—with zero remorse and plenty of profit." That doesn't help. She starts crying. My heart falls to the bottoms of my feet. I scoot my chair over to her side. My right arm shelters her shoulders, and like back there in the blood-smell summer pasture, she lets herself sob.

~~~

After maybe ten minutes, Wynne dabs her eyes and face with a linen napkin, and places bundles of *wasicun* documents into her beautiful woven bag. I think she loves that bag; I'm only fond of mine. The meal cheers her. Or seems to. At her request, the Pink lets us order from the dinner menu. She orders lobster salad. I have grilled salmon.

Her eyes are red and sagging. "What did you do today?"

"I popped into the O'Keefe Museum, but didn't stay long. I was more interested in seeing what was hanging at IAIA. That was fun. The day's been really nice, too, with plenty of clouds to keep the sun at bay."

"You don't like sunshine?"

"It's not that. We need sun to exist. But with interminable drought, I think both the planet and I need as many breaks from parching heat as possible. And the only hat I brought along on this trip is in the Little Nell garage."

"Do we need to get you a hat?"

"Thank you, but I'm fine. Especially with cloud cover."

"You know that ultraviolet rays penetrate those clouds, of course."

"Yes, and for me, it's mostly the heat. I'm not even a little bit fond of being too hot. Except when I'm in hot water, of course." Not so much as even a hint of a smile.

We're quiet. Every so often Wynne picks out a few pages, and scans them without reading. We stay a long time, but talk little. I pull a well-worn Louise Erdrige novel out of my bag, and give Wynne lots
~~~

of space. No one else is in the restaurant because, as it turns out, the Pink closes between lunch and dinner. The hostess lets us stay, perhaps because Wynne is upset, perhaps because Ms. Worner is a valued regular here. She even comes in to light the little gas fireplace, setting it to a tiny flicker.

Wynne says nothing more about her meeting, and understandably isn't her usually cheerful self. She smiles every now and then as we linger in the coziness of the Pink, and the romantic corner that is all ours; but under the surface, like having an irritating itch that you can't reach in public, she's clearly concerned. Nearly four hours into the afternoon, we get up to go.

Pretty petite unlocks the door to Old Santa Fe Trail, and partly sunny skies.

Chapter Twenty-One: You Called Me Gorgeous Today

Grimacing, Wynne tries to find a spot on her left shoulder where her bag's not so oppressive.

I immediately reach to help her hold it. "Let me carry that, okay?"

"I can handle it."

"I know you can, but you know what? My book bag's feeling a little too heavy today—possibly because there's an actual book in it. Maybe you could help me out by taking it for me?"

She gives me *the smile*. "You charmer." We trade bags. She looks at me. "It's heavier than I expected."

I look in her eyes as seriously as I can. "You know, that's because my bag only knows how to ride on a right shoulder."

This garners a weak chuckle. "And my straps have been carefully worn in for only the left."

I switch her bag to my left shoulder; she smiles, red eyes shining at me, and moves mine to her right. We saunter across to De Vargas and then up Canyon, enjoying the perfect, partly cloudy, Land of Enchantment late afternoon. She remains quiet. I decide to interrupt her solitude—it's an intuition-guided decision.

"I love late afternoon and early evening, although not as much as morning. Mornings are God's incredibly perfect gift to us: freshness, new blossoms, and rebirth every miraculous day, although the U.S. Government takes that gift away with Daylight Stealing Time. New Mexico evenings, however, are nothing to scoff."

I can't be sure she's listening, but my heart says to keep talking. "I love the subdued sun rays, angling low across this intensely painted, high desert landscape. Delicate sunset pastels highlight earth-toned, adobe architecture—or wash across cholla cacti, sagebrush stands or mountains and mesas near and distant. That light exposes the rich hues and vibrant colors of the unique Southwestern-ness that melds with your spirit here—an intrinsic, soulful art often in hiding during blanching midday heat."

She takes my hand as we scamper across ever-busy Paseo de Peralta. She lets go on the other side. "Was that a speech you memorized? Nobody talks like that, Matt."

"I warned you I was abnormal. Well, maybe it wasn't a warning. I probably made it sound harmless." Her laugh takes me by surprise. "I'm afraid that was indeed *not* a practiced piece of pedantic punditry."

She laughs again. "Really, how do you come up with this stuff?"

"Stuff? Oh, you mean *Matticisms*…just part of what I am. I can't help myself. Maybe it's a result of years of frustrated creativity."

She chuckles. "Matticisms." Her face turns serious again. "Frustrated creativity?"

"Instead of soulful writing and drawing, I pursued jobs—to make money, not to be happy. It was just maddening, not following my heart." I'm thinking we already talked about this.

"I do remember that from our first conversation, at the Club. I feel as though I'm getting more insight into you, though—an improved perspective." She reaches over to squeeze my right hand.

"Ditto." I squeeze back, but we each let go and readjust our adopted shoulder bags. Meandering our way into twenty or so inviting galleries, we delight in a bloom-scented evening stroll. The Canyon Road art district is definitely quieter than on frantic Fridays, but still filled with Sunday sightseers. They don't inconvenience us, though. We're enveloped in our own reassuring bubble.

Wynne is smiling again, and happy. "You said you were also an artist, didn't you? Tell me about that."

"More like an artist dilettante."

"Why do I not believe that?"

"For the last five years or so I've merely played around with concrete sculpture, drawing, and printmaking. Nothing serious. My most recent passion is abstract expression. I might get serious about that."

"You seem to me to be pretty serious about everything."

"Is that good or bad?"

"Neither. It's just your character, I suppose."

"You're right, of course. Unflagging solemnity is another personal growth project. My take is that I'm preoccupied: too deep in my head. Coming from heart is best—and where I'm concentrating my internal work these days." She just looks, probably wondering about something. "Back to art, I audited numerous art classes at the University of Colorado. One of my extracurricular watercolors garnered an Honorable Mention in the senior art exhibition. An art student girlfriend, who helped to hang the show, told me later that I actually took first place, but art faculty convinced the judge to reconsider because I wasn't a Fine Art degree-seeking student. Blah, blah. Anyway, visual art has not been a primary focus."

"So now you're doing abstracts?"

"In more ways than one, yes." She chuckles. I join in. "My most recent work is a series. I haven't finished it, but it's been really fun."

She takes my arm, and after retrieving her shawl, pulls it up and over our entwinement. "Come on, I want to hear more."

"The series started five years ago, when I experienced a collision of major life events. I mean, it was incredible—a primal, ingenious catharsis, during which I accidentally created my *coup de maître* piece."

"A primal, ingenious catharsis. Cool."

"That's several times now I've heard you say 'cool.' "

"Hey, I can be, you know, like, colloquial with the best of 'em, dude."

I grin. "Fair enough."

"Come on, I want to hear it all."

I pretend to whine. "Okay."

She squeezes.

I squeeze back. "If you get bored let me know. I can ramble on, you know."

"I think I might have noticed that."

I squeeze her arm this time. She squeezes back, with a big de Gracia smile. "I was studying during a cutting edge, contemporary media class at the Colorado Springs Fine Arts Center. One day, we were given big pieces of vellum to play with, using India ink. I put my vellum on the floor, and proceeded to let out all my hopes and frustrations around resigning my first library director position. I threw and splashed and dripped and brushed. I used differing techniques, surreptitiously adding a tiny bit of oil pastel and acrylic. I love that piece, and have thoroughly benefited by creating the series based on that one work. Hold up a second. I need some water."

We stop and Wynne turns my bag, still atop her right shoulder, toward me. I pull out the nearly empty water bottle, offering it first to her. The bag slips from her shoulder, but she catches it with her elbow.

"Does it have boy cooties?"

"Crawlin' with 'em."

She laughs and takes a long drink, but only half of what's left. I finish the rest and angle the bottle back into its assigned parking spot.

"So, tell me more. This is fascinating. I've never been much of an artist, so it's intriguing to hear about the personal process." She pulls my humble book bag back onto a pinstriped shoulder, and the four-year-old pleads, "Please?"

"Well, if you insist. What I discovered with that first big piece was—are you ready for more Matticisms?"

She laughs again. "Matticisms."

"What I felt, for the first time in a long time, and possibly for the first time ever, was total, impassioned, consciously rational release of emotion and expression, without any preconception or structure: a sort of visualistic diphthong."

"May I look that up in the dictionary in your book bag please?" She turns my bag toward me again, grinning over her shoulder.

I laugh heartily. "Matticisms aren't in most dictionaries—yet."

"When are you going to let me see your work?"

"Well, I've given most everything away."

Sounding much like youthfully playful Cassie as she says it, Wynne is intentionally melodramatic. "Oh, come on, Matt. I want to see your work. Please?" We wave at Frank, who barely returns a nondescript nod, as we walk by the guardhouse and into the sunset birdsong gallery of The Compound.

Wynne cajoles me in that sweet, sensual voice I am so unable to resist. But then, I really haven't tried very hard. "Come sit with me for a while." She pulls me along and sits us down, side-by-side, onto a worn, unpainted, wooden bench next to the fountain in the common courtyard. She does not let go my hand. Of course, I don't exactly try to pull away, either. With cascading water next to us, and the tiniest of breezes barely brushing heavily scented Compound fragrances through thick evening air, we sit silently and embrace sunset lavenders, tangerines and peaches; while patiently awaiting the inevitable fade, into dusk gray and white, of massive cumulonimbus clouds mushrooming in the southern vista. As our evening grows darker, the temperature drops noticeably.

Wynne suddenly breaks the silence with an energetic outburst. "Let's get some dinner."

"Okay."

She doesn't let go my hand until she reaches for the wooden front gate. We step under the adobe-style arch and across the garden path. She unlocks the front door. "There's some left-over lasagna in the freezer. Does that sound okay?"

"Sure. I could open the pinot we got at Kaune's." I certainly can't take sole credit for the wine, since Wynne paid for it. Hey, as a bonus, we can share the blame if it's vinegar, the accolade if it's exquisite.

"Oooo, good idea. I hope the lasagna's not freezer burned. It's been in there more than a month."

"I'll bet even if it is, we won't notice. I love lasagna, even though it's not the best choice for my diet." I watch her smile fade. My speaking before thinking habit strikes again—might be authentic, but it sure can blow a hole in the cosmic order. "Wynne, I absolutely love lasagna. It'll be perfect."

Her smile spreads right back. She brushes wavy golden hair from her eyes. They seem concerned, or maybe more sensitive, more vulnerable. I recognize them. "Well, if not, we'll go out and get something, okay?"

"Okay."

~~~

With a big stainless steel spatula, Wynne deftly transfers a half-lasagna from its cardboard shack to a gleaming ceramic plate sitting inside the microwave. I don't ever use those things, but I'm not saying a word. She hands me the empty box. "Will you put this in the recycle bin in the garage? It's all the way out by the door."

"Sure." While there, I notice the Prius' windshield is still extremely cracked. The Jeep is an older model Grand Cherokee with an efficient and dependable inline, six-cylinder engine. By the time I reenter the kitchen, it's already filled with the heavenly scent of lasagna. A few minutes later, Wynne places two handmade stoneware plates on the table, complimented by ancient silver flatware, fresh linen napkins, two glasses of water—no ice—and two crystal wine goblets.

I open a suspect drawer. "Where can I find a corkscrew?"

"In the top drawer, left of the stove."
~~~

Opening the bottle, I break the cork. Pouring each wine goblet to half full, I smell the pinot after swirling it each direction inside my glass. It seems unremarkable, but not sharp. The center of the table now has a single, lit, white candle in a short, plain, silver candlestick. The microwave dings. One minute later, dinner is served.

Wynne dims the kitchen chandelier, made of hand stamped Mexican tin. "I hope you don't mind. I like to enjoy dusk."

"That's perfect." My professional barriers are fading, like a dream you suspect you should remember, but that instead disintegrates instantly—the moment you awake. You're left with a few emotional sensations, and a vague idea that something important was once there. And is no longer.

After finishing the first bite of lasagna, sipping the pinot noir, and nodding her head with an approving little smile, she matter-of-factly states, "You called me gorgeous today."

I want to take my first bite from her silk neck, not from my Italian fare. Instead, I turn crimson, and cut away a one-inch lasagna square. The kitchen heats to about ten thousand degrees. "Sorry about that. My professionalism is slipping. I should have better control."

"No you shouldn't."

"But that was totally unprofessional."

"Matt, I want to believe we're becoming good friends. We're getting to know each other, and it seems to me a good deal of familiarity is just fine." Her eyes pierce into mine. "This conversation is a rerun. Relax. Give it up. Enjoy yourself, enjoy me, and let us enjoy each other. Okay?" She slips her fingers around the stem of her goblet, and, cupping its in her palm, raises it gradually to her lips.

That wasn't really intended to be so sensuous, I'm pretty sure. "I guess I'm finding it difficult to advise you, because you truly are gorgeous. In many ways."

On her elbows, she leans over the table, goblet in both hands, and asks, "Matt, are you attracted to me?" In both hands, the glass waits just under her lips, tilted so wine is less than a half inch from the brim, her head titled down toward the crystal, eyes looking up to mine. Those eyes…. Oh, my God.

"More than you can imagine." Quickly I avert my eyes and reach for my wine glass, too. I watch it intently, swirling the wine inside. I smell the bouquet, take a big sip, and let it linger inside my mouth. Of course, none of this silly diversion is useful. The wine is quite good, though.

"I'm attracted to you too, you know."

I want to disappear, or slip down in my chair to hide under the table. Instead I just sit there, frozen. I'm caught in a state of Salvador Dali confusion: a partially melted pizza of guilt, desire, clarity, and blindness—biochemical chaos. Surreal real life.

She notices my expression—whatever expression it is that I'm wearing. "Really, Matt. I'm pleased you find me attractive. The feeling is completely reciprocal."

I try to stop spinning.

"You have noticed, right?"

I'm melting. Melting.

"Matt?"

"I'm sorry. I'm feeling confused."

"About?"

"About being attracted to you. I'm supposed to have professional boundaries."

"Bull. Be who you are. Feel what you feel. No regrets. You would advise me no differently."

My mind is swimming, unable to respond. Raising the fork in my left hand, I finally engulf my cubic inch of lasagna, and don't look at her. The knife in my right hand might be quivering. I can't fall into those alluring gray-green eyes, can't be softened by that wild honey smile. Or gaze at the fine velvet arc of her neck and shoulder. I can't. It just isn't professional.

Reaching for the wine bottle, Wynne flatly and expertly changes the subject. "Let's have some more of this excellent pinot noir." She pours a splash into each goblet.

Immediately, I'm deluged with a flood of even more guilt. Or remorse. Or shame. Or—whatever it is, I am assuredly drowning.

"Life coach underboard. Life coach underboard."

Chapter Twenty-Two: Alone Together

It's like two not-quite acquaintances, having a self-absorbed chance meal, at a locally favored, warmly lighted restaurant's community table. We don't finish the pinot. It stands lonely on the kitchen table, an unstoppable green glass bottle, exploding with one refracted candle flame; alongside, and within reach of, two half full goblets of organic Oregon State pinot noir, displaying an unremarkable, yet not sharp, bouquet. All, gracing the otherwise bare, white linen clothed, nineteenth century New Mexican dining table: A table weighing perhaps seven hundred pounds, that features two, two-inch walnut axles that provide fulcrums for extensions adding another four or eight people to the ten it normally seats. The *comida* is warm not from heating a well-liked dinner in the microwave, but from smooth lines, flowing curves, soft textures, and heartwarming *ch'i* of southwestern adobe sensibility.

We wash dishes together. Well, I wash. There aren't many of course. She dries.

The request is vague. "Will you come for a walk with me?"

I'm eager to make up. "I'd love to."

She blows out the candle, which proceeds to smoke profusely. At the front door, she wraps her upper torso in another woven cotton shawl, a sturdy one, and plain vanilla, from the cloak closet. It perfectly compliments the satin blouse, pinstripe silk pants, and supportive walking shoes. She drapes the shawl across her shoulders, back and neck, crossing it over her heart, and pins it closed with a three-inch, sterling and turquoise clasp. We head outside, under that bountiful grandfather apple and past Wynne's beautifully planned garden, blossoms closed or open for the night, according to their preferences. It's dark now. The air is cool, almost chilly, and wet, heavenly fragrant, and dead still.

I venture further out on the gangplank, a rough sea below me, my ship being tossed around like a tot's toy. "What a delicious night, don't you think?" A shiny, sharp, medieval guillotine had severed the cord between us. I know it. I also know it was I who set the blade loose.

"Definitely. Was the lasagna okay?"

My voice quavers. "I loved it. It was like fresh from the oven."

Wynne laughs easily; smiling a smile that gives me hope all is well with the world. "A month old, and fresh from four minutes in the microwave."

"It was delicious. The wine, too. Robust but simple, as one expects from a pinot noir, and with an almost cheery bouquet." My ironic slip escapes neither of us.

She giggles, sounding exactly like Cassie from the tan leather back seat of the Lexus. "You mean cherry, I'm sure."

I dreamt what Cassie might be doing right now. Packing for school? Writing letters to friends? Connecting online? Remembering Browner? Getting ready for a night out in Aspen? Was she doing something I don't remember, or never knew, about being seventeen, especially in today's U.S.A.? Today's tiny little world, where the whole planet is at your fingertips, and in your face? I know for certain Cassie is *not* watching a stupid television. She's too alive for that. We sure can cover a lot of ground at light speed, in our dreams, and thoughts. I redden at my slip, and chuckle quietly. "Yes, yes, I did. Cheery indeed." Like my life depends on it, I back off the plank. "Wynne, I'm really sorry about what I said at dinner. I ruined our lovely evening."

"You didn't ruin anything. You were being honest. Perhaps we both needed to broach the attraction thing, and move on. You would advise me to do exactly that, I'm certain." My hostess deftly changes the subject. Again. "So, what might you like to do tomorrow?"

"Well, I haven't been to Tesuque for several years. And we could call Jerron and Francesca Whitten. I'd love for you to meet them. But, what do you have in mind?"

"I'm perfectly happy just hanging with you. I'm seeing Santa Fe with a new perspective, through your eyes. I guess I've become too familiar with the place, doing the same old things, seeing the same old sights, doing, mostly, the same old business."

"I'll call Jerron and Francesca tomorrow morning."

"That sounds wonderful. I look forward to meeting them."

~~~

We stroll up Canyon, away from galleries rather than toward. We say nothing; instead listening to our own footsteps, and occasional sounds of quiet lives from old, tiny adobes: simply enjoying an almost chilly high desert night. At Camino Cabra we cross over to Upper Canyon Road, striding next to what at one time was the Santa Fe River. Eventually our hike hooks back down Cerro Gordo. It's a long, lovely, winding walk: nearly three hilly miles. Back in town, we take our time strolling back down East Palace to Delgado, before turning uphill again, to Canyon Road and The Compound.

As we approach the guardhouse, Wynne stops, turning to face me. A friendly and not intimate two feet away, she takes my right hand in hers. Crossed in front of us like that, our arms create a much sturdier barrier than the one surrounding The Compound. The night is just-passed new moon black, but with glow from the guardhouse we can see into each other's eyes. Eyes tell everything, all by themselves. Words are unnecessary. Nevertheless....

"Matt, thank you for a wonderful walk. I've had a delightful evening. Please don't worry about familiarity, or professionalism, or anything at all. I really would appreciate it if we could simply enjoy our time together, okay? I want to unlearn more about myself. I want you to teach me to breathe underwater."

"I think you're already drawing breath better than I."

We enter the condo. I begin refilling my water bottle, and Wynne walks down the narrow hall to the master bedroom. She turns back around after she goes in, leans her head out with her body resting on the doorjamb. "Thank you for your honesty, Matt. I'll see you in the morning."

I turn my head to look down the hall. "Likewise, Wynne. Have a wonderful, healing, restful sleep." That's what I say to my birdies at night, too. And anyone else who might be there.

Wynne disappears inside, and I turn back to the gallon jug of water.

It feels like she's looking up the hall again. I finish filling the bottle, and turn to look, but she's not there.
~~~

Chapter Twenty-Three: Alone Lonely

It's dark, this Monday morning, when I wake early again. Another Santa Fe songbird concerto fills the guest bedroom through wide-open windows. I pull apart blood red curtains, patterned sparsely with gold-embroidered Native American designs—Great Lakes or Northeastern. This morning is windless and cloudy: high stratus, mostly medium gray, with an occasional dark layer underneath, like two different types of butter spread thick across a slice of toast. Smooth stratus underbellies like these mean rain. Especially when they descend upon what's below.

In the maroon bathrobe, I concoct morning maté in my now favorite Santa Fe mug. I carry the water bird into the study, sit down at Wynne's heirloom writing desk, and turn on her powerful desktop PC. After a glance at news headlines that I'm powerless, except for prayer, to affect, I check email messages. Only one real email is waiting, from a colleague at Colorado College. Daryll wondered if I could help create a computer troubleshooting presentation to a group of Pikes Peak Region librarians. I answer tenuously, explaining that I'm out of town right now, and might be too busy for a few weeks.

Then I compose an email to a new friend.

Hey Cassie!

Just wanted to drop a quick note to say I miss your smile, your energy, and your laughter. We didn't have nearly enough time to hang together. Thank you for being so kind to me.

Really like your mom.

Hope I'm not intruding on private matters. If so please do let me know. She told me about the San Luis water rights problem. Jeez, that's so huge. I can't imagine what she must be going through. She went to meet with the lawyers yesterday, and came away sad. Sounds like she's being pressured to sell out. You probably know this already. I hope I can help in some way.

Anyway, I know you're getting ready for school, and hope you find a little time to keep in touch. I'd like that bunches.

I promise I'll send maté, and bug you more than you want.

Best regards,

Matt Hale

Leaving the PC running for now, I wander outside, journal in one hand, maté in the other, and sit at the weathered table under the portico. I jot down notes on the last two days: random musings really, about flying and music and art, a dry Santa Fe riverbed, and professionalism versus true feelings, contrapuntally highlighted by emotion versus intuition: mind music. Perhaps Buddhists are right; detachment is key, though it is important to avoid confusing detachment with indifference. The front door opens and Wynne comes out, in a full-length teal terry robe and slippers with furry little faces on the toes. "Good morning. How are you?"

"I'm pretty well…slept okay, though I woke about two and didn't get back to sleep for maybe an hour or so."

She sits on the chair next to me. "I'm sorry. Is the bed not comfortable?"

"No. No, the bed's fine. My mind was just way too busy. Nothing to worry about." I point my eyes at the clouds. "Looks like rain today."

"As is the case in Colorado, New Mexico can almost always use rain. What should we do about breakfast?" Not waiting for an answer, she continues. "Would you still like to drive up to Tesuque?"

"I'd love to go to Tesuque, and if you don't mind two days in a row, breakfast at the Guadalupe would be fine, too."

"Sounds good to me. Let me take a quick shower and we can go."

She gets up, politely holding her robe closed, shuffling slowly back to the door. As she reaches to open it, I clearly see yesterday morning's joyous and sexy *fouetté*. I feel that deep sinking in my gut. Will I ever be done with that feeling, or am I addicted? "I'll grab a shower, too. By the way, I fired up your PC to check email. I hope you don't mind."

"That's fine. Please, do make yourself at home." She turns back inside.

After closing my notebook, I sit for a few minutes, listening to birds and being with the quiet grandfather apple. No one seems to have a specific message for me at the moment, so I meander in for a shower. Afterward, I pull a plum tee shirt over my head, slip on an unbuttoned, un-tucked, lightweight, dark purple corduroy shirt, and my walking shoes. Wynne sits in the living room, with two stacks of legal papers on the coffee table.

"Shall we go then?"

"Well, I left the computer running in the study. By the way, you should have a password, girl. Can I quickly check weather, and my Chinese horoscope?"

"Chinese horoscope?"

I nod enthusiastically. "I check in with this site almost daily. The astrologer is Chinese, so sometimes his English demands a bit of interpretation, but I find him uncannily accurate. Most of the time, anyway."

"Can I watch?"

"Of course!" She gets up to follow me into the study.

"I'm a Tiger. I guess I mentioned that, though."

"You know, I don't think so. I'd have remembered that. I presume that means you're tiger-like."

"You got it. I thought I mentioned being a Tiger at the hot springs."

Without smiling, her head shakes back and forth.

"Undoubtedly it was a mental conversation with myself."

She nods, looking over my shoulder. "Will you write down the website for me? I'd like to check it out."

"Sure. What sign are you?"

"I don't know. I'm a Taurus, but I don't know my Chinese sign. Are they called signs?" She goes away in thought. "Well, wait. I do remember looking at one of those paper place mats in a Chinese restaurant. I think I'm a Dragon."

"We can confirm your sign on this website."

She brightens a little. "Okay."

I brighten a lot. "Here, enter your birthday in that box." I watch, committing the date to memory.

"You were right, you're a Dragon. Let's check your element."

"Element?"

"In Chinese astrology, you have not only a sign, but even more specific to your exact birth date, you tend to have characteristics of one of the five elements."

She glances from screen to me, then back to the screen. "The five elements?"

"The five elements are fundamental to Chinese medicine and ontology. They're Wood, Fire, Earth, Metal, and Water."

"Hm."

"Fire generates Earth, Earth generates Metal, Metal generates Water, Water generates Wood, and Wood generates Fire. It's a circle of transformation. Two circles, actually: one generating and one degenerating. Water degenerates Fire, Fire degenerates Metal, Metal degenerates Wood, and Wood degenerates Earth. The elements do matter, but it's the animal sign that's most important." I peck a few more keys. "You're a Wood Dragon. I'm a Water Tiger."

"Hm. Are we compatible?"

"As a matter of fact, yes. I'm pretty sure a Dragon woman is better for a Tiger man than vice versa, but the pair is a good match. And, Water supports Wood."

"Hm."

I want to bring more optimism back into our pool, but feel afraid to delve any deeper. I'm a coach out of water—a fish, for once, out of words. I don't even bother to look at weather.

~~~

It's Wynne who remembers, as we finish breakfast. "Matt, we did talk about going to Ojo Caliente. Are you still interested?"

"You bet." I'm still trying to conjure ways to restore our broken connection. Maybe a day trip will work. The truly authentic act would simply be to bring up the topic. But it doesn't feel like the right time—and I don't wish to make matters worse. Time heals all wounds, the old saying goes, and allowing time does require patience. And faith. And trust. "Would you like to go to Ojo today? I'd sure rather do that than visit Tesuque, especially if you would, too."

Wynne's is a sanguine monotone. It often happens in life that we don't miss something until it's gone. "I'll need to go back to the condo for a swimsuit, and we can leave from there if you like."

With the biggest smile my face was capable of supporting without pain, I exclaim, "Let's go." Okay, that one hurt just a little around
~~~

those cracks at the corners of the mouth—a sure sign I need to drink lots more water. Without conversation, we tread across the gravel lot behind the Guadalupe Café, where waits the broken windshield.

~~~

It was the best of both possible decisions. I drive the Jeep north on Paseo de Peralta and turn right at the Masonic Temple. Gary will let mechanics from the Toyota dealer into Wynne's garage. We motor up Bishop's Lodge Road. Quintessentially Old New Mexico, not many tourists come up State 590, a narrow passage that isn't even shown on most maps. We can stop at Tesuque, on the way to Ojo Caliente. Today is about hitting many bulls-eyes with one arrow.

At the Tesuque Glass Works gallery, Wynne picks out a matching pair of hand blown, fourteen-ounce drinking glasses and a spectacular, red and orange, opaque-ish glass lamp, blown into the shape of the famous New Mexico Zia Indian sun symbol—the entire lamp glows when turned on. We didn't stay very long in the hyperactive kiln studio, watching co-op artists at work, pulling molten, multicolored glass like they're creating oversized taffy confections for birthday party centerpieces. Maybe the fire was too hot.

"The lamp is really beautiful, Wynne. What a find." We climb up into the Grand Cherokee and head just down the road, to stop in at Shidoni Sculpture Garden.

"Thank you. I think it will accentuate the condo, though I'm not quite certain where I want to place it."

This is the way it is today. Our conversations are stilted niceties, rather than heartfelt engagement. I'm uncomfortable as hell and afraid to talk about it. Wynne must be, too. For over an hour we stroll around the several acres at Shidoni, sitting on numerous benches throughout the site, munching on dried fruits and nuts from my trusty bag, basking in ambience of colossal, and even immense outdoor sculptures near and far. Given the emotional charge of the morning, it seems to me, and possibly to Wynne, though I can't really say how she's feeling, that we're stuck, exscinded in Salvador Dali's *The Persistence of Memory*. "It would have been nice if I had remembered to bring the leftover wine."

She smiles sweetly, and nods slowly. "Almost like a picnic."

Almost. I tried to not look hurt. Still, not my Wynne. Still, the new, plaintive Wynne, though it seems she might be warming up a tiny bit. I don't think I'm making that up.

Our being together on this overcast, cool, comfortably humid
~~~

Monday morning seems to be drudgery. In some humorless drama, we're playwright-actors, observing our own Act Three from outside our bodies, like hovering around the emergency room watching our unconscious accident victim selves being resuscitated.

We're together, but miles apart, like so many unfortunate people who spend a majority of life afraid, or unwilling to confront difficult problems and circumstances, perhaps ignorant that something can be done; or worse yet, somehow unconscious, by choice or otherwise—feeling condemned to endure rigidly intertwined and codependent existence, in utter disharmony. Bad *ch'i*. Okay, perfection or total harmony might be impossible to attain or maintain, in self or in relationships, but appalling dissonance in either is absolutely treacherous. Not to mention no fun at all.

It's way past time to do something about it.

Chapter Twenty-Four: Alone Alone

As morning blends into afternoon, a sudden, icy-cold, stiff northerly breeze whips our hair into our faces. I know what it means, as predicted by those stratus clouds in the New Mexican sky this morning. While we scurry for shelter in the Shidoni café, I pluck a hair tie out of my bag to wrap my ten-inch tail. Four-dozen other people enjoying the sculpture garden arrive at the door simultaneously. Everyone is cordial: smiling and laughing. We find a table for two, near, but not by a window.

Sipping a bowl of chicken-veggie soup, with a toasted tuna melt in my left hand, I watch Wynne watch clouds—now a wavy-bottom sea of heavy moisture. "Wynne, our conversations today have been strained. Would you agree?"

Continuing to look outside, she says, "I suppose so." Head turning to me, she looks across our tiny, white, metal parlor table. "Well, yes, definitely. I'm uncomfortable expressing myself, or my feelings. I neither want to lead you on, nor be led on. It's taking me a little time to adjust to the nuances of our relationship, but I'm sure if we're patient, communication will improve." She slowly turns back to look outside.

"The strain is drowning me, Wynne. I'm going to be totally honest, if I may."

I wait for an okay—that isn't coming. This escapade is to be my responsibility alone. I gulp half a glass of water, inhale a deep breath of aromatic restaurant air, and then take a plunge off this cliff, just beyond the well-worn path. Is that a crystal clear pool down below, or a volcano?

"Wynne, I've let you into my solitary heart." She turns her head back to me as I continue. "I absolutely adore you. I believe you've let me into your heart as well. I'm concerned because societal and professional standards say I should not be intimately involved with a client. I hope you haven't taken my reluctance to act on the attraction we feel as rejection. That is not at all the case." My gaze falls down to the tabletop. Putting both hands on my half-empty water glass, I just hold it.

"Wynne...." I hesitate, then take another plunge. "I want to hold you. I want to kiss your perfect lips. I want to nuzzle the downy softness of your skin, your neck, your shoulders, the small of your back. I want to take you in my arms, and hold you tight. This is how I truly feel."

A couple at a table near us looks our way, and avert their gaze as I glance back.

She stares into my eyes for a month of moments. Leaning forward, she quietly says, "Screw societal standards." She abruptly sits tall in her chair, head turning back to the view outside, transmitting disgust like she's a New York City radio tower. She whips back around. Fiery eyes match the demand. "Exactly which standards are we talking about?"

"As you know, a professional and client relationship implies mutual trust: a sincerity and honest openness that can be manipulated or misused by the unscrupulous. Thus, touching or otherwise becoming intimate isn't allowed. It's my duty to *not* act on my attraction to you."

"And you're being unscrupulous how? Especially if it *is* true that I've let you into my heart—and I'm in yours? Are we talking hearts, or semantics? Is this poetry? What does that mean? 'I've let you into my heart.' "

"Wynne, we're talking hearts, souls and spirits. Society is talking semantics, ethics, rules, and regulations."

"So you're a man of words, of societal dictates?"

"No. I'm a man of heart, who wants your heart, and who doesn't want to take advantage, be abusive, or act dishonestly. I try to live life by leading with my heart, being a spirit of feeling, analysis, and deduction—all served up as data available to intuition. It's a life, simply, of being. At the same time, we exist within a diverse culture, with customs and traditions. It's incumbent upon me to observe those as well, at the same time that I listen to a higher power. It's a question of balance."

"That's quite profound. On the flip side, at what point does observance of custom dissolve into one fractal among millions? Matt, are you in any way being dishonest with me?"

"Only by *not* taking you into my arms, like I ache to do."

She jumps up from her chair, clutching her napkin in a clenched fist. "Then what the hell are you waiting for?" The couple next door look our way again. So does everyone else in the restaurant. Kitchen staff peer out from the back of the house. Sculptures be damned, we're the main attraction now.

I look up from my seat. "I also don't want to be seen as a gold digger. You're of a social class that I cannot claim."

"Oh, give me a break!"

"Wynne, compared to you, I'm an Untouchable. What would the Fields or the Blairs or the Cranes say, when you and I walked together on Jekyll Island?"

She's still standing, but also leaning toward me like a boxer trying to sucker me into throwing an off-balance blow. As it turns out that's just my interpretation: Rather than feigning, the fighter lands a one, two, three. "Everything you've been saying is *mine* to decide, Matt Hale. You have no absolutely *no* right to decide what's best for me, life coach or not. *I* make my decisions, not you. And for your edification," she transforms into stone, head tilted just so—she's actually looking down her nose at me—and says, "Jeykll Island is for *Colonials*."

She throws the napkin on the table, snatches up her bag, turns and storms out the front door. The sixty-one unique expressions, on the sixty-one faces looking at me, would tell sixty-one different stories about how events in life are perceived, interpreted, and acted upon. Or reacted upon.

Gosh, that went well. I should've looked more intuitively before jumping off that cliff. Maybe it's time to get out of the pool.

~~~

I wander alone, dejected and somber, to the men's room to pee. My water bottle is empty: I'm not. I wash my hands first, as usual. Afterward, I open the door with my paper towel, and then make a perfect shot into the trashcan—nothin' but net. At least a dozen diners watch as I slowly walk out to the parking lot, empty water bottle in hand, bag slung over my left shoulder, to refill from the gallon we brought in the Grand Cherokee. The Jeep is gone.

For nearly two hours, I wait on a bench by the restaurant. The cutting wind only grows stronger. I watch blackening stratus
~~~

underbellies descend lower, while humidity grows dense enough to move with my hands. Then, the dark blanket overhead brightens a tiny bit, backlit by barely visible green where the sun must be. The wind subsides. Standing from the bench, I stretch my arms to the sky. Then, like an impala sloughing off the stress of outrunning a lion, I shake all over. Finally, I shout aloud. "Well, fine. I'll walk."

Question is—I ask myself, silently now, since the couple in an SUV that just pulled into the spot vacated quite some time ago by a Grand Cherokee is staring suspiciously—do I go north or south. Back to Colorado, or south to Santa Fe. Why am I even asking this question? Look at the sky. Smell the fertile rain in the wind. It's going to rain no matter what I do. I sit back down.

It's still early afternoon, with another seven hours of daylight. The couple decides I might be safe after all, and climb out to walk into the café. Dude, it's silly to even think about heading back to Colorado. Jeez, Santa Fe is only ten miles or so away. Jerron and Francesca will be happy to put me up for a day or two. I can either patch things with Wynne, or decide how to get back to Aspen for 'Bu and my stuff. Most of my clothes are in the guesthouse, along with my laptop and cell phone. Wynne would send my gym bag and small soft side to me. On the other hand, she was really pissed.

In my experience, people's deepest feelings and tendencies— around love, anger, resentment, fear—don't change so easily; definitely not without personal desire and motivation to make positive change occur. Sometimes there are biological or illness factors, too: Wynne's not there, though. But my connection with her is gone.

I haven't done my job, and I'm not supposed to have a relationship with a client. I want to, though. But dude, get realistic. Here you are. In New Mexico, bag over your shoulder, watching a serious storm maturing, instead of at home working on your projects. What the hell am I doing here? I shake my muddled mind, and let the tremor course through my whole body. Chasing some romantic dream. A dream. Chasing a dream. And it slipped away. I'm goin' back. Back where I belong. And, hello, I'm getting soaked no matter what I do.

I cross 590 and starting plodding home, or at least toward Aspen and Maroonbaru. As the rare vehicle comes up behind me, I turn and stick up my thumb. One, probably thirteen year old, red haired girl with mammoth braces, in the back seat of a black Buick Roadmaster from Missouri, sticks out her tongue as the family blasts on by. All the families blast by—four in the last hour. Time to think about this direction I'm taking.

Disheartened, I sit cross-legged on a boulder under a Siberian Elm, just as the rain begins. It starts light: feminine rain, as I learned it's called during my year teaching computer science in West Seattle. But I know it's just the beginning of this storm. This ain't intuition, baby. Well, duh, should've gone back to town, right? The black stratus blanket is now, maybe, a thousand feet overhead, looking more like ceiling than sky. The air is so wet it takes effort just to breathe. There's never been even a hint of thunder. I pull out the plastic bag that I keep rolled up, in case of inclement weather, at the bottom rear of my book bag. At least I can keep the mobile office dry. I put on my flimsy, but waterproof, survival jacket rolled inside the plastic bag. With no hood, it won't help much.

A few more cars cruise by, filled with folks who pretend to not see me. I've done that to hitchhikers myself. Don't look them in the eye. They might get to you, just like downtown beggars. Jeez, I don't even smell bad yet. And by now, I'm getting a nice shower anyway. My tree no longer provides any protection from raindrops that have increased in intensity from merely stinging to the size of water balloons. Wish my shirts were wool instead of cotton.

After, say, about 20 or 70 excruciatingly long minutes, following the onset of what is now officially a torrential downpour, an ancient Chevy stepside pickup, probably 1947 or 1948, rust colored because it is nothing but rust, dull even in the rain, painstakingly drags to a squealing stop on the other side of the road. I lift my head, a drenched mutt sitting in mud beside the pavement, lost and confused, nowhere to go, with sad eyes drooping. Who is this that is stopping in such a downpour?

Chapter Twenty-Five: Do You Know the Way to Santa Fe (Redux)

He leans out his window and hollers at me in Spanish. All I can make out is "what" and "where" since my eloquent Spanish is limited mostly to ordering food, or asking where is the toilet. I wave, and smile appreciatively.

"*Señor, señor, venga. Tú te vas a morir. Va a granizar! Ven entra.*"

I wave politely, and point up the road, tilting my head that way too.

He laughs heartily for a good seven seconds, rolls up his window, and then gets out to run across the road. He sits next to me on my boulder. We sit there in the stinging rain. A gust suddenly blasts steely and frigid. So what. I'd been unprofessional, bared my soul, and have been abandoned as a result. I deserve this misery.

Thunder bellows from not far up the quaint New Mexican state highway. I look north. A billowing, black squall line, maybe a quarter mile away, rolls steadily toward a dejected Matt Hale. Thank goodness I'm not judgmental or cynical—or stubborn, either.

The Samaritan takes my arm, and gently tries to get me to stand up. "*Por favor señor, venga conmigo. Va a granizar.*" I look up. His brown eyes are kind, gentle, and set in a face wrinkled with age and work and laughter.

Kindly, I reply, "*No, gracias, mi amigo,*" and gently pull my arm back. It's not like he was holding me with a death grip or anything. So he sits back down, next to me on the rock, and folds his hands in his lap. Two minutes later, lightning cracks a drought-dead piñon right in half, about 70 feet up the hill behind us. I jump up, heart racing, ears deadened and ringing, eyes big.

He just looks up at me, and smiles. *"Dónde vamos a ir ahora, mi amigo?"*

"Okay," I say.

"Okay," he says.

He stands, and puts his arm around my shoulder. Snug under my right arm, I clutch my big black book bag, wrapped tightly inside its big white plastic bag. We stroll across the road to his rusted chariot. When you're already soaked to the bone, hurrying loses all meaning. Except, perhaps, for that lightning bolt—there are now others—the cracks and thunder are deafening. Walking with me around to the passenger door, he reaches through its open window for the inside door handle. The battered door pops open with a loud crack, creaking in protest as he yanks it wider so I can climb onto a wet seat. There is no handle to raise the window. There is no window. After six laborious attempts the Chevy starts, coughing like Martin back there in Aspen, for a full minute, smoking almost as much; and then gradually begins to purr. I guess maybe Martin runs well, too.

His baritone voice is gentle. *"Mi nombre es Cambrio,"* he says, pointing at his heart. He doesn't extend his hand for a handshake. I like that.

I point at my heart, too. "Matt." My Sioux friends and relations don't much appreciate perfunctory, meaning-bereft hand grappling that is the *wasicun* (Sioux: let's just say a non-flattering term for white people) tradition. I agree entirely, except when society requires the act as a considerate acknowledgement of others. But then, the Sioux mostly aren't part of that society. And I'm not normal. I'll take a fist bump any day.

Cambrio nods, shoving the stick shift relentlessly until it finally crunches into first gear. He rolls down his window, and proceeds to stick out his arm, to signal to absolutely no one at all in either direction that we're coming out onto the tiny highway, then rolls the window up again. Letting out a chattering clutch, he looks over, nods his head, smiles a toothless grin my way, and says, *"Bueno, señor Matt, bueno!"*

I offer a heartfelt smile. *"Gracias, amigo."*

He looks back to the highway ahead. *"De nada, señor Matt, de nada."*

Accept your gifts when they're offered. They may not come your way again. *"Knocked while you were out—Opportunity."*

~~~
~~~

Someone once told me that George Bernard Shaw said, "Caring for the world is what remains after caring for yourself." Time has come, again, for me to care for myself. Lick my wounds. Here's how I interpret the Shaw quote.

It's kind of like Matt's revised version of Maslow's *Hierarchy of Needs*: Once you're able to take care of your own basic safety and security needs, and then progressively reduce your ignorance around how to live a good life, eventually you climb up to the top of the pyramid where you can actually *live* a good life. Then you can reach out to help others in ways within your self-actualized means. The path one takes up the pyramid is a matter of personal choice, often helped or hindered by random circumstances of one's birthrights or mountain passes already traversed.

Cambrio is a Samaritan. He's had enough of his own basic needs satisfied, I guess, that he was not going to leave me at the side of the road, alone, soaked, cold, sitting on a boulder next to a tree, in a hail storm with lightning striking all around—or striking me. Not exactly caring for the world, I guess, until one realizes that our worlds are all relative to ourselves.

Wynne's world includes raising Tobiano paints for a wealthy equestrian market, incubating golden eggs in the family trust basket, and managing resources in conscious ways to help improve global social conditions.

Driving a '47 Chevy pickup that hasn't quite rusted completely through yet, Cambrio perhaps has the means to eat wholesomely even without many teeth remaining, and certainly enough heart to pick up a stranded dog in a rainstorm—as well as enough sense to drop him off quickly. He lets me off at De Vargas Mall.

Before we squeak to a stop in the parking lot, I stick two very damp twenties, partly hidden, in the seat crease. I know he'll refuse if I offer. Intuition. Cambrio was just like that. I didn't understand much of what he said to me, but I still listened carefully, and felt his spirit. He's a good man with a very good heart. I embrace that image. Good men, in my experience, have been hard to find.

"*Gracias, Cambrio. Muchas gracias, mi amigo.* Thank you, my brother."

Chapter Twenty-Six: Reflecting Pool

Almost certainly still in at least a mild state of shock, I'm now in a dry, quiet shopping mall, on a very rainy Monday afternoon. I'm not dry, but my book bag is. I locate a water fountain to fill my bottle with jaded, Santa Fe tap water. Why is energy wasted refrigerating these water fountains, anyway? Room temperature water is far better for you. I sit down on a bench by the mall entrance and munch on tamari roasted pumpkin seeds and raw organic almonds.

Of myself, aloud, I ask, "What now?"

Myself answers, also aloud. "Well, the obvious thing is to call Jerron and Francesca." Myself responds to myself. "Seems like good advice to me."

I won't even touch the first pay phone I see: Bacteria on that baby are the size of cicadas. The next one has no dial tone. The third doesn't have a receiver. The fourth is hidden away inside the drug store, near the pharmacy, and my hand doesn't stick to it too badly.

"Hello?"

"Francesca! How are you?"

"I'm fine. Who is this?"

"It's Matt."

"Well, Matt Hale. How are you?"

"I'm good and wet."

"Are you at a hot spring? The caller ID says 'unknown,' so you're not at home."

"You've always been smarter than the average bear."

"Oh, stop it. Seriously, what's up? We haven't heard from you since we got back from Italy."

"I'm at the De Vargas Mall."

"You're in Santa Fe?"

"Yep."

"You didn't let us know you were coming. How long can you stay?"

"I'm not sure. I came down with someone, but at present find myself quite stranded."

"Stranded? Wait a minute. What did you mean, 'good and wet'?" Francesca's tone turns motherly. "Matt, what have you done?"

Frowning, I decide, once again, to be completely honest. "I flew down here with a client. We're attracted to each other, but I think she's feeling rejected because I'm trying to keep a professional distance. Not very successfully, I might add."

"Is she cute?"

"Drop dead gorgeous."

Francesca laughs. "Such a Matt thing to do."

"Thanks, Francesca."

She laughs again. "So you're stranded?"

"I had to hitchhike back into town. She dumped me at Shidoni."

"In the rain?"

"It wasn't raining at the time."

"You're defending her?"

"I really care for her. She's good people."

"Good people don't leave you stranded."

"So I could use a ride."

"The guest room is available. Bain's coming this weekend, but it's yours 'till then."

"Thank you, Francesca."

"Where did you say you are?"

"At the De Vargas Mall. I've made a home out of a bench just inside the main entrance."

"Quaint. I'll come and get you. Jerron is out on the tractor grading the road. The rains have done some damage, and he's improving drainage."

"Well, the good news is your well must finally be in good shape."

"Full to the brim. In our twelve years here, I've never seen it so full."

"I'll be the guy asleep under newspapers."

She laughs. "I'll need about ten minutes here, then I'll take off. See you in about 40 minutes."

"Thanks again, Francesca."

"It'll be good to see you."

~~~

I return to my bench home. Having found most of the weekend edition of *The Santa Fe New Mexican* laying abandoned on another bench over by the kids' play area at the far end of the mall, I look through the newspaper. It's pretty much the same news anywhere you go anymore. Pretty much the same town anywhere you go anymore. But a librarian, or rather, information professional, with a librarian's book bag with no books in it shouldn't be too choosy. I'm most assuredly not up for writing in my journal, no matter how dry it might be. I'm all wet.

After brusquely polishing off my bottle of obviously not-bottled water, I stroll back down the mostly empty, long hall of retail worship to get a refill of obviously not-bottled water, and use the obviously not-private restrooms. I wash my hands, of course, before using the bathroom. Some societal norms not only could, but should be broken, or at least bent. I keep my eye out for Francesca. Once I exit the *baño* that is.

Bored at the bench, I peruse the help wanted section. There are few jobs available, most paying seven to ten bucks an hour with no benefits. Welcome to the land of milk and honey. That'll take care of the three hundred thousand dollar mortgage on your three-bedroom, one bath, Santa Fe fixer-upper. Okay, moving along and cynicism aside, I feel pretty sad about Wynne.

Having avoided thinking about her for almost four minutes now, I'm due for a good wallow in self-pity again—it's a mud wallow. At least I can still move around in it. It's not cement—not yet, anyway. My mind strolls onto a well-walked pathway—could'a, should'a, would'a done this or that—there's a great way to drive oneself nuts, while achieving absolutely nothing positive. Well, it's possible to learn some lessons using the could'a, would'a should'a thinking, but usually it's simply a walk away from what is. But, really, I am heartbroken.

Maybe upholding social standards that he/she may not always believe in is how a life coach should practice, maybe not. Nonetheless, I feel it is appropriate for me to be concerned about the ethics of getting involved with a client. No matter how badly I want, no, desire, no, am honestly drawn, to get involved. On the other hand, whom the Creator has brought together, let no life coach pull asunder.

How do we know these things? I mean, how do we know when to bend the rules, or break them outright? I opt to contemplate these
~~~

questions; with the caveat, of course, that I've learned my intuition is always correct. After struggling to pull off wet, leather walking shoes, I also roll off soppy socks, and cross my legs under me: a half lotus. I'm good, but not full lotus good. Folding my hands in my lap in meditation pose, thumbnails just touching, I shut my eyes and listen to my thoughts—feel what's inside me. What *is* my intuition regarding Wynne? Surprisingly, my intuition answers right away.

~~~

"Matt?"

I open my eyes, blinking slowly.

Wynne stands before me, smiling sheepishly. "May I sit with you?"

"Yes. Please."

"Matt, I'm so sorry I left you back there. That was childish."

I lie. "It's okay." The internal jury's still out on whether this is also a lie. "I deserved it."

"No you didn't."

I start to say that I shouldn't have pushed, but she raises her hand, finger pointing in the air, just as I have done numerous times. "At first I was angry."

I give her a "You don't say" look.

She nods her sweet head, and looks down at the floor, but only briefly. "I called the restaurant as soon as I got back to the condo, but they said you'd left. I got worried, trying to decide what to do. So I drove back toward Tesuqué, but couldn't find you. Then I remembered Jerron's office—fortunately it's in the book. I convinced the office manager to provide a home number, and I called just after you did. Francesca was kind enough to agree to let me come to get you. She was very protective, I'll have you know. I was interrogated rigorously. I definitely want to meet her, by the way."

I start to respond, but Wynne stops me with a raised open hand, and the cutest, sheepish, guilty, little girl look she can muster. I find it most effective. "Matt, please forgive me. You were being honest, and I was being a spoiled child. It's been a very long time since I've met a man to whom I feel so attracted. I was hurt that you didn't want me, too. Then I was hurt that you did want me too, but were letting some dogmatic crap interfere."

I'm squirming—quite a lot. My wet cargos belt out a cacophony of squeaks, gurgles, and burps. "Wynne…."

She puts a finger to her lips, shaking her head "no." "Matt, it's no
~~~

more fair for me to ask you to overlook your professional standards...." She pauses, that cute little grin flashing as she gazes up from a bent down, suppliant head, "...No matter *how* silly they may be—than for you to make decisions for me."

Again she stops me before I start to speak.

"I have to respect that you feel professionally responsible, and just because I don't like it, doesn't mean I should leave you stranded in the rain. Snow, maybe, but not rain."

I laugh. In her eyes is a spark again, although she is crying. I take her hand. She doesn't resist.

"Matt, will you please forgive me? We don't have to talk about attraction anymore...." She looks at me, playfully seductive, and I nearly lose my virginity right then and there. "Unless, of course, you want to." Through her tears the grin reappears.

There's a stirring inside my cold, wet britches. Where is that choir I hear? Is that the chorus from Beethoven's Ninth Symphony? I'm quiet, since she hasn't yet let me spew an ill-spoken word.

"So, I really am sorry. Okay?"

My bag is between us. I reach over, and wrap both arms around her, pulling Wynne tightly to me: the bag, from mid torso down, keeping us safe, and her mostly dry. She begins crying again, head on my shoulder. I hold her for several minutes, stroking her hair, detecting that lavender in her hair, and feeling her warmth against my damp shirts. As tears subside, with a hand on each of her shoulders, I push her slowly and tenderly away. Her head stays down as she wipes tears on her sleeve.

"Wynne, I couldn't possibly stay upset with you for very long." She looks up. "I'm so glad to see you. Thank you for coming to save me." Quickly I add, "From this place." My own coy grin in place, I ask, "Will you take me home with you?"

She smiles, nestles my right hand in her left, and slowly stands. As I get up I slide my free hand inside the straps, awkwardly slinging my bag over my left shoulder. We walk then, out of the mall and into that dark, gray, life-sustaining downpour.

Chapter Twenty-Seven: To Have and To Robe

Wynne winds the Prius around Old Santa Fe. "Would you like Chinese for dinner?"

"I'm starving. That sounds great. Something hot. Maybe a green curry?"

"There's Asia Jē. It's quite good, and they don't use monosodium glutamate. We'll probably have to get it to go, though. The place is exceptionally popular."

"Great. And I'm looking forward to a hot shower and dry socks."

She does a u-turn, pulling immediately into a gargantuan parking lot with a dinky building, and we go inside. The place is standing room only.

"What would you like?"

"I'd like Chicken with Garlic Sauce. That'll be spicy hot."

Wynne orders Happy Family. On the way back to the car, she tosses me the keys. The Prius drives itself back to The Compound, parks itself next to the Jeep, and in no uncertain terms tells us each to go take a hot shower. Surprisingly, neither of us is in the mood to argue.

It's nearly seven-thirty as I emerge from a steamy shower, feeling much happier, though I was pretty happy before the hot water. As I look into the guest room closet, I realize that I did indeed pack very lightly. I reach for the maroon robe, hanging at the very end of the cedar rod. Commando, I slip into its loose softness and bulky warmth, then tie the belt in a martial arts double knot.

In the kitchen I go, for one of the apples from Kaune's. I'm hungry, and haven't had my apple for a couple of days. A doctor is probably just outside the back door. With the refrigerator open, I lean in, and immediately drop my apple to the floor as Wynne, who crept right behind me, suddenly says, "Don't spoil your appetite."

She's grinning. I fall, with great drama, against the open refrigerator, clutching my heart.

She laughs. She's wearing the teal robe she wore this morning. "I'll put dinner in the microwave. Would you mind starting a fire in the living room? I'm still a bit chilled. Pull the damper into the room to open the flue. Wood's in the garage."

"You're putting me to work already? After just giving me a heart attack?"

She grabs a hand towel and throws it at me.

I catch it and throw back. "I'd love to build us a fire."

The wood carrier is indeed empty. I pick it up and head for the garage. There I discover a large paper sack filled with perfect kindling, next to a cord or so of piñon, oak and other hardwoods, with some split cottonwood on the far end; all stacked neatly along the north wall of the garage. It's practically a mirror image of the south wall in my own garage back at Sleeping Bear Oasis.

After arranging a number of one-inch thick sticks to form a base, I carefully scoop a quart of dry leaves on top of a pinecone, and then sprinkle ponderosa needles like dark chocolate onto a coconut milk ice cream sundae. Over the heart, I stack a pyramid: first with twigs, then with sticks, and finally build a teepee of one to three-inch wide oak branches, all covered by pieces of quarter-split cottonwood. Four un-split, four-inch diameter piñon branches in each of the Four Directions finish the teepee. I go to the guest room for tobacco from my bag.

Sauntering back into the living room, I see Wynne standing in front of the fireplace, body swaying inside her robe with her dancer's grace. I hear no music. Man, oh man. She turns as I pad, in bare feet, into the living room. "This is the most beautiful thing I've ever seen."

Now I understand the music she's hearing. "What?" I query, looking to confirm intuition.

"I've never seen anyone start a fire like that. It's a little pyramid. You know, I started to crumple newspaper to stuff under the grate, but got a shiver. I immediately stepped away. Look at what you built there. It's art."

"Thank you. I've been blessed—by taking care of ceremonial fires. I was taught respect for Grandfather *Peta*. I say prayers while I build it, then pray with tobacco and give it to the fire, to send my prayers in smoke up to the Creator."

"I had no idea the extent that you hold Native spirituality in your heart."

"Thank you for being someone who would notice. You honor me, and I'm humbled. Now, the ability to make fire itself is, thus far, out of my range of skills. Where do you keep matches?"

Wynne tosses wet, sandy blonde waves, as she nods to a two hundred year old sideboard against the wall about five feet from me. "Top middle drawer."

"Perfect." It's a refillable lighter, butane, about ten inches long. I kneel down, offering the tobacco in seven directions before sprinkling it loose into the stacked wood, before lighting the bottom center of the pyramid, under the pinecone. Little flames furiously consume the leaves, ponderosa needles burning longer and igniting twigs. Flames begin licking up sticks, reaching splinters on the split wood. I stand up, our small fire living on its own quite nicely, thank you very much.

Wynne sidles up to me and gives me a one-arm hug. "Matt, thank you again for being here."

We turn our heads to one another. I'm hesitant, but start to lean in a tiny, tiny bit. She leans in, too, slowly. I feel the unmistakable pull. No intuition here, just hormones and soft, milky skin, moist lips, and damp hair falling around her neck and shoulders. The microwave bell dings. We stop in place, and laugh.

"I'd better get dinner. Shall we have wine, too?"

"I'll get it." At dinner yesterday I noticed a stash in the cupboard by the fridge, right where the wine glasses are. Last night's pinot is in there, topped by a rubber and copper stopper.

<p style="text-align:center">~~~</p>

Wynne strolls into the living room with a plate in each hand. "Can we sit together on the sofa?" We both know it's a loveseat.

"Sounds good to me." I'm all about being accommodating. It's an altruism thing.

She hands me a plate. I smell chili peppers: those little, skinny, nearly black ones. We simultaneously ease ourselves down, Wynne to my left, crossing our legs underneath to put heavy, oval shaped, nearly overflowing stoneware dinner plates in our laps. She had laid happy family down first, and then poured each plate with garlic chicken. Chopsticks in fingers, we eat voraciously.

This is, like, totally romantic: soft amber wall lighting on either side of the bookcase, track lighting turned down low over original works of art; and her new, New Mexico Zia blown glass lamp, glowing yellow-orange-red and now sporting an antique parchment shade, placed in the prosperity corner on that ancient wooden sideboard by the fireplace. The crowning touch? Flame-light dancing everywhere in the living room, bursting out from a Santa Fe adobe fireplace, molded softly, flowingly, into the southwest corner—like Wynne's delicious neckline, flowing into delicate shoulder, tucked under a teal robe. And I'm supposed to behave?

We don't talk—the fire is singing sacred songs. We simply pinch tasty bites, passing them onto grateful taste buds, occasionally hand feeding special morsels to each other. The organic pinot noir, good to begin with, was now more fragrant, smooth, and deep, having been open for twenty-four hours.

Toward the end of supper, we begin glancing at each other. I take Wynne's empty plate and mine, and set both on the coffee table, out of the way on the helpful people corner. I dribble the last third of our bottle into both wine glasses, and hand hers to Wynne. Curling up in her robe, she sinks comfortably into the corner of the loveseat, watching our fire. I get up and carefully place another hour's worth of wood, and then arrange cottonwood coals under the grate. I sit back down on my side of the loveseat, extending my legs to rest my feet on the coffee table, warming the soles and toes against the fire. With fingers of my left hand, I tickle her bare feet, where they lay right next to me. They twitch like crazy.

She giggles, and waves her hand at my arm. "Stop it." To keep my attacks at bay, she swings her feet over to the coffee table. Her robe falls open to expose a right thigh. We lay back, side by side, serene, cozy, watching and listening to our fire, sipping wine, breathing piñon and cedar.

"How did you learn to build a fire like that?"

"Many years ago now, I was acquainted with a Sioux roadman. He performed Native American Church ceremonies, and when he got to know me, he asked if I would help with ceremonial fires and other responsibilities. He paid me a great honor, asking me to hold head fire-keeper duties during a ten-day-long ceremony on the Fort Peck Indian Reservation. At the end of that ceremony, I was asked by tribal leaders to help with fire during Sundance."

"Really? How intriguing."

With Wynne lying there in her robe, in the firelight—I'm filled with desire. I take my feet off the coffee table and roll on the loveseat, turning to face her, my right foot planted on the floor. She's reclined: gracefully, luxuriously, at my side, our shoulders touching. Her robe is looser now, falling away from both sides at mid-thigh. I long to kiss the white velvet crease of her chest.

I'm going to be bad. Very bad.

"Please don't let me go out alone into the garage again."

She looks at me with curiosity, with glee, our eyes now only shoulders apart. "Whatever are you talking about?"

"If you leave me alone, with my imagination, I can no longer be held responsible for my impulses." With my right hand, I reach to the coffee table for my wine glass. My left hand is on top of the loveseat. I have no clue how it got there.

She grins, adjusting her body to more directly face me, feet still crossed on the edge of the coffee table. "Well, it's about time." Her robe slips open, just a centimeter more. I notice.

I lean over, at the same time setting my wine glass down. I reach for her right hand, carefully extricating the plain, heavy crystal wine glass and set it next to mine on the table. I'm looking at de Gracia lips, smiling a luscious version of the smile I will forever know: corners tenderly upturned, moist lips slightly apart. I lean closer to those lips, and lightly kiss the back of each of her fingers in my left hand, one at a time. As I pull the underside of her forearm to my chest, she rolls toward me. The back of my right hand reaches for her cheekbone, ever so lightly caressing. She closes her eyes, head tilting into my stroke. My fingertips slip under her left ear, slowly tracing imaginary paths around and around, down and into the curve of her silk neck—where I've been desiring to kiss since the first time I saw her, wearing that pomegranate summer dress, in the Little Nell marble lobby. Her head leans into my hand, eyes closed, lips barely touching and smiling. The index and middle finger of my left hand stroke her neck, from hairline to the end of her shoulder, so slow, only faintly grazing her skin, and then slide back up, above the hairline, my palm cupping the back of her skull, fingertips gliding up into her hair. She moans ever so quietly. My hand holding her head, I pull her toward me. Her eyes are closed: lips parted just the tiniest. I lean closer, and touch her lips with mine. Her mouth opens a little. I let my lips explore her upper lip, a centimeter at a time, then the bottom lip, and my tongue reaches just for the tip of hers; they meet only once, before I let my lips kiss hers again, touching her soul, exploring her spirit. Left hand still holding her head, those two right hand fingers circle her knee, and, almost not even touching, run alongside an ivory inner thigh, so smooth, how can I describe this? Baby soft…no longer covered by her robe. Her legs part just a little more. Her hips turn toward me ever so slightly. Then her lips pull away, not far, only a millimeter. Her hand reaches to tenderly ride on top of mine, as it still explores, lightly caressing her leg.

She whispers, "Matt, I'm thinking we'd better move a little more slowly here."

"All engines—full stop," barks Captain Commando, standing at full ready.

I halt stroking her thigh, and turn my hand over to hold hers—I don't let go of her head though—it remains heavy in my palm. I continue running my fingers through the fine hair on the nape of her neck.

"As you wish." I find my breath again, and nuzzle her neck with my cheek and nose. Her hand still resting in mine, on that delicious leg, I let go her neck, sit back up on the loveseat, and let out a sigh, with a happy, satisfied smile. She calmly, slowly pulls her robe a bit; knot still tied, our hands still joined on her thigh, and adjusts her sleek body to lessen temptation. I close her robe and hold her hand in mine, reaching for our wine glasses. Hers first.

Our fire still dances in her eyes. "Thank you, Wynne. That was, without equal, the single most exquisite kiss I have ever experienced. If I die now, already I have known the empyrean."

Grinning, she slaps at my shoulder. "I liked it, too." She punches my arm. "The empyrean."

She shifts a bit, and I raise our hands so she can completely close the robe—but my eyes guiltlessly linger, to the last possible nanosecond, on those incredible, strong thighs, and nearly exposed breasts: the awesome beauty at my side. Then my gaze rises back into the eyes of a woman I really barely know, with whom, at the same time I feel I've enjoyed a lifetime.

She silently lays me down along the loveseat, and then lies down between the fire and me, squirming to snuggle tight. One perfect leg gracefully opens its robe curtain, and lays behind her, and across me. Our heads are next to each other, hers resting on my shoulder, my arm around her, my head on the throw pillow lying on the loveseat arm, her hair right under my nose.

~~~

That's how we awoke, together on the loveseat. A jumble of
~~~

arms and legs, wound like a ball of twine a kitten has been playing with. Our nourishing Grandfather *peta* had faded quietly, peacefully, gracefully: prayers sent, coals glowing golden and black-bordered like an autumn aspen leaf, hissing with faint, crispy breaths. Wynne took my hand, and led me into her bedroom, where first her robe, then mine, fell to the floor, and we climbed sleepily into her king bed, easily snuggling back into each other's familiar body.

Chapter Twenty-Eight: Keeping In Touch

"Wynne, is it okay with you if I check email?" She's still in the master bathroom. I have maté in my mug, and a smile on my face.

"No need to ask, and, yes, of course!" comes the distant answer.

I've already signed in anyway. And gone to the Chinese astrology website. Today, Tigers might have happy love affairs; someone will prove their love; increased vitality and endurance—time to tackle difficult life problems. I check Dragon, too: possible lack of judgment and clear-headedness; tendency to intolerance; take measures to advance in personal and professional projects; rid yourself of negative thoughts about yourself. On to the aviation weather that site shows possible thundershowers later, and a mild cold front coming in within 36 hours from the Pacific Southwest. On to email. My new email provider does a great job of filtering out spam, helped immensely by mine being a new email address—it hasn't yet been discovered. I open Cassie's message, sent last night.

> *hey matt*
>
> *thanks for writing! miss you too. wish we coulda spent more time together but there'll be lots more chances.*
>
> *just get over the professionalism thing. not supposta tell u, mom really likes you too. lots! I'm totally down with that. go 4 it!!!! :D*
>
> *water rights thing is so not cool. been researching and have an idea. if you wanna hear it let me know. mom doesn't think it would work but I'm looking into it anyway. know what I mean? ;)*
>
> *leaving tomorrow. aspen denver chicago zurich.*

btw nothin new about browner. sheriff's got zilch. clancy said tire tracks and footprints inconclusive. butts because martin runs errands for widow Blane up road from us. been warned to use ashtray or be fined for litterin.

keep in touch, Coach.

lookin forward to my care pckg. ;)

hugs,

C

Wynne comes in and stands, hands on hips, framed in the center of the arched doorway to the studio office. She's wearing a pleated jean skirt and form-fitting red top, her hair wet. She's not wearing a smile. Instead, her jaw is set, eyes steely; equal parts doggedly determined and alluringly sultry.

"I'm heading over to Donovan's office. I decided this morning to refuse the so-called deal. If you don't need the car, I'm driving over there right now."

"I'd rather walk anyway, but thanks for thinking of me."

"I'll grab a bite at Kaune's. The spare door key is hanging next to the bulletin board. Will you take the cell phone again? I might need some extra courage."

"I doubt that, Wynne. I've seen you mad. You're following intuition, right?"

"That I am, Matt. That I am." She tosses the cell phone all the way across the room—a perfect throw—blows me kiss, does a *fouetté*, skirt flying, and heads for the garage: a dangerous beauty on a mission to not sell God. Good for her. Good for *Mde Wakan*. Poof! A cloud of dust, were any in the condo to be clouded upon that is, is all that's left. I sit a moment, mildly stunned. Dude, when a de Gracia makes up her mind about something, that's that! After the dust in my head clears, I drop the cell phone in my robe pocket, and return to answering Cassie.

Hey, girlfriend,

I'd love to hear about your idea. Your mom just now left for the attorneys' office. She's going to tell them she's not interested in the deal to sell out. The way she left, my guess is they're going to hear a little more than that.

She can be a tornado, can't she?

Have a comfy trip Cassie, and you can count on my not only keeping in touch, but probably being more of a bother than you can imagine.

Hugs back at ya', gorgeous!

Matt

p.s.   xxx

I sign off, stand up, stretch, and head for the guest bedroom.

Off comes the maroon terry, and on go a canary, un-ironed, athletic fit, button down short sleeve, and a pair of boot-cut jeans. Let's see, which of my one pair of walking shoes go with this outfit? Canary is my favorite color for the day. Yellow *ch'i* for good health and general well being. I head out the door for canary eggs at Plaza Café. Then I go back in the door for Wynne's cell phone.

At eight-fifteen, the morning is still fresh and almost chilly. The old apple smiles serenity in his gnarly, grandfatherly way—and, of course, all the songbirds that are anybody in Santa Fe have gathered in The Compound to send me off. There's a bounce in my step—it's nearly guilt-free. After breakfast I sit on a bench in the plaza, and pull out my journal.

While I finish composing a dry narrative about rain, hail and being all wet, an all-female mariachi band plays their way into the plaza. I grab the digital camera out of my big black book bag. You don't see female mariachi every day—or every year for that matter. Brandenburg Concerto Number Six, stirring inside my left front jeans pocket, interrupts a perfectly fine photo shoot.

A few people turn to see who is the culprit. I don't turn crimson. "Hello, this is Matt."

"I need to get out of here, *now*. Where are you?"

"I'm sitting in the Plaza."

"Where can I meet you?"

"I'll go back to the condo right now."

"See you in few."

~~~

Packing away my camera as I stride across the Plaza, I then jog up Cathedral, and diagonally cross busy Paseo de Peralta and Alameda, slaloming between oncoming, green-lighted traffic. Only one SUV
~~~

lays on its obnoxious horn. Glancing at the license plate as I run zigzagging across the street, I notice out-of-state plates. In stark contrast, all the New Mexico plates, and a California, slow for me, each of us smiling big, judging the other's actions, and smoothly adjusting. Good *Feng Shui*: harmony in motion.

As I stride vigorously up the gentle, long slope that is Canyon Road a not-so-obnoxious, compact-sounding horn taps tiny-ly, twice on my right. Focused on getting to The Compound, I sure as heck am not going to slow my pace. I let peripheral vision do the work. It's Ms. Prius.

I run around to the passenger door and jump in, mostly out of breath. "Are you okay?" I look squarely into her eyes.

"Yes I am." The response is short, insistent—matter-of-fact. She's a dragon, all right.

I wait patiently—sort of.

She demands, "What!" It's *almost* a pretend, melodramatic irritation, with a smile—yet let no question linger about the attitude underlying.

"*Lo siento, mi amiga.* One can't help notice you aren't your usual self, that's all. I don't mean to pry."

"Right now, I don't care to talk about it."

"You got it. I understand."

My head turns away to review the mostly tourists, moderate in number so early in the afternoon, strolling by galleries on a Santa Fe Tuesday. Some actually enter galleries while I watch. The occasional local is walking more assertively, on some mission or another. We turn into The Compound. I wave to Gary, who already has the gate swinging open—Wynne impatiently whips around the tedious black metal obstacle, heading for the garage. We get out of the car, garage door left open, and fly into the kitchen. Wynne slaps the car keys onto their hook, next to a sparsely populated bulletin board, and retreats immediately into the bedroom, closing the door gracefully, but with no-question-about-it solid certainty behind her.

I head for the refrigerator, grab a previously opened quart bottle of organic pomegranate juice, pour out about seven ounces into one of the new Tesuqué glasses, squeeze in a fourth of a lime, and top off the sixteen-ounce glass with sparkling water. This glass is blue and purple, with just enough gold to appear glazed. Just right for pomegranate juice. Reaching into my left jeans pocket, I squeeze my hand past my wallet and fish out Wynne's cell, and set it on the kitchen table.   Without cargo pockets, a phone is darned uncomfortable in blue jeans—especially since it's better for the spine to never carry or sit on anything in the back pockets—of any clothing. Back in the office, I place the beautifully blown drinking glass down on a cork coaster, and push the button on Wynne's computer. The operating system still requests no password, so I open the Internet browser. My only new email message is from Cassie.

> *Coach,*
>
> *Forget tornado, try hurricane. It's rare, but one hell of a blow.*
>
> *Packing for tomorrow morning, so can't talk long.*
>
> *Idea is to create something like a conservation easement, like land conservation trusts use. If we can do the same with water as with land, the rights could be left in perpetuity to a trust.*
>
> *Haven't researched it enough yet to know if it would work.*
>
> *C*

Wynne comes quietly out of the master bedroom wearing a white, mid thigh, lacy Mexican skirt, a manner of skirt I have always found to be an absolute turn-on, with a matching top; her feet staunchly uniformed in cross-trainer, leather sport shoes. Wrap-around black sunglasses hide her eyes, and the golden waves are hastily tied in a bun. Like my Ferrari F50, she's sleek and ready to go fast. Now.

I quickly log off and out, sans answering Cassie.

Chapter Twenty-Nine: Not Bourbon Street Busted

"Let's get some lunch."

"You bet. You know, I'd actually love to go to the Pink again. There's more on the menu I want to try, if you don't mind." I start the automatic PC shutdown process.

"Can we walk? Is that okay with you? But I know you prefer walking anyway." She smiles, offering her hand. I take it gladly, and rise out of the office chair, being not so gently pulled along.

We take the scenic route again, though a longer, far more strenuous, and crankier version, all the way up to Canyon's end, then back down Alameda and the Santa Fe River walk, before striding up Old Santa Fe Trail to the Pink. The sun is past midday high, but not by much.

"May I be honest, Matt?"

"Of course. I'll have it no other way."

"You seem cynical about life. I mean, you talk about living a good life, but then go into diatribes about Daylight Stealing Time, or rampant corporatism, and SUVs, and more than I can remember right now."

"Uh, oh."

"What's that about, Matt? Which is true, that you're teaching how to live an authentic life, or that you're a jaded man with a grudge against society?"

I don't know whether my face looks shocked, offended, or fearful. I answer right away, though, without thinking, of course. "You're absolutely right. I know I can be cynical—and judgmental. It's an inside joke. One that I realize is funny only to me."

"Well, there are times when it's cute, other times when it's poignant, and sometimes enlightening. The problem is, for me, anyway, that it's not infrequent. It seems like a big part of your personality. Sometimes I feel uncomfortable."

I look her right in the eyes, stumbling on the sidewalk as a result—well, I suppose I might also be a pinch nervous. I manage to catch up with her. "Thank you for your honesty. I appreciate it more than you know. I'll try to explain." I reach into my bag, lift out the water bottle, take a big drink, and offer it to Wynne.

She shakes her head.

"Cooties?"

She smiles. It's not the de Gracia smile, but also not perfunctory. "No. I'm not thirsty right now. Thank you, though."

"Okay, here goes. Let me know if you need me to explain as I go. Interrupt freely, okay?"

She doesn't look over. "Okay."

"I've mentioned before, that I have ample intuition and vision. I'm not making that up. Problem is, it's more a curse than a blessing. As is too much intelligence."

She nods.

"Anyway, I see right through ploys, propaganda and brainwashing: Or so I believe. A lot of what I say is opinion, based on relationship and professional experiences—and the way people sometimes respond to me. The discerning me sees that the American, self-determinate mind has been marketed to near-extinction. First it was consumerism: Buy this, buy that, and pretty soon everybody was accustomed to advertising—confusing and purposely misleading "information" became "normal." Then politicians and institutionalized self-promotion began using Madison Avenue more and more. Back in the 1950s, even Dwight Eisenhower warned the American people, while he was President, to beware the dangers of the military-industrial complex. But people didn't hear that. Or didn't pay attention. For what I think have been many years now, disinformation—another word that might apply—has become perfectly acceptable, and often not even noticed. Nowadays, so many folks have become so accustomed to "the way things are," that they have no clue of either "the way things were," or as I see it, "the way things could be." And public education has been reworked to produce minimally individuated, identical drones—rather than original thinkers and problem-solvers."

I take another drink, and hold the bottle in my hand for a moment before replacing the cap.

"I tried becoming more active politically, speaking at public meetings, municipal or regional sessions—other government or privately sponsored venues—but I saw effectively *no* positive results. And gatherings of only like-minded people don't often seem to really advance ideas or issues in a fashion allowing for alternative possibilities.

"I guess I feel cynicism is one of the few unbroken tools left in my bag to help people become aware of what's happening. I know, from observation over the years, that I've had some impact, but thus far it's not significant. I haven't discovered a single, truly successful way to be effective—but then, I also don't own media empires like some who manipulate our minds—so I frequently offer ideas and facts as satire, disbelief, or world-weariness; partly because I feel driven to talk about difficult sociological issues of the day, and partly in the hope that some folks will be inspired to gather data from a wide variety of sources, rather than blithely accept opinion or spin designed to *help* them arrive at pre-determined conclusions. I believe we need citizens that are redeveloping an innate capacity to think for themselves.

"I'd love to see America—and the world—but starting right here at home, transform the corruption, greed, and ignorance that has become normal, commonplace, even expected, throughout our culture. Imagine the good that would come if all the money spent on war and greed, were spent instead on public works; development of education, science, and technology; and repairing air, water, food, and earth—if we can learn to care about *every body*, and *every thing*.

"I've attempted straightforward documentary, satirical writing, fiction, and some philosophy of mind or ontology, but I'm wary of trying to publish; what I have to say seems to be misconstrued as anti-mainstream—a natural, convenient target of socialized myopia, or perhaps more appropriately, ignorance through enculturation. It's like people don't *want* to know, while simultaneously they're lured into a steadfast march toward the edge.

"Out of frustration—I'm a creative cynicism recidivist."

"A Matticism if ever I heard one."

I glance, as she chuckles delicately out the nose—bearing a smile too brief to determine whether it might be cynicism or mirth.

"I know it, I'm embarrassed by it, and I don't like it, but it's become habit. A habit I work on eliminating: that, and fits of anger. And I do attempt—I sure hope it comes across this way—to not snipe at other than broad societal, cultural, or political phenomena. I suspect personal attacks incite negative emotional response."

I drink more water—and don't offer. Wynne watches our way afore.

Squeezing her hand, I look for clues. "I often embarrass myself, like my episode when the windshield got cracked. Yet I still react, usually without thinking first. It never does any good, and in fact often makes matters worse—or impossible. It's become such a habit. I just don't seem to be able to totally rid myself of these habits. A large percentage of the cynicism and angry outbursts, I'm convinced, is a consequence of my abused childhood—and I continually work at not remaining a victim. Still, I *have* learned how to live a good life, by being authentic and genuine to the extent I feel safe, given whatever environment in which I find myself.

"Nowadays I actively support sustainable living practices, not just by speaking out, but also by growing my own vegetables, at home and in community gardens. I'd love to have chickens, goats, and honeybees, but where I live there is too much predatory wildlife. It's a wonderful way I can model by doing something positive. We all need to re-learn ways to take care of ourselves, our families, our homes, our food, and our planet. It is, thus far, the only Earth we have.

"To sum it all up, and I apologize for rambling, I suppose I want to be someone who helps develop an informed American citizenry: Citizens who, along with our leaders, will be totally honest; who will do what is absolutely in the best and highest benefit for all living things. A good start would be to discontinue proclivities toward presenting misinformation, opinion, or biased analysis—as unimpeachable fact—and, for me to keep working on being less reactive, in such a cynical fashion.

"So, I'm deeply sorry that you feel uncomfortable. No way do I want that. I never said I walk on water—I'd really appreciate your help in pointing out when I do what I do that prompts you to feel uncomfortable—it will help me gain awareness of what I do and say, consciously or unconsciously. Please remind me when I need to return to the same positive attitude I want for the world. Help me see myself, okay?"

I go silent. My vocal cords are tired. I get so intense. Take a breath, Matt. Breathe in.

"Okay." Wynne squeezes my hand, and slows our breakneck pace. "I understand what you're saying. I'm relieved to hear you recognize how little good cynicism really does. I'm sorry you haven't yet uncovered other ways to focus your amazing talents. You will. I see that in you. *That's* where I'll see if I can help." She stops in her tracks. "Let me think about it, okay?"

"What are *your* fees? Who's coaching whom here?"

"Who cares? You are helping me. I *am* learning, or maybe re-learning in your terminology, to find myself again—to be myself and be strong enough to assert what I think is right and good. You do bring that out in me, Matt. Donovan didn't like what I had to say today—but that doesn't matter. He is not paid to tell me what to do. He's paid to help accomplish the right thing. So, thank you. And thank you for your honesty. You speak with your heart. I'll vote for you as the next President."

I pretend being indignant. "I will only accept Benevolent Dictator."

<div align="center">~~~</div>

"So the upshot is, I fold to development or face legal battles to refute numerous eminent domain claims—both private and government."

"Wow. I'm sorry, Wynne. I've seen eminent domain used more and more by corporations and government." My fingers fly to make air quotes. " 'Government of the people, by the corporations, for the corporations.' That sounds cynical, yet I'm convinced it's absolutely true. Sometimes it's tough to tell the difference between truth and cynicism, especially when truth is well disguised, and so expertly twisted into being labeled the culprit. I am trying to be careful how I say things."

"That's important."

"Surely you've read about Super Slab, the private toll highway battle over in East Central Colorado. That issue has been quiet for, jeez, I don't remember, maybe, four years now."

Wynne nods. "I remember seeing something in *The Denver Post*, but I didn't pay much attention. Should I have?"

"It's a blatant, undisguised, eminent domain land grab by private enterprise—for nothing other than private profit. Don't misunderstand: I'm not even remotely against private enterprise, which I believe is often necessary for innovation and jobs creation, but I cannot support private usurpation of political power for profit.

When truths *aren't* hidden, people often do rise in opposition. Super Slab is like that. The Colorado legislature did change eminent domain statutes, probably only because of public outcry. I'm certain lessons are there that will help us—I mean—help you."

"One thing is certain, Matt; I need a second legal opinion."

"Back in Colorado Springs, I do know a former professor and college Dean who's a water rights specialist. Is it okay that I call him? Or maybe I'm butting in. You undoubtedly already have and know plenty other resources."

"Well, yes and no. Yes, I know other resources—and no, I'm not sure whom to trust right now. Please do ask your academic friend, when you get the chance; but don't trouble yourself."

"Wynne, know this—to the utmost of my abilities, I stand right here at your side."

We get up to go. She stretches slowly and gracefully, reaching for the ceiling and raising onto her toes. I do the same. Did we have lunch? What did I order?

Chapter Thirty: The Scent of Her Hair

As we leave the Pink I open the front door for Wynne—and instantly grab her arm to yank her back inside. She nearly falls.

"What the hell are you doing?"

"I'm sorry. There's somebody outside." I hesitate, trapped. "There's something I haven't told you." I glance out the window. A black SUV, with opaque black-tinted windows, is sitting just outside the front door. There is no sign of activity, or that if we were seen anyone is coming.

Pretty petite stands there, shocked, behind the hostess podium. "Is everything all right?"

"Sorry. Can we return to our table for a minute?"

"Yes, of course, sir. Do you need anything?"

"No, thank you. We just need a quick conversation." I have a second thought—more than intuition. "And a couple of waters please, no ice?"

Still concerned, she barely smiles. "Right away, sir." She whisks away for our water.

I take Wynne's hand and gently pull her toward the table. She resists—enough to let me know. She's not smiling—but there's been a lot of that this morning, anyway.

I pull out her chair. "Wynne, I think we're being followed. Remember the SUV that broke the windshield?"

"Yes?" She leans onto the table on both elbows, hands clasped with thumbs supporting her chin and fingers covering her lips.

I speak quietly; the restaurant is still busy. "We may not have much time to talk. I really don't know. But be ready for *anything*, okay?" I'm listening for the front door to open.

"Okay—what's going on?"

"I really don't know. That same SUV followed us into town—all the way to The Compound. I haven't seen it since, so I didn't bring it up. But it's out front—right now." I drink a third of my glass of water. "Not wanting to concern you, I didn't say anything. I wanted to be sure. I'm still not. Would anyone be watching you, to make you sure you're safe? Someone who'd be following us?"

"Definitely not. What's your intuition?"

"I have a bad feeling. We need to be careful. Please drink up," I say gently, pointing to her water glass. I'm still listening for the heavy, ancient front door to open. It hasn't. "I think we should get back to the condo, and decide what to do from there. Or we can call the police right now."

"You have my cell phone. Or we can use the house phone."

"You didn't you pick up your cell? I left it on the kitchen table."

"I didn't notice. Matt, I don't know what to say. You're scaring me a little. There is no one watching out for me. My parents know about the San Luis water issues, Patrick, and Browner, but I've not given anyone a reason to have someone keep any eye on me. There is one more issue I'm dealing with, but it's a very private matter. Are you sure this SUV is following us?"

"Well, no. As I said, I haven't even seen it since we first arrived at the condo. It could have been coincidence, but I'm not a big believer in that. It was going so fast that the Prius' windshield was broken, yet drove the same speed I did coming into town. Now it's sitting out front? Blocking traffic? I think we should call the police."

"I want to see this." She heads for the front door.

"Wait, drink a few ounces of water first, but not too much."

She returns, and picks up her glass while I step toward the foyer. She catches up quickly, and stays by my side. I peer out the tiny window.

"We can't leave this way."

"Why not?" She grabs a napkin from the podium, wipes her lips, and stuffs it in her skirt pocket.

"It's still out there."

Leaning into my shoulder, she looks too. The scent of her hair inspires me. It's tiger courage: protecting my family—the safety of a loved one. It's instinctual.

"So that's it—you can't see inside." She almost whispers, but she's not afraid. "Do you really think it's that dangerous?"

"I don't know. I'll tell you this much—I'd rather not find out by going out that door. Jeez, it's just sitting there in traffic, emergency flashers going."

She peeks again. "It's got *four* antennae on it. It looks like it could even be a government vehicle." She swivels around to lean against the wall, facing me.

I join her on the wall, inhaling again. "I don't see any winky-winkies."

"*What?* Winky-winkies?" She laughs quietly. "What are winky-winkies?"

"The lights on emergency vehicles." Pretty petite picks up her phone.

"Oh. Well, that makes sense." She laughs again. "Winky-winkies." I get a playful shove. "What should we do, Matt?"

Pretty petite says, "I've dialed 911." She holds out a white receiver. I begin to reach.

"Matt, somebody's getting out." Wynne goes back against the wall.

I jump to the window, and peer out the bottom corner. Holding the passenger door open and talking to someone inside the vehicle, is a guy in a plaid shirt, wearing a windbreaker on a breezeless, 80-degree afternoon—and there's a significant bulge under his left arm. I glance at our hostess. "Tell them we're in trouble. Is there another way out of here?"

Wynne thinks on her feet. "Let's go through the kitchen," she says, already bursting into the restaurant. We whirl around busy tables, as I hear the front door open.

"He's in." We sprint past surprised kitchen staff, and out the screen door. Small problem: The kitchen door opens only onto a patio that is, of course, in staid Santa Fe style, surrounded by a six-foot tall coyote fence. On the other side of the patio is the Dragon Room Lounge, the Pink's watering hole. We're in a box canyon. The only exit is onto Old Santa Fe Trail. I look back at the fence.

Coyote fences are usually made, well, haphazardly. Coarse, straight branches about two or three inches in diameter are held in place vertically by nothing but wire. These fences are normally unstable and difficult to climb. They're not only splintery, but the tops can be uneven, or even sharpened. This one does have a precious few metal posts for stability.

"We have no choice that I can see, other than go over the fence."

There's commotion inside the restaurant. Wynne moves first.

"Let's go."

There's a two-foot high, adobe planter built along the length of the fence. It's wide enough to stand on; or, to sit a patio chair on—which Wynne is already doing. Pulling off my bag, I put one of the long straps around my left shoulder, and slip my right arm inside the other, like a backpack, so both hands are free. A streamlined Wynne brought only her wallet, and that's in a buttoned skirt pocket. Standing on the chair, she starts to climb the fence. I stirrup my fingers under her right foot, lift her up and over, while glancing back toward the street. At least this fence doesn't have sharpened tops. Count your blessings. I stand on the chair to get solid handholds on the fence top, pull myself up far enough to kick the chair as far away as I can, and then pull my right foot on top, and lift my left foot up, too, so I can swing both over while I jump to other side. Through the coyote fence, I see the chair lying in a corner: just like the wind blew it there, maybe—count another blessing.

"Whew." I brush wood shavings out of my palms, and peck Wynne on the cheek, pointing an index finger her way. "You d' man."

"What?"

"The chair. Brilliant. You're brilliant, girl."

"Get out of my way, you idiot!" There's a loud crashing of metal. The Pink's kitchen screen door bangs open. A big pan hits the fence behind us, followed by eloquent Spanish cursing, and footsteps running into the Dragon Room, or back out to Old Santa Fe Trail. We don't wait to find out.

We run down a clean sidewalk, past numerous professional offices, and pristine xeriscape with pea gravel mulch. The complex opens onto De Vargas, just below the Pink, and then onto either Old Santa Fe Trail down the street, or South Capitol up the street. Hugging buildings on our right, holding hands, we tread tenuously toward traffic stalled on Old Santa Fe. The SUV would be facing uphill. I peer around a building corner at the end of De Vargas.

Backup lights come on instantly. The SUV roars to life, tires burning and squealing. It tries backing into a pack of vehicles stuck behind it. Blessings be.

"Run!" We hear the gut-wrenching sound of metal on metal, and glass crashing to the street. Don't see what happened, we just hear it. We're already sprinting the other way down De Vargas.

We're no longer holding hands as we run on by the office complex: That's another dead end. Just as the rear end of the SUV backs into sight behind us, we duck into an alley—another box canyon!

In one corner, construction to repair the adobe wall, in the other, no way out—just an eight foot wall. But there is a Siberian Elm over there, next to the wall, out of sight from De Vargas.

I shout and point, even though Wynne is right next to me. "Climb the tree!"

We sprint up to it. I shinny up to the lowest big branch, not quite as high as the wall. My heart pounds as I hear the SUV blasting up De Vargas—it goes on by the alley entrance. Standing on the branch, I look over the wall. A miracle! Only two feet lower than the top of this wall is another wide adobe wall, and a gravel parking lot. Planting my right foot in the branch nook, and the other on top of the closer wall, I squat, reaching down to pull Wynne up the tree until she reaches the branch. I straddle both walls to help her stand with me.

The SUV growls slowly, reversing back down De Vargas, getting louder as it pulls into the alley below us. We make the gentle jump onto the parking lot, which turns out to be yet another box canyon. The empty lot serves a retail mall on Old Santa Fe Trail.

This tiny cluster turns out to be mostly empty professional offices, and is devoid of people. In the plus column, it's full of recessed portals and wide porticos. Stealthily, we maneuver toward Old Santa Fe Trail. Behind a broad, shady portal we stop to catch our breath. Well, I stop to catch my breath: My hands go to my knees, as I bend over. I look up at Wynne. She's eyeing the street ahead, her face set like it was this morning in the condo archway, and not even breathing hard. What is she, a marathoner?

Chapter Thirty-One: Over the Mission and Through the Woods

Across the street from us stands the white stone Lamy Building. We can't stay on Old Santa Fe Trail: They'll see us for sure. Whoever *they* are. Unless we go back over the walls from whence we came—maybe not a great idea—our only choice is to cross Old Santa Fe Trail. Where they'll see us for sure. Well, we could go up or down the Trail, and be exposed far longer. Nobody is home in any of the offices or little retail boutiques we've passed. I know the Lamy. Behind it is a State of New Mexico employee parking lot and a visitor's bureau. Sirens begin to howl nearby.

"Wynne, if we can get across to the Lamy Building without being seen, we might be able to lose them in the parking lot, or dash into the visitor center for help. Are you okay?" Who am I asking? She's not even breathing hard.

"I'm okay. Nervous, but okay." She looks calmly my way.

Dude, I can see that little rip in the left side of your skirt. And your matching top is a bit scuffed, too. "Let's see how much closer we can get to the street before we try to cross."

She nods. We edge closer to the street, staying in the shadows. We're lucky to have come this way. We advance, crouched. All we need now are carbon nanotube ballistic vests and automatic weapons.

Down by the Pink (what are we, maybe a hundred feet up the Trail?), where the SUV no longer sits but a couple of cars are crunched into one another, there's a railing and a portico—and a probably three-foot, raised curbing. We've deployed into a twelve-by-twelve, recessed bench-seating quadrangle with a mural on one wall. We're almost at street-side, behind a two-foot faux adobe wall—from that, it's only six or seven feet to the street, after we drift around a large, maybe twenty-eight inch high and five foot long, white planter box in the middle of a wide sidewalk.

"Okay, this is as far as we can get without walking into plain view. Let's rest just a little more. Would you reach the water bottle?" I turn the bag on my back to Wynne. We both take sips. Wynne firmly settles the bottle back into its assigned spot.

Peering around the wall between our mural and the street, I report. "I don't see it. There are two police cars down by the Pink. Let's walk across like tourists, taking our time. Maybe we won't attract attention."

"I'm following your lead." Her soft hand slides into mine while we watch and wait. She squeezes my hand. Squeezing back, I don't let go. A nice looking couple saunters by, so we saunter onto the sidewalk right behind them, hand in hand, down Old Santa Fe back toward the Pink and Alameda. Wynne asks, "Maybe we should go back to the Pink?"

We didn't get four steps.

The shout comes from behind us. "Stop right there!" We both look back. Two guys are hopping out of the SUV, sitting behind us at the corner on Capitol. We start running, still holding hands.

"Stop or I'll shoot!"

My thoughts race—those guys didn't ID as law enforcement.

"Are they police?"

"Didn't identify themselves! Come on!"

Letting go her hand, I jump into the street without looking, Wynne right beside me. Tires screech—that was scary close. We run up the steps to the Lamy, and around the near side. I hear footsteps running after us. Heading toward the parking lot out back, we pass a four-foot low utility building of some kind.

"This way." I grab Wynne's hand and pull her around the corner of the white concrete structure. Her hair flies out of its bun. We duck behind a tall, slatted fence.

The big guy in the plaid shirt and windbreaker looks all around as he walks sideways, pistol in both hands, pointed to the ground, toward the State parking lot. We wait for maybe seven seconds.

Whispering, "Over here," I get up, remaining crouched, and waddle toward a portico right behind us, alongside the San Miguel Mission—immediately stumbling in a six-inch deep, concrete drainage culvert, twisting my left ankle just a little. Thank goodness for yoga. I keep moving with Wynne right behind me. We scurry about twenty feet to a metal, spiral staircase. Fingers on my lips, I silently "Sh." The outdated, librarian stereotype flashes into my mind—while running, probably, for my life. Funny what bursts into one's mind during critical events. We step quickly, and as silently as possible up the spiral. I raise my hand—we both stop—and hold deathly still.

Two police officers, one male and one female, run past and below, toward the parking lot—hands on still-holstered weapons. Eleven steps up, I climb under the railing and jump over to a gravel roof on the Mission portico, landing like a tiger—well, okay, at least on all fours. Wynne doesn't hesitate—just bounds over the railing—landing crouched. Dude.

There are old, tall conifers all around the roof. Going down the other side of the Mission's gravel roof, I slip and land hard, ripping the underarm of my shirt—and my elbow.

Wynne whispers, "Are you okay?"

"Have to be. Keep going."

Crawling low, we carefully maneuver to the rear of the Mission, and slide down its short, brown adobe backside. I've always loved soft forms of adobe construction, the gentle *ch'i*, but never so much as this moment—this is more like a playground slide than an eight-foot cliff. I help Wynne as she slides down on the soles of her shoes—a slide in a delicate lace skirt is tougher than in blue jeans. We advance toward tiny De Vargas Street, as tires screech. A big American V8 roars into our alley from Old Santa Fe, which is at most a hundred feet away. I glance around.

"Wynne, in here!" She'd gotten in front of me.

A small space, between two buildings, crisscrossed at the back by several horizontal utility pipes looking much like jail bars, is just wide enough for one slender fugitive—or two, side-by-side. It's another dead end, of course.

The black monster speeds on down De Vargas, past the Mission Café, turning right and into the first parking lot entrance. Whew. I turn to Wynne. We're both panting now, more from nervousness than exhaustion. I take a deep breath, as does she. "Maybe they think we're in the parking lot. I sure hope so." It's my positive offering.

Wynne looks down at my elbow. "Matt, you're bleeding."

"It's okay." It hurts like hell. I feel a hot trickle running down my arm. "See the trees over there on the other side of De Vargas?"

"Yes."

"Let's go. Try to keep cover."

We slip out of our crack. I peer both ways on De Vargas: around the building to our left and the four parked cars lined on our right. Hearing more, and closer, sirens, we run across to the Casa Vieja parking lot, headed for the trees. They're growing from the bottom of a ditch, with a steep, six-foot embankment. I slide upright and sideways down the bank, feet digging into loose dirt. Wynne follows. A police car, winky-winks winking, but sans siren, squeals up De Vargas.

We're out of sight; below the top of the embankment, trees around us, with a long building to our left. "We can go back to Old Santa Fe or follow the ditch."

She doesn't hesitate. "We take the ditch."

We crouch low, even though we can only be seen if someone comes right up to the precipice. I hear no footfalls, no menacing V8. At the end of the ditch, probably fifty feet from where we jumped in, is some beautifully done graffiti artwork on a four-foot tall concrete wall. There is also eau' d'urine and broken liquor bottles—with a few beer cans scattered around for textural contrast. I look on other side of the wall. "It's a tiny backyard and another dead end, complete with barbed wire. We can't get through." There's brief shouting from the direction of the State parking lot, followed by that now very familiar roar.

She nods toward the street below. "We have two choices: take that path down to Alameda—where we'll be exposed—or go back out onto De Vargas."

"Where we'll be exposed."

"Right. Let's stay in the best cover we have."

"De Vargas it is." I climb back up the steep ditch, and turn to help Wynne. We slither, hidden from the street, behind a tall wood fence. Then a *milagro* appears right in front of us—a path, not visible from De Vargas, winds behind the Mission Café. We walk carefully up the well-traveled dirt, and just as we're about to come back in view of De Vargas, at the back entrance to the De Vargas Retirement Residence, our miracle joins another path. Turning left, away from De Vargas, we sneak single file—once again hearing busy Alameda below.

Winding and quiet, with walls on either side, this path is shaded by old, tall trees, and is not clearly in view of either De Vargas or Alameda. Good *Feng Shui*. A smooth granite rock, big enough for two, is looking expectantly, right at us, as though we had made reservations. We look at one another, then sit down.

"Wow. You really know how to treat a girl to a good time." She reaches into my bag for the water bottle. Pulling the napkin from her skirt pocket, she pours a little water on it, and dabs at my elbow.

"Wow is right."

"We sure are stopping a lot." She hands me the open liter, after having a sip herself.

"Yeup."

"Yeup." She bumps my shoulder, grinning.

"And you know what? The more we rest, maybe the more difficult it is to find us."

"What do you mean?"

"Well, it could be that they expect us to be running like crazy, covering lots of ground. The longer we take, the more likely they might be to give up looking."

"Or the more likely they'll realize we've just been hiding and haven't gone far at all."

"Gee, thanks."

She chuckles, *con mucho gusto*.

So do I. "Wish I had Clancy's Glock."

"Would you know what to do with it?"

"For a couple of years I was a Colorado State fraud investigator. I have small arms and semiautomatic weapons training."

"Too bad you don't have Clancy's Glock."

I laugh again. So does Wynne. We're still quiet though—we're not that far away from De Vargas.

"I need the rest. My green beret training was many years ago now."

She's incredulous. "You were in the military, too?"

"*No.* I'm just pulling your leg."

"I can't tell when you are and aren't." A pause. "Well, sometimes I can. Especially when you give me clues. Give me clues, you jerk." She bumps me right off the rock. I catch my fall with my hands, and stand.

"Can't help but wonder if the police are after them, or us."

"Or both," says a wry beauty sitting on a boulder. "Right now, I'd rather wait and find out later."

We haven't been running since the ditch. In fact, we have now spent probably twenty minutes moving all of a couple hundred feet— if one were to draw a line on a map—from the back of San Miguel

Mission to this rock. But we've been out of sight. Probably not out of mind though.

"I don't think we're out of danger just yet."

"Nor do I." She smiles again, looking sweetly up into my eyes. The bloody napkin goes back into her skirt pocket, and she hands me our almost empty water bottle. "But you know, I feel good about this." Reaching for my hand again, she guides me back over to sit by her. "We're going to be okay."

I gaze, admiringly of course. "You know, I have a good feeling, too."

She looks away from my eyes and down at the ground. "Do you really think I'm gorgeous?"

Jeez, that came out of nowhere. I redden. She doesn't notice. She's still looking down, tracing little circles in Santa Fe dust with the toes of her shoes.

"Are you kidding? Of course I do. And, what's more—" A vehicle again roars up De Vargas from Old Santa Fe Trail. We take off running the other direction, toward Alameda.

Behind us, the roar passes on by. We slow to a stroll.

"I presume this path ends at Alameda?"

"I really don't know. I've never been here. I've never been in the ditch either, but it smelled like a popular hangout. I guess I don't get out much."

Chuckling again, with eyes closed, my head swivels side to side. "Your sense of humor, especially now, is so comforting." I stop, and squeeze her hand. "Thank you."

She leans over to kiss me on the cheek. I turn my head slowly toward her, slide my forearm around her waist, and gently suggest her head to mine with the other hand. She backs against the wall of concrete behind her. We kiss, our arms wrapping each other, her fingers in my hair and on my neck. I shiver, wanting her badly, then and there, right on the wall. We hear another vehicle above us, though it's somewhat more subdued this time.

"They're slowing down to take a better look." I let out a deep sigh. "I guess we'd better get serious. I don't think we want to be on a street, though, if we can avoid it. Let's look for more backyards and stinky ditches."

She laughs, taking my hand as we snake down the pathway, in the direction of Alameda.

Chapter Thirty-Two: Under the Bridge

Along the west side of our shady route is a tall, ancient adobe wall, with an equally aged wooden door built into the wall. There are thousands of these in Santa Fe. I try it, but it's not going to budge: probably hasn't been opened in fifty years. Another hundred feet or so and we'll walk out onto Alameda, which is coming into plain sight—our path now straight and true down to the boulevard. On the other side of the path is that familiar, six-foot high concrete wall, against which I kissed Wynne not a hundred feet ago. I jump up just enough to hold on and look over, before dropping back down.

"Nothing's there but that building—looks like it's being remodeled or something. The lot is big, with trash strewn around, some construction supplies, but no recent tire tracks and no people. Let's go over."

I cup my hands. The equestrian steps in, and swings her right leg up and over, straddling the top of the wall like a saddle. Heels digging into the ribs, she reaches across her body with her right hand, planting the left on top of the wall. Our palms and thumbs entwine, like a handshake. I dig my left hand and fingers into the rough concrete on the top, and then jump while doing a one-arm pull-up with as much effort as I can muster—it sure looks easier than this is in the movies— but it's Wynne's arm strength that hoists me so that I land, with much grace and savoir faire—on my belly. I recover quickly, licking my paws as though I'd planned the whole thing, and then swing my left leg over the top, straddling to face her—like two rodeo clowns on the same horse. "How did you get to be so strong? You continue to amaze me."

She grins. "Green beret training."

We let ourselves down the other side. The lot is barely visible from the street, but still we seek shadows, following the sides of the building. Trees from the Santa Fe River bed provide good cover as we approach the busy thoroughfare. A police car, lights flashing, slowly cruises up Alameda. I see no other traffic. At the boulevard end of the building, a chain link fence has a section torn away from a corner post, exposing a small path leading down to the riverbank. We aren't the only ones to use this route.

"After we squeeze through, let's walk, not run, and climb down into the riverbed. Birds of prey watch for rapid movement to expose their meals."

"Okay."

Our little path leads all the way down into the riverbed. Another jump is required. We keep low, so not to be seen from the street. About a hundred feet upstream, we come upon a small pool of water behind a short dam of rocks: a lovely little waterfall when water flows. We expose ourselves briefly while scrambling part way up the bank slope to navigate around a tiny pool of stagnant water, but otherwise we keep to the dry river bottom. We choose our steps through sand and rocks, under a bridge to yet another retirement residence.

We're being as quiet as possible. "Should we take the parking lot over to Paseo de Peralta?"

"Canyon's only a few hundred feet from there."

"But we'd be back in traffic."

Wynne takes my hand. "If we keep to the riverbed, we can go under the bridge at Paseo, and keep out of sight."

"Let's do that." I don't let go her hand while she leads me up the sandy bottom, and under the much larger Paseo de Peralta bridge.

The far side provides substantially less cover. Riverbank slopes are no longer steep, but gradual, and significantly lower. Now that we're pretty much in plain sight, I start looking for better cover. We're behind the first galleries at the bottom of Canyon Road. They all have parking lots or sitting gardens in the rear, are surrounded by serious security walls, and an iron fence with spikes on top. Not friendly, but more so than what we might meet on Alameda. Wynne points to a corner footing—solid concrete and painted gray— probably eighteen inches broad—and best of all, without iron spikes.

I help Wynne over, and then make the climb myself. We sit on grass, leaning against the shady side of the corner post, out of view from Alameda, which once again is busy with traffic. Wynne reaches for my water bottle. It's empty.

I'm still willing to speak softly. "So, what do you think? Do we call the police, or try to get to the condo and decide from there?"

"I don't like that the SUV looks like a government vehicle—I'm reluctant to contact the police. I'd rather get to the condo, and call Donovan first thing."

I nod. After a short rest, we head for a gated warning: "Drury Gallery, No Trespassing."

We trespass. In fact, we waltz right in the back door. It's a basement, with a framing and preparator's shop, and working studios. No one notices us. We quietly, but nonchalantly walk upstairs, and, after a sneaky peek around, stroll into the rear of the gallery.

Chapter Thirty-Three: To the Galleries We Will Go

I close my eyes, breathe deep, and in a normal voice say, "Ah, the smell of fresh oil paint."

Wynne chuckles, in a normal chuckle. "Always the artist, are you?"

We try to look like buyers. Wynne's lace skirt and top are soiled and roughed up from climbing ditches, walls and the occasional tree. I wear a torn shirt, and sport a bloody elbow and knee. I've no idea where the knee took a hit: My jeans aren't ripped, but that black stain leaves no doubt. We attract attention, but go on pretending everything is fine. Actually, we act very little, instead examining closely and commenting on a few of the paintings, stopping to look critically at several contemporary landscapes that employ surprisingly realistic use of nearly effervescent color. Very nice. Eventually, employees and visitors go on about their business—with only the occasional glance.

Outside, we do have to take a very short stroll up Canyon Road, but at least the sidewalks are filled with tourists and the narrow street is crammed with slow-moving vehicles. Only thirty feet or so later, we duck down onto the black asphalt driveway to 225 Canyon.

This compound of galleries is below and well away from the street: close once again to the riverbed, actually. Public restrooms are available, provided by the half dozen or so galleries. We wash up and drain our bladders. When Wynne comes out, I hand over my water bottle, filled with refreshing restroom tap water.

"Matt, I'm never again leaving home without a water bottle." She smiles, handing it back to me, and wipes her lips on her arm.

"There's a good idea. You never know when you might have to run for your life. Or pee in a ditch. Are you ready to try the last stretch up to the condo?"

"Let's go. It's a comfort having all these people around, isn't it?"

"We really are safer here, I think."

We're both tired. The cool, shady, guarded Compound sounds pretty nice about now. We cross over the private drive to Gallery 225, stepping in to briefly view an abstract show, but mostly to appreciate air conditioning for a spell. After a refreshing half hour, that I especially enjoy since this artist and I employ strikingly similar techniques, we walk on around the circular driveway, back up toward crowded Canyon Road, sticking close to nooks, crannies, gardens, and verandas.

"Gotta' love this Santa Fe style."

"I've lived with it all my life, and have never appreciated it more."

As we approach Canyon, Wynne sees it first. "Matt! Duck!"

In a garden set several feet below street level, we hide behind a huge boulder. It's a beautifully landscaped little garden, with mature trees next to the truck-size rock, providing shade and even more cover.

Always the brilliant bulb, I ask, "The SUV?"

She grins. "Who'd have thought it?"

"Well, duh."

We sure are taking this well: in good spirits, even with the SUV grumbling slowly up Canyon with the rest of the tourists. We wait a few minutes, pretending we're just sitting nonchalantly in the shade. Well, we are sitting in the shade, maybe just not quite so nonchalantly. When we carefully glimpse over the boulder, up Canyon toward The Compound, and then down toward Paseo de Peralta, we see no black menace.

"I'm thinking they're waiting for us at the condo, Wynne."

"I'm thinking you're right. What do we do?"

"Let's see if we can get to Jerron's office, over on Old Santa Fe Trail. I'm not sure how to get there from here, but we'll need to keep as invisible as possible."

Wynne is ready. "We need to cross over and go up Garcia."

"Okay with me."

I stand up, and stretch arms and body upward, hands interlaced—the first of the Seven Arrows that are *Pal Dan Gum*. It feels really good. Animals do this all the time. Stretch that is. Why don't we?

Wynne follows my lead, moaning pleasurably. I reign in my imagination once again, but make no attempt to hide my admiration. She is exquisitely sultry, in that tattered, innocent white, Mexican skirt and top, her slender, taut waist exposed by the stretch.

We saunter across Canyon, hand in hand, trying to not be conspicuous, or to appear as disheveled as when we intruded on the private parts of Drury Gallery. The 225 restrooms had provided a welcome oasis, and for this life coach, a first aid station as well—thanks, of course, to the baggie of emergency supplies in my book bag. My bet is that an anonymous financial gift will soon appear to help support those privately owned and maintained restrooms. We keep a careful watch, though, as we walk briskly up Garcia Street.

Completely residential, Garcia has not a single moving car. We stay close to ubiquitous adobe walls, weaving between parked Lexuses and BMWs, with the occasional Jaguar, and one old Beetle: one of those Seventies models with a pretend Rolls-Royce hood. It's only about a quarter mile to the next intersection. We reach the end of the street alive, and seemingly unnoticed. We look everywhere before crossing Garcia, to take refuge inside Downtown Subscription, next door to Garcia Street Books. We both already need to pee. No small wonder.

I purchase two bottles of Sparkling Grapefruit mineral water while Wynne is still in the ladies room. When she comes out, we sit outside in the back garden, in the corner, hidden behind xeric landscaping—next to the wall, just in case. We've become quite the team with this over the wall thing.

Wynne looks at her bottle. "This soda is delightful—citrus and not too sweet. Just what the life coach ordered." She grins my way. "An electrolyte replacement, eh?"

I grin back. "Constant fear and vigilance will take it out of you—and we *need* it."

She chuckles, but rapidly turns solemn. "Why didn't you tell me about the SUV earlier?" There's not a hurt look on her face, though: just genuine need to understand.

"Well, to be honest, I wanted to be sure I wasn't just imagining danger when none existed. I've had a tendency in life to make mountains out of molehills. Actually, I've also done the reverse, seeing molehills when there were mountainous cliffs soaring before me. I hope I haven't offended you. I wholeheartedly didn't want to concern you unnecessarily. You've had enough to worry about."

"True. Nonetheless, please feel free to let me know anything at all. I am pretty tough, you know, for a poor little rich girl." Dragon purring is so divine.

"So I've noticed." My turn to smile.

"What next?"

"I'm pretty sure we can get to Jerron's office, but I'm not getting a hit on what to do from that point."

"I'm not sure, either. But I do *not* like that vehicle. It looks too much like some Secret Service truck or something. With those antennae all over it, and the black windows, it looks evil. Okay, Coach—it *feels* evil. Maybe I've seen too many movies, but I'm not sure whom to trust right now. What are you feeling?"

"I'd say evil covers it pretty well. People running after you with guns drawn can't be good. Particularly when they don't identify themselves. Well, maybe we can get back to Colorado. You have people you can trust in Aspen?"

"Absolutely. And plenty of friends with secure hideouts in the hills. I'm talking about people with armed guards and security cameras and nuclear weapons."

I laugh aloud. Wynne grins a big one, and then laughs along.

"If it comes to it, Wynne, I do know an assistant district attorney back in El Paso County, and a retired state trooper, as well as a few District Court judges. I'm confident each and every one will be willing to help us."

"Well, then, let's see if the Cessna's safe, and fly the heck out of here."

"Do you carry a key with you?"

"No, but airport service keeps a spare for emergencies. I consider this an emergency." There's another smile. It's a rough way to have fun, escaping from unknown assailants in black scorpion SUVs, but we're managing. We're in this together.

Chapter Thirty-Four: Friends in Need

"Well, this is mighty fine, sitting here in the shade, relaxing. I know we need it—at least I sure do. But I am starting to get a little nervous. We've been here almost half an hour."

"I've been feeling that it's time go for maybe ten minutes or so. But we're having such a nice time. It's odd, I think."

"What do you mean?"

"First, I have the meeting with Donovan and leave feeling empowered, but still second guessing myself—though Cassie did agree with my decision when I called her from East Palace. I needed to hear her voice before she left the valley. She has such a clear, energetic mind, that daughter of mine—even as she's hurrying to leave the States for Switzerland. Of course, in June we shipped several cartons for her school year, but we always plan for customs to almost certainly imprison her belongings until September. She still has much to pack. Back to what I mean.

"It seems odd to have such a—sometimes—pleasant time, while our lives obviously are in danger, and yet I feel good about what's happening. And, Matt, I'm beginning to really—to really get it—you know, the feeling, the intuitive perception, as opposed to a purely rational, analytical viewpoint. We don't have enough data for well-reasoned analysis, yet the tendency is to go with whatever thought process, or deductive reasoning, that the rational intellect derives. Every cell in my body trusts that path, it seems—but it's what *feels* right, so far today, that has resulted in the most positive outcomes, the correct decisions, to the best of my recollection—which could be fuzzy—but I don't think so.

"Right. So, first Donovan; then my angry river walk—confronting you about your innermost personal flaws; then my confused diatribe—that you, the near-perfect gentleman—sit through at lunch; followed by your pulling my arm out of joint as we leave the Pink; followed by running like we're jail escapees in an old western movie, chased by guys with guns, and a sheriff's posse; to enjoying adept contemporary art in air conditioned comfort; to sitting in this lovely xeriscape garden for half an hour; to wondering how we get to your friends' office; to, okay, do we fly to Aspen where I know exquisite hiding places, or to Colorado Springs where you have superior reinforcements; to…." She inhales, blows out her entire lungs, refills them slowly, and while exhaling again says, "… Dude."

I burst into laughter. Leaning all the way back in my metal armchair, tilting my head so far that it bangs on the outdoor chair's roughish top rail—I laugh from deep in the belly. 350 miles away, Manitoids all over town are cupping their ears southward, going, "What's that?"

"Knock it off Matt."

To which I nearly fall out of the chair.

Everyone in the place is howling. Laughter is truly and wonderfully contagious. I'm in tears.

<div align="center">~~~</div>

We get up to go, both watching acutely for any sign of trouble, and leave the only way we can (well, there is the wall), through the Downtown Subscription front door. We're cautious, treading like a stout tiger and a hardy dragon, into the parking lot. The intersection is a five-way: Garcia Street and Acequia Madre stop here and keep going; Arroyo Tenorio, a tiny, winding, one-way dirt path barely big enough for cars, heads in the direction of Old Santa Fe Trail. So do we, not sure where this dust bowl might lead. But trusting intuition completely.

At the faintest sound of an automobile coming up behind us— since it is a one-way—we run for ample cover provided by curving adobe walls, five-foot salvias and brooms, or we duck behind beaters and luxury sedans parked on top of the powder. It's hot now, the air tawny in this tiny alley, especially when the rare car actually blows by rather than turn into some courtyard. Coming ever closer to the end of our journey, we hear traffic on Old Santa Fe Trail—and our senses heighten. My ears stand tall—twitching. Wynne's yellow eyes are vigilant—her dragon's tail ready to plant a pugilistic anchor. I wonder if she breathes fire—hmmmm. Never mind.

The good news is Arroyo Tenorio ends at the Trail. The bad

news is Arroyo Tenorio ends at the Trail. It has been peaceful, and we felt relatively safe on this quiet little dust road that, like De Vargas, is honestly what most of America calls an alley. Old Santa Fe Trail is a different matter. It's one of the only main arteries from the south into the Plaza District. Not only will we be totally exposed, with no handy side streets or helpful hiding places, but it's a forever-long four hundred yards down to Jerron's office.

We hold hands—for the first time since Downtown Subscription—and don't bother to try to look like tourists, rather than a couple on the run—from what or whom they don't know. Our hunters haven't found us. Maybe they are indeed waiting for us to reappear at The Compound. My gut, though, says the police have been looking for the thugs—and they *are* thugs—not us. Who knows? I open another heavy, antique wooden door, and hold it for m' lady, bowing and sweeping my free hand for her to enter.

The clean, cool humidity of the office is of great comfort, and for the first time since lunch at the Pink, I truly feel safe.

"Matt! What brings you to town?"

"Hi Sylvia. This is Wynne. Are the man or lady of the house in?"

"Jerron's in his office. You know the way. Francesca's gone out for something, I don't know what. Nice to meet you, Wynne."

We wind around the building, past drawing tables and framed drawings of fine Santa Fe residential and commercial buildings to Jerron's office. He looks up, surprised, and then smiles broadly when he sees us. Standing up immediately, he roars, "Matt! So good to see you. This *is* a surprise. And this can only be Wynne."

Jerron is tall, large in the manner that a grizzly is large, bearded and always well groomed, even for a bear. He always feels to me like a swarthy adventurer, who regularly hangs out with Hemingway or Cousteau. In fact, he is indeed an adventurer at heart and in life, and loves local histories as much as he loves good art—and good people. A renowned architect, his firm is most successful. He comes around the desk to give us both a *mato* hug. Ladies first: gentlemen friends second. Wynne keeps her arms loose, but still wraps him fully—I think she's feeling trust, but unfamiliarity, perhaps, is raising her scales.

I look at him, then bow to her, eyes to the floor. "Jerron Whitten, Wynne de Gracia Worner." She offers her hand. He takes it graciously.

Eyebrows raised, he inquires, "Of *the* de Gracias?"

Wynne smiles sensitively. "I'm not quite sure how to answer that question, except by saying—possibly." She looks my way, and I wink my right eye. "My family roots are in southern New Mexico."

Jerron smiles his knowing smile. Turning to me, he booms, "Matt, what brings you to Santa Fe? And you both look like hell, by the way."

"Wynne's a client. She has business here and invited me to join her on the trip. You know me—I'm not going to say no."

He grins at her. "Well, I should say not! Where are you staying?"

"Wynne has a condo at The Compound."

"How splendid." With a questioning look this time, he adds, "What can I do for you? Did I mention you look like hell?"

"Well, as a matter of fact, hell is quite succinct. We're being pursued and need safe haven."

"Pursued? By whom?"

"We don't know. They have guns."

"Good grief. No wonder you appear disheveled."

It was a gracious understatement, at which I resoundingly chuckle. "It's been quite a day so far, yes. We've been on the run for the last two hours or so. It seems we've lost them, whomever they are, but so I thought for three days until suddenly, they appear today."

"Matt, Wynne," he says, looking compassionately at Wynne, "how may I be of assistance?"

I answer. "Well, we're not really quite sure. We were thinking of flying back to Colorado."

"From Santa Fe? The only flights out of here are to Denver or Grand Junction, I do believe."

"Wynne has a plane. It's hangared at the airport. We flew down."

"From?"

"Sorry. Aspen."

His eyebrows go up again. "I see. Have you called the police? I did hear sirens just a while ago."

"We…." I glance at Wynne. "…Decided not to call the police. We don't have a clue who is actually after us. It's a big black SUV, with black-tinted windows and several antennae on top. Looks like it could be a government vehicle."

"Government? I hope that's not it. Why would you suspect government?"

I look to Wynne.

She gives a miniscule nod, but is no longer smiling. "Without going into mundane detail, I'm involved in legal matters potentially affecting large numbers of people." She's done. I understand. Then her face softens. She adds, "I am most certainly not on the wrong side of the law however. At least, not yet. That I'm aware."

"Understood. Won't you sit down?" He gestures toward two padded leather wooden chairs in front of his beautiful antique New Mexican desk. "Matt…." He looks at me, then to Wynne. "…From what you've told me, I might suggest calling the police. Armed and unknown assailants are chasing you. You have done nothing wrong that you're aware of." He looks at me, then toward Wynne. "I suspect you have resources available to assist you, should you encounter legal trouble. If government might be involved, you may be best served by asking government for help."

I haven't thought of it that way. "You're probably right on target. When one of the guys chasing us yelled, 'stop or I'll shoot,' he didn't identify himself. Usually, at least the way I was trained, law enforcement always says something like: 'Police. Halt.' That's why I decided to run. It was instinct."

Wynne speaks up. "I agree with Matt, Mr. Whitten."

"Please, it's Jerron. A friend of Matt's is de facto a first name basis friend of mine."

Wynne continues. "I suspect the issues I'm faced with have become more personal."

"All the more reason to contact the police. I know the State Attorney General. Let me call and ask his input. Is that agreeable?"

We look at one other. Damn she's beautiful. Wynne reaches over to take my hand. Jerron sees all this, smiling his broad, Whitten smile. We don't say anything right away. What's our intuition?

Still looking at my beautiful companion, I speak first. "I can't believe you've—we've—done anything illegal. My gut says he's right, we call the authorities."

Wynne, not smiling, squeezes my hand, and softly says, "Okay." Her head spins back to Jerron. She starts to speak, but—

The back door to the building opens, causing a couple of hearts to pound. Only moments later, Francesca bursts into Jerron's office.

"Matt! Wonderful. Oh, it's so good to see you. I see your friend found you."

I get up to give and get a hug. "That she did. Thank you for sending my angel after me."

"Well, she did have to convince me, but convince me she did.

And this, then, *is* Wynne?"

As the two women shake hands, Wynne says, "Francesca, it's a pleasure. I told Matt I wanted to meet you after you and I spoke. You obviously care for him a great deal, and know him quite well, I must say."

Francesca laughs her throaty, full-spirited laugh. "So do you, or you'd not have survived my interrogation. You *are* joining us for dinner?" She looks us both over, adding, "And perhaps a shower?"

Wynne looks my way. "I'm not really sure. Matt?"

I look at Francesca, who is very definitely no stranger to intuition. "Thanks to Jerron's objectivity, we're considering calling the police. We've spent the afternoon being chased."

"*Chased?* What do you mean, chased?"

"Someone with a gun is hunting us. We suspect it has to do with a legal issue Wynne is facing, but we really don't know for sure?"

"Have you broken the law?"

"No."

Francesca doesn't hesitate for a nanosecond, after first closing her eyes for an actual nanosecond. "Call the police," she says in her most matronly tone. Moms really have that down.

I look at Wynne, Wynne looks at me. I take her hand. "I'm feeling they're right. How about you?"

She nods, squeezing my hand. I squeeze back.

"May I please use a telephone to call my attorney?"

Francesca speaks immediately. "Come to my office." She turns and strides out, Wynne two steps behind.

I look warily back to my old friend. "Okay. I suspect starting at the top is almost always a good idea, especially when the top is a known entity, and specifically a friendly known entity."

Jerron flips to a card in his old-school Rolodex, and picks up the phone.

Chapter Thirty-Five: Friends Indeed

"Ma'am, your situation is actually within the jurisdiction of the Santa Fe Police." This State Trooper is polite but professionally brief. This is not a social event. "My orders are to get you home. SFPD will be waiting for the hand off."

I've never been in the back of a police car, or in this case, a black and white, well, a black with a white door, New Mexico State Trooper car. I know in the seat of my soul that I don't want to be here again anytime soon—especially on the wrong side of law. This is definitely a mini jail cell on wheels. Wynne doesn't seem uncomfortable, though, so I buck up.

"What about airspace over New Mexico?" she asks our protector. "Who has jurisdiction over air space?"

"Ma'am, I'm not really sure about that to be honest. I believe that jurisdiction would be FAA, with the Air National Guard handling State of New Mexico problems. I'm sorry, I really don't know. It seems the FAA could answer that question."

"Thank you, Officer."

My stomach takes a dive. "Wynne, are you concerned about our return trip?"

"Well, it does seem as though we should be prepared for any eventuality." Her smiling lips are upturned and sly. "Following lunch today my life coach said something similar to me—just before we climbed our first coyote fence together."

I chuckle. "I think I heard about that. What can we do?"

"I'll check in with the New Mexico Aviation Division when we get to the condo."

"Well, all right then." That's the best I can do for a response? I'm trying to look ahead on Canyon, through the dense metal mesh separating us from the front seat. Instead, I settle for looking out the side windows. We're almost at The Compound anyway. The SFPD car sitting in a no parking zone just before the driveway is a dead giveaway. Our cruiser pulls in as far as the closed gate.

He leaves the jail cell running, air conditioner working hard to keep us all cool. "Ma'am, from here Santa Fe will take over." As he climbs out, I notice this trooper could easily be an NFL linebacker. He opens the door for Wynne. Ladies first. Gary is already out of the security station, and a second guard, whose name I don't know, is still sitting inside, looking quite serious. That might be because a uniformed Santa Fe Police officer, whom I recognize as one of the two running by us at the Lamy, stands next to him. The cop comes out to greet Wynne.

Another uniform appears from behind us to open my door—there are no handles on the inside, of course. It's the female officer, also from earlier today. We should've hailed them three hours ago. Who knew? Sometimes intuition becomes clouded—particularly when emotions are running high above flood stage and you can breathe under water but you can't see too far ahead.

I'm polite and friendly. "Thank you, Officer."

She smiles. "You're welcome, sir. We thought about just leaving you in there."

I laugh nervously. "Well, it is very cozy."

She turns, laughing along with me, to walk back up to the car in the no parking zone. I walk around the front of the Trooper's car, as he begins backing out of the driveway.

"Mrs. Worner?"

She smiles sweetly. "It's currently Ms., Officer, and yes."

"I'm Lieutenant Cole, Ma'am. I'm in charge of your safety."

"Thank you so much for your assistance. We've had a challenging day."

"Yes, Ma'am. Ms. Worner, we have a watch on The Compound and your residence. I'll remain in my car. It's in visitor parking for your unit. I've a patrol car on Canyon, and another at the rear of the complex. We have other units in the area and an APB issued for a black SUV with black tinted windows. Two detectives in an unmarked unit are waiting to speak with you. Is this Mr. Hale?" He's not going to shake any hands, which is always fine by me, but is respectful and professional.

"Yes sir. Matt Hale."

"May I see your identification, sir?"

"Of course, Officer." I pull the tri-fold leather wallet out of my left front pocket. I'm not asking why he needs my ID. I'm just happy to see these guys. And gals. There is more than a small measure of comforting safety conveyed by professionalism. I open the wallet for him.

"Will you remove the license, please sir?"

"Yes, of course. I'm sorry, sir."

"You're from Colorado, Mr. Hale?"

"Yes sir. Born and bred, as they say."

He jots something down in his little notebook, about the same size as my cargo pocket notebook: my address and license number I assume. He hands it back to me. "Thank you, Mr. Hale."

"Yes sir." I put the license back under the plastic window in my wallet.

"Ma'am, sir, if you'll come with me I'll escort you to your residence, Ms. Worner."

"Thank you very much, Lieutenant Cole."

Gary walks by my side. In front of us the Lieutenant stays next to Wynne, while we wend down the gentle asphalt slope shaded by tall, old willows. Sure enough, down in the flats, a police car sits in Wynne's visitor parking, with an obvious unmarked vehicle right beside it. I can't see the third patrol car. It's nice to see these guys are taking this seriously. Wynne and I certainly have been. Two plain-clothed detectives, a male-female team, exit their gold Crown Victoria as we approach.

"Ms. Worner?" the brunette asks. She's pretty and obviously athletic, even in a khaki-colored, professional pantsuit that nicely compliments her short, wavy, auburn hair.

"Yes?"

"I'm Detective Pratt, this is my partner Detective Grayson." She extends her hand to both of us, as does Detective Grayson. "We'd like to ask you some questions if you don't mind."

"Not at all. Please come in." Detective Pratt nods once, and we all four stride through the front gate and into Wynne's lovely little low-water garden. The apple is glowering—I swear.

Behind us, Lieutenant Cole closes his car door. I hold open the weighty wooden front door as the entourage enters the subdued mellow of Wynne's Compound condo, her new Zia lamp on the sideboard, glowing its handsome orange and red onto adobe walls painted every pastel color ever seen in these New Mexico sunsets.

~~~

"I'm starting the recorder now. This is Detective Lorne Grayson, Santa Fe Police Department, interviewing Mr. Matt Hale of Colorado Springs, Colorado. Today is Tuesday, August 30, 2011. The time is approximately 3:18 p.m. The interview is taking place at the Canyon Road residence of Ms. Wynne de Gracia Worner. Mr. Hale, you have the right to remain silent. Anything you say can and will be used against you in a court of law. You have the right to speak to an attorney. If you cannot afford an attorney, one will be appointed for you. Do you understand these rights as they have been stated to you?"

"Yes sir."

"Do you wish an attorney?"

"I can't believe that's necessary at all."

"Will you please answer yes or no."

"No."

"Starting at the beginning, please tell me everything that has happened since you arrived in Santa Fe. Leave out nothing."

Well, that takes easily twenty minutes. Then, in his charcoal gray, two-piece suit with white shirt and black tie, Detective Grayson gets down to business.

"Would you be able to identify any of the persons chasing you?"

"The one guy I saw, yes."

"How long have you lived in Colorado?"

"I was born in Colorado, and except for a few years in Southern California, a summer in New Orleans, a summer in Philadelphia, and a school year teaching in the Seattle area, I have lived in Colorado."

"How long have you known Ms. Worner?"

"She contacted me by telephone last Wednesday, and I drove to Aspen to meet with her for the first time on Thursday, the 25th."

"Of August 2011?"

"Yes sir."

"Do you know any of the individuals involved today?"

"Other than Wynne, no sir."

"How long have you resided in Colorado?"

"Nearly all my life. I was born in Colorado Springs."

"How have you spent time when you were not accompanying Ms. Worner?"

"Primarily in museums, or writing in my journal."
~~~

"Can you describe the vehicle that you believe was chasing you today?"

"It's a late model SUV, I don't know what year. American made, though I don't know which manufacturer—it is a General Motors vehicle. It's completely black, with black tinted windows so dark that I could not see the interior or its occupants. It has numerous, possibly four, antennae on top. It has chrome or magnesium wheels, probably original equipment rather than custom. It has a very throaty exhaust sound, rather than quiet. I did not see license plates. I can't recall anything else."

"Can you describe Ms. Worner's relations with her family?"

"Exceptionally warm and loving, from what I know up to now."

"What are the call letters on Ms. Worner's aircraft?"

"N7—you know, I didn't really pay that much attention."

"Tell me about the vehicle you own."

"I drove my 1993 Subaru Legacy wagon to Aspen. It's maroon, or winestone I believe Subaru calls it. It's the 25th Anniversary Edition. It has only 140,000 miles. I also own a 1986 Nissan standard bed, two-wheel drive pickup, white, that I purchased new. It now has 277,000 miles, and is still near-perfect."

"Describe your relationship with Ms. Worner."

"We have a professional relationship. I'm a lifestyle consultant. We have, however, been feeling attracted to one another. That has caused a bit of contention."

"Do either of you hold ill will toward the other?"

"Absolutely not."

"Do you have family?"

"My parents are both deceased. I have a brother who, with his wife, lives in Manitou Springs, Colorado."

"Can you describe the weapon you observed?"

"The fellow was holding it in both hands, so I didn't get a good look. Judging only by the stocky barrel, it may have been something like a Smith & Wesson M&P."

"How is it that you are knowledgeable about guns?"

"I have firearms training and experience from a short stint as an investigator for the State of Colorado."

"Do you own firearms?"

"I have a vintage .357 Magnum from my law enforcement jobs, and a CO2 carbine."

"Who else are you acquainted with in New Mexico?"

"I have old friends here in Santa Fe: Jerron and Francesca Whitten. I also know a man by the name of George Shaw, who runs an antique shop downtown. Some academic friends of mine moved to Las Cruces. I have visited them several times."

"Why would someone be chasing you?"

"There's no reason for anyone to chase me, that I am aware. However, I do believe that someone entered my hotel room in Aspen to observe my professional journal. I have kept notes regarding my interactions with Ms. de Gracia."

"Please describe in the greatest detail possible the persons chasing you today. Take your time. It's important that you remember even the tiniest detail."

"I only saw the guy who was on foot, and chasing us." I close my eyes. "He was about six feet tall, ruddy complexion—his face was a little bit pock marked. His hair was very short, as though his head was recently shaved. He was big but not overweight. I'd say he was around 225. He wore a red, white and light blue plaid shirt—small plaid, like one-inch squares. He also wore a tan, almost gold windbreaker—very lightweight. He had a shoulder holster under the left side. He had on pressed khaki pants, but not cargo-style—more business casual. His shoes were black. I didn't recognize them except that they were sturdy—perhaps military, with traction soles and high ankle support. I didn't see any jewelry or rings, and he did not wear glasses. His eyebrows were kind of bushy." I open my eyes, blinking. "That's the best I can do."

"Did the individual with the weapon have facial hair?"

"No sir."

"Where is the main Santa Fe Post Office?"

I close my eyes, and trace my way there with finger on an imaginary map. "Sir, it's on South Federal, by the courthouse."

"How did you know to take the route you did while being pursued?"

"With all due respect, we believed we were running for our lives. We simply went where we felt safest—from moment to moment. Neither of us had a plan, or knew where we were going. We did initially try to get back to Wynne's condo so she could call her attorney, but gave up on that and went instead to the Whitten Firm."

"You have admitted to seeing Santa Fe police numerous times. Why did you not seek police assistance?"

"That's a really good question. And when I think about it, the answer doesn't make a lot of sense."

"Please just answer the question."

"We were concerned the SUV might be a government vehicle. Given the magnitude of the water rights issue she and her family face, and the fact that government entities as well as corporate seem hostile about procuring the rights, I believe the feeling was that we could not trust government interests any more than private."

"Why do you feel you cannot trust government interests?"

"Do I need a lawyer present?"

"Mr. Hale, you may request a lawyer if you wish before any further questions. I am nearly finished however. As I stated before any questioning, you have the right to remain silent. Anything you say can and will be used against you in a court of law. You have the right to speak to an attorney. If you cannot afford an attorney, one will be appointed for you. Do you understand these rights as they have been stated to you?"

"Thank you, Detective Grayson. I have done absolutely nothing against the law that I am aware. I can only speak for myself, and only do so now. My personal belief is that, in a broad and general construct, government interests at any level may or may not be in collusion with private and/or corporate interests, for the furtherance of private profits, and goals not necessarily in the best interests of the citizens of the United Sates of America."

He stares at me long enough to shake that one off before continuing his line. "Do you feel such is the case as regards Ms. Worner?"

"I have absolutely no idea."

"So your immediately previous statement is Ms. Worner's opinion?"

"No sir. It is entirely my own."

"Has Ms. Worner ever made a similar sentiment known to you?"

"No sir. Not to my recollection."

"Then why did you earlier state that 'We were concerned the SUV might be a government vehicle'? And that 'the feeling was that we could not trust government interests any more than private'?"

"I understand. Under the circumstances, we were not thinking altogether clearly. Furthermore, given the enormity of water issues facing municipalities and states around the country, and in this case, the Southwest and California, I believe Ms. Worner has received threats of unknown magnitude regarding transferring her family's water rights to serve interests that are corporate, government, or both. I have certainly not pressed her for details—her affairs are private. I can say she *is* under a great deal of duress in this matter. That's the main reason she engaged my services—to try to help her personally cope with pressures that, other than legal assistance, she is facing on her own."

"Thank you, Mr. Hale. Have you anything else you would like to say?"

"Not at present, sir."

"Then, again, thank you for your time and assistance. I'll show myself out. Have an enjoyable evening, sir." Click. He puts the black pen in a shirt pocket, flops closed a blue spiral notebook, and picks up the recorder.

"Thank you, detective."

We both get up, and I follow him to the door that he opens and closes behind himself without saying another word. Jeez. I guess interrogation methods have changed a smidge since my days.

~~~

After reliving our day to the detectives, interviewed separately by our respective sex in separate rooms, we were left alone, finally. I thought it a bit sexist. I would've had each of us interviewed twice, once by each detective. But that was another of my former careers. Wynne and I sink into the loveseat together, again. Clothed. I prefer robed.

"Whew!"

"Whew!" Wynne agrees.

She reaches for a black remote control on the coffee table, presses three buttons, and from every corner of the condo wafts soft, pleasant instrumental music with a distinctly southwestern flair: soothing, comforting, relaxing, meditative. Wynne's head falls onto my shoulder. I reach for her hand. We say nothing at all, and just relax back into the loveseat.

We both jump. I don't know what startled me. Maybe one of us was dreaming. My neck hurts from my napping position: head tilted back onto the top of the loveseat. I've given myself whiplash, relatively speaking. We both glance at the grandfather clock just as Winchester chimes hammer seven o'clock. We've been asleep for nearly two hours.

"What just happened?"

"I don't know. I startled myself awake, I guess. I don't even
~~~

remember falling asleep."

"Neither do I. I feel like I could go to bed right now, and sleep until Thursday."

"Me, too. I feel like I've been drugged and have a nasty hangover." My belly roars to life. "Sorry, I guess I haven't eaten since those few pumpkin seeds and almonds we had on the trail."

Wynne laughs. "You bet—the trail. That sure was a pleasant hike." Then she adds, "You know, I'm hungry too."

There is precious little vitality in my voice. "I don't really feel like going anywhere. Should I see what's in the refrigerator?"

"I'm with you. I've had enough excitement for today. Though I don't think there's much in the condo to eat."

"You'd be surprised. I'm a master at making soup from nothing."

"Let's have a look-see."

I can't remember hearing that term since my grandmother. I follow Wynne's disheveled, tattered skirt and blouse into the kitchen. That outfit is probably beyond repair. Black and brown smudges are everywhere. The skirt has a long, sexy tear up to her mid thigh on the right, and is also ripped and unraveling along the bottom, the hem stripped out. Some people pay a hundred dollars for that look, new. I try to think about food.

Wynne goes to a cupboard, opens it and removes a can of organic tomato soup. Setting that on the counter, she reaches back in to hold up a box of quinoa elbow pasta. "How about soup?" She's smiling. We're both waking up slowly, only minimally rested.

In the refrigerator I find a desiccated lime, various condiments, apples, some bottled water and organic soft drinks, and two bottles of Santa Fe Pale Ale. "It looks like we have tomato soup with pasta, and beers, with apples for dessert."

"How about the freezer, Matt?"

"Oh, right." In the freezer are unopened bags of green beans and sweet corn, maize tortillas, packages of ground organic turkey and pork, along with another dozen or more unidentifiable items opaque with frost. "Hey, jackpot! We can have a great soup! Turkey or pork?"

"Pork sounds more substantial to me, but either is fine."

"Pork it is, then."

"I'm going for a shower."

I let coconut oil melt into a saucepan, slowly thaw and brown the pound of pork, drain off fat, add more coconut oil, then sauté *the other white meat* with green beans and sweet corn, oregano and curry, over high heat, while quinoa elbows boil quietly in a quart pot. We don't need a big meal, or at least no leftovers, although a bite to eat for the flight back to Aspen might not be so bad. Detective Pratt said it was okay to leave New Mexico, and they'd contact us as needed.

They don't have a lot to go on, other than a black SUV with dark windows, license unknown, and a vague description of one fast, big guy in a plaid shirt and tan windbreaker. They'd let us know if they come up with anything. They were concerned, though, because a gun was *allegedly* involved.

After draining more fat and lowering the heat, I squeeze the entire lime into the pork pan, add about three tablespoons of fresh olive oil, stirring gently, and then immediately turn off that burner. After pouring the contents of the pan into a two-quart pot where the tomato soup is now hot but not boiling, I add on-the-verge-of al dente quinoa pasta, rinsed, in a colander, four times with cold water, and sprinkle the top of our soup with parsley and thyme. My ale lasted only five minutes after I started to cook, and I now have a disorienting alcohol buzz going. So I open the other one, too.

"Dinner's ready."

"Be right there." She comes out in the furry-headed slippers and pajamas.

"I drank both ales." I hold up the bottle. "Well, this is the second and last one. Can I get you some wine?"

"Thank you, but I'm really tired. I think I'll pass on alcohol."

"A wise choice."

We sit at the dining table, side by side. No candle, and with paper napkins. Wynne's left hand comes lightly to rest on my right jeans leg, just above the bloodied knee. Her fingertips circle the spot. Suddenly I'm not feeling so fatigued.

"Matt, this is absolutely delicious! The pasta's perfect! And the lime! *Rico!* You may certainly cook for me any time!"

"Flattery will get you everywhere with me, girl."

Chapter Thirty-Six: Santa Fe Escape

The telephone wakes us. The sun hadn't. Untangling ourselves is downright fun. Wynne's silk pajama top is up around her midriff, our arms and legs wrapped around each other like a Picasso abstract. We're under only the sheet, the bedspread strewn across the floor like a spilled plate of spaghetti. I sit up.

"Let the service get it," Wynne says sleepily, stretching her arms overhead, and kicking the sheet over to my side of the bed. I suck in a cubic yard of oxygen. Sometime during the night she removed her chartreuse pajama bottoms and now wears only plain white, cotton underwear.

She just smiles, nonchalantly pulling her pale top down to about eight miles higher than the knee. This helps me precious little. Well, actually, temptation is now *mucho mas* delicious. "Sorry, Matt. It was a little warm in here for me last night."

"Uh, no problem—really." I fib for sure, and lay back down, staring at smooth lines of adobe crown molding. "You're a temptation, clothed or not."

"So I see." She grins, looking at the sheet tent on my side of the bed. "I'm starting to lose my resolve, Matt."

Eyes and other parts hopeful, I roll onto my left side. The sheet falls behind, exposing the waistband of my blue boxers. "Really?" I think for a moment, and very softly add, "Then what the hell are you waiting for?"

She laughs, rolling onto her side, facing me. The long silk top flows in waves, beaching itself loosely around her shoulder, abdomen and hip. "I suspected that might eventually come back to haunt me." She chuckles, smiling seductively. "I'd like to see who called, and get us back to Aspen. There will be another day."

I give her my finest pouty face and puppy dog eyes.

With two fingers, she traces outlines around the gray-red embroidered mandala on the chest of my forest green t-shirt, then reaches up with thumb and index finger to push my melodramatic lips into a smile. "Anyway, I need another shower to rinse off more *running through the ditches, and over the walls, of Santa Fe yesterday.*"

"*To the galleries we will go,*" I sing, finishing the verse. "I don't mind."

"You're sweet," she coos, pinching my cheek, and then rolls onto her back with arms and legs outstretched. Wynne spirals over and out of bed, headed for the cell phone on top of her ancient, heavy, you know the drill, dresser—a bounce back in her step, swagger restored to her hips, that pajama top dancing—my tent now a languishing big top on this side of the bed. Shameless. With arms and legs sprawled out, I release a sorrowful moan.

~~~

I've never had a police escort before. Don't want one now. Well, maybe I do. We haven't seen the black scorpion since Canyon Road yesterday. Neither, apparently, has the Santa Fe Police Department. The Prius' new windshield is clear as the morning sky. The water issue is unresolved. Browner is gone. Cassie's on her way to school. Wynne and I, though in pretty good spirits, are sore and tired, and ready to be back in the Roaring Fork Valley. I haven't brought up my concerns about black SUVs waiting for us there—one step at a time. We can talk about it in the plane—and this pilot won't announce that we need to turn off cell phones.

Lieutenant Cole follows us through the gate to the private hangars, and stays in his car while ground service pulls *Wambli Gleska* out of the hangar. I back the Prius into the hangar, grab our bags, and trod up bouncing metal stairs into the gleaming Cessna. My arms are way too full, and all the bags fall, thumping around the Berber carpet. My book bag, though, is safely atop my left shoulder. Wynne doesn't notice the chaos—she's already wearing headphones. I stroll back to close the hangar door.

The powder room is heavy, and I proceed to pour the pail's contents onto the Tarmac. Lieutenant Cole's partner (why didn't I get her name?) watches all this—with amusement aplenty. The passenger window glides down as I start back toward the plane with stainless steel swinging in hand.

"Mr. Hale," she calls out, "can you spare us a moment?"
~~~

"Yes ma'am." I stride over to the Camaro—white, with red and blue stripes and Zia, and those low-profile winky-winks—a fast ride with a beefy suspension.

Her jaw is set, eyes narrowed. "Mr. Hale, I'm pretty sure that was illegal."

I open my mouth but nothing comes out—probably a good thing. Maybe I'm getting better about the speaking without thinking thing.

She giggles. "You should see your expression!" She's not just a pretty face, after all. "We plan to stay until you're off the ground, and another ten minutes just to make sure you're safely en route. State Police have established radio contact with airport security, and will continue to monitor your progress until you leave New Mexico airspace. Miss De Gracia seems to have friends in high places: The 58th SOW from Kirtland is assigning an HH-60G Pave Hawk to monitor your flight until Aspen. Do you understand?"

"Yes ma'am. Except for all the acronyms."

"A helicopter will be keeping an eye out. You'll probably never even see it—let's hope."

"Yes ma'am. I'll relay the information on to the captain, ma'am." I grin. "But honestly, thank you very much for helping us." I bend down to look over at Lieutenant Cole. "And thank you, too, Lieutenant. You've been very kind." He just grunts a little and lifts a hand off the steering wheel to toss a tiny backhand wave. My smile is nonetheless genuine—he *was* in his car all night at The Compound. I straighten my spine, and resume the trek to the silent, high performance twin-engine aircraft.

With headphones on, Wynne's voice is a little louder than usual. "Are we ready?" She's poised to get the Hale out of Santa Fe.

"I just need a moment to stow our gear."

"What?" She turns her head, gingerly, slightly my way and pulls the headphone from her right ear. "Sorry, what did you say?"

"I just need to stow the bags. Do you need yours handy?"

"Thank you, but no. I've got a full water bottle here, and my flight bag." Her head turns all the way around to the cabin. "We can eat for a week on the contents of your bag, if needed."

I laugh. She does too, while adjusting that gorgeous pomegranate sundress. She must like it as much as I do. Copilot Hale climbs into the cockpit, straps in, and pops headphones over his ears as if he knew what he was doing. The engines whirr, roaring to life. Wynne immediately eases off the choke, letting the engines warm for several minutes while she tips her water bottle, making certain I notice. I give her a big smile and a thumb's up. We both need lots of water to continue flushing toxins from yesterday. And we're good—we have a five gallon stainless steel potty pail.

We ease toward the runway, while I carefully record communications and aircraft operation in my pocket notebook. Another lesson is at hand, and I'm a darn good student. Maybe someday I can pass the exam.

"Cessna November Six One Zero Delta George, you are cleared for takeoff on Runway Two." Santa Fe's small airport isn't very busy, so we're not waiting to lift away.

Wynne taxies us onto the runway, adjusts manifold pressure, and gracefully, smoothly, pushes the throttle levers all the way forward. Man, this acceleration is outrageous. We dip a bit as we escape the Tarmac, my solar plexus giving me another roller coaster thrill. Air de Gracia Cessna 414 RAM VI, flight number two en route to Aspen, Colorado, is on its way. Woo hoo!

Chapter Thirty-Seven: Passing Time

We fly back on a standard Taos–Alamosa vector: no sightseeing this time around. Wynne doesn't say a word as we approach Colorado and the Upper San Luis Valley. I know she has a lot on her mind. I know I don't want to impose. So off I go, my vision flying back to Manitou Springs, to Sleeping Bear Oasis, to my friends and to 'Toids.

I wonder how Fountain Creek, prone to flooding, is fairing. Wynne and I have seen some rain, though not a lot, both in Aspen and in Santa Fe, since I left home to enjoy the gorgeous Rocky Mountain drive to Aspen in Maroonbaru. Has the wonderful late summer monsoon abated, or worse, gone away completely? Have drought-depleted reservoirs been replenished? Is my xeriscape garden holding its own without additional water? After seven years of weeding, I feel confident that at least I won't return to a field of weeds. I prefer the fields of my dreams. Speaking of fields, my heart sinks as I think about Browner. Nervously, I gaze below as we fly past Alamosa and over unseen aquifers.

"Matt?"

I snap out of it, feeling my stiff neck. "Whoa! Sorry, Wynne, I was daydreaming."

Looking a little sleepy, she smiles that sweet smile, letting me know she's just playing, joking, understanding, and approving. "Really?" She really does look tired. "Do you think you'd mind taking the wheel for a while?"

My heart instantly races. And not NASCAR driving around in circles, either; this is Formula One *ch'i*: serious, fast, treacherous, demanding diversity of curves and driving elements. "Wynne, I'd love to." I smile, more than a bit tenuous.

Showing no emphasis or concern, she says, "Well, I think you might need to. I'm suddenly feeling faint enough that I might pass out."

I almost yell, "What?"

Her eyes aren't shining with dancing light. "Matt, I'm not feeling well at all." In fact, her eyelids are sliding down like a hangar door.

I reach for the yoke. "We're on autopilot, aren't we?"

"Yes. Denver Regional Service Center should be contacting us any minute for instructions."

We're just entering Colorado, but I know that Air Traffic Control watches planes closely and takes action well enough in advance to both preplan and be ready for any contingency. Having that understanding is comforting right now, and I need every little bit of comfort I can find.

She's nodding away in her seat, head falling down. "Wynne!" Oh shit. "Wynne! What should I do?"

She mumbles quietly with her eyes closed, head turned toward me, chin on her shoulder. The last word I barely hear is "radio."

~~~

"Mayday! Mayday!" I press the button on the yoke so hard my thumb hurts. Soon it starts tingling. "Mayday! Mayday!" After several minutes with no response, my mouth is dry as the high desert below me. I let go the yoke and Comm. button to grab my water bottle. I notice something out the right window. It's a menacing-looking helicopter.

"Mr. Hale, this is Captain DeAngelus, U. S. Air Force. We are right here and will keep a close watch on you for the duration of your flight. Right now, Denver is trying to contact you." He waves from his window, gives me a thumbs up, and the giant dragonfly zooms ahead to take a position above and to the right of *Wambli Gleska.*

"Cessna November Six One Zero Delta George. This is Denver Regional Air Service Center. We read. What is the nature of your distress? Please release the Comm. button after completing your communication, sir."

My water bottle goes between my legs, my hand back to the yoke, and I press the thumb button. "My pilot has lost consciousness. I am not a pilot. Repeat: I am not a pilot." I release the thumb button this time. Well, duh.

"Cessna November Six One Zero Delta George. This is DSC. We read pilot is unconscious. Does anyone on board have flight experience?"
~~~

I press the thumb button. "DSC, negative. I'm the only passenger." I'm getting the hang of this. I'm nervous, but have people to talk to. And the plane is flying by itself. So far.

"Is the craft under autopilot control?"

"Yes."

"Good. Remain on autopilot. Kirtland Air Force Base has an aircraft escorting you."

"DSC, the helicopter is close to me and going the same speed."

"We show the aircraft registered to de Gracia Family Trust. Registered pilot is Wynne de Gracia Worner. Is this correct?"

"DSC, affirmative."

"Please identify yourself."

"This is Matt Hale, business associate of Ms. Worner."

"Mr. Hale, is the pilot's condition serious or life threatening?"

"I don't know. She seems to be unconscious."

"Please check the pilot's pulse, eyes, and breathing. Is pulse normal? Are the pupils normal and responding to light? Is she breathing?"

I reach over and put two fingers on Wynne's carotid artery. Lifting her right eyelid, the pupil immediately closes against the light. Her chest is waving up and down, as it was when I watched her sleeping last night.

My left hand went back to the yoke and the Comm. button. "Ms. Worner seems okay. Pulse feels normal, or maybe a little slow."

"Is the pilot bleeding or displaying any other sign of gross trauma?"

"No, sir."

A different voice—this one female. "Remain on autopilot. Relax. Keep breathing normally. We will assist. You will be fine. Repeat: you will be okay. Do you understand?"

"Yes."

"Please adjust to heading seven-four-eight and climb to 12,500. Do you understand?"

"I understand, but I'm not sure how to do that. Can you help?"

"What is your name, sir?"

"Matt." Brevity, normally foreign to me, is sometimes in direct relationship to nervousness.

"Thank you, Matt." Her voice was nice. Smooth, calm. How do they know I'm a sucker for that? Well, I suppose most men are.

I press the button. "You're welcome."

"Matt, everything is okay. Do you have any flight experience?"

"This is my third private flight. I did pay close attention and took notes when we flew to Santa Fe, and Ms. Worner showed me how to fly the plane manually." It might be best to not say anything about my getting to try my hand at the yoke. Wynne's hand was really in control anyway.

"Matt, do you believe you are able to fly this aircraft?" Her voice remains steady, calm, patient, friendly.

"I believe I can try. I think I can keep it in the air. Landing is a different story."

"Matt, if I promise to give you clear, careful, specific directions, do you feel you can fly the craft and land also?"

"Do I have a choice?"

There's a quiet chuckle on the other end. "No sir, as a matter of fact you don't." I can hear her smile. "I'm confident you'll do very well. Do you know the location of the autopilot toggle?"

"Affirmative."

"Don't do anything yet, okay? I will instruct you and then let you know if and when to toggle autopilot off. Do you understand?"

"Yes, ma'am." My body temperature is nearly a thousand degrees. Salty sweat stings my eyes. I know it's salty because it's also dripping from my lip into my mouth. My shirt is getting damp. No Cambrio is here to save me from this rain.

"Matt, I'm not ma'am. I'm Julianne."

I laugh aloud, thumb on the Comm. button, grateful for the humor. I'm speaking with a professional, who understands the situation completely. Thank goodness for competence. And for the U. S. Air Force.

"Please call me J."

I'm actually beginning to relax again. It's that or drown. "Okay, J. Thank you."

"Matt, what we need to do is gradually increase airspeed to 200 knots, by moving throttle levers up, but only until RPMs reach the middle of the yellow range. As your airspeed increases over 180 knots, adjust the autopilot altitude control to 12,500. Do you understand?" Julianne's voice sounds more relaxed, too. And a little sexy.

I press the button. "Affirmative, J."

"Great! It's absolutely critical that everything you do is done gently and smoothly. Very, very smoothly. Okay?"

"Yes, absolutely." I drive a Ferrari, remember?

"You are approaching Saguache, Colorado. We can take you to a small landing strip at Buena Vista or elsewhere on your current heading, or bring you to Aspen. We believe insufficient medical facilities may exist along your current route. We prefer directing you to Aspen. What do you think? Closest or Aspen?"

"Aspen, please."

"Matt, Aspen it is. You'll do fine. I've flown a Cessna just like yours, and really, it practically flies itself, agreed?"

"I sure hope so. Though is a great time for a really good lesson."

Julianne chuckles again. "Please begin acceleration to 200 knots, and ascent to 12,500 starting at 180 knots. Can you do that?"

"I'm on it." I push both throttles forward gently, slowly accelerating to 180 knots. Following what I watched Wynne doing, I adjust altitude for 12,500, and *Wambli Gleska* begins a rapid climb, giving me one of those familiar little thrills. I'd better be careful, I think to myself, or I might start having fun. And having that Air Force helicopter over there to my right is a huge comfort as well.

"At 200 knots, disengage autopilot and watch for a highway below heading northwest. When you see the highway, it will be the only one in that direction, please begin a left turn by smoothly turning the yoke to the left, maintaining 200 knots. Please watch the attitude indicator and maintain a ten percent attitude until you are over the highway, then level out again over the highway. Climb to 12,500 if necessary and maintain that altitude. Then resume autopilot control. Do you understand, Matt?" She said the "do you understand" part with a kinder, sexier voice than she used while instructing me what to do. Okay with me.

"Yes, Julianne."

"Your course change will take you over Cochetopa Pass, above Colorado Highway 114, toward Gunnison, Colorado. Have you flight maps available?"

"J, affirmative to flight maps, and I am actually very familiar with 114." Colorado 114 is nearly my favorite Ferrari drive. It has almost no traffic, and is very fast, being gently engineered. I, of course, never go over the speed limit.

"Fantastic. Once you are above Colorado 114, stay above the highway at 12,500 until you approach Gunnison, Colorado. I will contact you again with further instructions before then, and will continue communications constantly."

I press the autopilot button and the blue light fades instantly. *Wambli Gleska* doesn't even flinch. I gradually move throttles forward again, listening to growling engines rather than watch the tachometer. At 200 knots, turning the yoke to the left like Wynne taught me over the Taos Valley, spotted eagle turns gently.

I jump in my seat at Julianne's voice—I was concentrating on my speed and turn, not on the headphone. "Matt, one correction: At heading seven-four-eight, level out your turn by watching the attitude indicator until level. Continue gradual acceleration to 200 knots and climb to 12,500, then maintain airspeed and resume autopilot. Understood?"

"Yes, ma'am. Thanks for being so nice and so professional."

"You're welcome. I'll be quiet for a short time while we contact Aspen tower and plan your approach. I will remain right here for any communication you need to send. Okay, Matt?"

"Affirmative, J. I'll miss you though."

She answers chuckling a bit. "Flattery will get you everywhere, sir."

Chapter Thirty-Eight: Timing Passes

It's actually becoming painful. My water bottle is nearly empty and my bladder complains loudly. I've been reaching over every now and then to check Wynne's pulse and eyes, but the effort is now nearly explosive. The stainless steel bucket shines there right behind me, stowed under its seat, mocking me in a friendly way.

Given the autopilot blue light, I take both hands off the yoke, very gently, and very, very slowly. I hold them there suspended in the air for probably five seconds, ready to grab the yoke again. *Wambli Gleska* bumps, and I nearly pee my pants—not much of a surprise in any case. I grab the yoke so hard I push it upward, although the plane doesn't even blink. Captain Autopilot knows better than to trust me completely. If only he can also land us.

Unbuckling the seat belt, I'm out of the copilot seat before the belt is even out of the way. I move quickly but gracefully, so not to jostle the plane. I grab the bucket handle and slide back into the seat, breathing fast. After belting myself back into the soft leather, I pull the lid off the bucket and unzip. Ahhhhhhhh. I hear a faint voice, and look around. Headphones! Oops! Julianne's voice gets louder as I lift the headphones with my left hand to my ear.

"Matt, are you there? Please respond! Matt, are you there?"

"J, I'm sorry. I was taking care of some personal business."

"You had us worried. Please notify us of any time you might be unable to respond or communicate. Do you understand, Matt?"

"Yes. I'm so sorry."

"No problem. You are approaching Gunnison, Colorado. What is your altitude and heading?"

"My heading is seven-four-eight and altitude is 12,500. This is a little higher than Ms. Worner was flying."

"Matt, we need the altitude to get you over the mountains. Given the uncertainty about Ms. Worner's condition, we're guiding you the most direct route possible to Aspen. Do you understand?"

"Yes. Thank you, thank you, and thank you."

"Your current heading will take you west of Crested Butte and then over McClure Pass. Maintain speed and altitude. At 200 knots, you will reach the Colorado River and Interstate 70 in about 20 minutes. As you approach the river, we'll have you turn east and southeast to proceed up the Roaring Fork Valley. Do you understand?"

"Affirmative, J." Man, it sure is a good thing I took notes and worked hard to learn as much as I could on the way to Santa Fe. I look over again at Wynne. She seems to just be sleeping, but she sure is going to have an even stiffer neck.

~~~

McClure Pass is indescribably more beautiful from 12,500 feet than from my trips on the highway below. This is one of those Colorado mountain vistas often photographed, especially during fall when the aspens glow gold. From up here, almost 4,000 feet higher than the summit of the pass, the view is jaw-dropping spectacular. To the east are Castle Peak, Maroon Peak, and Capitol Peak, along with all the other jagged mountaintops and deep green valleys that are part of the headwaters of the Crystal and Roaring Fork Rivers. This is why I've always wanted to fly—to look upon Creation from a perspective that truly allows you to take in the awesome beauty of it all, to be overcome with joy at the sight of the greatness of nature. I feel that fullness behind my eyes that occurs when tears are on the way. I also really need to pee again.

I have to hold it though—Mount Sopris is directly ahead, and Carbondale only minutes away. Autopilot is a lot easier than flying manually, though probably pretty boring for experienced pilots, among whom I of course am not. Change heading, attitude, or airspeed and the plane does exactly as directed effortlessly and perfectly. But then, we had been blessed, the unconscious Wynne and I, with nearly windless and almost cloudless skies on the flight to Santa Fe. Not so on this trip.

There definitely have been the occasional bumps or turbulence, and some roller coaster drops in altitude, especially as *Wambli Gleska* took us over mountainous wilderness, but the Cessna instantly and perfectly corrects itself. Things got pretty tense as we flew toward
~~~

North Pass while following Highway 114. That pass over the Continental Divide was just over 10,000 feet and we were flying at 12,500 but it sure looked like we could have been higher. Mountains growing taller and bigger as you fly toward them at a very rapid speed are just a little scary. For the most part, though, we had come over the lowest mountain passes possible, and they were right on the route Julianne was taking me, that was straight as could be. Nothing short of a miracle in my book bag.

"Matt, how are you doing up there?"

"I'm lovin' it."

"Great. What's not to love, right? Okay. It's time to prepare for your approach to Aspen."

My heart rate doubles. You can know something is coming, and still lose your calm, your peace.

"If you want to refer to your approach map, you'll be using Roaring Fork Visual Runway 15 CVFP, but it's not necessary. In fact Matt, you'll probably want to just concentrate on verbal instruction. Your choice. At this time, please gradually reduce airspeed to 170 knots, and begin a gradual descent to 10,000. Got that?"

"Yes. I'm nervous, but I've gotten to know this plane in the last 50 minutes or so. I can do this."

"You absolutely will. In a few moments I'm going to hand you over to Aspen Tower. I will remain patched in to your communications, but your communication will be with Aspen Tower. Understood?"

"Julianne, I understand. Thank you for everything. You've been totally great."

"You are most welcome. Please change over to ATIS 120.4, NAV One to 118.85, NAV Two to 288.3, and UNICOM to 122.95. Understood?"

"J, please repeat." I grab my little notebook and pen.

"I'll speak a little slower. Please change to ATIS 120.4, NAV One to 118.85, NAV Two to 288.3, and UNICOM to 122.95. Understood?."

"Got it. Setting Comm. channels now."

Humming along at 170 knots and 10,000 feet, Carbondale is ahead to my right.

"Cessna November Six One Zero Delta George, this is Aspen Tower. Do you read?"

"Aspen Tower, I read." I already miss Julianne. I look over at

Wynne, smile, wipe a little drool from the corner of her perfect mouth and onto my cargo pants, and quietly say, "We're almost home, Sweetie."

Chapter Thirty-Nine: Aspen Visual

"Cessna November Six One Zero Delta George, this is Aspen Tower. Do you read?"

"Affirmative, Aspen Tower."

"Aspen Tower: After slowly reducing airspeed to 90 knots, use the turn coordinator to execute a 120-degree right turn over Carbondale and proceed on heading three-two-two above the Roaring Fork River. At Basalt begin a 15-degree glide slope until 8,000 feet. Maintain 8,000. Due to the nature of this airport and weather conditions we cannot fully employ Ground Controlled Approach. We'll give you easy instructions. You'll do fine."

"ASE, understood. Reducing airspeed to 90 knots." This controller is all business, but then I'm going to land this airplane now. There is zero room for error. My heart pounds, eardrums thumping inside the headphones so loud I can barely hear. "ASE, approaching Basalt, beginning 15-degree descent." Palms on the yoke, they're almost too sweaty to have a secure grip. I start breathing in and out, yoga breaths, breathing underwater. Matt, you can do this. Breathe. "ASE, maintaining 8,000."

The helicopter gradually slips closer to me. "Mr. Hale, it looks like you are doing fine. There's not much more we can do, so we're heading home. You've done very well. You'll be fine." He waves again, and the bird turns away and disappears from view.

"Matt, as Sardy Field comes into view," now that's better, "turn coordinate a 12-degree right turn until red blinking runway lights come into view, then immediately go zero attitude. Is this understood?"

"Understood, sir."

"At zero attitude, contact us immediately." He's talking slowly and carefully now. "We will radio transmit the landing glide slope to your Instrument Landing System. Autopilot will control your altitude as you approach the runway. When I say GO, engage landing gear, enrich fuel mixture to maximum, and increase propeller attitude to maximum. Do you understand?"

"I understand." I had watched Wynne do the same process, so fast I hadn't been able to take notes. But it seems to me that the process is the same as engine compression braking in a car—that I do understand. I can do this. Piece o' cake, Matt, piece o' cake.

"Okay, Matt, the next steps are critical to your safe landing. One: Watch the glide slope indicator closely. Two: As you get ready to touch down, and you see the aircraft has leveled itself, disengage autopilot. Three: Immediately increase manifold pressure to maximum and go to maximum down flaps. Maintain yoke straight. As you touch down, wait until the plane is ONLY on the runway. You cannot be in the air at all when you apply brakes or up flaps. Is that understood?"

"Yes sir." The runway is coming fast, and our altitude is leveling.

"Four: As soon as you are firmly on the runway, go to up flaps, and then apply brakes very gently at first followed immediately with increasing pressure. If you begin to skid or swerve let off brakes a little and then reapply, until you come to a complete stop. Is this understood?"

"Holy shit!"

"Matt, I have you in visual contact. I will walk you through as you land. You're going to do fine. You can do it, no problem. It's really very easy." Keep saying that, I thought to myself. "Matt, this is it buddy. Ready? <u>GO</u>."

<div style="text-align:center">~~~</div>

Flashing lights are everywhere and sirens are screaming. I barely recall following instructions like Wynne's life depended on it. I know I landed hard, bounced pretty badly, and swerved a lot trying to get the hang of braking. We did come to a stop, and not even in a ball of flames. After returning manifold pressure, fuel mix, and propeller attitude to normal, I switched off the engines. Faintly, in some distant parallel universe, I hear the hatch door pop.

A medic in white jumps to Wynne's side, rocking the plane, and yells to someone outside. Another medic rushes in. The first unbuckles her, straightens her head, and gently lets her body weight fall out of the seat, into his arms. I just watch. I can't move. My white knuckles still grip the yoke.

225

The medics lay Wynne down on the carpet. The first guy talks into a mike on his shoulder. Some kind of sling appears through the door and the two pick Wynne up carefully and lay her on the sling. They lift it slowly, and disappear out the hatch door. A uniform appears next to me.

"Mr. Hale? Mr. Hale? Are you okay sir? Mr. Hale?"

I can't make my mouth move. I try to nod. I'm just staring at the Tarmac in front of me. Red and blue lights are flashing everywhere through dull daylight, all the color and life washed out. I hear a snap. Ammonia burns my nose and I cough, throwing my head to the right. I yell out, "What the hell?"

"Mr. Hale? Are you okay sir? Mr. Hale?"

I look groggily over my left shoulder. My eyes, feeling like I've just had them dilated, have to focus again in the darker cabin.

"Sorry, sir. Are you okay, Mr. Hale?"

My lips are numb and huge, like shot full of Novocain. My nose stings from the ammonia. My hands and fingers tingle. "Wynne?"

"She's in the ambulance, sir. She's unconscious, sir, but doesn't seem to be in any immediate danger. I'll stay here beside you, sir. Let yourself come back as slowly as necessary."

I don't respond. I feel drugged. Everything is blurry, surreal. Dali-esque. Again.

"Sir, maybe you should let go of the yoke now."

"Thank you—sir. Yes—yes, you're...'slutely right." I put my blood-drained hands in my lap, palms up, and gently start making fists to get some feeling back. After a few minutes I unsnap the harness buckle. I then promptly fall out of the seat.

Chapter Forty: Home, Home on the Ranch

Wynne has been forever in the Emergency Room. I had an early dinner about four o'clock—a hamburger patty and some mixed vegetables from the cafeteria—later I'll enjoy nuts and dried fruits for dessert. Every now and then somebody comes out into the waiting room to let me know she's going to be okay, but remains unconscious. That's all they'll give me, no matter how much I plead to know more. Eventually a doctor emerges. I know because he's wearing light wool slacks and Italian shoes, along with a pristine white smock. No stereotypical stethoscope, nope.

"Matt Hale?" He looks around for an answer. There are nine people in the waiting area—counted about seven hundred times now by yours truly.

I jump up. Slowly. "Is she okay?"

"Mr. Hale, Ms. Worner gave me express verbal permission to speak with you before we sedated her. She should sleep through the night. She'll be perfectly fine, but she's going to be disoriented and have a severe headache for about twenty-four hours. Ms. Worner was administered a drug at some point today. It's a very fast-acting anesthetic that blocks motor control before the recipient loses consciousness. The dose was non-lethal, and will have no permanent negative effect. We've moved her into a private room for hydration and observation overnight. I assume you'd like to see her, though please remember she has been sedated and won't know you're there. Would you like to come with me?"

"Thank you, yes." I bend down for our shoulder bags, sling hers over the right, mine on the left, and follow him through swinging doors that read "Authorized Personnel Only."

~~~
~~~

At first the nurses weren't going to let me stay with Wynne after visiting hours. An ER physician kindly asks them to relax hospital rules, given that I just landed at Sardy Field with her, flying her airplane. Even though a bed would feel a lot better than this gray metal hospital room side chair, I am relieved to see her breathing comfortably—though the IV is disconcerting. I awaken many times during the night, each time with my neck stiffer than the last—even with the two pillows that a really nice, very tall, brunette nurse brought in for me. Eventually, I lay myself down on my right side, next to Wynne, my arm across her waist—on the bedding, of course, not under.

"Matt?" We're in Santa Fe, running through dusty red winding streets without end, my legs so heavy I can barely move—I'm struggling brutishly hard, but desperately failing to keep up with Wynne, who is nearly out of sight ahead of me, disappearing around the side of an adobe. The harder I try, the slower I move, and the slower I move, the harder I have to try. If I stop struggling at all, I come to a complete halt, unable to move. A big, dirty, bloody, hairy, tattooed hand grabs my shoulder from behind. "Matt?"

"Matt, are you okay? They're getting ready to check you in here at the hotel."

Wynne has pulled the chair I spent most of the night in over to the bed, and sits there, her hand on my shoulder. "Wynne! Are you okay?" I rub my eyes—almost never a good idea, that. "I'm sorry, I fell asleep. Are you okay?" It hasn't really dawned on me yet that I'm lying on a hospital bed, while she sits, by my side, on the room's only chair. I altogether missed dawn this morning.

"Well, I have a hangover I haven't felt since I was, like, twenty-two, and my neck is essentially immobile, but I'm fine. Dude, you flew!"

I laugh, struggling to sit up, not hung over but soggy. I cross my legs under me on the bed. My neck, also, is mostly unmovable. "I'm so glad you're okay! I was *so* worried. Do you know what happened to you?"

"You're sweet. I was drugged. Airport security recovered my water bottle. The lab here confirmed it contained something I can't pronounce or remember. It's some sort of anesthetic that knocks you on your butt but isn't deadly. Crashing the plane, on the other hand, which was most likely someone's plan, would have been sufficiently deadly—but you got us all the way back to Aspen! I'm so proud of you." She stands, bending over the edge of the high bed to hug me. We both fall backward onto the bed—well, it's more like greasing through molasses air, while carefully holding our necks in place. And—I might have grabbed her waist and pulled her just a little, teensy bit.

"I had lots of help, Wynne. If it hadn't been for Julianne—" I let that statement go as we sit back up, legs swinging over the bedside like a couple of six-year-olds. "What about the water bottle?"

"No fingerprints. No sign of anything. It was the bottle I keep in the Cessna. Somebody got to it. The sheriff is checking with the hangar service, both here and in Santa Fe. Whoever this is, is pretty careful about not getting caught. Who's Julianne?"

"One of the controllers who helped keep us alive."

"Should I be jealous?" She's grinning.

"Not even a little bit."

"Good. Let's go get breakfast, before someone refuses to let you leave." Sliding off the bed, while keeping my neck from moving, I reach to the floor to grab my big black book bag and pull it, carefully, atop my left shoulder. Wynne, bag already on her right shoulder, takes my hand in hers as we gingerly meander down the sterile-smelling hallway. She'd refused the wheelchair. Staff here has learned it might be preferable to not confront Ms. Worner once she's made up her mind.

<p style="text-align:center">~~~</p>

Clancy waits outside the automatic doors in the Lexus, and jumps out as soon as he sees us not dancing across non-slip mats in front of all the doors. Our luggage is in the back. He helps Wynne into the passenger seat, perhaps because I walk like I should still be in a bed inside the building we just exited. I climb into the back seat, on the driver's side. He closes my door for me—very un-Clancy-like, if I do say so myself.

Wynne speaks first. "Will you please drive us into town for breakfast? Annie's will be fine."

"Yes, ma'am. Miss Worner, you had me worried for sure. Doc Weisman said you were fine, sleeping overnight, and not t' worry. So I stayed at th' ranch. Hope that's okay."

"Absolutely, Mr. Sandstrom. That's why I pay you the big bucks—for you to keep an eye on the homestead. Something, by the way, we need to begin doing double duty. Sheriff Burress came to visit me this morning, and the department will be watchful. You're aware of what has occurred?"

He nods.

"Please call Johnson and Pack. We need at least one of them with you at all times until further notice. Get anyone else you need. Please. Understand?"

"Of course, Miss Worner. But are you okay?"

"I'm a wee bit woozy, and my sight is still blurry—probably from this damn headache. I'll be fine. I just need quality rest." She has to turn her whole body in the seat. That's an experience with which I'm definitely feeling empathy. Our necks may be catchy for a while, though I am trained to massage away most of our problems.

"Everything is fine at home, I trust?"

"Yeup."

At exactly the same time, Wynne and I each respond, "Yeup." We giggle like teens in body casts. Clancy just watches the road—no change in expression whatsoever. I love this guy.

~~~

The ranch is absolutely verdant. Our miraculous August monsoon has been busily blessing Colorado while we were away in Santa Fe. Wynne's world is littered with diamonds and emeralds. Sienna puddles cover depressions in the road, and shining mirrors fill every possible low spot as far as blurred vision can see. It's just after 10:30 in the morning, and the sun here and there perseveres at breaking through a partly gray-cloudy sky. What we breathe is that clear, clean, crisp Rocky Mountain air that could change the world—I have my window all the way down—hair down and blowing in a slightly chill, thick breeze. Browner still is not out in the pasture. Everyone else is, though, and sending neighborly greetings. Clancy leaves the Lexus in the circular driveway, and gets Wynne's luggage. He sets the bags by the foot of the staircase. We three head straight for the kitchen. Clancy helps her ease onto the nook bench. He turns and heads out the kitchen door. Never said another word.

"Thanks again for breakfast—Annie's was perfect. Would you care for a maté, Wynne?"

"Yes, please. Thank you." She sits looking beyond those pale yellow curtains. Yellow is good—the central *bagua* color fosters health and happiness. We can use hefty doses of both. While I'm heating water and gathering maté fixin's, Clancy comes back in, wiping his boots on the bristly mud mat in the entry hall by the kitchen door.

Wynne looks over, smiling broadly, neck seemingly swiveling
~~~

more easily already. "Clancy, how are you, anyway? I apologize for being so self-absorbed."

"I'm fine, Ma'am. So's the place. Had big rain every day you were gone. Been somethin' wonderful. Just cleared yesterday so you could get here okay, I guess." He glances at me, extending one barely perceptible nod, before looking back to Wynne. "Need anythin', Miss Worner?"

"Clancy, I think we're okay for now. Let me get settled a little bit. I'm sure you've kept everything absolutely perfect, as always." She looks out to the pasture again briefly, then back at Clancy. "Anything new from the Sheriff?"

"No ma'am, sorry. They got nothin'."

"I'm learning to suspect as much. Can we get you anything, Clancy? A maté?"

"No thank you, ma'am. I'm fine. Need to get out t' th' summer pasture. Too muddy. Need t' move 'em to higher ground. Been puttin' 'em in th' barn nights, too, 'least for a while. Need t' make some calls."

"Perfect. Thank you for checking in."

He walks over and extends a hand to me. "You did good." I give it a good solid Sioux handshake. He nods, ever-present Boonie bobbing just a bit, turns and heads out the kitchen screen door. He's not wearing the Glock. Yet.

Wynne turns her body, wincing just a little, and gazes for a few seconds into my eyes, from across the breakfast nook. She stands, moves away from the bench, and stretches. "Thank you for the maté. I'm going to unload the car and lay down for a while. As always, do make yourself at home."

"Thank you, Wynne. Let me get your luggage, though. Clancy brought everything in. I'll carry them up for you."

"That's sweet. Thanks, Coach." She smiles a drawling de Gracia smile.

"I'll go out to the guest house and unpack my things—that is, if you still desire me to stay for a while."

She goes moderately wide-eyed only for a moment, and then smiles. "Please don't go anywhere just yet, Matt. We're not done, you know." She spins around—no technically gorgeous *fouetté* today—her wrinkled pomegranate dress flying away just enough to be tantalizing—to me anyway. But we know I'm easy. She walks carefully into the living room, and keeping a left hand on the staircase, winds gracefully up a grand, beautifully finished, curved wooden staircase. My arm dangles over the back of the breakfast nook. I still have a leg up on the bench seat. It takes a minute or two before I stretch, and lag behind to get luggage.

~~~

It appears modestly rustic from the outside; undoubtedly once a cottage for hired help. As one now expects however, the guesthouse is comfortable. A soft, emerald green Berber carpet covers hardwood floors everywhere but the kitchen, and maple thresholds foot each door. The kitchen is tiled with the same stone as the main house, as is the bathroom, though the carpet extends there, too, to the end of dual vanities, before transitioning to tile. Thick Navajo rugs are thrown on the Berber in high traffic areas. I peek into a utility closet, and admire a Swiss-made, on-demand hot water heater, serving every water need including hot water-heated floors—and the most curious electrical box I've ever seen.

My bags are waiting in the bedroom. I use the telephone on top of a heavy New Mexican desk to dial Josh.

"Hello?"

"Josh! Matt."

"Dude! Hey, how's it goin' up there in Aspen?"

"Pretty well, I think. It's been wild, though."

"Wild?"

"Yes: We've been to Santa Fe and back. I landed her Cessna here in Aspen."

"Dude? Her Cessna? Airplane?"

"It's a long story."

"I got time."

I tell him the whole saga, of course omitting romantic complications and private details.

"Yeah, that's pretty wild."

"No kidding. Hey, can you do me a favor?"

"Sure. Whacha' need?"

"Will you drive by the Oasis and make sure everything's okay? Sue's bird sitting, and hasn't answered the phone this morning—or her cell. Given what's gone down, I'm concerned."

"I'll go right now. I'll cruise by every now and then, too."

"Thank you, my friend. No need to call here unless there's trouble. I left her messages."

"Dude, what's your number there?"
~~~

"Yeah, I guess you'll need that, right? Got my cell with me now, too."

~~~

I fall onto the sofa for a nap. Right about twilight, I get up, wash my face, and go to bed.
~~~

Chapter Forty-One: An Aspen Garden of Eden

As I first blink tired eyes, blood-red velvet curtains glow royally—Sirens calling my name, softly, luring me. "Matt, come touch us. Look how soft and radiant we are: warm and cuddly, exotic, erotic, quixotic. Come feel. Come caress." I do as tempted. Sunrays shoot into the bedroom like God's own hand stroking 500-count organic cotton sheets and emerald wool carpet, fingertip pads sensually smoothing across tactile pleasures that these fine fabrics so selflessly offer.

Outside the window, the entire floor of Wynne's Snowmass Creek valley is black, soaked through and through by rainwater. High stratus clouds provide a sky blanket, wavy underneath with every shade of gray, little round pails everywhere waiting to pour down upon always-thirsty earth below, while *Wi Ate* shines brightly, for now, rising underneath buckets o'rain and atop distant mountain peaks.

Every leaf, every blade of grass, every spider web, every tiny insect wing beating, glistens and glints. Hundreds of Pine Siskins and American Goldfinches fill the firs and ponderosas along Snowmass Creek, singing sweet Rocky Mountain Colorado joy to second broods. Those cloud-bulges are becoming more burdensome, though. There will be only brief sun showers this morning.

Through wide-open windows, fresh, mid-August, high meadow morning air rushes in, lightly toasted by the warming sun, and so heavy with lush fragrances it needs to be spooned into my lungs. I raise my arms and come to standing prayer position, joyful at the beauty—the gift of life. My neck, much to my surprise, is surly but fine.

Blissful and breathing deep throughout my *Pal Dan Gum* and yoga routine, I contemplate the five thousand back in Manitou, the six hundred thousand around Colorado Springs, the millions throughout America, the billions on the planet. How many can take time, or will, or do, to feel the morning sun, to smell the fresh gift of another day, living in Eden? How can I, simple lifestyle consultant that I am, reach them all, touch them somehow so they, too, might experience joy, enlightenment, the grace of God—if for only a moment, each momentous morning?

I pray for help and guidance. Guidance is here. Always has been, always will be. I've known that for decades now, after having suspected it for all the years before the knowing came—even childhood moments when I was alone and abused. So much wisdom is laid across our paths to trip on, should we choose to fall. I've been fortunate. I have lots of bruises. And I'm grateful.

I kneel down in Japanese meditation posture as tiny, salty tears tickle my nose. There's a knock at the door—a bright, brash bringing of the world, crashing solidly into One's whole being.

Wiping away *Mde Wakan*, I holler, "Be there in a minute!"

First folding into extended child's pose, I flow into plank, stretch on up into a grand upward facing dog, feeling that twelfth vertebra soulfully pop into place, and then reverse into downward facing dog—releasing my entire pelvis—with the added euphoria of stretching hamstring tendons at the ischial tuberosity—and then with a feather's touch, jump my feet to my hands, reverse swan dive up, and bring my palms together into prayer for about seven seconds, thanking the Creator and all who may be here with me. Last night I spotted another canary terry robe in the cedar closet—otherwise birth-suited, I remain grateful.

Wynne's upstairs bedroom door never came open yesterday afternoon that I am aware, and I haven't seen her out the window this morning. I visualize her outside the front door, under the cottage's full porch, knocking politely, wearing that first Santa Fe morning violet nightshirt with the little purple bow. I head for the front door, looking like a giant cockatiel that hasn't yet morning-preened his long yellow crown.

"Mornin' Matt. Say, have you seen Miss Worner?" He looks to the main house, then back at me. "Usually she's up an' at it by now, but I haven't seen her."

"No, I haven't seen her either. Not since she went upstairs, right after we got back yesterday."

"Everythin' all right, you think?"

"I'd say yes. We were both really tired. I went to bed a little after seven myself."

"Yeup. I'm gonna run t' town for a bit. Need a tarp for th' tractor, an' a new seal for one'a th' well pumps. Just wanted somebody knowin' where I was. Pack'll be here 'round nine-thirty. Back in an hour or so." He waves from the waist and turns to go. "Thanks, Matt."

"You bet. Let me know if I can do anything around here."

Clancy waves backward, on th' way t' his cottage. He stops abruptly—performs a perfect about-face, and steps back—along the way, detaching the holster from his belt. "Hold on t' this for me. 24C. 15, point 4 O rounds. Second magazine on th' backside o' th' holster. Safety's always off."

"Understood."

I head for an on-demand hot shower. Might just take another look at that junction box in the utility closet—I've never seen anything like it.

~~~

My Thursday morning maté is nearly gone—consumed with gusto as I prepare breakfast for two—just in case—in the big house. Seeds and nuts, accented by the occasional dried fig or date, won't provide the high octane I need this morning.

The sun is now above our heavy ceiling of rain buckets. Hey, a cloudy day is nearly always fine with me. People that want nothing but sun, no rain, or no snow, should move to a real desert. There're plenty of them, and lots more on the way. Take your particular prayers and move to where they're fulfilled, eh? Don't try to make them happen where they don't want to. Or shouldn't. Man, I really shouldn't be left alone, should I?

Hearing slow shuffles coming through the living room, I look left to see Wynne doing the shuffling. Hair tussled, and wandering groggy, she's wearing a short, red silk robe over matching pajamas—and marmots. Not real marmots, of course, but cute, dark brown fake fur slippers with round little marmot heads on the toes and round little tails on the heels. They must need to go on little marmot diets, the way she's dragging her feet. Her face is drawn, her eyes puffy.

She takes a shot at enthusiasm. "Good morning."

"How are you feeling this morning?"

"I've still got a headache, and can't move my neck. Honestly, I'd rather still be drugged." Red eyes look up from a hanging head. I can
~~~

just make out the little grin.

I laugh. "Cute."

"Thanks. I'm learning from the best. I am, however, famished."

"Then it's good that I made breakfast for two."

"You're sweet. For a saint." She notices the Glock.

"Clancy needed to go to Miner's for a pump seal. He said Pack, whoever that is, should get here about 9:30."

She shuffles over, leans my way with a straight back and neck, and kisses me on the cheek. "If you don't mind, Matt, I'm going to go back to bed."

"Good idea. You've been through a lot."

She points her right index finger to her head. "Nail," she says without emotion, and then makes a fist with the same hand and hammers slowly. "Head." The other arm is occupied by holding up said head.

"Would you like a maté?"

"Might interrupt my self-pity, so no, thank you. However...." The nail finger flies up. "I will *definitely* have some of whatever scrumptious meal you're preparing. That aroma brought me down here. Quite the sacrifice, I might add—the stairs simply *were* torture."

"I'll carry you back up." No response. I already have two wide, gold-rimmed, Spanish dinner plates next to the stove. The bottom of each one is signed illegibly, and stamped "Cartagena 1816." I cover each with half a vegetable frittata, without meat or seasoning, but with crumbled goat feta on top. Gentle food is the order of the day—or certainly, the order of the morning.

Chapter Forty-Two: Salient Horse

Maroonbaru is still safely, I presume, underground at the Little Nell, so of necessity I make my way to the de Gracia auto stable. A bulletin board by the kitchen door, not unlike the condo corkboard, holds a few notes to herself, and several more notes and such in what looks like Clancy's corner down in the lower right. In the upper left are numerous little manila envelopes with dates written on them, presumably enveloping tickets to various events d'art, and four sets of keys. In the center, a photograph of Wynne, Cassie, and Browner— immediately I recognize him from the vision I had while coming back from New Mexico.

I see the Lexus keys, and chuckle at a familiar *cavallino rampante* silver horse on a black leather key fob sporting a single key, and then spot a set just like the Santa Fe Prius keys. I snatch those, and open the screen door. The four-car garage and workshop are detached from the ranch house. More good *Feng Shui*.

First, I have to unlock the door—a solid metal fire door. The garage is brick, with a stone roof matching the ranch house—and the guest cottages, come to think of it. The hybrid Lexus, shining clean and silver, is waiting there in stall one. Next to the SUV I can see the front of an also gleaming, mica green Prius—I had chosen my keys well.

I press the second-closest button of the four next to me on the wall, stiffly clank the heavy metal door shut behind me, inside its metal frame, and turn the key in the double bolt lock. As the number two stable door grrrrs up, letting in more light, I see on the other side of the Prius is an industrial strength riding mower, and the now-familiar ATV. Then my heart stops—dead in its taps—like when Wynne first walked into the Nell.

Holy shit! My chuckle at the bulletin board was premature. I, too, own a Ferrari key fob—for 'Bu's keys. But in this stable, in that farthest fourth stall, covered with an obvious layer of fine dust, is a Nurburgring gray, 599 GTB Fiorano. Wow!

Mostly in life I try to not be a motorhead—well, once I graduated from my teens, that is. Or maybe my mid-twenties. Or maybe it was my forty-third birthday. Well, okay, maybe I never really got the diploma. I like my comfy old Maroonbaru wagon just fine, thank you very much. I might pretend 'Bu is a Ferrari, but the Pininfarina lines on this Gran Turismo Berlinetta are seductive, impenitent art. Not daring to touch *this* piece, I circle it slowly, taking in every line, examining every detail, peeking into each window. Nowhere is the Ferrari name. The bonnet emblem is identical to the key fob. The rear panel displays only a chromed, six-inch high, prancing horse— *cavallino rampante.*

I lay myself down, onto a sparkling clean garage floor—sliding under to see what a magnetoreological damping suspension looks like. I suppose it's mostly a guy thing. On the other hand, I also suppose this steed might not be Clancy's.

I get up from the cold cement floor, lift myself onto a workshop bench built along the entire length of the east wall, and just sit there, admiring this machine. Every so often I hop down to stroll around it again. Eventually, a lack of detachment glaringly obvious even to myself, I open the Prius door, and drive, pining, but economically, into Aspen.

Chapter Forty-Three: Aspen Public

Aspen Public is to me a very familiar library. Winding the Prius down into the deepest cool of City Parking Garage, I wonder how my director friend is doing. She escapes my thoughts the moment I begin to wind my tired physique out of the Toyota. Scrapes—lingering reminders of Santa Fe—are stinging and itching at the same time, and while my stiff neck feels okay but tenuous, I definitely have numerous troublesome muscle pains. And I have to say—my right knee, with a scab the size of one of those jumbo de Gracia eggs, hurts like hell— no itching there. I'm taking the elevator.

Stepping out, I experience a mighty wave of nostalgia— immediately regretting no longer being a library director. The smell of a contemporary library is like none other I know. The scent of paper of a vast array of ages, fresh ink from the most recent magazines, sorry, I mean periodicals, combine with the smell of sixty computers running nonstop. Libraries communally provide otherwise exclusive resources that hide modern pirates' treasure—information and knowledge. One of the reasons I left high-tech careers to be a librarian was outrage over corporate power that purchases and privatizes information—subsequently charging for access to previously freely available data. I don't feel that money should be a barrier to knowledge. An informed citizenry, workforce, or society, has always seemed to me to be the best path to success of any country, commonwealth, or other form politic. So is that judgment, cynicism, or plain truth? I'm not sure. I suppose it's all in the intention.

After stopping at the reference desk for a one-hour visitor use pass to 'Net access, I sit down and pull my red journal-slash-notebook out of my big black book bag.

Needing to search water rights in general, and case law databases specifically, nationally and within Colorado, for water easement precedence, I'm ready for lots of typing. With only thirty minutes left in my hour, I change my Internet queries to Colorado law resources. In addition to restricted-access case law sources, I need to look at the most up-to-date Colorado Revised Statutes regarding water, water rights, and conservation easements.

Eureka! Cassie had been right on. I locate a 2003 Water Resources Legislation Memo, stating the Governor has signed HB03-1008, *Conservation Easement for Water Right*. I also find a February 2003 Periodic Legislative Report from an organization called Colorado Coalition of Land Trusts.

"Authorizes the record or beneficial owner of a water right appurtenant to a land or water area to create a conservation easement in the water right."

There isn't a lot of detail, and one might stir up some paranoia about "appurtenant," but here is positive confirmation that water conservation easements are a probability. After making sure my notes are succinct and clear, and completely answer my questions, I sign out, and walk across Main, under a torrential downpour, for lunch at La Cocina. We need more research, but I'm sure Cassie will be thrilled—I can't wait to email her.

Chapter Forty-Four: Corralled

Wynne looks rested and is comfortably dressed in almost-loose-fitting, faded blue jeans with a gorgeous silk southwestern-flavored sash, a definitely-loose-fitting turquoise blouse, and an elegant, Native, turquoise and coral sterling necklace. She walks toward me as I clank the fire door.

She's smiling. I'm glad. "Did Cassie's Prius behave for you?"

"Wynne, I hope it was okay to borrow it. I didn't want to bother you to ask permission."

"I did say to make yourself at home, right?"

"Yes ma'am."

"Permission granted. I take it you noticed my other favorite stud horse?"

"You mean the silver one in the barn right behind me here?"

"Yeup."

"Nope."

"Liar."

"Yeup."

"So what's for dinner at Ché Coach?"

"Well, let's just go have a look in the fridge. I should be able to whip up something mighty fine in *your* well-stocked kitchen."

She takes my hands in hers—see, one of the less-appreciated benefits of a man-bag is it leaves both hands free. "I'm just kidding. You've cooked for me quite a lot recently. Excellently, I might add. Let me treat you to dinner."

"Yeup." This dialectic response might be habit forming, though I definitely don't wish to insult Clancy. "I'd like to drop off my bag in the guesthouse first, and maybe freshen a bit."

Wynne's jaw drops in mock shock. "You're not taking your book bag?"

I nod, most seriously. "Every now and then we need to take some space from each other—builds a stronger relationship in the long term."

She chuckles. "Give me a shout when you're ready to go." She lets go my hands, turning toward the kitchen door. I walk around the side of the ranch house, underneath the cover of tall, broad willows.

I do want to take a short shower. I've spent all day in town. The hour at the library, nearly an hour at lunch catching up with *The Aspen Times*, three hours just walking my favorite streets and watching disc football in Paepcke Park, and three-quarters of an hour at Salon Tulio having Chris trim my hair for the first time since May a year ago. I love Aspen.

Opening the cedar closet, I nab my teal, short sleeve button down shirt, a fresh pair of cargo pants, and dress clogs. When I finally walk back into the main house, Wynne is on the office computer.

"Cassie says 'Hi.' " Wynne turns her body toward me. "She's settled in at Le Rosey, and waiting for a maté shipment. What have you started, Matt?"

"Did I forget to mention maté is addictive?"

"Yes, you did forget to mention that. You're kidding, right? You're ready to go, I take it?"

"Yes, as far as I know. And yes; but—you can only borrow it."

"Cute." She turns back to the computer, types a few more lines, presses the send button, signs out and turns it off.

"Wynne, I'm pleased to see you leave your PC off when not in use."

"Why is that?"

"It's far more secure, as you know. Reduces the risk of prying eyes or snooping bots—as does having a wired network, like you have, rather than wireless. Does the router have a firewall enabled?"

"It surely does. I picked up a nasty worm around Christmas two years ago. I eventually had to replace the computer. Literally nothing would work anymore, and Aspen Tech Dudettes couldn't get her going. Now I do everything possible to avoid a reoccurrence—and I do regular system images."

"Awesome."

"Thank you. Lately, I'm feeling significantly more concern for safety than ever."

"No kiddin'?"

She mimics me. "No kiddin'. Let us away!"

~~~

Okay, sure, I want to take the Ferrari. But, as mostly anyone can tell by its layer of fine dust, that is one horse that isn't ridden very often. And we have light rain today.

Probably I should only have limited access to a machine like that. I'd love it to death within sixteen years. Expensive habit. The Ferrari 599 might even gather a little dust in my garage, too. Nah, probably not.

From around a quarter till six through nearly eight o'clock, we devour a huge and exquisite dinner. Me, a rib eye Chicago Style: with seafood chowder, sugar snap peas, and sweet potato au gratin, covered with sheep feta, and caramelized. That main course I follow with a mixed salad of organic fresh greens, blue cheese crumbled at the table by our stunning, redheaded forty-something waitress, and chili-tamari dressing on the side. Wynne absolutely devours a spectacular salad, in only olive oil with nasturtium and day lily petals; an eight ounce porterhouse medium rare, vegetable and spelt dumpling soup, steamed and then garlic sauce braised mixed root vegetables, and black cherry cheesecake with organic dark chocolate sauce. Dude! And that's not counting the Latour. This may not have been our most life-coach-approved meal together—but dang was it fun. And tasty? OMG.

Like the first night we met, we laugh the night away and share stories. After dinner we take a stroll downtown, and sit by the fountain, listening to J.J. play guitar and sing originals. Wynne folds a tip and drops it into his guitar case as we leave. We even consider a movie at the Wheeler, but decide that early to bed is assuredly a better idea.

I open the Prius' door for Wynne, and walk around to the driver's side. Pulling out of our Hallam Street parking place, I grab the right side of my neck. "Yeow!"

Wynne turns her body to see what's the problem. "Your neck again? Are you okay?"

"Yeah, it'll be okay. I just need to be gentle again for a while. It didn't bother me all day. I forgot to be careful."

"What happened?"

"I turned to look at a black SUV over on Monarch. I didn't even get a good look. I'm just paranoid, I guess."

"With good reason. I've been on the lookout too, believe me." Wincing just a little, she turns her head and body straight again,
~~~

speaking to the windshield. "While you were in town this afternoon, Sheriff Burress called. He said he spoke with Lieutenant Cole in Santa Fe—there's been no sighting, statewide, of the SUV. Bill assures me his department, the Aspen Police, both Garfield and Eagle County Sheriff departments, and even the Colorado State Patrol, remain on the lookout. His call helps me feel more comfortable, but I'm still wary. So, by the way, is Clancy."

"I'd sure like to hear about some arrests or something. Our necks have had enough for a while."

Her smile quickly morphs into a slight frown. "Do you not like the Lexus?"

"Oh, no, that's not it at all. I do like the Lexus. Except for the day I got out of it so indelicately." Wynne chuckles at the memory while I continue. "I'm a sucker for environmentally friendly options. Unless those options happen to include a 599 GTB, of course." I glance over, with my peripheral vision. We're quite the impaired pair. "In fact, I'm really proud of you for having hybrids. Well, and the inline six-cylinder Jeep in Santa Fe. I know the de Gracias do their part. And then some, I'm more than sure."

"Thank you. With my neck like this, it might have been easier to get in and out of the Lexus. That's also the only reason I didn't suggest taking Fiorio—although I usually don't drive him in inclement weather—even this light rain."

"I totally understand. Fiorio?"

"The Ferrari. See, I do name things. But they have to be pretty special, Coach." She hesitates for only a second. "I knew you'd love Fiorio. We'll have more time, I promise."

"You're right. I love the Ferr … Fiorio. Wow. *Wambli Gleska* and Fiorio, too. Life doesn't get much better."

"Sure it does. Wamblee Gleshka?"

"The Cessna. Sorry. I was just trying it out. I should have mentioned it to you."

"Oh, stop with the worry already. What does Wamblee Gleshka mean? Is it Sioux?"

"It's Sioux for spotted eagle. Golden eagle to most folks."

"I think I like it. I'll have to let it sit for a while before I have it painted on the side of the plane though, if that's all right with you."

I laugh. "Okay. As I'm sure you already know, some Native cultures say the eagle flies next to, and brings us closer to the Creator. I only mean to show respect for the ways I've been allowed to learn—

a tiny bit. I'm just a toddler on the "Red Road," although it's closer to my soul than any other road I've traveled."

"I understand."

'Bu suddenly pops into my head, just as the roundabout comes into view. "Hey, should we go back and retrieve Maroonbaru from the Nell? It's probably costing a fortune to keep her there. It's been a week now."

"*Her?* I'm not concerned about the cost, but would you like to have your car handy?"

"It's not necessary. If Maroonbaru was around, though, I might be less tempted to sneak into your garage and steal Fiorio."

She grins. "You can only borrow him."

"*Him?* Well then, let's not bother tonight. I'm pretty tired, and ready for an early night."

"As am I, Matt, as am I."

~~~

As I pull the Prius into the garage it's still raining lightly; feminine rain—the gentlest—tiny droplets or sometimes drizzle, falling slowly and without malice, though I'm not sure rain ever intends malice.
~~~

Chapter Forty-Five: Horse's Rear

I sleep until nearly seven, and open this morning's Siren-less, dullish red curtains to a gorgeous gray day. Everything in sight is soaked dark and happy. Following yoga and stretches, I brush my hair, dress casually of course, and head for the big house. I bring maté.

The house is quiet. So then, am I. After wool-sock-footing across kitchen tiles to start the water kettle heating, I silently enter Wynne's office and start her computer. My antique portable is just so slow. I'm in luck. She has no password for this PC either. I return to the kitchen to make tea while the Internet connection fires up.

With maté in mug, I settle into Wynne's ergonomic office armchair. The Chinese horoscope says that today, Tiger's sentimental life is intense and possibly illusory, that circumstances are uncontrollable and everything is conspiring against me—swell—and I'll lack self-confidence, so I should avoid panic and anguish. Tomorrow I should ignore provocations and ill-intentioned criticisms, try to recover my self-confidence, and I won't exactly accept changes life throws my way. Swell, times two.

Dragon may want to have the last word in couple, and a breaking off is inevitable. Tomorrow small problems will make Wynne angry, so she should avoid exasperation—risks of complications and delays in amorous life may occur. I'm thinking I should go back to bed for two days. As is another my habits, I save the best for last. It's an email from Cassie. It turns out to be brief.

Coach,

Mom told me what happened in Santa Fe. Thx for getting her home safely. This is way scary. I'm worried. Are you two in danger? I want to come home.

This really sucks.

C

After tiptoeing back into the kitchen to extend my maté with more hot water, I head back to the office, where I proceed to sit pensively in front of the keyboard. How do I respond? Reclining in Wynne's comfy leather chair, sipping reheated, slightly diluted maté, I decide to simply start typing and see what comes out. I press the reply button.

Hey, beautiful!

Your concern is on target. You're worrying because you love your mom.

You know, I think it's going to be okay. We haven't seen any sign of trouble since we got back, and police everywhere are watching out for us.

BTW, it looks like you were right about the conservation easement idea!! My gut feeling is that when we get the water right situation dealt with, this other stuff will all go away. Maybe we should focus on easement creation.

I did some research and found out that water conservation easements are possible by Colorado law (HB03-1008).

"Authorizes the record or beneficial owner of a water right appurtenant to a land or water area to create a conservation easement in the water right."

We need more info on this, but it might be the answer. I don't want to step on any toes, yours or your mom's or your attorneys' or whomever. So do you want to follow up with this?

I won't suggest you not worry. I believe we should fully experience our feelings. Really, Cassie, I think we're okay. I feel that whoever was after us is after the water. That's the problem that needs to be solved. That's what I'm intuiting anyway. For some reason I don't get a solid gut feeling about it all just yet—but I will.

Please let me know if you think I should go ahead and bring it up. But an easement is your idea.

What do you think?

Remember, Clancy and I are here, as well as some other guys—twenty-four-seven—and really, the sheriff, the state police, totally everybody is watching. We're safe.

Keep on breathing girl. And drink lots of water.

Hugs, Matt

P.S. Maté will come soon, I promise. As soon as customs will allow.

I press the send button. The little envelope appears, seals itself, and fades into the distance on the screen. Hearing marmots in the kitchen, I sign out of email and leave the PC on.

Wynne is behind an open stainless steel refrigerator door.

It's time to be positive, worry-free and upbeat. Time to focus on opportunities while they're knocking. With a big smile I exuberate, "Good morning!"

"Good morning. I thought I heard someone down here. How did you sleep?"

"I slept soundly. How 'bout you?"

"I went out right away. But I did wake up about two and then just napped off and on until about four-thirty. After that, I just laid awake, thinking. My brain's been going about seventeen places at once."

"That's a pattern I know intimately. You have too much on your mind, my friend."

"And what's there is likely to persist, a least for a while."

It seems best for now, intuitively and all, to avoid bringing up breathing techniques, diet, exercise, or stress reduction activities—uh, coaching, in another word. "I understand. May I make us breakfast?"

"Oh, Matt, you don't need to keep taking care of me. I can do things myself, really."

"I'm completely certain of that, Wynne. But I haven't eaten either. I'm more than happy to whip something up for the both of us."

"Well, okay. Thank you. I'll go shower and get dressed—be right back, okay?"

"That's great! Any preferences?

"Surprise me. See you in a bit." She turns slowly, holding her neck stiffly on those lovely shoulders, and the marmots pad back up the wooden staircase.

~~~

"Matt, thank you for agreeing to again come down here."

"You're welcome, of course. Both of us can use it. I've already confessed my hot water addiction."

"There are worse. And thank you for driving the Lexus."

"I honestly don't mind at all. This is a beautiful automobile. Frankly, it gets better gas mileage than my old Subaru."

She smiles. "Maroonbaru."

"*My* Ferrari."

She laughs, poking me in the ribs with her finger—the nail. "Yeah, *her.*"

At least it's not the hammer. "Are you jealous?"

Coy, she's way too cute. "Maybe."

"Good."

She laughs. "I hope the hot spring isn't crowded. I'm feeling unsociable. I'm inclined to barricade myself into my tower and not come out until my hair reaches the ground."

"That's not like you, is it?"

"No. I'm still jittery. And a bit depressed. Maybe I'm still having after-effects from being drugged. I'll tell you this, though—I'm again feeling uncertain what to do about the water rights. Maybe I should just accept the developers' offer and be done with it."

"That's not you either. Especially after being so strong in your conviction not to sell. Dude, you were a quark-gluon plasma fireball. Give yourself some time to start feeling better, don't you agree?"

She's grinning—it's a good look on her. "A *what* fireball? You silver-tongued devil."

I smile and chuckle, puffing air from my nose.

She rubs her neck. "I suppose you're right. Maybe the hot water will help this neck."

"I enthusiastically hope so."

The parking lot is only two-thirds full—a good sign. We each head for our respective gender's locker room. Wynne waves gingerly from the hot end when she sees me looking for her. After setting my gym bag on a wooden bench, I pull out two water bottles and set them on the deck behind her.

"Don't know about you, but I have *not* been drinking enough
~~~

water. One's for you, if you feel the need. You will feel the need...."
My jaw is set and eyebrows ferocious. "Won't you."

She smiles the sweet smile. I like that one a lot, too. "Thanks,
Coach."

I walk over to the steps, wade down, and breast stroke right on
over to her side.

Chapter Forty-Six: Turning Up the Heat

Glenwood Hot Springs is indeed not busy. There are just seven of us in the hot zone, and one woman swimming laps in the Olympic pool. The morning is exquisite: quiet, no breeze, feminine rain dusting our hair, thick steam rising like clouds blushing the summit of Independence Pass. Awesome. Life is good. Note to self: Remember that.

"This is great! Thanks for suggesting it, Wynne."

"*De nada.* I'm simply returning the favor."

"Would you like me to work on your neck?"

"Work on it?"

"Massage."

"Ohhh, yes please!"

I lift my hands out of the water, and begin doing what I've seen called an "artist's stretch." It's a hand, wrist, forearm workout. From pinky to thumb, one finger at a time, you create a tight fist and then release, shaking from the forearms out through the fingers.

She watches.

"Warming up, you know."

"Hmm."

We're side-by-side on the narrow, submerged, built into the pool, bench. "My best work here will occur if I can scoot in directly behind you. Tell you what. I'll spread my legs, and let's see if there's enough room for both of us to sit here on the shelf. Is that okay?"

She nods. There's barely enough room for her to balance on the edge.

"Let me know, Wynne, and I am adamant about this, the *moment* you feel uncomfortable for *any* reason whatsoever. And definitely please tell me, continuously, on a scale of one to ten, what pain levels you feel. I don't want us to go over five or six."

I don't wait for a response—I'm in the zone, baby. "You probably already know that muscles have memory but they don't think. So, for instance, in a whiplash injury, the muscles instantly *learn* and *memorize* how to compensate for radical cervical movement in order to minimize damage—but because muscle tissue doesn't think, after the trauma, the tissues need to be instructed to *learn* to let go. Otherwise, they simply tend to hold onto the trauma and not return to normal. At least, not as fast as we'd like and often never completely. I've worked on several women with sacral and coccyx problems caused by horse riding falls—accidents that occurred thirty years earlier."

"Really? I know a few people with those very problems. You know, Matt, you really seem to be a jack-of-all-trades. Perhaps it was unfair of me to call you eclectic."

"And hopefully a master of at least of few. When did you call me eclectic? Which I am, of course."

"That was a year ago, on the phone."

I chuckle. "Oh, right. My website bio."

"Yes."

"Excellent. In addition to whether you feel uncomfortable for any reason, including our tight seating arrangement, and pain levels one to ten—I need to be aware of referred pain or nerve responses. I don't want to be on nerves. I know the locations of major nerves, but I don't walk on water."

I can tell by the change in ear position that she's smiling. That sure is good to see, even if my only view is the back of her head. "Just *in* it." She giggles exactly like Cassie—on purpose, I bet.

"Then do I have your permission to go deeper?"

"You most certainly do."

"Okay. I'll start on your shoulders, then work into the armpits, and finally the neck."

"Armpits?"

"Yep. When I get there, you'll feel why. The number of trigger points that will fire into your neck and shoulders will amaze you. Remember though, let me know about referrals, or any nerve sensation, and to let me know if we get over that five or six range. Okay?"

"Okay."

After about ten minutes, she finally says something—other than moaning. "Wow. This isn't about sensuality, or even relaxation. You really are a therapist, aren't you?"

It's a rhetorical question, but it feels good that she asked. "I prefer to think so, yes."

As predicted, trigger points in Wynne's axillary regions refer into her neck and shoulders, and we uncover referrals to chronic headache patterns as well. After thirty or so minutes, I plead, "I need to stop. My hands and arms are getting tired. Why don't you dip into the water another time to warm up your neck and shoulders, and then I'll do a little Swedish to smooth things out. Okay?"

"That does not sound as okay as continuing what you're doing for a day or two, but we don't want you hurt—any more than is already the case." She slips away from the shelf between my legs for about the tenth time, stays under hot water for half a minute or so, then arises to sit on the edge again.

After ten more minutes, I have to stop. She turns her head slowly from side to side. "Matt, I can't believe how much better my neck feels. You're a miracle worker!"

"Well, let's not exaggerate, but thank you. Be careful not to overdo things, though. You run the risk of pushing too far, too fast, because it feels better for now. Be gentle, okay?"

"I'll be careful." She slips in up to her chin, and turns her body around to look at me. I dip down too, to warm up. She gives me a de Gracia smile, and moves next to me again. "I'm going to come down here more often. Thank you again."

"You're very welcome. It's totally my pleasure."

~ ~ ~

We enjoy another early dinner at Mi Casita—it's on the way back to the ranch. I have my usual *carnitas*. Wynne tries the special— featuring numerous *casa* specialties.

"Matt, this is the best Mexican food in the Valley. Thank you for enlightening me."

"I'm glad you like it. There are a couple of other places I can show you."

She looks across the table. "I gave some thought to water rights while you were working on my neck. It was nice of you to remind me of the resolve I had in Santa Fe."

"You were a super-hero—solid, firm, and following your heart and your intuition. I'll take that any time."

"I've allowed the SUV thing to get me down. This is about

what's right, not what's easiest."

"Life's often that way, don't you think?"

"Definitely. I know most people think I enjoy a pretty easy life. But the truth is, we all have burdens to bear."

"Amen, sister. Unfortunately, many of us tend to focus our attention on sadness, failures, and pain, rather than opportunities, successes and joy. As you know, I'm still working on the latter myself. Should we head back? Or is there something else you'd like to do?"

We are, and have been as we linger, imbibing the house red.

"I think I should go to bed. It's got to be about eight." I notice she's not wearing a watch. How long has this been going on? Do I remember her *ever* wearing a watch? "I'm tired, and more relaxed than I've been for what seems like eons—another early night will be a good thing. I hope I sleep better."

"I bet you will."

She offers no wager.

<div align="center">~~~</div>

The Lexus knows its way back to the ranch and into the garage. As we climb out, I again admire walnut and brushed stainless appointments. This truly is a beautiful vehicle—and hybrid as well. Works for me. And for Wynne.

Just outside the garage door, Wynne turns and leans over to kiss me on the cheek. She misses. It's a feather light, lingering kiss on my neck, back behind my ear. The fine hairs on my neck stand up—and that isn't all. "Thank you for another wonderful day. Let's have breakfast again in the morning, okay? My treat."

"I'm already looking forward to it."

The dancer having made a comeback, she flows toward the kitchen door. I follow the voices singing from Snowmass Creek by the guest house. Feminine rain still falls like an Avalon mist, as it has all day, and did all last night. Like it probably will all night tonight. Tomorrow?

Mde Wakan. Sacred water.

Chapter Forty-Seven: The Kettle Boils

It's another beautiful day in paradise. Yawn. This is almost getting boring—nah, just kidding. I left the guesthouse windows open, again, all night. Every room is fragrant, humid, welcoming—and chilly. I also didn't close the bedroom curtains. Past dusk, there's no light, other than stars or moon, to enter the cottage anyway. Following a shower and an hour of yoga, I stroll over to the big house.

Rather than maté, I enjoy Eldorado Natural Spring water from my trustworthy liter bottle, and unwrap a bar of organic 85% dark—eight thirty is a little early even for me, but I haven't enjoyed nearly enough chocolate lately. Wynne's computer is already powered on, and in standby mode. Not seeing or hearing her, I'm quiet.

Going straight for email, I don't bother with horoscope or aviation weather websites. There's no need to be reminded of the horoscopes I read yesterday, and the weather, for today anyway, is predictable—continuous feminine rain. Ignoring news headlines, I open Cassie's email.

> *Coach,*
>
> *Thanks for helping me feel better. Still worried, but not as much.*
>
> *Got your message, emailed our Aspen attorney and copied Mom. Hope she doesn't get upset. We usually email every day. Been two days now.*
>
> *Anyway, thanks for the encouragement.*
>
> *C*

Okay, now to stay out of the way. I'll just see what Wynne needs from me today instead of going back to the library, although I plan to do more research about easements—just for the joy of knowledge gathering—and out of concern for *Mde Wakan*.

> *Hi Cassie,*
>
> *Glad you're feeling more comfy with the situation here. You and your mom will work out the water stuff.*
>
> *I don't know what more I can do as a lifestyle consultant around here—your mother is hip to all my tricks. She eats well, is healthy as can be, and already knows how to live a good life. I'll probably suggest I head back to Manitou Springs unless she needs anything I can actually do for her.*
>
> *And, I can ship maté to you from there. Hope your studies are awesome, and I look forward to hearing from you soon.*
>
> *Hugs,*
>
> *Matt*

After closing email, I start to look at weather back in Colorado Springs just as the front door opens. A winded Wynne comes into the office. She has on a black running outfit, and is soaking wet. She bends over, hands on her knees, stretching her hamstrings. "Good morning, Matt."

"Hi, Wynne. Have you been out for a run?"

"Yes. To the end of the road and back. Round trip is seven miles, and fairly treacherous."

"Wynne! I knew you were in good shape. Now I know why."

"Before that, I took a ride on Tillie."

"Tillie?"

"Tillie is Browner's favorite girlfriend. I haven't been riding or running since perhaps a week before I called you. I thought it high time for me to get back to taking care of myself."

"Well, your neck must be a whole lot better this morning."

"That it is, Matt. I attribute the miracle to your massage work. I'm going to take a quick shower. Are you going anywhere right away this morning?"

"I hadn't planned on anything. Last night you mentioned breakfast, and I wanted to check in with you first thing. I guess first thing for you was pretty early this morning."

"Yes. I need to talk to you. I'll be back down in about twenty minutes. Is that okay with you?"

"Of course. What did you want to talk about?"

"I'd rather wait until I come back downstairs, if you don't mind. Let's go into town for a nice breakfast." She's not smiling.

Before I can emit a word, she turns slowly to go upstairs. I return the PC to standby, and stumble a couple of times on my way back to the guesthouse for a water bottle refill—I suspect I'm going to need plenty of water today. I think I'll even stick a second bottle into my book bag. I sure do miss the *fouetté*. I'd die for even a *petit*.

~~~

Wynne drives the Lexus. I don't bring it up—whatever *it* is. And she's quiet—so I keep quiet, too. Sure, I'm nervous. I concentrate on deep breathing, and do my best to stay calm—without success. Every so often, with peripheral vision, I look for any type of sign from her face or countenance. I notice zero. Until we come to the roundabout.

"I apologize for being so quiet, Matt. I realize we ordinarily enjoy substantive conversations, and that my silence must be somewhat unnerving for you."

"That would be an accurate observation, yes."

"I'm sorry, really. I have so much on my mind, and to be honest, I'm finding it difficult to keep my head organized. There have been so many upsetting events recently that my mind is swimming in confusion—and emotions." She goes silent again as we go through the 7th Street turns and head up Main.

I dive from the cliff top. "Is there anything I can do?"

She pulls over by Paepcke Park.

"Matt, what I want to talk about are a few things that are making me uncomfortable."

My medulla oblongata starts buzzing and the world goes blurry.

"I'm truly grateful for all that you've contributed to my quality of life." Uh oh. "Our closeness has been a relief. At a time when I had given up on men completely, you arrived and showed me tenderness, understanding, respect, and rekindled the possibility of love in my heart."

I want to say, "Then what's the problem?" But I know better. I have to let her finish. And if ever there was a time for me to choose my words carefully….

"First there was the craziness in Santa Fe, where you seemed to like me enough to want a great deal more from our being together. I
~~~

tried to let you know I felt the same way, but you stayed distant. Then you practically attacked me on the loveseat. Since our return to Aspen, you've been even more distant. I need consistency, not a roller coaster.

"Even so, I would have been willing to keep trying, until I discovered you've been carrying on with Cassie, too. She's gorgeous, you say. She's beautiful, you say. Then there's somebody named Julianne on the Cessna radio. And you take in every sexy woman you see. I know that look in your eyes."

Smoldering is over—this fire has ignited and is spreading hot and fast. I feel an inch tall, and brown, round, and only a little elongated.

"But the last damned straw is your meddling in our personal affairs. I told Cassie I didn't like her easement idea, and then you go behind my back!"

I start very slowly, with a wavering voice as calm as I'm able muster. "Wynne, I'm so sorry. I would never mean any harm at all. I've really come to…."

"Skip it. I don't need to hear another bunch of bull. I can see with my own eyes. You're just another user. A tease. What was your plan? Get in my pants and my daughter's too? Sucker me into a relationship with you, and then slap another palimony lawsuit on me? You men really are all the same."

"Wynne, sweetie, you're mis…."

"Don't bother. Sweetie, my ass. Send me a bill and take a hike. Go back to your tiny little slum house and get the hell out of my life."

Stunned, I reach into the back seat for my black bag buddy. "As you wish. I'm so sorry. I'll easily be able to take care of things from here, so if it's all right with you, I'll just hop out now. If you should change your…."

"Nothing will change my mind. Just go."

After climbing down from the tan leather seat, I stop to look back. She's staring out the driver side window. All right then, I'm out of here. I do my own shaky *fouetté* and quake my way into the park.

~~~

That was bizarre, at least from my perspective. Well, maybe not. I should have stuck to my professionalism guns. Never entertain a relationship with a client. There is solid ethic and common sense underscoring that rule. Walking angrily straight to the Little Nell, I see nothing around me, in front of me, or behind me. The feminine rain kissing my face is little more than a nuisance. My mind flies a million
~~~

miles a minute, toward no particular destination. Nonetheless, I maintain focus on retrieving Maroonbaru and heading back to Manitou—back to my tiny little slum house—to Sleeping Bear Oasis. To my birdies. Back *home.*

No valet is around to open the door at the Nell. How appropriate. Steffan isn't at the desk. I stride on up anyway, and a twenty-something brunette opens her shapely little mouth. "How may I help you, sir?"

"My name is Matt Hale. I need to pick up my car please."

"Are you a guest, Mr. Hale? I don't remember your name."

"I was a guest last week. Steffan allowed my car to remain here while I attended business in the area."

"Let me check for your keys, sir."

"Thank you."

She scurries back from the manager's office. "Yes, of course, Mr. Hale. Your car will be brought up immediately."

I reach into my left front pocket for my wallet, wrist snap it open, pull out a Visa card, and extend it to the pretty young desk clerk. Wynne is absolutely right. I notice women. Well, when last I looked, I *am* single. Hey, I notice beauty. Period.

She smiles, nodding her head at my credit card. "We won't need that, Mr. Hale."

This time I'm a teensy bit abrupt. "I insist on paying."

She smiles kindly—authentically. "The bill has already been taken care of, Mr. Hale."

I ease up, and take time to notice her nametag—nothing reshaping my brain, my heart, or my ocean, is her fault. "Thank you, Shandra. You've been most kind."

She smiles again, pleased to be acknowledged. "You're welcome, sir. Have a very nice day, Mr. Hale."

I turn toward the glass doors, open one, and proceed to pace to and fro under the portico like a tiger in his cage. Feminine rain still falls in its tender, loving way. "Tender. Loving. You bet!" I bellow aloud—a valet glances. "Sorry. It's been a rough morning. I'm just letting out a little steam."

"No problem, sir. We'll have you on your way momentarily."

Maroonbaru arises from the underground parking ramp, lights on, like a true and trusted old friend—carrying a fresh-baked pumpkin pie, winding up the walk to my front door on a blustery, subzero winter day with no sun and no snow. And I just started a blaze in the fireplace.

The driver opens 'Bu's door, climbs out, and stands aside to close it once I seat myself. I reach for my wallet to fish for a tip. He raises his hand, just like Renate, smiles understandingly, and shakes his head "no." I drop my bag onto the passenger seat, slide onto smooth velour, readjust the seat for my own height, and drive away, turning left down Original Street and then right onto Colorado 82 East.

Chapter Forty-Eight: Independence

Maroonbaru is happy to see me; the feeling, of course, is mutual. These firm, plush seats are plenty comfortable and my old Subaru is a pleasure to drive: responsive, and all wheel drive sure-footed. I'm already passing the East of Aspen trailhead when I remember my things—still at the guesthouse. My thinking is not yet precise. At the first opportunity, I do a u-turn, not dangerously at all, but nevertheless in front of a giant RV that's about a quarter-mile away. My mood is not suitable for puttering along. Back in town, I scorch down Main, miraculously without attracting the attention of always-observant Aspen Police. Soon enough, as I twist through the turns on 7th, I decide to slow down—in numerous aspects.

Wynne has her reasons. I'm not perfect. I know that. I shouldn't have made a pass at her. I shouldn't even have flirted, though in my defense, avoiding flirtation was nearly impossible. Nonetheless, I should have stuck to professional principles, after all. *De gustibus non est disputandum.* Could'a, should'a, would'a—a little advice to self: Don't do that to yourself.

On the other hand, I *am* in love with her. Not the thought of her. Not her heritage. Not the Berlinetta. Not the Cessna. Not the ranch. *Her.* Her smiles. Her kisses. Her walk, her grace—and yes, her beauty. Her intelligence. Her compassion. Her quick mind. Her gentle touch. The softness of her skin. Her wavy hair. Her understanding. Her vision. Her principles. Her styles of dress. Her little mannerisms. Her smell. Her authenticity—as a mother, a person, and a friend.

I shouldn't have meddled with the water easement idea. Probably I ended up getting Cassie in boiling water, too. And Cassie! Jeez, no way would I ever seduce Wynne's seventeen-year-old daughter. That's not even realistic. Mini-Wynne is gorgeous—and I'm old enough to be her father, or uncle, or whatever. Protector and mentor, anyway. I glance at the speedometer as a Pitkin County Sheriff car passes by on the other side of the highway.

I'm fine. The speedometer shows 57, and this is a 55 zone. I turn onto Owl Creek Road. According to Wynne the southern route from here is longer and slower, but I want to enjoy the beauty of Old Snowmass valley and *El Rancho de Gracia* one last time. Sightseeing my way through the golf course, I head on up Divide Road through Snowmass Village, eventually turning north on Snowmass Creek Road. There's no other way to go. Taking my time on this drive, I notice more of Martin's butts littering the gravel. I slow to ten as I arrive at the south edge of the ranch. The familiar granny apple green fence guides me down a road of sorrow. Where Browner fell the summer pasture is still flat and black. My heart is pounding like a sledgehammer.

I approach the ranch house with care. If Wynne is home, the Lexus has to be in the garage. I don't see Clancy *et al* anywhere. I turn gingerly into the drive, attempting to make no noise whatever. 'Bu is not a Lexus though.

Pulling as close to the guesthouse as possible, I swing out of my soothing seat, and leave 'Bu running. Don't even close my door. There won't be much of this wonderful feminine rain that finds its way inside the car. Grabbing my things as quickly as possible, it takes three trips to toss my stuff, unpacked, into the back seat from the open driver's door. I slide back in and click the door—it does close quietly, solidly. 'Bu is in great shape for a '93. Of course, she has low miles and I take loving care of her. I back up, turn onto the pavement, and drive out the gate—back onto crunchy wet gravel. What little is in the big house 'fridge will stay. I can't bear to go inside.

Poking along at twenty miles an hour, I soak up the valley on Snowmass Creek Road and Wagon Divide. Pools of rainwater remain everywhere, mirroring the sheer, soft, gray cloud blanket overhead. This place is absolutely gorgeous, just like Wynne. I take the right turn onto Colorado 82 back to Aspen—back to Independence Pass—back to my little Oasis in the foothills on the eastern slope of these Rocky Mountains.

Wynne is rapacious in my mind. I simply cannot avoid seeing her sweet smile, smelling her hair, and feeling the smooth satin of her neck and shoulders, her cheeks, her face. I relive that first night in the Little Nell—her pomegranate summer dress dancing to a graceful, sensual gait. And then there's the violet *fouetté* that first morning at the condo—OMG—an image chiseled forever in the marble galleries of my mind.

This time on the way into town I watch my speed ever more carefully. I'm hustling heart and head to be completely present, to recover calm physiological stasis, while filling my lungs with wet Roaring Fork Valley air—all the windows down—feeling sorry for myself.

That's okay. It's best to go with your feelings, to experience them fully, admit your grief, your sorrow, your anger, your despair, and your joy. Not necessarily driving down a highway maybe, but one does what one has to do. I have to leave behind the woman I've come to care for too much, and head back to JustLikeEverywhereElseVille. But, I do have a full tank of high-octane petrol in my Ferrari, eh?

Okay, maybe I'm not a man's man, whatever that is—salty tears drip in slow motion next to my nose as I wend through and away from Aspen. Still, I am looking forward to getting back to Manitou, back to where Manitoids know my name. Back to my life—my own good life. Back to helping others live lives of grace.

Back to what, today especially, has rooted deeply in my soul. I have become, and am still becoming—Matt Hale—a pretty decent guy, who isn't out to hurt anyone.

<div style="text-align:center">~~~</div>

Independence Pass is quiet. No traffic is heading east, or at least I haven't had to try to pass anyone yet, and only an occasional caravan follows an RV down toward Aspen. That's surprising for a late August Saturday, especially since it's not all that early—just a few minutes after eleven. It's okay—I don't mind quiet.

Maroonbaru hums along peacefully at 45 as we cruise past the micro-delta at the base of the pass. The Roaring Fork River meanders gracefully through this fertile bottomland, mostly in view of the highway, though sometimes it sneaks off behind stands of willow and pine. Feeling grateful, as *almost* always, for overcast skies and ever-so-light rain, I relish clean, cool, fragrant mountain air with all the windows still down. There is no need for air conditioning.

We flow around the first ninety-degree curve, where the valley narrows and a gradual climb becomes more demanding. Still, the summit bathrooms are miles away. I've had no maté and not a lot of water yet today, so there is no pressing need to be overly hasty about visiting my friends on the summit. The bag of organic raw almonds from my bag is open, on the console. As I approach the first section of dangerous, one-lane mountain highway, I slow to a crawl, peeking around the corner.

No one is coming. I press the accelerator to get through the thousand feet or so of one lane road as fast as safely possible—it's often best to move quickly out of trouble, rather than slow down and hang out in it. Ditto for the second one lane stretch. Passing Weller Lake, I keep a steady, modest pace—enjoying fertile beauty all around. It's not like I'm rushing to meet a new client. My heart sinks into my knees. That's when I notice a black SUV in the rear view mirror.

I know it can't be the same one. It would've been spotted, right? My heart rate shoots skyward, adrenaline spreading through me like I'm standing where lightning is about to strike. Or like when Wynne wouldn't tell me what she wanted to talk about. The fine hairs on the back of my neck stand straight. Just ahead, immediately beyond a tight curve and not visible to the SUV behind me, I know there's a paved pull-off, with ample parking. Frequented by hikers, bicyclists, and other outdoor enthusiasts, Lost Man Trail trailhead is a popular spot, hidden behind a giant rock outcropping looking down at the highway and two extremely sharp hairpin curves.

On this midday Saturday, the lot is packed, with two available spots at the far end. I pull into the very last diagonal parking space, closest to Highway 82, with my front wheels turned to the left— toward the exit. Leaving the keys in the ignition switch, I open my door, fish the cell phone from my book bag, jump out of 'Bu and sprint about forty feet, stopping so I can just see Highway 82—and then decide a little cover might be a good idea. I turn on my phone. The SUV does not go on by.

As I turn my head back to the parking lot behind me, I see one couple, daypacks in hand, walking the other direction, away from their silver BMW station wagon at the other end of the lot. I *also* see the black menace coming in—fast. It pulls into the other empty parking place, about six cars down from 'Bu. Running for my trusty steed—I glance at zero bars on the cell. I get to Maroonbaru and jump into the driver's seat—but the door won't close—the same big guy from Santa Fe has his huge, hairy hand on it, and a pistol with a silencer pointed between my eyes.

A vehicle enters the lot from this end, and I start to open my mouth to yell for help. The big guy, who obviously hasn't shaved in at least several days, and wears a different plaid shirt, leans his body into my open door to free both hands—cocking the slide while dropping the pistol to waist level—and rapidly says, "One word and it's a bullet in your brain—they won't hear a thing." The car's already past us anyway, and there are no more parking spaces. After it exits the lot at the low end, I hear a door open and close.

Another person walks our way—hard sole shoes clicking across the pavement. I start to look, but plaid commands, "Eyes forward—don't fucking move." A drawling male voice says, "Get 'im out of the car and behind those trees. Keep his eyes away from us at all times." Plaid waves the pistol, about twelve inches long with the silencer, motioning for me to climb out—which I do, making certain to keep looking away.

As we're walking away from the parking lot, cold, round steel is pressing—hard enough to be not merely obvious—into the right side of the base of my skull. "Stop here. Don't fucking move." We only went thirty or so feet, just behind a stand of firs. I recognize the sounds of my car doors being opened, as I stare toward the forest about two hundred feet away. There is nothing but beaten down grasses, dirt, and stones, between any cover and me—except for back to the parking lot.

Fifteen minutes passes like fifteen days. I've got sweat pouring down my arms, my forehead, the back of my neck, and my legs. I breathe quietly and as deeply as possible—keeping myself oxygenated. I've been standing absolutely still so long my legs begin to tremble, and my low back muscles are starting to tighten painfully. All this time the silencer has been shoved down into the crook between my neck and right shoulder. From the parking lot I hear the other guy. "I can't find it. Ask 'im where it is."

The silencer digs deeper into my neck. "Where's the envelope?"

"I don't know anything about an envelope."

Something bashes the right side of my head—a sharp pain stabs my inner ear and shoots across the temple—into my left eye, which goes blurry for several moments. Cold steel jabs back into my neck.

"I swear I don't know what you're talking about."

I hear the hard soles walking closer. "Manila envelope the bitch gave you."

"Ms. Worner gave me nothing—fired me and kicked me off her property."

Hard soles says, "I couldn't find it. When I get back to the truck and start it, kill the fucker and shove him under the trees."

He clacks over the fifty or sixty feet. I hear a door open—*and voices at the trailhead*—as the door closes. The steel slips slightly—in a tae kwon do move, I step my right leg forward simultaneously spinning 180 on my left foot and lowering to fighting stance—both arms and fists blocking as I turn. The gun flies from plaid's hand as my left forearm strikes it—I snap-kick his left knee with my right foot, stepping aside with that foot as it comes down—and sidekick his right knee—it pops like a plastic ketchup packet being stomped—he screams as he crumples.

I jump away from his reach and grab the pistol—point it at him—he's writhing on the ground, both hands on his knee. I turn to the SUV—windows black and up. I aim carefully and fire at the driver-side doorpost—it makes a metallic snap and the rear window crackles into a jigsaw puzzle. I fire several more silenced shots at the doorpost—hoping to sew it shut—p-p-p. The trailhead voices are shouting. "What the hell's going on?"

I yell it loud. "These guys have guns! Get outta here!"

I hear running—including my own. Hope the keys are still in the ignition—I shove the pistol inside my waistband and reach for my wallet—where I keep a spare. With twelve inches of steel across my pelvis and sprinting for my life, I can't get the wallet out yet.

I run to Maroonbaru and around the passenger side—shut both doors, slam down the rear hatch, run around to the driver's side door, shove the passenger door shut, reach across the door jamb to punch the hood so it slams down, and slide into my seat—the keys are still there! I turn the ignition. 'Bu fires immediately. Simultaneously I drop the shift lever into D, release the parking brake—and push the accelerator through the floor—just as an RV with a line of cars behind wallows by on the way down to Aspen. Reluctant, I aim 'Bu up the pass.

The Independence Pass ascent, east from the parking area, is a twisting, turning, mountain road race track—much more demanding than the first half out of Aspen. Standing on the gas pedal, I perform smooth acceleration and deceleration, braking into turns, accelerating out, and taking curves in four-wheel drifts—the real thing this time.

My traction is still quite good on this gnarly pavement—a little slippery with light rain. 'Bu has low profile, all wheel drive, and *really* nice tires. My Ferrari and I know this tortuous pass—we've driven it briskly at every opportunity. In all the hundred and more times I've been up and down, I've never seen a State Trooper up here. But, we don't put ourselves or anyone else in harm's way—ever—until, perhaps, today. Glancing in the rear view mirror, there is still no SUV. It should take a while to get plaid guy up and into the passenger seat.

I cajole, praying aloud, " 'Bu, my life may depend on you, old girl." I steadily press into the accelerator, heart rate now officially higher than the altitude and a headache like someone's slowly shoving an ice pick into my right ear—there's a warm trickle down the back of my neck.

"Okay, Matt. Think it through." Yes, I talk to myself—no one else is here to listen, that's for sure. "You know the pass. Drive hard, but don't go over the edge. Above all, keep calm, keep breathing."

Maroonbaru and I take curves far faster than ever before. I keep glancing to the rear view mirrors. Nothing yet. We still have several miles of tight curves ahead, before the road straightens for the last two-mile run to the summit. There'll be people there. Always are. Peeing, watching marmots, walking up to the summit, trying cell phones. But just like those tourists, my cell won't get bars on the summit.

The curves are almost done now. Soon I'm vulnerable. I stand on the accelerator, then brake into and accelerate out of the first big hairpin on the final sprint. 'Bu's tires squeal through the drift, not necessarily in delight, and in spite of damp pavement. Shooting up the incline, I glance back and about five hundred feet straight down. The SUV is still at least a thousand feet from the hairpin. I have a good lead—and need it.

Several tourists, out of their cars at the ghost Town of Independence lookout, turn to stare as I blast by, my foot to the floor and 'Bu hitting seventy uphill. One yells, flipping a middle finger—universal sign language for *"How are you today, my friend?"*

More than one driver coming down the pass does the same, horn blasting. I slide across both lanes through curves now, trusting that no one wide will be there at the same time. 'Bu simply is not powerful enough, even riding her with my best skills, to outrun the SUV—leaving no choice but to go like hell and take chances. Faith is what I have left. And fight or flight response.

On the large, sweeping uphill curve just before the summit parking area, I look back to see the monster gaining fast, a cloud of dirty gray-black exhaust following it. It's closing—probably less than two thousand feet.

My foot's to the floor already.

Only three cars at the summit. I have to keep going—I won't endanger anyone else.

The east descent is always treacherous. I should be able to keep some distance through curves and speeding downhill. At the bottom, though, they'll catch me for sure—if not before. "Please, God, somebody with the miracle of cell service up here call 911." I don't have time to fish the cell phone out of my right front cargo pocket—even if I could get reception up here.

It's a mile and a half—through three sharp curves—from the summit, to the first of three, rapid succession, big-time hairpins. Maroonbaru's expensive radials are hot now, grabbing damp pavement well—my time around curves is now twice as fast as it has been. Maintaining about sixteen hundred feet of separation from the monster for now, I brake into the first hairpin.

'Bu breaks traction in a perfectly controlled drift through the curve. The smell of burning rubber stings my nose. If I lose a tire, what the heck, I'm likely to die soon anyway. But not without a fight—though I've already used four shots from an unknown quantity.

Almost every time I traverse this pass, I wonder what it would be like to fly off the side, down one of these thousand or two thousand foot drops at the edge of the pavement. Maybe today is the day. I'm okay with that—I'm ready to meet my Maker—but not if I can help it.

The SUV gains a couple hundred feet on the straight after the first descent hairpin. It's damn close now, maybe twelve hundred feet. I see an arm come out of the passenger window. I hear the firecracker snap as a bullet passes my window. Never heard a report, though.

Flying into the second downhill hairpin, I press the brakes smooth but too hard.

"Damn ABS!"

The automatic braking system chug-chug-chugs me into the turn instead of letting me drive. I take my foot off for a nanosecond—it's enough. Bench pressing the steering wheel and braking gently I maintain a full drift through the tight curve. I stomp the accelerator and we dash down the slope.

One more hairpin—the tightest—is not quite a mile away. This one is a two-mile-an-hour turn at any speed. It'll be a bitch. The grade here is tremendously steep. I hit seventy in a heartbeat.

I yell encouragement. "Come on, 'Bu!"

A wall of rock to the left, a dinky guardrail to the right with a two-thousand foot drop—the monster now only five or six hundred feet behind!

"Shit!"

This last, straight stretch has always been bumpy, washed out, and contains a dozen deceptive little curves, like swerving through cars, in and out, in and out. Chicanes, if you're on a Grand Prix track—one after another—swerve, swerve, swerve, swerve. Halfway down I yell, "Shit!" An RV coming uphill!

"Shit!"

SUV now a hundred feet from ramming me! I hear another pop at my window.

A huge chunk out of the road—in this lane! End of the next swerve! Can't slow down—they'll ram me over the side! Hit *that* hole—over the side!

"Shit!"

I flash my headlights right in front of the oncoming RV—flick my wrists left—head-on into the RV at the start of the chicane—RV stops dead—flick right—around the pothole.

"We missed it! A miracle baby!"

Another seven hundred feet—the last hairpin!

Eyes on the curve and the slope into it—brake into the last chicane—swerve—accelerate! Smooth! Every action—smooth, smooth, smooth! At the hairpin!

I step into the brakes too hard!

"Damn ABS!"

'Bu looses traction. We screech sideways across the highway into the turn—off the blacktop! Onto the sand pullout! Her tires dig into the sand as we slide broadside to a stop—an eyelash away from a steel guardrail post. I press the accelerator smoothly to the floor and shout, "Go, 'Bu, go!"

The front wheels are pointed out of the turn. All four tires kick up sand and gravel—sounds like a hailstorm. Shooting onto the blacktop, we force an oncoming car to slam its brakes. I yell, "Sorry!"

I fly into soft curves next to the White River wetland at the base of Independence. Ahead of me I see smoke, or dust.

"What the hell?"

Then it hits me. "*Yes!* They didn't make it!"

Probably hit the hole I missed. I let off the accelerator. Not a lot though. I'm not sure of anything yet. A quick glance tells me the

SUV is not close behind.

Sure enough, across the bogs I see a twisted, glinting carcass. A darkened trail of black dirt and broken trees climbs a breezeless mountainside, from the marshes all the way up to the chicanes more than a thousand feet above. The SUV took that flight I have only imagined. I don't need to wonder anymore what might happen. Better them than me, baby.

Nothing of that vehicle is recognizable, except tires. It's a crushed ball of gnarled metal lying motionless in a cloud of smoke, steam, and dust. I keep going. There are no signs of life—and my Good Samaritan side is in hiding right now.

Okay, maybe I should have stopped to render assistance. But they sent at least two bullets snapping by my head. I doubt the intention was to miss. No way was there much assistance to render, in any case. I do not dawdle the rest of the way through the Rockies to Manitou—I also don't do anything to attract too much attention. Sixteen minutes after I drove by the SUV, the first State Trooper whizzes by me going the other direction. It's a motorcycle, and must be doing at least 115. But then, this stretch of Highway 82 next to Twin Lakes Reservoir is wide and smooth. I pull over in plain sight and stop when I see it coming, which of course is the law, but thankfully it keeps going.

Trooper two, in a familiar silver Crown Victoria, screams by a few minutes later. He also doesn't stop when I pull over. I'm relieved—to say the very least. I can go home now. Further down the way, on Highway 24 East, with no one coming toward me, I swerve onto the other side of the road to toss the pistol out the driver side window, way down into the Arkansas River.

Maybe that wasn't such a good idea.

Chapter Forty-Nine: Sweet Home Oasis

The first Manitou Springs exit from Highway 24, near the bottom of Ute Pass, is a most welcome sight. As I brake down the long hill into Manitou, listening to 'Bu snarl just a tad with my foot off the accelerator, I let out an enormous sigh. Fountain Creek has been singing for the last eight miles, and when I ease past Soda Springs Park and 'Toids Café, the prayers are loud and clear. The creek is swift, robust, and joyful. Feminine rain falls here, too, as it has the entire trip home.

I wave to Becky and Michael as they sit at my golden table inside 'Toids. I nod to Police Chief Harris as we glide by one another in opposing directions. There's Mark, taking a late day walk—he probably waited to see if the rain would stop before finally giving in and taking off for his daily regimen. I love Manitou. It's good to be home.

After coasting underneath the iron arch, where Manitou Boulevard changes into Colorado Avenue, and Manitou Springs into Colorado Springs, almost immediately I turn left onto Princeton, and bear left on Holyoke to Grinnell. 'Bu and I enjoy the winding streets up to Sleeping Bear Oasis. Good *Feng Shui*.

I pull easily, deliberately, onto my old, cracked, cement driveway. There we sit for a minute, letting her motor idle smoothly, exhaust still growling just a teensy bit, before switching off the ignition. The gas gauge is well below empty—I didn't stop anywhere along the way today—a risk even under ordinary circumstances. I'll leave 'Bu in the driveway tonight rather than the garage. She deserves a good rest, and to be cooled and caressed by the delicate touch of heavy mist.

I swing my legs out together, and stand up. Stepping onto the mulched garden path, I stretch for the sky with a deep *ujjayi* inhale, perform an exhaling swan dive down to the ground, and reverse all the way back up with another *ujjayi* inhale—a couple of lumbar vertebrae clunk back into place—and pull my hands together into prayer.

> *"Tunkashida, Wakan Tanka, Wi Ate, Canku Asnihan*
> *Mani, hiye miye, ece wakiya. Wiyochpeyatan kin yan, he*
> *Mitakuye ob, wani kta cha, pada miya, pada miya. Thank*
> *you for my life. Mitakuye Oyasin."*

The garden is exquisite—sweet with blossoms open and closed, and exuberant in blues, purples, yellows and oranges. I open the wooden north gate, and walk around the garage to the back garden, stopping for a few minutes to let my eyes focus over Sleeping Bear to individual, tiny trees atop the mountains. The bird feeders are half full, meaning it has been a normal day here at the Oasis. Sue has done her job well. I can't help but wonder, though, why I never got a call or even an email. Opening and closing the south gate, I enjoy the red and orange penstemon, cacti, and five foot datura on the desert side of the Oasis.

The front door is locked. I whistle the signal, and Gizmo, my twenty-one year old cockatiel, immediately starts screaming with excitement. I unlock the door and step inside. Ah, a nice, cool house. I relax into familiar smells of home. Verdito is also glad to see me—bursting into his finest joyful melodies—even though he's beginning his seasonal molt. I open both their house doors. Giz comes out onto the drawbridge to whistle me our song while I nuzzle his new-feather-stubby crown with my nose. Verdito flies over my head to the kitchen window to perch on the café curtain rod, again singing with a heart four times his body size.

While surveying the house, I open all the windows, and let down the glass on the front and back screen doors. The backyard is filled with the sounds of birds. There are even a few pine siskins—unusual because they spend summers in narrow mountain valleys with running water. And probably two hundred fifty grackles grackling. I grab a gallon of Eldorado Natural Spring water, sit at the kitchen table, and spend an hour just resting there, 85% dark melting across my tongue, taking it all in while Gizmo eats voraciously and Verdito flies back and forth—buzzing the top of my head with each trip. How good to be back home. I finish the entire gallon. Then I go to pee.

~~~

Carrying a dry change of clothes on top of my gym bag, I'm off in
~~~

Number Ten, my trusty old Nissan pickup. 'Bu needs the nap, not to mention a tank of petrol. Ten is great—it's been nearly a month since he's been started, but he fires right up. Take care of your stuff, your family, your friends, and yourself, and they take care of you.

Hot water sounds really, really nice. After thirty or forty minutes in the whirlpool, I'll do a little sweat lodge ceremony in the steam room, singing sacred songs and praying, to express thanks and gratitude, ask for help and forgiveness, and for guidance and health, for all my relations. The Y won't be busy. It'll be seven o'clock by the time I get there, and everybody will be home watching Saturday night TV.

The locker room is indeed nearly empty. Right away, off goes the television. After a first shower, I step down into the whirlpool. This private area is adult men only, and swimsuits are disallowed in the whirlpool. That's good. You can massage the low back, sacrum, and pelvis under powerful jets. Can't speak to a dress code on the women's side.

After forty-five minutes I saunter in for a brief shower, then step into the steam room. I employ the hose to spray the entire hot, dry, empty, tiled room. Once it's steaming hot, I sit on a towel, kick off my sandals, cross my legs in half lotus, say a prayer of thanks, for the best outcome for Wynne, and for the spirits of the SUV guys. All four rounds are done before some of the evening guys start to wander in. I pay my respects, and throw open the lodge door.

"*Mitakuye Oyasin!*"

Rob is in the whirlpool. He waves. "Haven't seen you for a while, Matt."

"Hey, Rob. Yeah, I went to Aspen."

"Aspen, huh? That sounds like fun."

"It had its ups and downs. It was a business trip."

"Business in Aspen. Yeah, sounds like tough duty. Hope you got combat pay."

I chuckle. "I know it sounds rough, but it really wasn't so bad. I also flew to Santa Fe."

"Flew?"

"Yeah, a private twin-engine Cessna."

"Excellent."

"It was excellent—most excellent. Even the emergency landing in Aspen coming back."

"No way! Emergency landing?"

"Yeah, my client, the pilot, passed out in flight. I had to take over."

"I didn't know you were a pilot, Matt."

"Neither did I."

~~~

I enjoy lasagna at Adam's Mountain Café, where only the newest wait staff ever ask me what I'll have at dinner. When Number Ten and I arrive back home, I find a note from Sue, thanking me for the check and letting me know everything was perfect while I was gone. I paid her for the entire two weeks, plus another week as a tip.

Off go the lights, and in my studio go I. Everybody should have his or her own private room. Not a bedroom, but a space set aside for just their intimate, personal life. Here is my art, my library, my guitars and violin, my drum, my moccasins, my wolf-bone choker, and my cedar box—my inner life. My room is where I hold the space for myself to be absolutely, completely myself.

My diary has no entry since Wednesday, August 17. It's going to get one now.
~~~

Chapter Fifty: Meanwhile Back At the Ranch

The Lexus sits in the driveway. Clancy comes through the kitchen door, wiping his feet. Wynne isn't in the nook. He keeps walking. There she is, at the dining table, papers strewn everywhere, head in both hands. He removes his Boonie hat, holds it in his left hand, and stands at ease. The Glock is on his right hip—the belt also holds extra magazines, and a horizontally mounted scabbard with a black-handled knife, probably ten inches long.

"Miss Worner?"

"Come on in, Clancy. Please, have a seat."

He hesitates, and then sits in the chair next to her. "What d' you need me t' do?"

She looks up, reaching to place her right hand gently on a sandy salt and pepper cheek. "Thank you, Clancy." Then with the same hand, she reaches down for a spiral-bound writing pad on the table. She picks up the pad, flips to a new page, and sets it back down, nestling a maroon fountain pen between thumb and fingers.

"I'll write it down for you. Let me know if anything here makes you feel uncomfortable." She looks at Clancy with damp, narrowed eyes—steel-hard, under eyebrows just noticeably knotted above the nose. "Promise me that?"

"Yes, ma'am."

"Okay. Thank you, Clancy." She looks back down at the pad and prepares to write—then turns her head back to her ranchman. "Before I start, there's something you should know. An SUV tried to force Matt Hale off Independence Pass yesterday afternoon. He's probably okay, but no one has spoken with him yet." Again, her palms cradle her forehead. "It's my fault, Clancy, it's my fault." She looks up again, eyes fierce. "This crap is all going to end—*now*."

"Ma'am, how d'ya know it was Mr. Hale?"

"Numerous witnesses reported his University of Colorado license plate. The State Patrol has been here."

"Yeup."

"You're going to hear things on the news—what, I'm not sure. Two men were killed when the SUV went off the road. That's all I know right now. My position, and therefore yours, too, is that we have no comment—we're letting the police do their job. Okay?"

He doesn't nod. "Yes, ma'am."

"I'd like you to call Denise, Gregg Kearney, Grant Foster, and Carolyn Worth. I'd like everyone here for lunch at twelve-thirty tomorrow. I know it's Sunday, but contact everyone you can or leave messages, and call again first thing tomorrow morning. If anyone hesitates, tell him or her that this is an extremely urgent matter. If they still won't come, come get me and I'll talk to them. I need you here, too. Are we okay so far?"

"Yeup."

"Okay. Please call Daniel at the bank, ask him to come, and to bring paperwork necessary to add three people as signatories to the ranch operating account." She finishes writing that all down, and looks up to Clancy. "Got that?"

"Yeup."

"Okay. Then, I need you to call Carrie's ZG Catering. We'll need lunch for seven, two vegetarian, the rest chicken, steamed vegetables, and house salads. And a good red table wine. Four bottles. No dessert. Ask her to bring all the settings. Full service. Okay?"

"Yeup."

"I'm going to the office now. I've about ten thousand calls to make." He gets up as she does. "Clancy?"

"Yes, ma'am?"

"I'm going out of town for a while—perhaps quite a long time—six months or a year. I need you to be completely honest with me."

"Yes, ma'am."

"You've never broken my trust in you during our seven years together, but this is really, really important. Okay?"

He lays his hat on the table, and clasps his hands together. "Yes, ma'am."

"Clancy, you've talked about retiring someday soon. I need to know if you've given that idea more thought, or have set a date."

"Really haven't put my mind t' it that much, ma'am. Reckon this ol' body'll hold out a good five, six more years anyway. Long as I don't push real hard."

"May I count on you to stay here with me until you decide to leave in five or six years? And to arrange for any help you need, at any time you need it?"

"Ma'am, could be longer. You know I'd die an' be laid t' rest here if you let me."

"You can count on that, Clancy." She leans over and hugs him hard and close. "Thank you, my dear friend. Thank you."

<center>~~~</center>

I sleep in until six before getting up for my morning routine. At my PC, I down a second liter of water while I check weather, horoscopes, and email. I decide to send an email.

> *Dear Wynne,*
>
> *I'm sorry about all that has happened.*
>
> *I have truly enjoyed meeting you, and wish you the very best always.*
>
> *Because I feel our time together was not professional, I cannot possibly accept payment for services not rendered.*
>
> *I hope you can forgive me someday.*
>
> *Best regards,*
>
> *Matt*

I leave it at that. I could have written a book. Maybe someday I will.

Maroonbaru smiles big as I exit the front door. Rain has washed off some of the road grime. She starts right up, purring softly, though with that little growl she acquired with the new muffler four years ago—a growl that is always more robust following a road trip in the Rockies.

"We'll have to do that more often, eh, 'Bu?" She doesn't answer. Just keeps purring—that's answer enough, eh?

I stop for gasoline right away, at the Sinclair as usual. The Manitou Sinclair has one of the only remaining, original Sinclair dinosaurs in the entire United States. Rumor has it that this had been the only one left in the entire USA. It was airlifted out, to where I

278

don't know, to father a whole new generation of five-foot high, green dinosaurs, one of which was presented as a gift to the station. The faded grandpasaurus is now partly protected behind shrubs, gazing lovingly at his shiny new counterpart. According to the Subaru owner's manual, Maroonbaru has a twelve-gallon fuel capacity—she laps up nearly 12.1.

Manitou is not very busy for ten o'clock on Sunday. Maybe it's the miraculous rain still drifting down on us. Maybe it's because I need more quiet time. I also need maté, and the voice of Fountain Creek.

My table is waiting for me. Lounging in the booth, I sip maté, with coconut milk and stevia, while devouring a couple of steam-poached farm fresh eggs with locally grown organic tomato slices, fresh Parmesan, and crushed, homegrown organic basil and thyme. And spelt toast. The door bell bings.

"Matt! What's happenin', my man?"

"Hey, Josh. I'm just enjoying breakfast—and being home."

After our old-school hand-shake-palm-glide-fist-bump-explosion, I sweep an open hand toward the other booth seat. "Join me?"

"Sure. I'll get a maté—be right back."

He comes back to set the paper cup on the table, then plops down, and reaches for a slice of my toast. "How was it?"

"Aspen?"

"No, Antarctica—Dude—Aspen, wild new client, Santa Fe, crashing airplanes?"

"I didn't crash it. It just wasn't pretty. And I don't remember saying 'wild.' "

He emits a few laughs from the sternum. "Awesome. So—how was it?"

"Nothing new since I called you—just got dumped, fired, kicked out of town, hit in the head with a gun butt, shot at, chased over Independence Pass, and killed a couple of guys."

"Whaaaat?"

"That's how it was. Just another day."

"Dude, you serious?"

"Afraid so."

"Killed a couple guys?" He sternly brushes a toast crumb from that deftly trimmed, auburn beard.

"Nah. They killed themselves. Went over a guardrail on Independence."

"Whaaaat?"

"Just as they were going to ram me from behind."

"You're makin' this up."

I swivel around. My hair is carefully trimmed to the scalp around the gash, and it's covered by a gauze compress taped in place with a two-inch round bandage.

"Whaaaat?"

"Like it?" I turn back around. "Take a closer look at my right eye."

He leans across the table, squinting. Josh refuses to use his glasses. "Damn. Dude, over the edge?"

"Down a thousand feet at about an eighty degree grade."

"That'd do'er, all right."

"Did. I expect cops, like, any minute now."

"Whaaaat?" Josh slumps back, hands behind his head on the high-back booth seat,

"I didn't hang around. Somebody's gonna be asking me some questions, you know?"

"I suppose so. But you did nothing wrong, or so it sounds."

"Other than winning the Independence Grand Prix?"

"Meaning…?"

"Dude, you should see my tires. I went through some of those turns at sixty—and more."

"Whaaaat? On Independence? You're makin' this up." He huffs. "Independence…."

"True story."

"True story?"

"Scout's honor."

He removes his hands from behind his head. The left hand reaches to stroke the beard. His eyes close for about ten seconds— they pop open. "Gotta take off bro'." He jumps up. "Gillian's got me repairing sub flooring to stop squeaks—as we speak I'm at the hardware store getting screws. Dude, I want to hear more about this trip. We'll have you over, right?"

"Sounds good to me. Let me know. I'll bring wine."

"Right on." He extends a fist, I bump, and he turns, refills his cup, snaps on a to-go lid and is gone with a ding.

Bryant comes in to sit for a while. He just returned from playing keyboard at a friend's wedding in Hawaii. He shows me photographs and tells stories.

Becky and Michael drop in for maté to go. Becky is going out to clients' gardens, in spite of the rain, but isn't in much of a hurry. We talk about permaculture. She's an environmentalist, a very dedicated one, and a mentor in such endeavors. We're great friends. Michael is her man—a classical guitarist by trade, part-time gardener by default.

Dana is next to join me. She's a writing buddy. We often sit here together and write. She's working on a juvenile fiction piece that sounds pretty good to me. She heads off to a quieter table to get some writing done when Jan walks in, grinning.

Jan knows where I've been. "So, Matt...." Cheshire cat grin on her face, she commands, "Tell me all about it."

"I'm not sure I'm up for it, Jan."

"What? Come on, I have to know. Are you in love?"

"Yes and no."

She gives me the evil eye. "Well, thanks. That sure narrows it down. Come on." She's gesturing with both hands—come on, come on. "Let's have it!"

"Yes, I fell in love. No, I can't be in love."

"What does that mean?"

"She never wants to see me again."

"What? Why? What happened?"

"The story is too huge to tell. And I'm still processing it. I'm just not ready."

"Okay, the condensed version, then." She's apparently not going to give up easily.

I submit, sighing laboriously. "Wynne is gorgeous, and possibly the most authentic, loving, intelligent and creative woman I've ever met. Outside of yourself, of course."

She chuckles. "Yeah, right. Go on."

"Turns out she has a nasty legal problem." Her eyebrows rise. "She hasn't broken any laws. It's unknown people, probably corporate, maybe government, after family assets. Anyway, we flew her private plane to Santa Fe."

Again with the Cheshire grin. "Oooo. Sounds romantic. Did you...."

"A gentleman never kisses and tells, and no. I wanted to, but it never happened."

She gives me a sad face. "Aww. Still, it sounds very romantic."

"It was. Until we were chased by guys with guns."

"What? You're kidding, right?"

"Not kidding."

"Matt?"

"Yeah. Anyway, they didn't catch us and we flew back to Aspen. But she passed out and I had to fly the plane."

"Passed out? Do you know how to fly a plane?"

"She was drugged. No, I don't know how to fly a plane. Well, a little bit now. I landed it in Aspen without killing us both."

Jan's expression has long since turned from Cheshire to serious.

I keep going. I'm on a roll now. "After we got back, things got weird. I guess I meddled too much, or maybe I was too much myself, or took too much for granted. I don't know. You know how I am, Jan."

She nods. "Yeah, I think I do. So, what happened?"

"She got mad at me and told me to take a hike. I left, and was chased by an SUV over Independence Pass."

Her eyes get huge. "Independence Pass? I can't go over that pass at ten miles an hour without peeing my pants. Independence is *deadly*."

"It was—for them, as a matter of fact."

"Meaning?"

"Meaning they, whoever they were, crashed their SUV. Went over the guardrail and down about a thousand feet."

"Are they dead?"

"I didn't stick around to find out, but I don't see how anyone could have lived through that wreckage. It looked like it went through a junkyard crusher. I got the hell out of there."

"When did all this happen?"

"Yesterday."

"Yesterday?"

"Yesterday."

"No wonder you're still processing things. I'll leave you alone."

"Not necessary. I could really use company. I just don't want to talk about it anymore. Maybe later."

"I understand."

"So, what's new with you?"

"Well, I did book a new band at Marcy's."

"Marcy's. Jan, that's a big venue. For Colorado Springs, anyway. Tell me about it."

"They're a five piece—mostly covers so far. They play old school rock: Doobie Brothers, Dire Straits, Pearl Jam, REM, New

Pornographers, stuff like that."

"Jan, that sounds fun. I'd like to hear them. Let me know when they're playing somewhere, and early. You know me, I'm a real party animal."

She laughs. "Yeah, an in-bed-by-10:30 critter."

"Hey, sometimes I'm up 'til 11. Fourth of July at Josh and Gill's...."

The bell on 'Toids door bangs as two short hairs in gray suits walk in. This can't be good.

Chapter Fifty-One: The FBI and I

Only one guy in Manitou Springs wears suits, and they never fit him well. I suspect he sells real estate, but I'm not sure—and have never asked. I've been known to wear a Harris Tweed jacket or four, and gabardine slacks, but only when I have some professional or social engagement. Several hand-tailored pinstripes are entombed in the closet in my studio—haven't worn one for nearly a decade. Around here, suits stick out like a hitchhiker's thumb. These guys are definitely cops.

They each look right at me as soon as the door dings closed. Walking lightly up to my table, they look down at Jan and me—mostly me, but the shorter one checks out Jan, too.

Displaying his badge in a black leather case, the darker gray suit asks, "Matt Hale?"

"Yes sir, I am. Am I in some sort of trouble?"

"Can we talk with you outside, sir?" asks the shorter one, in the light gray suit. Both men even have stereotypic black ties. Kinda' scary, those.

"Absolutely. Will you excuse us, Jan?"

She just looks at me with big eyes. I get up and lead them out the door, over the old stone bridge, and to a picnic table next to the creek. I want *Mde Wakan* close by. I sit down. They stand—one on each side, facing me. I feel a stiff neck again as I look up at them.

Dark suit does introductions. "Mr. Hale, I'm agent Ballard. This is agent Diggs. Federal Bureau of Investigation."

Light gray Diggs says, "Mr. Hale, we just want to ask you some questions."

Dark gray Ballard asks, "Mr. Hale, may I call you Matt?"

Slightly nervous Hale responds, "Yes, of course. Thank you, sir."

Ballard asks, "Matt, were you driving a dark-colored Subaru station wagon on Independence Pass yesterday about midday?"

"Yes sir, I was. Flying would be more accurate." I attempt a smile, but neither agent is impressed.

Light gray Diggs asks, "Were you fleeing from a black GMC sport utility vehicle on Independence Pass, Mr. Hale?"

My head swings his way. "Yes sir, I was most definitely fleeing."

"Matt, did you know the occupants of the SUV?"

I swivel Ballard's way. "No sir."

Diggs asks, "Had you seen that vehicle previously, Mr. Hale?"

I swing my head his way. "I can't say for sure, sir. A business associate and I had an encounter with a black SUV some days earlier in Santa Fe, New Mexico. But neither of us saw that vehicle well enough to identify it, or for me to say with certainty that the vehicle chasing me on Independence Pass was the same one. Sure looked like it, though."

"Matt, do you have any idea why you were being pursued?"

I swing my head back. "Not specifically, sir. I believe it might have had something to do with legal issues my client, Wynne de Gracia Worner, was dealing with while in Santa Fe."

"Did you at any time see any weapons, either in Santa Fe or on Independence Pass, Mr. Hale?" My already tenuous neck begins to try getting my attention with shooting pains.

"Yes, sir. In Santa Fe a man chased Ms. Worner and me across Old Santa Fe Trail and behind the Lamy Building. He was holding a handgun, in both hands. He didn't see us." Presumptively, I go ahead and turn toward Ballard, then look forward, roll my neck around, and massage it for a few seconds.

"Matt, did you recognize the type of gun the man in Santa Fe was holding?"

"No sir. Sometimes I can recognize a pistol grip if it's a common make. I know a retired state trooper and sometimes I browse through his gun periodicals. Some years ago as a State of Colorado investigator I did receive firearms training and certification." I turn to Diggs.

Ballard—which by the way is not fair at all—again inquires, "Periodicals?"

"Yes, sir. Magazines."

He nods. I have to turn back to Diggs—at least he's shorter. "Mr. Hale, would you be able to identify the man who pursued you and Ms. Worner on foot in Santa Fe?"

"Absolutely. Yesterday, it was the same guy that chased us in Santa Fe who held me at gunpoint on Independence Pass, while another fellow I never got to see searched my car for a manila envelope." No longer sure which way to turn next, I look at the creek and rub the back of my neck.

They both move to the other side of the picnic table and sit down.

Diggs: "Did they find what they were looking for?"

"No, and I have no idea what it was."

"Matt...." I look at Ballard, who looks at his notes. "...So far, it seems you've told us that you were pursued in Santa Fe and on Independence Pass. You don't know if it was the same vehicle in both cases, but you would be able to identify one of the assailants. You also would not be able to identify the weapon you saw in Santa Fe, and you never saw a weapon yesterday. Is that correct?"

"Sir, that is correct—except that yesterday some hikers surprised the big guy holding the gun on me. I was able to kick his knee and grab the weapon. It was a Smith & Wesson M&P with a silencer. Also, both SUVs were black, and both had numerous short, black antennae on top. I would also add that on the way down Independence Pass, between the second and third hairpin curves, someone stuck an arm out of the SUV and fired a gun at me. I was driving very fast and only caught a glimpse of the arm coming out the passenger side window. At least two shots were fired because I heard two bullets pass my open driver side window."

Diggs: "Mr. Hale, how did you know a bullet was fired at you?"

"I heard a snap, like a small firecracker exploding. I know military veterans who describe that sound as a bullet passing by, followed usually by the report from the weapon. The bullet, as you know, travels faster than the speed of sound. Since I saw an arm out the SUV window, and heard two snaps, I presume that two shots were fired. I did not, however, hear a report." Diggs nods. Ballard writes in his notepad.

"Matt, do you have any idea how the SUV pursuing you ended up at the bottom of a hillside yesterday?"

"No sir, I don't. I had nothing to do with that, though. I was too busy trying to stay alive and just drive my car without killing myself or someone else—or being killed."

He nods and smiles. "Thank you, Matt. You have no need to be concerned. You're not in any trouble here. We're just trying to understand what actually transpired. You did leave the scene of an accident, but you were involved in that accident only to the extent that you were being pursued, with a perceived probability of serious harm or death if you could not escape.

"We have two eye witness accounts that confirm a gun was pointed in your direction, though no one heard a shot. The SUV hit a very bad section of road traveling, as best we can tell, about 70 miles per hour.

"That road hazard caused the vehicle to bounce in the air. The right front end landed on the safety rail next to the highway, causing the rear of the vehicle to slide across the highway. The vehicle then flipped on the roadway and rolled several times, before rolling over the safety rail, and down the side of a thirteen hundred foot embankment. Both occupants were dead on the scene. Several weapons were recovered from the wreckage, including two handguns, not recently fired, both with silencers, and a high-powered rifle.

"We are aware that you own a cellular telephone, and were probably unable to call for help. Reception might have been a problem up there anyway. You have been deemed acting entirely in self-defense, even though you were driving somewhat over the speed limit, sir." He smiles. "The Pitkin County DA is totally understanding about the circumstances, although Lake County was a different story. We were able to prevail, however, and convince the District Attorney to be more understanding. Do you have any questions, Matt?"

"Thank you, sir, for telling me what happened—and that I'm not in trouble. This whole thing has been scary, but being chased, and almost rammed from behind on that pass was—traumatic. More so than a landing an airplane with no pilot experience."

Ballard smiles, barely. "About the airplane—did you see which water bottle Ms. Worner drank from within half an hour either before or after departure?"

"Yes, sir. Wynne, Ms. Worner, drank only from a bottle she had left in the airplane when we landed, to the best of my knowledge."

"Mr. Hale?" I look at Diggs. "Is there anything else you would like to say, or that you believe we should know, or that we haven't asked you?"

"Well, sir, a lot went down, that's for sure. I made some notes last night about what happened, but they're far less thorough than what we've talked about today. They're more personal and emotionally reflective, I suppose, than factual—it's a diary entry."

Diggs: "Mr. Hale, where is the firearm you retrieved on Independence Pass?"

Uh oh. "I threw it into the Arkansas River just after I turned onto Highway 24—I felt certain they were no longer after me, and I wanted to get rid of the thing. I tossed the magazine into a large thicket of shrubs beside eastbound Highway 82, about five hundred feet before the marina turnoff."

Diggs: "Are you willing to take a lie detector examination to confirm those statements?"

"Dude, bring it on."

Ballard nearly grins. "Matt, it really is unfortunate that you didn't retain the weapon. It would have been useful to us in many ways. I understand your sentiment, and that you might not have been thinking clearly at the time. Still...." Agent Ballard's head slowly shakes back-and-forth.

"Is this going to cause me trouble?"

"We will ask that you accompany us to the location, so we can see if it's retrievable."

"I tossed it down a steep gorge area."

"We still have to try to find it—and will require your assistance, Matt."

"Absolutely. We'll need rope in that spot. And wetsuits—I suppose we're talking seven feet deep—maybe twelve or more."

"Matt, can you be more specific about where you threw the weapon?"

"Approximately two thousand feet after turning south on Highway 24. I drove into the northbound lane to make sure I could fling it into the deepest section of the gorge."

Diggs: "Mr. Hale, why did not you not seek law enforcement assistance, or try to report this incident at your earliest opportunity?"

I look right in his eyes. "I just wanted the whole thing to go away. They were no longer after me—I just want it to go away."

"Matt...." Ballard's left hand pulls away the left coat lapel, as he reaches for the inside left jacket pocket, exposing a shoulder holster, though I'm pretty sure that was not his intent, and pulls out his plain, non-embossed business card. "...If you think of anything else important, will you please give us a call?"

"Yes, sir, I will. May I ask how the FBI is interested?" I take the card and slip it into my wallet, right on top of my own cards.

"We're not at liberty to discuss details. However, because of the very high likelihood that interstate crimes have been committed, or at least that criminal activity was likely conducted across state lines or in federal airspace, the agency is obligated to investigate.

"Once the case is closed, or if we need your assistance again, we may be able to give you more information at that time. Thank you very much for taking time to talk with us, Matt. Please call if anything else comes up, okay?"

I nod enthusiastically. "You can count on that, Agent Ballard. Thank you—you know, there is one more thing. Who were those guys?"

"So far, Mr. Hale, we've been unable to identify them. They carried no identification, and the vehicle was reported stolen from a fluids transmission services corporation in Dallas. In the vehicle were eight counterfeit license plates depicting various states, including Colorado plates attached at the time of the incident."

They stand—so I also climb up from the bench seat. They extend their hands—I extend mine. It seems they're on my side, and have spoken on my behalf with local law enforcement—hopefully I'm not going to get in trouble for tossing the pistol. What *was* I thinking? Shaking their hands authentically is the least I can do, and I darn sure will call if anything else comes up.

Ballard starts to walk away, stops, and turns back toward me. "Mr. Hale, you should be aware that you might not be out of danger. Please keep your cell phone with you at all times. Do you have a handgun permit?"

"Concealed?"

"Yes."

"No sir."

"You might want to think seriously about it. Use my name as a reference and emergency contact."

My heart is suddenly thrashing. I have no idea what my facial expression might be—other than not cute.

"Just a safeguard, sir. I'll be in touch—you have my number."

They turn and walk west toward the other end of Soda Springs Park, alongside the humid cool of Fountain Creek. I sit back down on the picnic bench to gather my wits, and listen to water song for a spell.

I shake off stress, my body tense, and medulla oblongata buzzing. I shake some more. Animals do that, too, after stress. They shake it off, rest, and go on with life. I'm doing the same. Well, I am still learning to read my nervous system's physiological messages and responses, so I can monitor and dissipate them as needed. Otherwise, just like with muscle memory, we hold onto trauma—sometimes forever—or at least for a muddled and often unhappy lifetime. Process your emotions as they arise—ditto for nervous trauma—whether or not you *think* nothing's there.

After seven minutes I stand, face west, looking up Fountain Creek, watching *Mde Wakan* flow toward me. Extending arms out and up, I breathe deep—and emit gratitude, visualizing prayer smoke, with my exhale. Then I walk back across the hundred-year-old stone bridge, over timeless water.

<center>~~~</center>

"Is everything okay?"

"They just wanted to ask some questions about what happened. I *was* worried, though, because, A, I reached outrageous speeds, B, drove in ways that possibly endangered others, and Three, left the scene of an accident—if you could call it that. Oh, and D, I did not attempt to render assistance."

"To people wanting to kill you?"

"I know, right? It's part of my wanting to do the right thing."

"The right thing was getting the hell out of there."

"Thanks, Jan. Seems the feds don't disagree."

"They were feds?"

"FBI."

"Wow! You're in deep, huh?"

"I'm not in hot water, Jan, just dancing on it."

"Okay, what are you talking about?"

"Sorry. I'm associated with whatever is going on, or went on, only because I was with a client. I'm an innocent bystander. And a damn good driver."

"A good driver?" Having been a passenger in my vehicles, Jan has some reservations regarding my driving skills—while I think she might be a little too cautious behind the wheel.

"I made it, they didn't. My old Subaru versus their giant SUV— Matt versus Goliath. They were maybe six feet from ramming me from behind and sending me over the edge. And I mean—*six feet*. I got lucky. As you know, I have friends watching over me."

Chapter Fifty-Two: Postmortem

Settling into my ten year old, gray synthetic fabric executive chair, before my golden oak laminate desk, I check email—after visiting aviation weather and the usual horoscope websites. I scan through eleven days of messages, over a hundred and sixty in all, looking for a recent one that really matters. 'Tis not there—but last night my clever buddy Cassie sent me a missive with the subject: "YOkay?"

Matt,

Mom told me what happened. I'm steamed.

You're just trying to help. It almost got you killed. The FBI came and asked Mom and Clancy questions. Told her you were chased over Independence. Dude! You okay?

Two guys are dead, squished like bugs, and mom sends you packing just for being there! I screamed at her over the phone when she accused you of flirting with me. No way are you skulking me. Dude, I totally get affection and honesty.

In my youthful experience, you're one of a kind. Especially when it comes to the dorks mom hangs with.

Anyway, maybe she'll come around. She gets this way sometimes. Like, she freaks and later gets real again.

She was totally pissed about the conservation easement. Gregg called her to talk about my email. I guess I should have asked her about it first, but I knew she'd just say no.

Guess what? Gregg says it's perfect! Didn't know if it will work, but he's looking into it. I don't get what Mom's objection is. I'm, like, Mom, don't you want to fix this?

Don't give up on her. She's just trying to deal.

C

Since returning to Manitou Springs, I've not spent much brainpower on water conservation easements—mind's been elsewhere. What was it Wynne repeated so often? "Life must go on."

After turning off my capable, older PC, I slip into the studio for private time—like there's anyone else here from whom I need privacy. Sitting on the floor in a half lotus, I light my sacred fire—a votive candle—smudge and say a prayer for wisdom to react lovingly on the road ahead. I add prayers to the tobacco I roll, set the cigarette by the fire, and pick up the *I Ching*. Six times I drop the three Chinese coins that an old friend, with whom, by my own lack of contact, I have lost touch, gifted me some twenty years ago.

It's time "After the End." Things are readjusting and realigning following a brief state of perfect equilibrium. I must avoid complacency or apathy, and apply coming changes in circumstances to develop inner awareness and caution. Above all, I should not maintain the "illusion of the ideal." Doing so would be to delude myself, and not in harmony with the cosmos—placing myself in danger. Hmm, Ballard did propose a concealed weapon permit. Problems might develop in social or interpersonal relationships—*might?* Well, isn't this just darling—a pep talk from the oracle, just when I most need it. Okay—knock it off, Matt. Dude, you are on the road—merely be cautious from which cliffs you depart. If you must dive—aim well.

A diary entry logs that hexagram, along with an immodest piece on how I've been seeing and accepting feelings—while smoothing reactionary tendencies. I'm deep down underwater in my ocean, breathing easy, and my swim is well lit by daylight, diffusing from the surface—displaying diluted, muddy colors through the deep, with its muted, echoistic sounds. Along floats a bubble—a crystal ball streaming the video of a friend, the host of an open mike night whereat occasionally I embarrass myself on guitar, who recently asked whether I was trying to sound like the whole band. He said, "Just be what you can be—if that's a whole band, well grab a recording contract—if it's just you going solo, ditto; but sounding like the whole band is a lot to ask of yourself." After lifting my staff from the wall, I lean over my candle fire to light the tobacco and go outside.

The staff I shove softly into thick, wet soil in the center of the back yard, facing west. Without inhaling, I pull on the tobacco, offering to seven directions. The whole time I pray, a big male crow in the Ponderosa pine on the north side of the Oasis, gives me the what-for—for-what I'm not sure. I lay the last of the cigarette on the ground and pull my staff out of Earth, emptying the tobacco into the hole before covering it over.

I turn to gaze, repeating his what-for, although I know less Crow than Spanish, and demand, "What?" His jet head turns sideways to eye me closely. He chatters at me only a moment, gives me the what-for again for about ten seconds, and lifts from the top—a single, powerful stroke into the breeze—then open winged, he glides over the stone hill a hundred feet to the east and southeast, a geological battlement that deflects the immense, jittery vibe of six hundred thousand on the other side. His cackling gradually fades from earshot—but he never did let up—just kept chatting at me. Messages are all around us, if only we take time to notice, to gain the wisdom to understand. Don't know what the heck he was talking about—but I'll take the time.

~~~

Wynne sits alone now at the dining table. The steely resolve she has commanded for the last four and a half hours is only minimally diminished—determination witnessed and embraced by her team, translated and conferred about, from initial brainstorming through a final workable set of actions that will effectively and efficiently dispose of matters while she's away. Unsettled still, though more at peace now that details are agreed upon, contracts and promises signed, sealed, or hand-shaken, a steady palm lifts a crystal goblet to her lips.

She tilts her head back to rest on a rounded, old oak, high-top dining chair, eyes closed, letting the Saint-Émilion rest on her lips. The glass goes back down on the table. She breaks off a single rectangle from one of Matt's German chocolate bars left in the fridge, and lays it on her tongue to melt slowly and sensually, the way he does.

She picks up the wine glass, the dark chocolate, and stands—stretching straight and tall—and then slowly ascends that spiral staircase to draw a long, hot bath.

~~~

I fell asleep on the loveseat somewhere around four, and slept without waking for two hours. Now I'm totally groggy. After a shower and shave, I make maté, with coconut milk and organic maple sugar. I take my Martin and a guitar stand with me when I go out the west kitchen door. Sitting on the deck, I watch the evening age and enjoy a Macanudo—my second of the year—whilst sipping, like it was four hundred year old añejo tequila, a glass of filtered Colorado tap water, alternating with the maté. There's weeding and deadheading to do in the garden. Maybe I'll get to that tomorrow.

The sun goes down in a magnificent blaze of red, orange, and pomegranate strokes bursting through monumental cumulous billows, opened here and there like rips in the fabric of God's robe—Pikes Peak and the mountains of Manitou suspended from the cloud cover like stalagmites and flowstone. Finches, sparrows, doves, grackles, siskins, hummingbirds, woodpeckers, chickadees, nuthatches, the four sibling crows who've hung together for two years now, and even a pair of magpies, have been gorging themselves ravenously since rain stopped. I'm not sure when it stopped. By the time I finally stand to go—with fingertips a bit sore from not enough playing time recently, but my singing voice solid and sure—faint twilight, opaline atop the clouds, is all that remains of the light of day.

I slip into blue jeans, a gray Martin guitar t-shirt, and add two early twentieth century African necklaces made with ebony, coral and bone. Sipping three ounces of inexpensive Chilean cabernet, I pick and solo through four songs I've been working on for about sixteen months, and then lay the guitar back in its case, returning both humidifiers to their place. As my forest green Radio Paradise hoodie goes over my head, my neck lets me know it is not at all pleased with today's activities. 'Bu starts right up, as always. I back out of the garage, melt into her comfy gray velour seat, and point my girlfriend downhill, on my winding little lane. It's going to be another Adam's Mountain Café lasagna.

Manitou is hopping on a Labor Day weekend, Sunday night. Tourists flood the streets. Locals sit and watch, or walk their friends and dogs—everyone wandering sidewalks and parks as though time doesn't exist. Right on. I walk across another of Manitou's five stone bridges, stopping to hear a busker playing and singing Americana covers.

The spinach lasagna is huge, fresh and delicious. I chew with intention, long and slowly, to squeeze every molecule of nutrition and gourmet flavor, watching people outside: singles, couples, lovers, families with children throwing stuff into the creek and climbing on anything and everything. Life in the village. Life as it should be. After dinner, I stand, stretch, thank the others dining here at the community table, and saunter back outside to find the apex of another hundred-year-old stone bridge. Smells of popcorn, salt water taffy, and caramel apples fill the air. I lean on old cold stones as *Mde Wakan* runs red and swift below.

Chapter Fifty-Three: Crow Brought the Message

A crow in the crabapple out front wakes me about five forty-five. It hollers relentlessly until I open the burgundy curtains in the master bedroom. I can't tell if it's the same guy from yesterday. Crows tend to look alike until you get to know them better. Except for one-foot, that is, whom I fed along with her mate over the winter.

I call out from the open window, loud enough to get the bird's attention, but not so as to startle him. "Crow person, what do you want?"

He blinks a black eye at me, staring intently, and bobs his head up and down, tail flicking to maintain balance on the branch. He starts chortling, and then makes the continuous clicking sound that crows sometimes do when talking to their buddies. Either way, this is obviously a conversation between familiars—like a fist bump and a hug. He never takes his eye off me.

"What?"

He bobs his head, and lets four shrill cries fly into the morning air. His wings open out and up, sinking his body weight down on the branch, and with four powerful wing beats he springs away from the tree to silently glide over the top of the house toward Manitou. It's *one-foot!* I run over to a window on the west side, in the walk-in closet room. Through the trees I still see her, unusually solitary in September, soaring, with a few wing beats here and there, over the valley toward west-northwest. Crows aren't among my totems, and other than one-foot and her man, I've never had a close relationship with one—certainly not like with some magpies I've known. One-foot and her mate didn't really want anything to do with me. They just dropped by to eat, usually with her companion keeping a watchful eye from above. I haven't seen her since March, but have prayed for her happiness and health. I watch until losing sight of the apostle as she dips beyond yonder foothills.

Lingering long in the open window, I rest my chin on my forearms at the high windowsill. Birds of morning fill the Oasis with activity and song. Everyone is conversing, and competition for feeders is aggressive. Second broods are out there, too, learning about life. There's always plenty of food though. No spirit goes hungry or thirsty if I have anything to do with it.

It's the lost lives of nature that I mourn most—those who lived their lives with song and suffering, who did no harm other than that required for survival, who took only what was needed, leaving the rest for the prosperity of all.

A visit by crow is not to be ignored. Especially someone you know.

~~~

Wynne awakens sometime after six. She had gone to bed early, after that long hot soak, but slept fitfully. Even so, she's energetic again this morning. There's more to finish. First on the list, call Switzerland before Cassie goes to dinner and evening activities. Twin marmots race each other to the triple mirror vanity in her bedroom. She closes the journal after reading her entry written last night, puts it away, closes and locks the drawer; leaving the key in its usual place— the cut crystal bowl on top of the desk—a bowl that holds buttons, ticket stubs, hairpins—tiny stuff of memories, harbingers of sentimentality. She reaches for the landline.

"Good afternoon. May I please speak with Cassandra de Gracia Worner? It's her mother."

The girls don't have telephones in their rooms. All calls come to the only common telephone, outside the house monitor's suite—and inside. Some might say Le Rosey is old fashioned, although it has successfully prepared sons and daughters of fortune for international social, cultural and political leadership for more than two hundred years.

Cassie's voice finally comes on the line. "Mom?"

"Hi sweetheart. Am I interrupting?"

"No, of course not. I was reading. What's wrong?"

"Why would you think something's wrong?"

"Mom, you don't often call unless something pretty big is up. We just email. So?"

"Okay. I just need you to know I'll be out of touch for a while."
~~~

"What do you mean 'out of touch'? You're never out of touch. Mom, what's happening?"

"Cassie, do you have pen and paper handy? You'll need to write a few things down."

~~~

With a damp cotton rag I dust my near-perfect 1973 Raleigh Superbe; and then pump new-rubber-smelling, gift from a buddy, German made tires to sixty-one pounds. I haven't ridden my trusty old English three-speed since early July. Foot-hilly terrain and reluctant physiology, combined with lots of rain, have been sufficient deterrence. This, though, is a perfect morning for a bicycle ride to Manitou; cool from yesterday's rain, cloudy before this afternoon's rain, and nary a breath of wind.

Downhill from the Oasis, uphill on El Paso, downhill on El Paso, uphill on El Paso, downhill on El Paso, uphill on Lovers Lane, uphill on Cañon to Soda Springs Park and 'Toids. *"Over the hills and through the woods, to Manitou Springs I go."*

~~~

Four and a half hours or so from 'Toids, just over three and three-quarters in a Ferrari, from inside a stone-roofed, brick garage, next to Snowmass Creek in Pitkin County, Colorado, arises a thunder more heart stopping than most people have ever heard. Formula One engineered and tested, twelve cylinders effortlessly roar to life, and gradually roll down to a surly growl. After a few minutes, white reverse lights flash on, and a slightly dusty Nürburgring Gray 599 GTB Fiorano backs out of its protective dark cave, into the mist.

~~~

After maté and a quick read of last Thursday's *Colorado Springs Independent* at 'Toids, I spend several hours riding around Manitou, at least where steep mountainside streets aren't going to kill me, stopping to visit friends. After pedaling back to Sleeping Bear Oasis, I check email, heart thumping—*nada.*

I commence building a huge pot of buffalo-vegetable stew, and after almost an hour and a half, leave it to simmer—while I return to the office to check email. Hearing unusual noise out front, I pad wool sock footed to the living room and look outside. *Nada.* I go back to the office. A few minutes later, the front door chime chimes.

I am not in the mood for a door-to-door anyone right now, so I ignore it. Another chime. Okay, do I see who it is, or ignore it? Maybe it's a neighbor. Maybe it's one of my circle of friends. Maybe
~~~

it's Agent Ballard. Whoa, cancel that thought. Ding-dong.

The screen door glass partitions are open wide to let in cool, moist air, filled with crisp Sleeping Bear garden fragrances—making it a bit difficult to pretend no one is home—not to mention the scent of my delicious stewing. Haydn also flourishes from the kitchen.

"Matt? Matt, are you here?" It's a voice I recognize.

Chapter Fifty-Four: Scion

The straps of that beautiful woven bag in both hands, her arms dangling from drooped shoulders, Wynne looks a little worn, but her hair shines as usual. As soon as she sees me, she looks down. My hopeful heart drops through my stomach, on its way down to somewhere around my knees.

She's wearing an above-knee, pleated jean skirt; the leather sandals she wore when we first met at the Little Nell; a delicately lightweight, barely pink crew neck cashmere sweater; and a simple silver chain bearing a tiny heart with a pearl mounted in the center. Wynne de Gracia, as usual, is stunningly gorgeous, although her sandy blonde hair is a bit windblown, and falling out of its bun.

As I pad up to the door, she still looks down. Finally she raises her head just a little. Sheepish eyes look up at me. My heart shatters. Without saying a word, I hold the door open. She silently comes inside.

"Mine is a shoes-free home. Would you mind removing yours?"

"No, of course not." She sits down on the pine foyer bench to pull off her sandals, sliding them under the seat next to my several pairs of shoes. "Thank you for seeing me."

"You're welcome, of course, though I am a little surprised." My head jerks upright as the source of the snarl I heard earlier penetrates my mind—I glance out the front door. In my old, cracked, narrow cement driveway is Fiorio, dull from traveling over rainy roads, and pockmarked from the sprinkle that's just starting.

"I hope you don't mind. I parked in your driveway."

"Not at all. That would be the first ever *real* Ferrari to rest in my driveway. I'm honored."

"Oh, come on. It's just a car." She looks up a little, but still her eyes won't meet mine.

I kneel down at her feet, place my hands on her ankles, and gaze up. She looks into my eyes, with tiny round tears beginning a tedious crawl down her face.

"Matt, I'm really sorry. I didn't mean to hurt you."

"Wynne, I'm not sure what to say. I'm leery of saying anything at all."

She looks down at the only slightly soiled light tan throw rug. "I understand."

I reach up, tenderly put my left hand under her chin, and lift her face back to where we can see each other's eyes. "It's okay, Wynne. I'm really happy to see you."

The corners of her lips upturn a tiny bit. She moves her woven bag from her lap to the bench seat and, hesitatingly, puts her arms around my neck. Her hands dangle behind my back.

I wrap my hands around her forearms. "I just wish I didn't care so much. I'm confused."

She starts to pull her arms back, but I hold them right where they are. She relaxes, and loosely clasps her hands behind my head. "It probably won't help much, Matt, but I'm confused too. I'm scared. I don't know what to do. But I can't stand having you mad at me, or hurt. I'm so sorry, Matt—I'm so sorry."

"Wynne…." I'm not about to call her sweetie again, at least not yet. "…It's all right, really." She pulls me closer, so my head rests on a soft, cashmere shoulder. I take a few more careful words. "Except for one thing, that is." Her breathing stops. "I need to get out of this position or my legs are going to fall asleep."

She allows a restrained chuckle. "Oh Matt, it's so good to see you." She tightens her grip to hold me hard against her. I smell her hair. I smell her skin. Cashmere is making my stubbly face itch. She releases her grip. I take a little time there, my nose snuggled into the nape of her neck, and wrap my arms around her waist. Squeezing, I visualize my masculinity merging with her femininity, our two bubbles of energy, our two magnetic fields, becoming one. She squeezes back. We stay there, silent, holding each other, until I let go to get up.

I take her hand and lead her to my wool, camelback loveseat, facing the fireplace.

"Is that one of your abstracts?"

"Yes, it is. That's my current *coup de maître* work. Do you like it?"

"It's stunning."

"You're just saying that."

"I'm absolutely serious. It's really good. You've adeptly applied several techniques, and the image immediately captures the imagination. It draws me in and entices me to look deeply. I'd be proud to have it in my living room."

"Wow! Thank you. That's quite a compliment, coming from you."

I watch her face fall from smiling to horrified.

I take her hand again. She doesn't resist. "No. Perhaps I misspoke. What I meant is that I have come to know and respect your artistic sensibilities. I'm grateful that, with your experience and superb taste, you like the piece so much." I hesitate, think it through, and add, "I love it, too, Wynne. I feel it's the best work I've ever done."

"Why don't you frame it?" It's an excellent question.

"It's a challenge to come up with a way to mount it. It's an odd large size, and because it's on vellum, it's actually extremely fragile. And I want it to hang free. I'll get to it someday."

"Is it for sale?"

"Um, well, yes and no."

"What does that mean?"

"It means that I might sell it to the right person, but at $27,547 I doubt anyone will purchase it."

"I'll buy it. Why wouldn't anyone buy it? It's great! Why the unusual price?"

"The price is the cost of my Master's degree. I call it *36 months*. It represents the ecstasy and agony of the three intense years I spent earning that degree and then having my fledgling career as a library director destroyed by—um, perhaps not the greatest library trustees—and by my own exhausted persona with too little fight left. I don't think anyone will purchase it because the price is so high. I'd be embarrassed for you to buy it. I'd rather make it a gift to you."

"You would do that?"

"Of course I would."

"Matt...." She pulls me to her side. "...I know you're being honest, as usual. I'm flattered—relieved—and grateful."

"So would you like the penny tour?"

"Penny tour?"

"Well, there's not that much to see. I can't really charge a nickel."

She chuckles through mineral deposit remnants of dried tears.

"Matt, the garden alone would take an hour. Give yourself credit, love."

My hopeful heart rockets up to my throat.

Chapter Fifty-Five: Life Does Indeed Go On

"Each level is 1100 square feet." Grinning, I sweep my left arm around the room. "This is the living room. One of my favorite things is a picnic in winter, in front of the fireplace."

"Ooo, that sounds romantic." She gets up from the loveseat to look at the secretary. Her fingers run over the wood inlay. "This is nice."

"It's a reproduction, but I do love that scene. The consensus is that it's Italian, but no one has recognized the village—maybe it's fictitious."

"It's really quite lovely." She walks over to sit in Dad's rocker.

"It was my father's. He passed away ten years ago, and my Mom two years ago."

"I'm sorry, Matt."

"It's okay. You know, they were both ready. Part of the reason they were so hard on me is that they had difficult childhoods and lives, too. I suppose they did the best they could. The rocker dates from somewhere around 1900. I think it came from my grandmother, but I never thought to ask Dad. Too often, people are gone before we realize they might be."

"Like Browner."

I offer a reverent nod. "Like Browner."

"This lamp is really unique." It's the reading lamp beside Dad's rocker. "Is it all wood?"

"Yes, except for the harp, of course. I'm not sure what type of wood it is, but it looks similar to the mahogany of one of my guitars."

"*One* of your guitars?"

"I have four."

"Four?"

"One for each hand."

She laughs. "Where are they? Will you play me something?"

"Sure. Come with me."

We walk down the hall, hand in hand. It's a short hallway, and I don't want to let go.

"This is the guest room. The dresser stores art supplies, and under the bed I keep my prints and drawings—the house is stuffed so full that I have very few places to store items flat."

"So you're going to show me your work, right?"

"We'll see."

She squeezes my hand with a strong grip. "Come on, Matt. I know what 'We'll see' means—I *am* a mom."

"We'll see. The next room is my studio."

Reluctantly, I let go her hand, but only so I can open the Martin case. I lift out my favorite guitar, sit on the stool and play a G scale up the ebony fret board and back down, then launch into one my songs. "This one is about finding a love you never want to leave. Like most love songs, I suppose." I proceed to knock out the best rendition ever.

"That was really good, Matt. You wrote that?"

"Yes, and I'm still and working on it. I want it to be perfect for you."

"Knock it off."

I laugh, and set the guitar in the stand facing my Acoustic amp. I reach for her hand and pull her out of the rocking chair—the only chair in the studio.

"But I want more."

"After dinner, okay?"

"Well, alright," whines a familiar four year old.

"The office."

"It's very professional. Three printers?"

"One for each hand."

She chuckles.

"Bathroom."

"Two vanity sinks. Nice. Oh, and I love these double towel rods. Great color combinations, too—I love the occasional reds."

"Good *Feng Shui*—fire to balance the water."

She nods like an old pro. "And the houseplants—wood to be nourished by the water—like you and me."

I smile like a proud teacher. "You got it, girl."

We head on down the hall. "The kitchen is relatively small, but totally serviceable. Our dinner is on the stove."

"So I've noticed. What are you making?"

"It's a buffalo and veggie stew: local, grass-fed bison; turnips, carrots, Hopi Gold squash and garbanzo beans from my garden; greens and onions from the farmer's market; and oregano, basil, and rosemary, also from my garden."

"Matt-food—I can't wait." She walks over to the picture window. "Nice view. That's Pikes Peak?"

"Yes, and Manitou straight across the valley."

"You're right in the foothills. This is sweet, Matt."

"Thank you. Downstairs is a family room—that's where the rarely used TV and video setup lives. There's a utility room, a furnace room, and the master bedroom suite."

"That you're not going to show me?"

"The last girl I showed the entire house to never came back. Now I'm bit shy about making anyone uncomfortable."

"Her loss—hopefully, my gain. It *is* your job to make me comfortable, you know."

The garden tour takes less than a half hour, though as a precaution I turn down the heat on the stew before we go out into feminine rain. Wynne loves everything she sees. There's no affectation, no flattery, no guile, and no pretense—just the Wynne I had fallen in love with. Am still firmly and completely in love with.

"So, are you ready for stew?"

"Yes, sir, I am. Actually I'm famished. All I had for breakfast was goat yogurt with dried cherries, and maté with coconut milk and maple syrup—all organic of course." Her eyes smile. "My wonderful life coach taught me how to eat like that. He taught me a very great deal, actually."

"Flattery will get you everywhere with me." I slip my arms around her waist, and kiss her tenderly—though briefly.

~~~

After our scrumptious stew sprinkled with paprika and goat feta, we sit on the deck and sip filtered water, with a squeeze of lime and a dash of organic pomegranate juice. I point out Red Rock Canyon to the south, and the west face of Cheyenne Mountain, where Gold Camp Road used to join Old Colorado City with gold ore from Cripple Creek. The trees and shrubs all around us are filled with ecstatic birds. Wynne's happy. So am I.
~~~

"Why do you call this place Sleeping Bear Oasis? I understand the oasis part, because you have definitely created an Eden at the edge of the city. But, where does Sleeping Bear enter the picture?"

"Look at the red sandstone formation over in the northwest corner."

"Yes?"

"Look closely."

She stares for a little while, and then turns to me. "I'm not following."

I point, even though it's impolite. "Look at the top of the formation. Let your eyes start at the closer end, and then follow the top to the north end. The bear's head is resting on the very south edge here, and you can see his body lounging on top of the rock, with all four legs lying under and behind him. He's just sleeping there."

"Oh my God! Matt! I see it! That's incredible! It looks just like a huge bear. That's so unusual!"

With rain now steadily increasing toward downpour stage, the tin roof over the deck starts to leak. We scurry inside. She seats herself at the kitchen table.

"Can I get you another drink? Or would you like anything else?"

"Another of these wonderful concoctions would be perfect!"

I cut another lime, squeeze a half into each glass, pour in a quarter cup of pomegranate juice, and this time fill the glasses to three-quarters full with sparkling Manitou mineral water from the Twin Spring. After adding four drops of chlorophyll to each glass, a couple of ice cubes are laid lightly into each. I hand the golden Tesuque glass to Wynne, pick up my smaller blue and purple glass, and lean against the kitchen counter, smiling, looking at the beautiful woman sitting at my 1970s Formica table—someone who, like, really, really likes me. This is a different outcome than I had imagined a few days ago—and for some reason, it's not surrealistic. It feels more like the last piece of a jigsaw puzzle fell into place, effortlessly—or no, this is like the spirit of life intended. No puzzle has been finished. The water has simply always been this calm and warm—a perfect temperature for an extended swim.

"These are Tesuque glasses, aren't they?"

"You've a good eye, girl."

"Thank you." She stands up, reaches over to take my hand, and leads me back into the living room. It's almost seven o'clock now. I'm secretly wondering about the length of her visit. I don't want to ask—not wanting to learn that she will drive back to Aspen this evening. The flip side, however, is that probability favors her staying right here: Why force the return trip to Aspen in the dark night of a New Moon in its midlife? She sits us both down on the loveseat, keeping my hand by her hip so that I sit right beside her.

"Matt, thank you for the water conservation research. It turns...."

"I'm sorry I butted in. When Cassie mentioned her idea to me, I thought it might be worth researching. It was a mistake to intrude—and a lesson learned."

Wynne smiles, her eyes absolutely radiant. I'm not making this up. Sometimes, these are fleeting moments. Other times, like this right now, we realize that life, our living of it, has been and is always this way.

"Matt? Matt? Where did you go? I want to be there, too."

My eyes remain in hers. "Ah, my dear, I've been so deeply enjoying our togetherness that I took a little side trip."

"Where?"

"Into a state of grace."

"A state of grace."

"I'll describe as best I can. Haven't you experienced a moment or two when it seems like everything is perfect? Just—perfect. A moment of ecstasy—where everything fits together just right and you know it—you're right there in it. You are it."

"Wow. Where *is* the wine cabinet?"

"Hahahaha. Haha. I'm sorry—waxing poetic, I guess."

"If that's your poetry, I can't wait to see your art."

"Hahahaha. Haha. Hah. Oh jeez. You're great, girl. You—are—just—great." I throw my arms around her and give her a bear hug, spilling some of my limagranate.

"Yuuuugh."

I let go the hug as my lips leap to hers. My eyes close. I kiss her long, with energy and fullness of heart, mind, and body, letting my spirit merge with hers. When I begin to lighten up, I pull back a little, and she follows me, her lips finding mine. I nuzzle her sweet, sweet neck. I smell behind her ear. "Well, I've spilt my drink."

She bursts out laughing, and playfully pushes me away. I set my glass onto the August 13 *New Yorker* on the coffee table, and wipe my hand on my khaki cargo shorts.

"Now *that* was a kiss."

"Let's do more of that."

"Let's do."

"Now that was a kiss," she says, mimicking, but not mocking me.

"Where were we?"

It's a sweet Wynne smile. "Well, if you'll let me finish, I can say that as it turns out, a conservation easement may be the perfect solution. Gregg Kearny, my Aspen legal counsel, is looking into it. We could save the water, and probably the valley."

I start to talk, but she stops me—lightly touching my lips with an index finger.

"I owe you an apology. Well, several, actually. I reacted badly to your involvement with Cassie regarding the easement idea. Every man in my life, except Dad, has either tried to "help," or attempted outright control of my management of de Gracia affairs. These days I resent that so much that I overreacted to what you were doing.

"Cassie, by the way, minced no words regarding my accusation that you flirted with her. She allowed me to realize that was a stupefying slap in not just your face, but also hers. She's absolutely right."

"Thank you, Wynne. I have a few things to say, too."

She stops me with a raised hand. "There's more I need to get off my chest. Please? When I'm finished, you can take a turn, if you still want to."

"Deal."

"You know that I was raised in a loving family. I never experienced people willing to lie or connive and contrive their way into, or out of, your heart and life—not even in school. I'm not saying my ex-husband did that. With him, I simply had no idea that two people wouldn't get along famously, or that they could have separate interests that keep them apart; or that anybody can love something more than each other.

"For years after my marriage ended, I felt unbearably alone. I've always had the closeness of family—love and devotion from those who care for you with all their heart. I raised Cassie by myself. I dated a few men here and there, but they weren't able to reach my soul. I need togetherness. I need to be touched, and to spend time together, laughing, crying, and being happy. I want a soul mate to hold hands with. Having money, though, is tough. Once people find out, they get weird or want things. I'm still astonished at how people are willing to use others. I just was not raised that way, and, I suppose

I lived a more sheltered life than I thought.

"Patrick came along and gave me what I didn't get in my marriage, or from anyone else I knew. It wasn't weird. But after a year or so, I began to see that we had very little in common. Internally he was vacant, or absent. In his superficially giving me what I needed, I was moved to enable *his* fullness—not *our* fullness, as a couple."

Wynne lets go my hand, and reaches for her glass. She takes a big drink, puts the glass back down on the end-slash-coffee table, and takes my hand again. She turns to face me on the loveseat and places our hands in her lap.

"So, please accept my most heartfelt apology for my temporary insanities. Please also keep in mind, however, that I am prone to these attacks from time to time. They often erupt without much warning, and I'm told medical research has yet to discover any effective treatment, let alone a cure."

I chuckle and knowingly nod my head. "Let me know when *that* cure is found. How about a fire?"

"Oh, that would be nice."

I get up and light the seven candles that always sit on the grate in the fireplace. "It's nice to have a little fire on a rainy, early September evening." I return to my designated seat, and put an arm around her—on top of the loveseat.

"The candles are nice. At first I thought it a bit kitsch, and now I have to say they look and feel like a fire—if you know what I mean."

"I do, Wynne, I do. It's all in the intention."

After another long drink, she sets her golden, hand-blown glass down on the coffee table, reaches over, without saying a word, and takes my glass from my hand to set it down, right next to hers. She turns toward me, one leg cocked into the loveseat. Déjà vu. I move closer to her, and take her hands in mine.

We speak at the same time. "Wynne...." "Matt...." Then we laugh at the same time.

"You first." "You first." More laughter.

I jump. "Wynne, I'm really happy you've come to see me." I squeeze her hands. "I've missed you so much."

"Matt, wait."

"Wynne, I need to say this. I want you to know how I really feel. I haven't been completely honest with you."

"But, I need to tell you...."

"I have to say this. Hear me out, please."

With a shrug, she gives in.

"When I first heard your voice on the phone, I loved it and couldn't wait to meet you. When I saw you walking toward me in the Little Nell, I thought I was dreaming. You were stunning. Gorgeous. Sexy. I was instantly and overwhelmingly attracted to you. Well, I was attracted the moment I first heard your voice. I've wanted you since before I even met you. I tried to not want you, because I was there in the capacity of life coach."

She rolls her eyes.

Undaunted, I continue. "It wasn't appropriate, but I couldn't help myself. Then, as we spent more and more time together, I traveled well beyond physical attraction, beyond immediate infatuation."

She smiles, squeezes my hands, and then eases her grip.

"I like absolutely everything about you. Well, you seem to overreact a little from time to time." Her smile changes to a frown. "Hey, you *know* I understand. I overreact, too. Remember the trip into Santa Fe from the airport? Or my ridiculous attempt to hitchhike back to Colorado? You're sincere, authentic, intelligent—well, I've said all this to you before. My mind hasn't changed at all."

I gaze into those gray-green eyes—her soul blazes out.

"Wynne, I'm in love with you. I love you. I've loved you since the beginning." Her eyes open wide. "Had I been truly honest, I would have told you before now. I know you're aware of the reasons why I didn't, but I should have. I can be a little secretive."

She snickers endearingly.

"I jump to conclusions too quickly. I see things that don't exist, and often make a bigger deal of stuff than I need to." Even I can tell I'm starting to ramble. "The bottom line is, I love you. I'm head over heels, not hopelessly but hopefully yours, regardless what happens next. Though I hope what happens next is a classic love story where we live happily ever after."

She looks down at our hands together, picks them up and shakes them gently for a moment. "Is it my turn now?"

"Depends on what you're going to say."

She smiles, and leans toward me, slowly tilting her head. It's a sweet, tender, lingering kiss. Our lips explore each other's softly, caressingly—love's language of communication, connection, and grace. She sits back up, our hands still together.

"I love you, too, Matt."

My endocrine system floods me with ecstasy. I have to be careful—I may not have so many of my nine tiger lives left.

"When I first met you, I was intrigued. I found you to be smart, handsome, and fun. You were willing to share intimate details about yourself—including flaws—without even knowing me. You really were genuinely interested in *me*, wanted to truly get to know *me*—and wanted me to know *you*. I don't know if that's been rare in my life, or if perhaps I've always taken complete and honest connectedness with another for granted—and have assumed it was there when in fact it may not have been. But the day I really knew I was falling for you was in the pasture, when you encouraged me to cry, to grieve, to let it out. You held me tight, and I felt so safe, so supported, so loved. I just kept falling deeper after that. I tried to show you, but it seemed you didn't want to respond."

I start to speak, but it's Wynne's turn—she puts a finger to my lips.

"I agree with you—we've been over these events. I think we both know and understand each other—and love each other. I've felt that from you from the moment you answered the door today. Your spirit reached right out and gathered me into your arms."

She lets go of only one hand, and stands, leaning away to pull me along. "There's something we need to do now."

She leads me through the kitchen, and down the Berber carpeted stairs into the tiger's den. I lean in front of her to push open the French doors to the master bedroom. This suite of rooms is cool, private, with its own energy, distinct from the rest of the house. I close the doors behind us. Pulling me along, Wynne takes us to the side of the bed. She hasn't said a word. Neither have I. I reach to pull the covers back.

She slowly unbuttons my shirt, and runs her fingers up and down my chest. I lean into her and kiss her tenderly. My lips envelop her upper lip, and in semicircular motions, massage that soft cushion from left to right, and then I move to the bottom lip. Wynne's arms, wrapped around me, squeeze me tight and close. I kiss up her cheek to her left ear, before gently moving to her forehead. With slow, tiny kisses, I move across each eyebrow, and then toward her right ear, where I kiss the lobe lightly, before taking it between my lips. I kiss down and up, then behind her ears. My lips move to her neck. Man, I love this neck. She presses against me, and I slide an arm slowly down her back to the small of her back and the sacrum, pulling her strong against me. Both her hands are behind my neck and in my hair, pulling my head into that little crease, just underneath the jaw. Our lips meet once again, and we kiss hard now. She responds, her lips parting just a little. Only the tips of our tongues meet for a slow dance.

She leans away, and I slowly pull that delicate, pink cashmere sweater up, and then over Wynne's golden waves. I watch every millimeter of her being uncovered. She slips out of her sports bra. With my arm under her waist, I lay her gently down on the bed, and starting at her feet, slowly stroke her legs bottom to top, inside and outside, letting my hands glide up under that faded jean skirt.

Leaving one hand on her left leg, with two fingertips of my right hand I stroke up and down her neck, below her ear, then move up to kiss her soft lips again, lingering long to savor our energies entwining. As I begin kissing down the front of her neck, her head arches back. I pull her skirt up toward her waist as she raises herself, and my fingertips caress the whiteness of smooth inner thigh. I look up. Her eyes are closed, and she's smiling—lips slightly parted. I slide closer to her, kissing her chest, all around her breasts, then down her abdomen, and slowly pull her skirt down her legs, over her feet, and drop it to the carpet.

My left hand caresses between her legs, just barely touching her, from bottom to top over wet panties, and then both hands slide slowly around to the sides, and little by little drag them down her legs, and off her feet. A hand on each inner thigh, I pull her legs apart, and start kissing first the tops of her feet, then her ankles, then her shins, and inside her calves, the backs of her knees, and up each inner thigh. Wynne moans quietly, and begins to writhe, almost imperceptibly at first, as I lay my chest into her pelvis and kiss her belly. She moans while strong hips begin writhing more intensely against me. I raise myself, and move down to kiss those creases where the pelvis meets her legs. Gently at first, then with more pressure, both her hands pull at the back of my head, pulling me into her mound, as she starts moving with my kisses. My tongue explores every millimeter.

I move slowly and more tenderly for a few minutes, letting my fingers softly stroke her thighs and legs. She starts pressing up into my tongue again, and I slide my hands under her, grabbing firm butt cheeks in both hands, and start moving her with my arm strength, faster and faster, until she writhes in time with my hands, now rocking her whole body under my mouth. Her hands clasp my head—she lets out a high-pitched hum as her whole body begins quaking and shuddering non-stop. I keep going this time, harder and faster, rocking her body with my hands under her, and not slowing down until her quivering begins to subside. I stay there, kissing gently, until she pulls me up on top of her.

She whispers, "It's your turn," and rolls us over so she's on top of me, and slips me inside her. She starts slowly and gently, too, moving with just the tiniest forward and back motions. With both hands, I stroke the curves of her waist, and then in perfect time with her rhythms, let my hands glide over her butt, her sides, her back, her arms, and her shoulders. I begin to feel the buildup of energy in my body, the thrill of release on its way. I start rocking with her, arching my back and pelvis far off the bed, hard against her. As she responds stronger and stronger, I reach up to cup her breasts, rubbing with light pressure in rhythm to her on top of me, and lean up to kiss, and lick, and take her between my lips. I can feel it coming: the release, the volcanic explosion. Wynne's moaning is coming faster and faster; she's moving with me in delirious fury. She starts a quiet scream: "Ohhhh!" I arch into her, both our bodies wriggling and writhing in ecstasy, and press into her with all my strength as we both shudder and shake for minutes, until slowly I lay back down, pulling her close on top of me, my arms around her, holding her tight.

~ ~ ~

We linger for a brief eternity, wrapped around one other under pastel yellow sheets, while birds outside, and Verdito and Gizmo upstairs, create an orchestral sunset suite. We touch, caress, kiss, and smile. Caressing, kissing, stroking, gazing into each other's eyes— these are truths that will not belie intent. What we feel is real, not merely a moment of physical passion but a drama of love for one another, of desire to bring us together into blissful rapture. This is gestalt: the crowning perfection of creation, an ultimate, intimate harmony of harmonies.

Chapter Fifty-Six: What, No Lasagna?

"May I buy you breakfast, love?"

"I cherish hearing you say that."

"What?" It's a quiet grin. "That I want to buy you breakfast?"

My face relaxes into a soft smile. Shaking my head back and forth, I say, " 'Love.' Don't be so enticing, sweet lady, unless you never want to leave this bed."

"I don't."

I slip a leg over her, and with a downy touch, use the index and middle fingers of my right hand to trace her eyebrows, cheekbones, nose and lips. My open fingers carefully comb wavy hair, as she closes those gray-green mirrors. Softly, I suggest, "Then don't."

"Well, we do need to eat sometimes—but you may never be able to get rid of me now. I feel treasured."

My lips caress her neck. I slide them up under her ear, kiss the lobe, run the tip of my nose around her ear and kiss back down the side of her neck into that exquisite, silk nape. "I love you." We kiss gently, sensually, and, enduringly—when an empty tiger belly growls.

"Okay," she says, grinning—giving me a mischievous shove. "…Back to the having breakfast thing."

"Be that way!" I sit up, pouting—then turn swiftly and jump back on top of her. We laugh, and try to keep each other from getting out of bed first, until she wins by pinning my head under her princess pillow. I stuff that big, fluffy, solid core pillow on top of my thin, firm posture pillow to gaze contentedly as Wynne performs a nude *glissade* around the bed, and away toward the bathroom. Once she's around the corner, I get up too. In maroon boxer shorts and a threadbare, sky blue Bear Butte t-shirt—my pajamas—I begin my morning stretching routine until she comes out from the bathroom.

"I need to get a few things from the car. I'll be right back. May I borrow your robe?"

"Sure. Later you can choose from a few spares in the guest room."

"Thanks, love."

"Have I mentioned how much I enjoy hearing you say that?"

"I don't recall. Did you?"

From my squat, Stretching the Bow stance, my right palm graces her firm butt with the faintest slap as she passes by me to pull my robe from the near end of the wardrobe.

As she returns, she shoves me over and runs, giggling, out the French doors. Pushing my upper torso from the carpet, I move back into my squat, a brief Crow, and then flow though Downward-facing Dog, *Chaturanga Dandasanga*, into Upward-facing Dog, pushing back again into Downward-facing Dog, and then jump my feet to my hands, with a Reverse Swan Dive into an extended spine, with a reverse bend—"ahhhh"—straighten, take eight final breaths with arms swinging and crossing above my head. I watch birds at the feeders, take one more deep, life-giving breath, and stride tall into the master bath to brush my teeth with alkalizing toothpaste.

Wynne reopens the French doors carrying a smallish bag. "May I use six or seven hangars?"

"Please. Spares are at the far end of the lower rod. Take as much room as you need." I restart my routine from the beginning. Wynne says nothing until I again perform Stretching the Bow.

"Is that a martial art form?"

"Not really, though several of these poses do resemble that. My routine is comprised of *Pal Dan Gum* and Yoga poses."

"Pal Dan Gum?"

"A set of Asian exercises—supposedly Taoist. At some workshop or another many years ago, I was given a handout with drawings of the seven positions. Since then, I've researched to know more, but never found any information at all."

"You look like a warrior—I think I'm getting turned on."

Jumping at her from my pose, I pick her up and toss her on the queen bed. As I jump to land on top of her, she rolls out of the way, giggling.

"Enough play, boy—we need to get food into your belly."

"There's plenty of time for eating. Come back here, you." I reach, and she hops off the end of the bed.

Hands on her hips, I get the mean mommy look. "I'm going for a shower—then we're having breakfast."

~~~

"Josh!"

The door jingles closed. He strolls over to my table.

"Hey, Matt." We high-five, then fist bump. He looks down at my plate.

"Yep, already finished my toast. This is Wynne de Gracia." I lay an open, supine palm toward my sweetie, sitting across from me—so our eyes can slow dance, while bare feet stroke one another's legs under the table.

Josh doesn't say a word. He looks back at me, eyes wide.

His head turns back to Wynne. She extends her hand. "It's a pleasure to meet you, Josh. I've heard about you, you know."

He shakes her hand like she's made of fine, hand-blown glass. "Well, it's not true."

She chuckles. "I can see it's pretty accurate, Josh. Besides, Matt doesn't lie."

"Yeah? Sure he does." He turns to me. "All the time."

Always gracious, Wynne asks, "Would you care to join us?"

He looks back to her. "Nah, I can't—already late to set stage at Pikes Peak Center." He looks at me. "Besides, Dude ate my toast."

He goes to the self-serve to fill his stainless travel mug, and puts two bucks in the tip jar—those in the know bring their own drinking vessel.

"Glad to see you in good spirits, young man." We fist bump. He turns to Wynne, and reaches for another handshake. "And I can see why. It's a pleasure to meet you, Wynne." He bows. "I really am late. Catch you later." With a hand wave from behind his head, Josh dings out the door.

'Toid's bell rings as we depart to embrace a sweet, cool, damp late morning. The sun is still low, and thunderheads are only beginning to bud along the foothills tips. We take a brief Manitou Springs walking tour. Wynne surprises me by tossing me the key as we approach Fiorio. I recognize the fob from the ranch bulletin board.

I search into her eyes. "Are you serious?"

"I'd like to have the auto tour now. We've got, what, all day? You should be able to provide the hundred dollar tour, right?"

"In Fiorio, my dear, I can give you a tour of Boulder and be back here in two hours. But I promise to keep him under one-sixty."
~~~

From Manitou we sprint south over 26th Street—not, of course, for the hill climb curves on 26th; it's just the longest way. We dip down through Bear Creek Park and onto Cresta. I turn down Cheyenne Road and take Mayhurst—not, of course, for the hill climb curves; it's just the longest way.

"These are very expensive homes."

"The Broadmoor is one of the oldest and finest residential areas in the county, created around 1890, by Silesian Count James M. Pourtales. He laid out the meandering, genteel subdivision himself. Pourtales also established many Broadmoor traditions, including a men's cooking club and land for polo fields. And back in the day, a casino."

"You know I want to see more than signs of opulence, right?"

"Oh, of course. It's just…this area is gorgeous, and I simply must drive Fiorio down Sycamore—around my favorite, fast car curves. When in college, I drove it nearly every day in my old Datsun roadster. Numerous times each winter, I four-wheel drifted him through seven inches of fresh, untouched powder. 'Course, we don't get snows like that anymore."

"Datsun roadster?"

"Precursor to the Datsun Z sports cars. Similar to the early British roadsters: Triumph, MG, and the like."

"Okay. I'm not sure I've ever seen one."

"When we get back to the Oasis, I'll show you some photos. Fiorio has a twin up here, and about a half dozen fathers and uncles."

"Looking at these residences I don't doubt that."

We rumble past the old Broadmoor Hotel, turn onto Pourtales, take the right onto Westgate and then shoot up Cheyenne Mountain Boulevard to Marland Road South. Well, it's not a shot—I keep Fiorio at a canter because of the speed bumps. They need to be there. Not for me, but for the *other people*.

"I was fortunate to live in that house," I say with a head nod, "for the five years of my undergraduate university career. The back yard is the twelfth fairway of the Broadmoor South course."

"Five years?"

"I enjoyed a beautiful place to live and study, and took advantage of an opportunity to expand my collegiate experience. I took essentially enough Letters, Arts, and Sciences that I could have graduated with a double degree."

"You never cease to provide me with surprises."

"Good to hear. I like it that way."

Fiorio growls as we wind through Pine, Thayer, Upland, and Plainview to Penrose Boulevard, where I turn into North Cheyenne Canyon. A Nürburgring Gray, Ferrari 599 GTB snarls up the twisting pavement to Helen Hunt Falls.

"Fiorio sounds very, very serious up here. It's not just the canyon and all these granite walls. He sounds mean enough to have all the black bears running the other direction."

"When Cassie and I went to Manarello to finalize the purchase, we were offered a modified exhaust silencer planned for the 599 HGTE. It produces, as you put it, a "meaner" sound. I totally get it—you chose today's tour route not to impress me with the neighborhood, but to control my horse like the thoroughbred he was born to be."

"I hope you don't mind. I don't think I've pushed any limits at all—though you haven't been along when I'm driving a racecar."

"Not to worry, love. You handle him like you did *Wambli Gleska*—with smooth, precise, graceful mastery. Like last night."

"Please repeat that—a little closer to the microphone."

She leans over, whispering into my closed fist. "Like last night." She then kisses my fingers and slips one into that inviting mouth. I'm having an immediate reaction....

"Yeah, baby. Got it on tape now. Hey, let's take a hike up Helen Hunt Falls—oh, but we probably shouldn't leave Fiorio."

"It's just a car, Matt."

"Yeah, right. Just a car."

"I want to go up the falls—look, there are even stairs. Pull over—pull over."

"Okay. You don't have to convince me. I love water—almost as much as you."

"So I understand."

We hike up steep, plentiful wooden stairs to the top of Helen Hunt Falls, climbing and relaxing on boulders around and in Cheyenne Creek. On the drive back down into Colorado Springs, I stop so we can check for apples on the oldest apple tree I'm aware of in the county. They're freakin' incredible. And not yet ripe.

"How 'bout Mexican for lunch?"

"You know I'm always up for that."

"I want to go to Vallejo's with you. It's my favorite. I've been eating there since I was eighteen."

"So, that's what, ten years ago?"

"Girl, as you know, flattery will get you everywhere with me—you're taking advantage." I turn my nose up and away. "If you don't stop I'll have to smile."

She laughs, and lays her hand on my thigh, leaving it there for the sixteen minutes it takes us to turn north onto South Corona to Vallejo's.

~~~

"Thank you for bringing me here. It reminds me of growing up at the New Mexico ranch. This is freshly prepared, exceptionally clean tasting, old world Mexican. I'm impressed—again. Will you ever stop impressing me?"

"I'm not trying to impress you."

"I suppose you just can't help yourself."

I chuckle *con mucho gusto*. We laugh, and I get up to pay the bill at the counter. I holler through the window to the kitchen. "Thanks, Lydia." She comes out to give me a hug, wiping her hands on an apron soiled by what will be a twelve-hour day.

"We don't see you enough these days, Matt."

"I know. *Lo siento*. I'm trying to drum up business."

"I understand," she replies, nodding. "This economy is terrible. And doesn't seem like it will ever get better. Philip works around the clock to find new customers. Who is that you're with? A new girl?" Not waiting for me to answer, she strides over to our table—I follow.

"I'm Lydia. Matt's been coming here for years, but he's never brought such a pretty lady."

"Thank you. I'm Wynne."

"You going to take care of my boy, here?"

"He seems capable of taking care of himself, but I might make him an offer or two."

She turns to me, and pats me on the cheek. "He's a good boy. You can't go wrong."

"Of that I'm sure."

I'm standing here not turning red.

Lydia says, "It's nice to meet you." She extends her hand and two of my favorite women shake each other's hand.

After lunch we indulge in a menacing-sounding Palmer Park tour, stop at the lookout, and climb from the Ferrari so I can point out some history. "Over here to the right is the University of Colorado campus, my undergraduate alma mater."
~~~

"Where you graduated with honors in business."

"You're getting to know me too well. From here on, I'm gonna be more careful what I say—or post on Facebook or my website."

She punches me in the arm. Girl packs a wallop.

"See the formal, almost gothic stone towers in the downtown area? Where all the tallest trees are?"

"They look like churches?"

"Precisely. The tallest is Grace Episcopal. The closer one is Shove Chapel—on the Colorado College campus."

"Cassie's been considering studying pre-law there. We haven't visited the campus, though."

"It's an awesome college, and I guarantee the most prestigious law schools are quite familiar with CC graduates. We'll cruise through there next."

"Why didn't you attend?"

"In fact, I was offered that opportunity by a CC trustee, but one of my CU mentors—a Harvard D.B.A.—suggested I might find the undergrad degree from one of the nations top public Colleges of Business more immediately useful. Being a pragmatic critter, I followed his recommendation."

"How very Capricorn of you."

I respond with a hearty chuckle.

"I had no idea Colorado Springs is so big."

"The population is approaching six hundred thousand, especially if you include folks from surrounding communities. Personally, I think it's sad. When I grew up here, this was a paradise of 70,000 people. Nowadays it's overrun with folks who come here for the beauty, and then have little or no respect for that very grandeur." My melodramatic arm sweeps across the 280-degree vista. "This urban sprawl demonstrates both a lack of consideration for efficiency, and even less preparation or vision for the future—but I suppose that's merely one man's opinion."

It's the disapproving mommy look. I understand—mommies can't help themselves once they've mastered the craft. Besides, it's endearing as can be.

"*Lo siento*. I do still get cynical. But just by looking at voting results for the last ten years and more, it's clear that most current residents, especially I suspect, recent arrivals and the transient military population, don't open their hearts, not to mention their wallets, for even a pittance of a tax to help preserve and maintain the area—let alone restore the damage they've done. So I'm not sure what I'm expressing is cynicism.

"We all, as citizens, should contribute fairly to our nation—and to our community's maintenance, repair and services. Those critical needs aren't free. If people think what we currently pay for water and electricity, for instance, is too high, let them purchase those essentials from a for-profit, unregulated corporation. Or WTF, give everyone an option: pay taxes or buy services privately. When my sewer or water line breaks, my taxes will bring the highest quality help to my street. Those who opt to pay privately can do so. Enjoy."

"Well, the place is huge."

"The rest of the city, what's been built since, maybe, I don't remember—probably 1990—is behind us: we can't even see it from here. What you see from this vista is now maybe a third of the entire city."

"I recognize Cheyenne Mountain. It looks different from this angle than out of your kitchen window or from the deck, but the communications antennae give it away. So that's the Broadmoor area, too."

"My road race course, you mean?"

"So where did you grow up?"

"Three blocks from Colorado College."

"Cool."

"Very cool. Many of my most enduring friends are CC grads. Let's visit CC—and then—may I buy you dinner, sweetie?"

"That should cover about a hundredth of the car rental for the day."

I pretend I'm going to punch her arm for a change.

"Don't you dare!" She puts a hand over her shoulder, and scampers, shrieking with glee, to Fiorio—with me in hot pursuit. She gets the door open, but I catch up to her and tickle her mercilessly. She falls, breathless with laughter, legs still dangling outside the car, into the passenger seat—skirt slipping into her lap as she kicks at me to stop. Yet this time, I am relentless. My body weight presses in between her legs, and my arms pin her shoulders into the leather seat as I lean in to voraciously kiss her.

<p style="text-align:center">~~~</p>

"Hi, Michelle. This is Wynne."

"Hello, Wynne. Is this guy treating you okay, or should I call 911?"

"I see you know him well. So far, so good, Michelle."

"Good. Can I get you two something to drink?"

"Two glasses of water, no ice, with lemon, please; and a bottle of the sustainable vino." I look at Ms. Saint-Émilion. "It's a blend—cabernet, zinfandel and merlot—all organic, and the winery operates as off-grid as possible. They're working toward a completely carbon-neutral footprint."

"Awesome." She looks at Michelle. "We'd better have two bottles. We can take home what we don't use, right?"

Michelle matches Wynne's grin. "Absolutely. Are you ready to order, or would you like to hear the specials?"

"I definitely want the halibut special. It sounds scrumptious. I noticed it on the board out front, while we waited for this lovely table by the creek."

"Would you care for soup or salad?"

"Your house salad and dressing, please."

"Dressing on the side?"

"Thank you. Please."

Michelle collects Wynne's menu, then turns to me. "Lasagna?"

"Actually, I'd like salmon enchiladas with lentil soup."

"What, no lasagna?"

"Please don't have a heart attack. I'm trying to impress Wynne."

She looks at Wynne. "How's that working for you?" Michelle politely nods the side of her head my way, and adds, "What a case, eh?"

Wynne laughs with restful ease. "What a case indeed."

"I'll get your orders in and return with your drinks. It's good to see you, Matt."

"You too, Michelle."

Wynne looks at me, grinning.

"This is one of my three favorite lasagna fixes. I nearly always order it."

"I noticed Michele almost passed out. A lot of people seem to know you in Manitou."

"Manitou is where I live, really and truly. Here, and to a much lesser extent downtown Colorado Springs."

"It's fun. I feel like I'm dining with a celebrity."

"A colossal exaggeration." I bestow her my entire heart through my eyes. "And thank you."

~~~
~~~

After a cold start outside Adam's Mountain Café, Fiorio growls to a smooth idle under my absorbing palms at ten and two o'clock on the steering wheel, while Wynne asks, "I wonder if a room is available again tonight at *Hôtel du Sleeping Bear Oasis?*"

"Gee, I'm afraid not."

Her smile fades.

"However, there is one queen bed that contains only one occupant. I think I can squeeze you into that room. There would be a discount, of course."

"You rat!" She slugs me again. I need to find ways to turn the other shoulder her way for a while. She leans over to kiss me on the right cheek. I reach for her, and turn my head to hers for a sweet, exploratory, lingering minute. The engine needs to warm up anyway.

During the entire drive back to the Oasis—well it's only just over two miles, although I stretch it into sixteen by going up Ute Pass to Cascade before turning back to Manitou—better for the V12, you know, to allow it to run thoroughly whenever it's started—slender fingers caress my neck and twirl in my hair. The bulge in my cargo shorts doesn't go unnoticed.

"It seems you like to be touched like this."

"I like being touched by you, period, Ms. de Gracia. Please expect to get no sleep whatsoever tonight. The hotel will be busier than you imagine."

"Tease." She grins, leaning over to stroke my prominence a few times, kissing up and down the side of my neck. This really helps.

Chapter Fifty-Seven: High Dive

We did get some sleep. We also did not get more sleep. We talked, rolled, caressed, made love, talked, caressed, and made love, and touched, and rolled and talked, finally falling asleep around two—tangled up in each other as completely as possible. We awake a little after seven, as a subdued sun peeks over the hill east of the Oasis, underneath a low, heavy, dark cloud cover. Following this 24-karat gold, humid, totally breezeless sunrise, there will be rain.

Leaning forward on my left elbow toward my sleepy friend, lover, and partner, I kiss her lightly—lingering just a second—on the tiny corner of her mouth, where those soft lips come together. "Good morning sweetie. I love you." I stretch my arms, legs, and head and neck away from my torso. "Ahhhhh."

She rolls onto her side and throws a leg over my waist. Her mouth moves slower than her words. "Goo' mor'in'."

"Did you sleep okay? After I crashed, I don't remember a thing."

She yawns large and long. "I s'pose another hour 'r two would have been nice...." She gives me a slow-forming, contented de Gracia smile. "...But I feel safe and snuggled. By the way, you don't snore— that's a monster-size, plat'num star next to your name."

"Thank you. Keep 'em coming." I stretch out my arms and then clasp my hands behind my head on the pillow. I turn toward Wynne—our eyes meet. Hers contain miniature reflections of morning sunrays streaking onto the soft, West Seattle green-mist walls of the master bedroom.

"Wynne—I'm happier than I can ever remember. Sometimes I wonder if I'm going to wake up—discovering this is only a dream. You get my spiritual side. We're emotionally honest and straightforward with each other. You're so smart I don't have to watch my words—I can talk freely and wordsmith my way through our dialogues. And physically...." I lean in to again gently caress her lips with mine. "I imagined us this way that first morning at the condo, when you came out to the portico in your nightshirt. Your *fouetté* turned me on so much I couldn't think of anything but you. That vision has never left me."

"It's too bad you didn't follow me back inside. I was so horny for you I couldn't imagine you didn't know."

I roll onto my side, keeping her leg lying there so lightly, across my waist. My head resting on the palm of my hand, I gaze in her eyes and bathe in comforting, encompassing energy—waves flowing, dancing jubilantly from all around and inside me, into her, and from her into me—two flesh, bone and blood magnets with unwavering, mutually attracting, interwoven fields.

"You, my dear, are the most wonderful companion ever." Barely touching, I slide myself over her, her left leg still embracing my waist—our body weight eventually drawing her onto her back. And, oh my, there's that satin crook in her neck.

~~~

Bending over the sink, Wynne brushes her teeth with a new yellow toothbrush I gave her last night: a permanent addition to my porcelain, surfer-woodie-Studebaker toothbrush holder. I snuggle up against her backside, my chest tickling her spine, arms wrapping her torso.

"May I make you breakfast, Ms. de Gracia? It's on the house."

"You truly are a superb hotelier, monsieur. *Oui, oui, s'il te plaît.*"

After brushing my teeth, I do a quick *Pal Dan Gum* set. Wynne joins me in the wide-open room I call my walk-in closet—there's enough space for four to practice yoga in here.

"I'll cut my routine short and get breakfast started. Unless you need me to supervise."

"You just like to watch."

"Darn right."

From her supine, Pilates foundation position, she tries to kick me in the butt. Smoothly, I sidestep and snatch her foot. I begin nibble-kissing her instep, then behind the ankle, and slowly move up the soft side of her calf.

"Breakfast. You said 'breakfast.' " She closes her eyes, and waits, limp, until I reach the inside of her knee—before yanking away the leg. "Breakfast. Hop to it." Through still-heavy eyelids, she gives me
~~~

a big, soft smile. And is ravishing in bed-tussled waves of sandy-blonde hair and rumpled, pearl satin camisole.

"Yes, dear." I grin, and then pop out of melodramatic deference. "My guess is—we've both worked up a bit of an appetite." I swing my purple bathrobe around my shoulders, hunch my back, turn like a vampire, bare my fangs and hiss, sweeping the dark cape over her as she lies there on the carpet—"Ha, ha hahahaaa"—then bound up the stairs into the kitchen.

"Good morning, birdies," a jubilant voice calls. Gizmo responds with a cheery chirp.

Verdito gets uncovered first—he's the young stud at age seven—and is raring to go. Gizmo—at twenty-one—is okay with a gentler awakening. What's that in human years? Like a hundred and sixty?

"Hi Gizmo," he says, from under his fuzzy, yellow cotton, night-cover blanket.

"Hi Gizmo," say I.

"How you doin' birdie?" he asks.

"Never happier buddy. How you doin' birdie?" I fold the front half of the yellow, same color as his crown and tail feathers, blanket over the top of his house, to harbor the upstairs rear in warmth and bask the living area in morning light and fresh air—nothing though, is so welcome as the mutual pleasure of one another's company.

My feathered teacher says, "I love you."

"I love you, too, birdie." The moment his door is open, he slowly wobbles, stumbling, out to his patio for a morning nuzzle: the tip of my nose feather light, stroking his yellow crown, the top of his head, and down the back of his neck just to the shoulders.

Wynne emerges from the entrance to the tiger's den. "Do I have time to take a shower?" She chose my ancient, silk, made in Hong Kong, turquoise robe: delicately embroidered with pagodas, bridges, and flowering fruit trees—and at least twenty-five inches too long for my taste.

"No problem. I'll be about an hour, with taking care of the flock, too."

"How are they?"

"They're their usual, wonderful, selves."

Verdito hops onto his second floor balcony door, and takes flight around the kitchen, clockwise, buzzing so close to Wynne's head that her hair waves lightly in his wake.

"Whoa!"

"He must like you. I should be jealous."

She chuckles. "I remember you mentioning your open door policy. It's wonderful."

"The birdies would agree. Being a great-great-great-grandpa cockatiel, Gizmo doesn't fly anymore, but he does love to hunker down like right now, there on his drawbridge—especially right after breakfast. He grinds his beak and takes a post-meal nap."

She tiptoes over to Verdito's house. He's already flitted back inside to sing his brightest morning song—understandably hoping this new girl is impressionable. "Hey, little green canary. Your name is *Verdito*, right?" He stops singing. Wynne looks at me, eyebrows raised and with a downward twist of her mouth—a worried four year old, ready to cry.

"It's okay. He doesn't want anyone, including me, to get too close. Neither bird will abide a hand either. He's fine. Not to worry."

"Okay. *Lo siento, Verdito.*" She sideways-steps the four feet to Gizmo's house and leans toward him, hands folded behind her back. Verdito instantly resumes exuberant melodies.

"Hi Gizmo."

"He talks! Oh my god. Hi Gizmo."

"Hi Gizmo."

"Hi Gizmo."

He slowly, agedly bobs his head. "I love you."

Time for me to interject: "Hey you, that's my line."

He looks at me and purrs. "That's his name for me—a kind of purring sound. I repeat it by fluttering my tongue on the roof of my mouth." I proceed to demonstrate—whereupon he purrs again.

He says, "Hi Gizmo," then looks back to Wynne.

She chuckles, and says to him, "I love you."

"I love you."

I step over and put my arms around her, applying a big squeeze. "My birdie buddies like you. That's a big compliment. They're most discriminating."

"Well, I like them too." She straightens, and spins around to face me with my hands still around her waist. Her robe falls open a few inches, and I lower my neck and head to kiss the sweet spot where the jaw meets her throat. Using an index finger, she lifts my chin to hers. "I'd better get that shower. I've already used some of my 60 minutes."

"That's right." I kiss her. She kisses me. We kiss each other. I pull her close. "I am totally in love with you, Wynne Luis Maria

Caveza de Gracia Brockman."

"You remember my entire name?"

"Of course."

"Forgot the Worner part, though?"

"Ignoring the Worner part. Like you haven't noticed." I kiss her again, and give her a Sleeping Bear hug, lifting her from a chilly, linoleum kitchen floor.

"Yuuugh."

I squeeze again.

"Yuuugh."

Chuckling, I let her down and turn her loose. She skips barefoot from the kitchen, down the hall, into the bathroom.

I palm handfuls of birdseed mixes from the freezer, let them cascade into ceramic bowls, and take them to warm, out on the front deck, in any-moment-to-be-cloud-obscured morning sun. I cut and shape fresh, unbleached, recycled paper towels to replace yesterday's top two sheets on the floors of both bird homes—each house has a thick carpet of six layers of paper towels. Then I clean and refill both birdies' water vessels.

A light dollop of coconut oil gets rubbed into each of two, brushed-steel breakfast skillets—an eight-inch and a ten-and-a-half. I open the fridge and pull out favorite organic ingredients: sweet potato (not yam), delicata squash, buffalo andouille, a purple carrot, an anaheim pepper, green beans, spinach, a giant collard green leaf, four fertile eggs, and two slices of no-wheat, sprouted-grain, cinnamon raison bread for toast. I prepare raw veggies for Gizmo and Verdito before padding in my lightest wool socks to the bathroom, where the door is ajar and the shower is showering.

"Is buffalo and veggies okay for breakfast?"

"Anything *you* create is certain to be exquisite, so—yes."

"Thank you for having the door cracked. I like it open so the houseplants and my guitars get a little extra humidity. That okay with you?"

"Sure. There's nothing here you haven't already seen."

"Or kissed." I sneak over and reach under the shower curtain for an ankle. She shrieks, and then laughs.

"You rat! You're gonna pay for that."

"I'll go get my checkbook."

"You won't get off that easy, bud."

"Take your time gorgeous, I'm just getting started in *la cocina*."

"I won't be long."

I open the door onto the west deck, take seven fully lung-expanding breaths, hold each one a tiny while to absorb fresh oxygen, exhale deliberately, and then stand in prayer position to give thanks for this day, this life, this wonderful new companion. I flow down the four stairs, retrieve feeders from inside the garage where I keep them safer from bears at night, add fresh birdseed, and finally empty and refill the birdbath with fresh water. Back in the kitchen, I turn a tad more heat under the skillets, and proceed to slice, dice, and shred. Wynne performs another graceful *glissade* through the kitchen, that turquoise robe folded over her forearm.

"Woohoo! Yeah, baby. Come over here, girl."

"No, no." She runs to the stairs, stopping at the landing.

"How shall I dress for the day?"

"Just like that will do fine."

"Don't you ever think of anything else?"

"Maybe in a hundred years."

"Cute."

"I haven't made any plans, sweetie. That's a team effort. What would you like to do?"

"I was thinking about Mt. Princeton Hot Springs?"

"Oooo, good idea. Yeah, I'm good with that. You'll need a swimsuit. I'm pretty sure none of my suits will fit all of you."

She grins. "I brought my own, just in case."

"The case is afoot, Watson."

"I shall go immediately to prepare, Holmes."

In mere minutes, she bounces back upstairs, wearing another white lace skirt and complementary low-cut top, accenting a turquoise and sterling bear claw necklace with matching earrings.

"You know what dressing like that does to me."

"Want me to change?"

"No way. Besides, breakfast is nearly ready."

"It smells wonderful."

"And so it will be. Would you like water, maté, another tea? I can do coffee, but it's a bit more complex—I'm totally out of practice." I open a top drawer and the cupboard above it, to reveal something like two-dozen tea options.

"I see you're having water, no ice, with lemon. I must do likewise, Holmes."

"Excellent choice, Watson." I start toward the only kitchen

cupboard that has no door, to grab my other Tesuque glass.

A traffic cop hand stops me. "I'll get it." She tenderly waves a finger in my general direction. "Don't you dare leave that stove."

~~~

Facing one another in our pool of hot water in Chalk Creek, I massage her feet.

"So, Matt. Here's the thing."

"The thing?"

"Yes, the thing."

"Fire away. I'm ready for anything."

"Good—I want you to head the newest de Gracia Foundation enterprise."

My hands freeze in place, thumbs still embedded deep in her solar plexus points—the centers of her soles. "Okay—I'm ready for *almost* anything."

"Hear me out, love."

"I'm all ears, sweetie."

"Since you want to be part of me, you'll likely need to be part of who I am and what I do."

"I'm a whole with you, baby, not a part."

"Right. Here we go."

She straightens her back, hyperextending her ribcage as she inhales a deep, monumental breath—holds it—and releases. I follow her cue. We're about to take a dive—from a cliff taller than any from which we've yet leapt. Another breath—and away she goes. I follow off the edge into that blue pool way down below.

"Matt, I feel from the depths of our ocean that you truly do love me—and want us to partner. I've felt that in the core of my being— multiple times."

I chuckle, undoubtedly wearing a smug expression. She slugs my quad. That one, without question, will bruise.

"Water is the tip of the de Gracia iceberg. The San Luis water rights issue is real as a heart attack—to be colloquial." She gives me an impish, "I told you so" look, and then turns somber. "And there is more at stake—potentially a lot more."

Eyes locked on hers, I slither into the bottom of our ten-inch deep pool for two to get hot again, using a wide, smooth, river rock as a pillow for my head. Alongside sixty or eighty feet of riverbank, are nine of these little pools, formed by placing stones and sand in a circle or semicircle—to contain hot spring water seeping up from
~~~

underground, and to direct cold water flowing down Chalk Creek. With her feet on my abdomen, I resume the reflexology treatment, working around the large intestines and upward along the spine.

"Do you remember the solar and wind installations in the Canadian Creek ranch?"

"Of course. Not every day does Matt, while flying his sweetheart's twin engine Cessna, observe zebras, Riwoche ponies, and power transformers, all within a few feet of each other—except perhaps somewhere in Africa? I don't know, maybe a zoo. Are there problems with the green energy research?"

"Hold on to your handsome jammer swim trunks. The Foundation is close to a plan to manufacture and install solar and wind on every building in America."

My jaw drops to my chest. I'm lying on the river bottom—it's not a fall so far. I almost exclaim "holy buckets," but stop myself—to listen without interrupting.

"The envelope couriered to Denver with Clancy and Tom Pack, that somebody assumed you were transporting, contained signed original documents—creating a non-profit organization, and outlining implementation plans." She pauses. My eyes open wider, as I crush acid crystals in her powerful feet, up around the adrenals, kidneys, and spleen—soon I'll flush out her ankles and lower legs. Then I'll sit up, and cleanse those upper legs, too—always, toward the heart.

"The goal is to promote very locally manufactured equipment and technology—built, installed, maintained, and repaired entirely by self-employed Americans. Promotion of insulation and conservation is, of course, a part of the process. We will recoup only costs of operations and materials. Some funds may be retained to assist with ongoing research and development, but our Foundation hopes to continue providing those resources, as well to engage additional philanthropic partners. Along this journey, we did request federal R&D grants. Perhaps at least in part due to America's more than one-hundred-year-old political tradition of giveaway corporate welfare, our controversial, not-for-profit requests were turned down."

I can't resist. "Controversial? I've not heard a word of this. And I pay attention."

"It's controversial within mahogany-paneled walls. The controlled media has not allowed word of this to go mainstream. I've been told there have been a few mentions of affordable, every-rooftop concepts on MHz Networks, and an occasional European newscast.

For what are now perhaps obvious reasons, I've not been unhappy with a lack of publicity. However, word got out that we were closer than *they* thought.

"The economy of America will almost certainly never return to that which people have become accustomed. We no longer manufacture much of anything, citizens no longer have jobs, and the end result is a population unable to continue the rampant consumerism that it has been brainwashed to regard as representing *growth*—and, unable to place money into savings to earn even sub-pittance interest returns of less than one-half of one percent. More fortunate Americans have seen portfolios lose and not regain value. And then there's environmental and ecological reality.

"With wars and induced unrest, mostly about oil—and now, of course, water—combined with nuclear accidents and truths still-untold—not to mention more frequent natural and man-made disasters; the destruction of already disappearing underground water supplies through drilling or other resource extraction processes; and life becoming extinct everywhere on Earth—we're ready to launch our green energy on every rooftop project.

"Time has come for everyday Americans to reclaim their own personal destinies—to relearn to live without corporate controls dictating to them how to be and how to think. I can't do all of this myself." She looks at me—determination steeling her face—and then grins. "Well, perhaps I can—but make no mistake—I look forward to your competent help, once you accept the challenge.

"Matt, I'm convinced your business and information technology background, cogent ethics, admirable intelligence, solid grasp of oligarchic ownership of political and economic systems—*and* strong survival skills—have prepared you to be an ideal leader to watch over this baby, in partnership with a Board of Trustees including Cassie, myself, and other minds yet to be decided. Are you up for it?"

Plash! Plash! This is ice water. And this is no pool, baby—this is a Great Lake.

Chapter Fifty-Eight: Plunging Deep

"You know, 'Bu really is a sweet little car, Matt."

"Thanks, Wynne. She's been good to me. We have a lot in common: a few years under our belt, relatively low mileage, very well maintained, operated with respect and understanding."

That earns a chuckling smile. "These seats are nice: soft velour, comfy, great low back support. And in your hands, the ride is also nice: smooth and stable."

It's my turn to chuckle—as I quickly cover my right shoulder with my left hand.

She just gives me *the smile*. "You forgot to mention another thing you two have in common."

"That being?"

"An insatiable libido."

"Maroonbaru pretends to keep that attribute pretty well out of sight—until events conspire to get her aroused. In fact, I'm surprised you noticed her appetite."

"I didn't so much notice, as intuit—given all that you two have in common—well, and her ability to outrun a vehicle twice her size over Independence."

"There was some luck, too. I saw a hole in the pavement. The SUV couldn't react."

"What was the admonition I recently opened in a Chinese fortune cookie? 'Good luck is usually the result of good planning.' " Her left hand and fingers slip around the nape of my neck. OMG. "So, have you thought about directing the new project?"

Click. My energy switch flips from fantasy to analytical. "Yes and no."

"I'd appreciate your being more cryptic." She smiles big, tipping that golden-waved head as though she's looking around a corner at me. "All this straightforward response is driving me crazy."

"*Lo siento, mi amor.* It's been, like, six years since I've headed an organization—almost seven. Now I enjoy a quiet private practice. I know I can handle the responsibilities, it's just that we're talking about a radical lifestyle change for a guy who's settled into a very comfy routine."

That earns *the smile*: innocently seductive, softly alluring, soothing and reassuring. "Who do you think you're kidding? You're dying to get started."

"Well, water easement on a national scale seems—more manageable, for this relatively low mileage unit."

"Water easement is included in our goals—especially after I read Interior's, *SECURE Water Act*. Major efforts have to happen now—we're *all*, all out of time."

"I haven't seen that report. Anything new?"

"For those who set aside a little time to pay attention, perhaps not—except that the revelations seem irrefutable—and in the hands of Congress." Her head tilts. She smiles sweetly, and with soft emphasis says, "You didn't answer my question."

"Your question?"

She slugs my shoulder before I can safely cover it. She's quick—this girl. And always accurate.

Wearing a melodramatic grimace, I rub my shoulder. Eyes narrowed and flat-lined lips, I ask the rhetorical question. "You're not gonna let this go, are you?"

A four-year-old bombshell looks up with big, round eyes, under raised eyebrows, chin tucked under just so.

Damn. "Yes—of course I'll do it."

Bouncing up and down in the passenger seat—hands waving in the air—she cheers. "Yea! Yeah. All right. That's the spirit." Raising a right-handed fist in the air, she looks me in the eyes and says, "We'll be a great team." Then, gazing my way, eyes soft, showing a lips-closed, wide, contented smile, quietly, she says, "And then, we already are." That fist begins to fly across her chest, on an unregistered flight path to my heart.

My left hand snaps away from the steering wheel, morphing into a fist as it passes my right shoulder. We bump with precisely equal pressures—gentle, yet assertive—a solid thump that feels like we've been doing it for eons.

"Is it only me, or are we awesomely good together?"

Like it was only two minutes ago, I see Wynne standing in the arched doorway to her office in the condo, determined to not sell out San Luis water. At this moment, I also see her silent, contentedly fascinated, gazing out 'Bu's front seat passenger window, watching rainfall—as it drags inky wisps of dense, wet clouds to the ground, like wave after wave of charcoal-colored, velvet stage curtains—marching across the expansive South Park plain.

Lifting my right hand this time, I tenderly, scarcely, brush her cheek, temple, and ear with the backs of my fingers and knuckles. "It's the team concept that I most look forward to." I turn my eyes back to Highway 24, and its post-Labor Day holidazed occupants. "I do want to be your partner—in every way you want to be."

The side of her head leans into my fingers, eventually hugging them against her shoulder. Her steady eyes regard mine. "It may not be simple. What we're talking about here is altering, albeit not overnight, the way energy is done in the country. Well, not just here in America. These concepts have appropriate applications in developing and underdeveloped nations—places where a cell phone sized solar cell, pre-amplified when feasible by a tiny, popup breeze venturi or miniature wind turbine, can be used to charge a deep cycle battery that provides an energy lifeline more important to a hut-dwelling family of thirteen, than a four-gigawatt nuclear plant to a hotel-dwelling family of four. There are many political, social, and economic interests on whose treasures we will tread. It's dangerous.

"More so now, particularly at the outset, than later, when we're in full swing. It's during startup mode that...." She leans forward in the passenger seat, to ensure that I notice she's making finger quotes in the air. "...Accidents—can happen. Like the man down South— where was it? Missouri? Georgia? He developed a tamper-proof computer voting machine—then accidentally met head-on with a truck while on the way to deliver the invention—end of fraud-free voting, it would seem."

"You know, I remember that. And of course, what ensued was another election with questionable accuracy. I remember a documentary, from the League of Women Voters I think, that interviewed a voting machine company guy—exposing flaws, and probably outright plans to alter voting results. The same video also points out a county in Texas that tabulated, I believe, hundreds, if not a few thousand more computer votes than the tiny population of the entire county."

Her mouth twists into a wry smile. "Accidents happen. Hey, I'm getting hungry. I haven't heard your belly growl, my tiger, but those dates and pecans from your book bag can't hold you much longer. Shouldn't we stop for a bite?"

"We can, though I recommend we get back to Manitou, at least. Any afternoon, especially on Wednesday after Labor Day weekend, can easily involve several miles of backed up traffic winding down Ute Pass—another reason I was reluctant to bring Fiorio."

"Okay, then what say you to an early dinner at a favorite restaurant. One you haven't shown me yet. Someplace different— where we can celebrate our partnership."

"Manitou Inn it is. They serve wild game, grow organic veggies and herbs, and locally source other ingredients. And the wine list is— well—extensive."

"And the lasagna?"

"Don't serve it."

"What? I don't believe it. Sounds interesting. Let's go. You were right about traffic. It's only two-thirty and there's nothing but cars as far as we can see. In a rainstorm."

"It's a slow drive, but that's cool—the trip's gorgeous. There hasn't been this much green since the last, honest, monsoon. August—seven years ago."

"This is a pretty route. I love seeing all the buffalo. There must be at least two thousand."

"Isn't it awesome? Multiply that number by a hundred, and we're seeing what Arapaho and other Native American nations hunted up here in summer—a thousand years ago. This is buffalo ground— cattle aren't native to North America."

"Can we take a quick stop on, what's it called? Wilkinson Pass?"

"Wilkerson. I need to go, too." I lift my water bottle from the center console. "This is the third liter, just since we left the Oasis this morning."

"Walking his talk, ladies and gentlemen, is Mr. Matt Hale—life coach *extraordinarius*." Her eyes squint, under curled eyebrows—she snatches the bottle from my raised hand and finishes it.

"Been brushing up on your Latin?"

"Only as regards the legal system."

"Speaking of which, what am I getting myself into with the Foundation?"

"Legally?"

"Well, no, not legally—you'll have all that covered. Tell me more about the project."

"This project will install, as literally as possible, green technology on every rooftop in America. It will self-employ millions of people. Mass scale, dynamic machining and manufacturing capacity needs to be built, or better yet, ecologically retrofitted into vacant buildings across the country. What we intend to do is create engineering uniformity—so that as technology continues to improve, existing equipment can be easily and inexpensively re-fitted."

"Like a Vox AC-30."

It's an obvious question.

"*Lo siento.* A classic, electric guitar amplifier."

"Ah, okay. I like the simile. So, it has been necessary to purchase some patents, but for the most part, we're creating a business model and engineering paradigm based on "open-source" concepts, like free computer software—ensuring the lowest possible price for everyone. Patents or proprietary specifics will not be in place to ensure profits or eliminate competition. And perhaps most importantly, as you're aware, anyone at all can add and improve intellectual capital.

"The goal is full employment in America—millions of people— all working for themselves, on their own or in community cooperatives—but every one self-employed. Rather than making wads of money for the few, millions of citizens will be the moneymakers: They'll manufacture, install, maintain and operate solar, wind, and thermal—including molten salt, and more yet-to-be discovered storage capabilities of every size—and other Earth, citizen, and environment friendly solutions. This is not hyperbole.

"Foundation research is already doing, or is close to achieving, everything I've just detailed—in small scale, methodology-proofing implementations around the globe. We're also experimenting with biological, water-living organisms that are capable of consuming carbon, methane, and other greenhouse gasses, thereby emitting electrical current, while processing an incredible range of commercial and residential waste—with a by-product—clean drinking water."

"Dude."

"The philosophy is entirely about re-creating a sense of togetherness, community—and strengthening those bonds, where they have survived. We can achieve this: by saving families and growing food and water; by reducing, and maybe even eventually eliminating pollution of air, water and soil. The result can be improved quality of life for everyone and everything: plants, animals, water creatures, humankind—everything.

"Time has come for the world, every country, every person, to get involved in changing personal economics—empowering people to have opportunity to work for their own benefit, to achieve the freedom and leisure time to garden and grow their own food, and to begin distilling or condensing water in those geographies where *Mde Wakan….*" (I can't keep myself from a big smile at Wynne's use of the Dakota.) "…Is scarcest and most polluted. And thanks to you and Cassie, we're expanding to include safeguarding existing water resources as well—to preserve water for people, rather than for corporate profits.

"Once everyone alive benefits from low-cost, clean energy, water, and air; when every person benefits from their own food production; then concentration of political and economic power is no longer so important—except to provide those resources people cannot easily provide on their own. Health care; police, fire and other safety protections; infrastructure like roads and transportation; recreation; education: These are among services that can be provided by larger, non-governmental organizations, as well as governing entities—wherever it truly makes sense to pool resources on behalf of everyone—to genuinely, authentically, leverage efficiencies of scale on behalf of all, rather than profit for the few.

"Millions will be working to install, maintain and repair energy harvesting, storage, and transmission technologies. Millions will be working to teach and operate urban and local farming—all the way down to the apartment-dweller level. Open-source technology will thrive and improve, requiring continuous upgrading and re-fitting of uniform infrastructure developed specifically for physical, environmental and ecological requirements of any geographic circumstance. Again, I do not engage in hyperbole.

"We have seen presidents, governments, political systems of *every* type and description fail at protecting and fostering the Garden of Eden and all its occupants. We, as planet Earth people, must adapt how we experience life—return to a focus on *living*, day-to-day, week-to-week, decade-to-decade—rather than laboring for the profit of a miniscule few.

"The vision, simply, is a renaissance of community togetherness, individual freedom, self-reliance, and restoration of personal responsibility for health and happiness—as well as the liberty to do so as guaranteed in the Constitution. It's a near elimination of outdated principles of the Industrial Age—which may have been important when banking and corporate power procured dominance around 1900—but that ideology has outgrown efficiencies of scale to favor concentrating power and wealth, to the detriment of everyone except the tiny few who manipulate that concentration. Not that accumulation of power and wealth are unique in history…."

She goes silent, while my thoughts buzz like a hive of a thousand bees—not a single one angry, because bees very rarely are mad or mean, unlike some wasps, but each one busily, happily, individually or in teams, industrious.

"It would be nice to end the practice, also started around 1900, of taxing income from labor. If only profit were taxed, massive relief would fall to the vast, vast majority of Americans—freeing impoverished middle classes to begin carefully spending and living again. That, however, is an ideal, and not a goal of our greening project." She goes quiet.

I wait. And wait a little more. Then a tiny bit longer just to be sure. And jump in.

"And *I'm* supposed to lead *this* charge?"

"Why not?"

"You're kidding, right?"

"I'll be there, too, serving on the Board, and overseeing the rest of the job."

"The rest of the job?"

"Matt, you certainly don't believe this can happen without monstrous legal and communications efforts."

"You mean, if we don't get neck-shot."

Her eyes fall, her mouth turns down, and color flees from those cheeks.

"I'm sorry. Damn it. *Why* do I do that? Why do I say hurtful things? Why do I fall into the pit of negativity? Thank you for being a part of my seeing and learning to reverse that tendency."

She looks me in the eyes. "Dude…." I smile as another healing wave surges through me—hair on my nape stands like lightning is about to strike. "…You have to be aware—because you have taken responsibility for your own health and happiness—that you have no intent to hurt me. You're simply making a point, Matt—an important point."

The healing wave sucks away from the shore, churning underneath itself before the joyful tsunami rising above it.

"So yes, if we don't end up like Browner. Look at it—*it* being whatever may happen—as potential sacrifice for saving our planet, our peoples, and all that walks, crawls, flies, swims, grows, or otherwise coexists with us."

"*Mitakuye Oyasin.*"

"Are you with me?"

I look into those big-hearted, gray-greens—and watch four hundred thousand buffalo running toward me. "I'm with you, sweetie, I'm with you. This is gonna' take an army—I mean, huge numbers of unarmed, dedicated people."

"An army with no armory."

"It's about time."

Chapter Fifty-Nine: Underwater Breathing

"Well, if it isn't Matt Hale. It's good to see you again."

"Thank you, Caroline. It's good to be seen."

"Two for dinner?"

"Yes, please."

"You're early. I can seat you in the southwest bay—but it is reserved for seven-thirty."

"Great. We can be done in three-and-a-half hours."

I watch Wynne's eyes, and say, "It's my favorite table—but it's everyone's favorite. Last time I planned a birthday dinner for myself, I reserved it ten months in advance."

"I can't wait. Why so special?"

"The view south and west is spectacular. The table is in a top floor, corner room under two gables, each with a big bay window. It seats eight, and more if need be, so if it feels too large for just the two of us, we can sit elsewhere. It seems we have the place to ourselves."

She looks at Caroline. "I'm Wynne."

"Welcome, Wynne."

"Thank you. I'd like to be seated at Matt's favorite table." She covers the side of her face with her hand, pretending I might not hear her, and in a totally un-hushed tone, says, "Sometimes he struggles a little to ask for what he wants."

Caroline smiles broadly. "We might have noticed that."

"Okay you two. Knock it off."

We follow Caroline upstairs, winding through the Tudor-style stone mansion. My plain pine table and eight, leather padded dining chairs—each chair with four layers of cured leather—graces what might have been a servant's quarter, or perhaps a little girl's bedroom. Ambient, restrained elegance simply glows onto rounded and whitewashed stucco walls and ceiling, accented with a crown molding of what might be, like, hundred-fifty year old oak, all supported by 16-inch, source-matched varnished oak beams. From that ceiling hangs, by a three-eights inch, solid brass smithed chain, a modest Nineteenth Century chandelier, sporting brass candle holders converted to electricity, and now LED lighting—something like a hundred crystal white lamps drawing a total of maybe 10 watts every four hours. The room is perhaps 600 square feet, with two, 10-foot wide, oriel bay windows that are sufficiently open to allow for rain-scented, September mountain fragrances; letting in cheerful and bright daylight, or the quiet nightlight of the mountain foothills town that is Manitou Springs. A granite fireplace sits silent in the center of the north wall, below a period oil portrait of a teenage girl. Standing in the center of a thick grate is a single, clear glass storm-cover that surrounds a chocolate-color candle, sixteen inches tall and maybe five inches thick. The whole room at once is common and smart: a fine venue for a comforting family dinner.

"Would you like a wine list, Mr. Hale?"

"I'd love for Wynne to see it. Yes, please."

"Wow—so polite. He still trying to impress you, Wynne?" Caroline looks back to my eyes. "Two waters, no ice, with lemon?"

"I do miss coming here."

"As you should." She takes a faux-dramatic, haughty stroll to a two-shelf Pembroke table topped with a coronal, scarlet-blossomed, Vancouver Centennial geranium potted in antique cloisonné porcelain: Menus and wine lists lie on a low shelf. "Anything else for now?"

"I think we'll be fine."

"I'll be back in a few minutes with your water. Jeff will wait your table this evening. Thank you for stopping in." Her head tilts to us each as Caroline says, "...Wynne, Matt."

Spine straight and tall, wearing an un-pressed, white silk dress shirt and no tie, Jeff saunters in carrying a walnut two-top. He sets the table down in the west bay window, picks up and carries two dining chairs from our family-size table to the more intimate venue, pulls out the chair facing the mountains, and looks invitingly at Wynne.

She smiles a de Gracia smile toward Jeff, then me as I get up to pull away the chair she's sitting in at the big table. She moves gracefully to the two-top, and slides silently and effortlessly into her waiting seat.

"Thank you, Jeff."

He nods slowly, and once I sit across from Wynne, he looks first to her, then to me, back to Wynne, and asks, "I see you have the wine list. Is there anything I can bring?"

~~~

"How is the Grenache?"

"I like it. It's heavier than I expected, and the raisin finish lingers like a port. Awesome."

"Oh, good. This is a new vintner to me, so it was a bit of a risk—I like it, too."

"To health, happiness, and prosperity for all."

"Health, happiness, and prosperity."

It's a solid clink, unlike the delicate twinkle of Wynne's goblets at the condo. She slips her arm and glass around mine. We sip simultaneously.

"To a partnership that helps heal Earth and her people—the first of many collaborations to come."

"Hear hear."

We untangle arms, and both tilt, deeply, the first glass. Our second bottle—an Australian Shiraz-Voignier—is already open and patiently waiting its turn. We've only a mile or so to drive home to Sleeping Bear Oasis.

"Oh my, that's tasty."

"Fairly potent as well."

"Who's trying to get the other tipsy?"

"And more importantly, to what end?"

"Let there be no end." Clink clink.

~~~

Precisely as Wynne finishes her house salad, Jeff enters the room with lime sorbet to clear our palates. He takes Wynne's salad bowl, pours us each a full seven ounces of wine, and silently leaves.

"Why didn't Jeff bring your salad?"

"He will. After my meal."

"Does everybody in Manitou know your preferences?"

"Noooo—besides, as you know, a salad finish is quite European."

She grins. "It does seem that wherever we go, people know what you want, or how you want it."

"I've become predictable."

"Because…."

"Because I know what makes me healthy, and I strive continuously for that health—well, as much as is reasonable."

"You do walk your talk. I'm thankful to have found you."

"Thank goodness for the website."

"The website did point me to a lifestyle consultant—I *found* you."

"You flatterer, you."

"Is it working?"

"Doesn't have to, and yes. Flattery will get you everywhere with me."

"And has."

I chuckle. A foot nudges my shin, just as Jeff arrives with our entrees. He removes sorbet cups, and then carries Wynne's Plum Mango Grilled Marlin with two hands, gently setting the plate in front of her. Demonstrating gender equality, he similarly sets my Smoked Diamond Back Buffalo Filet before me, and then refreshes our water glasses from a heavy, molded glass pitcher containing water, no ice, with lemon: lots of lemon.

"Will there be anything else for the moment, ma'am?"

"No, this is fine. It looks spectacular."

"Thank you. I'll forward your appreciation to the chef." He looks to me. "Mr. Hale?"

"Not a thing, Jeff."

"Shall I check back with you two, in, say, five minutes?"

"Perfect. Thank you, Jeffrey."

Silently, he spins and leaves.

"So, speaking of finding me, may I ask what attracted you to me? I mean—we're from different worlds." This nudge to my shin is not so gentle. Though it's not a particularly healthy practice, I cross my legs—and move out of range under the table—after first slipping a foot out of my clog to softly stroke her kicking leg.

"You know, I really just needed to clear my head—maybe rearrange, or prioritize. However, you obviously had a crush on me." There's *the smile*. "That felt refreshingly honest to me."

"A crush?"

"What would you call it?"

"A crush."

"It was nice to meet someone who presumably didn't already know who I am—a guide here to help—who was genuine. I'm sure you understand what I'm saying."

"I do, sweetie."

"From the moment I spotted you, I felt your soul soothing mine."

"Wow. I thought I've become pretty adept at camouflaging certain sides of me."

"Well, perish that conception. Dude, you're an open book."

I laugh. "I don't know why I laugh when you say dude."

"I do: It's because you still have me up on that damn pedestal." Her foot swings under the table, finding only air. She grins loudly, sliding down in her chair to kick at me. I jump up. She laughs as I run behind her, and reach down to ferociously tickle her quadriceps— both legs. She squirms, giggling hysterically. I stop almost immediately.

"How did you know I'm so ticklish there?"

"You're an open book, too. All you sandy blonde, ballerina types are ticklish there."

"And you know this how?"

"I've tickled hundreds of you."

She laughs. "Fair enough."

"More please."

"More what?"

"No, really, what attracted you to me? Our backgrounds really are different."

"Different? We're close to the same age. We both have blond genetic sources. We're both fit and athletic. We both have college educations and advanced degrees. We both have a modicum of cultural refinement inculcated when we were very young. We both have a passion for life and living, and simply living well while doing as little damage as possible. We both understand that political and socio-economic realities are doing harm to people unaware of what's happening." She grins. "And we're damn compatible in bed."

"Yeah, baby."

"Your turn, Coach."

"I was completed infatuated by your beauty and graceful style— gliding across the Nell lobby. I was so attracted to you—it's a good thing I tried hard to remain professional, or I'd have done or said something really stupid—and turned you off forever, maybe from that very first minute."

"The savvy, contemporary woman has learned that men nearly always react first with hormones—only later do we find out whom they really are."

I clear my perfectly clear throat. "Your strength in the face of loss and difficulty, and your unflinching trust in me—uphold my heart—I feel like I've known you for ages. Sure, I did continue to find you sexy—I guess I still do…." She lands another kick under the table: a gentle one this time. "…And it was how completely authentic you are with Cassie, with Clancy, and with me—how you give totally of yourself and your true feelings—no pretense, no guile, no bullshit—just, 'Hi, I'm Wynne. Here I am. Hope you like me.' But most of all, you accepted me for who I am. You warmed immediately to my kidding around; you understood and didn't ridicule my cynicism—too much. I know you witness my flaws, yet it's my heart and soul you embrace. We share so many insights and perspectives. In my mind, no doubt exists that our souls belong together, and we'll keep growing together—like two cypresses, rooted in deep water, trunks and limbs entwining. I love you, Wynne de Gracia."

We lean toward one another, soft lips at first touching, then moving away maybe half-an-inch to pause in the gestalt, before touching lightly, again and again, before finally lingering together, pressing with the knowing firmness that only lovers admit. She pulls away, to whisper only…"I love you too, Matt." I slip my hand around the back of her neck, and ever so easily pull her back to me.

Chapter Sixty: Forced Out of the Water

When the sun comes up over the hill east of the Oasis, a little after seven, we wake. It's Thursday—and another monsoon morning—complete with a low, gray cloud cover that the sunlight streams underneath, for perhaps another twenty minutes or so. We lie snuggled tight, spooned into a natal ball of arms and legs. My right arm, under her shoulders, is a lump of tingling goo.

Into the mass of golden waves matted to the back of Wynne's head, I say, "Good morning, gorgeous." I bury my nose deeper in her hair, and breathe deep and slow.

"Good morning, love."

"I have never slept so soundly—a miracle."

"My sentiment precisely." She raises her torso, and as she's turning toward me, I reach with my left hand to lift the dead right arm, and carefully lay it back down in front of me. While I lay there, gazing into her sleepy gray-green eyes, my arm slowly starts coming back to life—a buzzing, stinging, tingling mass of bone and flesh. I definitely don't mind the temporary discomfort.

Wynne gently pushes me onto my back, and slides tight into me, draping her right leg across my waist, and rests her head on my chest. Her fingers begin to comb my very disheveled blond strands. I hold her tight with my good arm, as her fingers slide from my hair, down my chest, to my waist, and gently squeeze an already prominent body part.

~~~

We're almost finished with breakfast when Wynne drops the bomb. "Matt, I'm going to have to go away for a while."

I don't quite scream. "*What?*"

"I'm sorry. I wanted to tell you, tried to tell you when I got here,
~~~

but you wouldn't let me. You insisted on speaking first. After all that you said, I couldn't bear to say anything. And I'm glad I didn't, because we've just enjoyed the most delightful days of my life." She looks down sheepishly, like she had when she appeared at my door. "I was selfish. I wanted to make love with you, to experience us together. I wanted to hold hands, and feel myself in love again—or maybe for the first time."

"Yeah. So now you're going away? For how long?"

"To be honest, love, I'm not sure. It may be six months, maybe more, maybe less."

"Six months? You're joking, right?"

Her head shakes side-to-side, sad eyes exploring mine.

"Wynne, what's going on? You can't go *now*...."

The doorbell chimes. The digital clock on the stove displays precisely nine o'clock.

"Will you let me get that? It's for me."

I peek around the corner when she opens the door. It's Agent Ballard. He sees me and looks around Wynne's head toward me. I duck back into the kitchen. I don't know why.

Wynne speaks quickly and too quietly for me to hear, and then pads barefoot back into the kitchen.

"What I wanted to tell you before, Matt, is that I'm going to spend some time in federal custody."

Jumping up, this time I do scream. "*What?*"

"Ms. Worner?" Agent Ballard is already in the kitchen, his hand on the weapon under his armpit.

"It's okay. Matt is just understandably upset. Please?" She looks at him—I know the look. Those eyes can melt glaciers.

"Excuse me; I overreacted." He goes back outside to stand by my front door.

"Wynne, what the hell is going on?"

"Please, love, sit down and let me explain."

"Wynne, I don't understand—this can't be happening. You're joking right? This is some sort of joke?"

"It's very real, Matt. Please, sit back down and let me explain."

I was a flood, no, a category seven hurricane of emotion. What the hell? Custody? Wynne? I sit down all right. I'm actually getting lightheaded. Custody? Independence Pass? Wynne? Running for our lives through the streets of Santa Fe? Browner? The ranch? Cassie?

"Matt, all this happened because…" She stops as I raise my hand, shaking my head slowly. Old, life-long learned habits streak through my consciousness, nervous system, and endocrine gyroscope: the knifing knot in the solar plexus, the thickening brain stem and dulling occipital buzz, the tingling tail-hair-raising pulse of nervous energy in the coccyx and back of my neck. These are all habituated fight or flight responses since childhood, infanthood, and probably before, and all now on the verge of frying my very being in a massive, systems-wide short circuit.

"Matt? Are you all right?"

I just raise my palm again, looking down at the table, but not focusing on anything—enduring a disorienting flood of surrealism. I'm gasping for air underwater, outside space and time. They never teach *this* in enlightenment school. This is the school of hard shocks. Wynne needs me to be present. I know that. I start shaking my body and exhaling hard and fast, like an animal, like a tiger, shaking off trauma. Finally I look up into frightened eyes.

I nod, the back of my head buzzing with a deep ache. "I'm okay Wynne. I've just used a technique where I allow myself to recognize my nervous system's physical sensations, and then release them. It's a technique that helps to release trauma."

Still concerned, she takes both my hands in hers.

"I'm okay, really. It's just that this is a huge shock. I'll need more time to process it all, but, please—go ahead."

She studies my eyes.

"Really, I'm fine now." I pause. "Well, maybe fine is a little optimistic. I'm okay, though, really. I need to understand what this is all about."

She nods. "Matt, a little more than two years ago," she says quietly, calmly, slowly, and clearly, "a close friend in Aspen, Clara Joiner, asked me to fly her to Puerto Barrios, in Izapal, Guatemala. She desperately needed a large order of fabrics she had custom ordered for her dressmaking business in Aspen. She told me she had received a big order to create clothing for several Russian diplomats' wives, who were accompanying an entourage to Guatemala and Belize. The embassy desired clothing informed by cultural dress of the region."

"*Fabrics?*" I know my voice sounds a little irritated. I am. "*Fabrics?*"

"Hear me out here, Matt." Wynne isn't smiling either. She's

deadly serious. I resolve to stop interrupting, and carefully hear what she has to say. I nod.

"Clara was internationally known for her formalwear and original designs. She told me her business had fallen on hard times, though, and she was desperate for the perfect fabric to complete this very lucrative order. It was a tremendously difficult flight, but the distance required only one refueling—at the airport in Puerto Barrios, for the return trip. We made it there and back safely, though, and Clara was deliriously grateful. Within two weeks she reimbursed me for all the expenses we incurred. I thought no more about it, except that the mileage meant I had to have extensive maintenance performed on *Wambli Gleska*."

I perk up a little—Wynne smiles, squeezing my hands on the table.

"What the hell is Ballard doing out there?"

"Ah, you've met."

"Almost the minute I got back to town."

"Well, it turned out that the fabric was a shipment of pure cocaine—six hundred pounds as a matter of fact. Clara and I have known each other since I first arrived in Aspen. I had no reason to think she was up to something other than what she told me. Well, about a month after we got back, the FBI showed up at the ranch to arrest me for transport of a controlled substance across international borders, along with another dozen or so other charges, unless I cooperated with them. But of course, just like in the movies, they first scared me to death, with threats of two hundred years in prison.

"I'm not kidding. Two hundred years. Anyway, the deal was that if I could help identify the source of the South American contact, I would walk away. Donovan, however, let me know that the feds had to prove I did something knowingly—which of course I didn't. I had no idea what was going on. The problem is, the fellow who met Clara and I at the airport happened to be a major international drug lord. To ensure she could swing the deal, Clara told him I was a new drug runner, with European connections. So he made a point to meet me at the airport, and began saying how happy he was to find a new "transporter." When I asked what in the world he was talking about, he seemed confused for a moment, and excused himself soon after.

"The FBI monitored what was going on. I'm told extradition is under way to get the drug lord guy brought here to the States, where he can be tried...where I am to testify. I was supposed to be under witness protection, but you've seen what protection that offered.

"You and I flew to Santa Fe so I could consult with de Gracia Trust lawyers about the water rights, it was true, but also about what to do next. I was rightly frightened that Browner had been killed. That could have been Cassie. It very nearly *was* you."

Me, I'm still in shock, sitting at my own kitchen table, beside the woman I'm in love with, listening to the unfolding of a story I wouldn't have imagined in my wildest dreams. And I've experienced some wild dreams in my life, conscious or unconscious. I don't intend to drown today, though, under the waters of temporal reality. Not here. Not today. This is Wynne. I'd found her. Well, she'd found me, and she loves me. I'm not going to lose her. Not now.

"Wynne, this is all hard for me to get a good, solid grasp on, but maybe witness protection is a good thing. I don't want to lose you. Who in the hell were those guys in the SUV?"

Wynne continues. "Matt, I have no choice about protective custody. And to answer your question about the guys in the SUV, Ballard and Company haven't yet been able to identify them. They suspect all of this has been an attempt to keep me from testifying. A couple of Texas arrests were made a long time ago actually, and we've just been waiting for trials—and extradition."

She stops. Her eyes search mine again. "So, I wasn't exactly being truthful with you either. You just thought you shouldn't tell me you loved me. What I was hiding turned out to be life threatening. Big difference." She smiles that melt-your-heart Wynne smile. "You're forgiven."

I laugh. She squeezes my hands. I squeeze back, and soften my expression. My resistance to this situation is not going to help. Won't change a damn thing. I look again into those gray-green eyes, realizing I might not get to do that again for who knows how long. I take in her soft, beautiful skin, and reach my right hand up, caressing her temples and cheeks with the backs of my fingers, slowly, tenderly, and lovingly. She closes her eyes. Tears begin to slide toward my fingers. I lean toward her, and kiss them from her face.

"Ballard is here to collect me. They're concerned for my safety after what they're certain was an attempt on your life. I'm going to an undisclosed location to be placed in a safe house until several trials are over. Then I can come home. And come home to you, if you'll still have me."

She goes silent. Looking into my eyes, Wynne squeezes my

hands. I squeeze back.

"Can I come visit you?"

"No, Matt, it's too dangerous, for all of us."

"What about Cassie, and the ranch, and, and everything else?"

"Cassie knows everything now. My parents have been named Cassie's guardians, with Gregg Kearney, and yourself if you're willing, as alternates. The ranch is in good hands. Clancy will watch over things, and I've assembled a team to handle absolutely everything while I'm away. *Wambli Gleska* will remain hangared, but will need to be started and flown every three or four weeks.

"I've arranged flight lessons for you if you're interested. And Fiorio needs regular care and exercise. Matt, you drive him like you flew the Cessna—and like you make love to me: smoothly, sensually, with perfect discernment and attenuation of our capabilities, needs, desires, endurance, and happiness. Will you keep him here for me? I've arranged for my insurance to include you on the policy. All you need do is call my agent's number." Wynne gets up and walks into the living room. She returns to the kitchen table with a stack of file folders. The top one is titled *Insurance*. "These folders contain copies of everything legal, medical, and otherwise pertaining to my personal affairs. I'm asking you a huge favor: to start up the foundation, and to help keep an eye on things while I'm gone."

I look deep into wet, red eyes, while tears well up in my own.

"I've arranged for a money market account to be created in your name to pay for any expenses you incur. I mean *anything*, Matt. Go see Cassie if she needs it. Learn to be an eagle so we can fly together in *Wambli Gleska*. In fact, feel free to bring the Cessna down here if you learn quickly and get your license. There are excellent private air services at Colorado Springs Airport."

I feel embarrassed, sheepish.

Wynne takes my hands again, and lifts them. She kisses each of my fingers. "Please don't feel guilty. I know you. I know that's what you're feeling. Give it up, love."

She smiles. I try. "Matt, I love you. Please help keep things in order. Get the foundation started on a solid footing: I know you can easily do that. Pay yourself—and you're aware of what this level of service is worth—don't make me send an enforcer. Rent office space outside your home. Hire an assistant. You have all the information you need in those folders, Matt—just go with it. Be Cassie's friend and confidant. She loves you, and trusts you like I've never seen her trust anyone before."

I nod. "You bet. Will you come back to me? When this is all over?"

She smiles painfully, and starts crying hard. "Matt, of course I will. I've been looking for the missing piece to my puzzle forever. You're it, my love—my missing piece. I love you."

I wrap my arms around her, and hold her close: two pieces each completing the other's puzzle. We're both crying as she gently pushes me away.

"I'll be mostly unavailable until after the trials. Not even email. If anything comes up, you'll hear from Donovan in Santa Fe, or possibly Gregg or Agent Ballard. You can get messages to me only through Donovan or Ballard."

"Wynne, I can't believe this is happening. This is so unfair. Especially now." I sit up, and straighten my back. "But *know* I'll be here for you—and for Cassie, and in any other way you need."

Tears are streaming down our cheeks. We hold each other close. I kiss her again, and again and again.

She pushes me away, not playfully this time, but gently, lovingly, eyes smiling, mouth sorrowful. "Matt, I have to go now. Ballard was kind enough to give me time with you to explain, but we need to be in Denver so I can be flown—to where I don't know."

"I can't let you go, Wynne."

"You have to, love. You know I don't want to go, but surely you can see I've no choice in the matter."

She stands and starts for the door. We're hand in hand. Agent Ballard ambles out of his gray Ford when we come out of the house. Wynne stops at Fiorio, reaching into the back for a single piece of carryon luggage and an over-the-shoulder travel bag. She starts to pull up the handle to roll the bag. I stop her, and pick up the bag. It's heavy. I take her hand again and don't let go. Ballard is standing there, looking down, holding the back door of the car open.

"Ms. Worner," he says, still looking down, "we really must go." Then he looks over at me. "Good to see you again, Matt."

I don't answer. What's happening isn't his fault, but I need someone to be pissed at.

He extends his hand. The shake is firmly gentle and friendly. I can't give him a Sioux shake though. I'm mad. Wynne hadn't known what the cargo was. This is damned unfair.

Wynne turns to me, crying. "Matt, I love you so much. I hope you can wait for me. Maybe I'll get lucky somehow and this will all end sooner than anticipated. I just don't know. But...." She sobs. "...I don't want to lose you. I've never been happier—or more sure of love. I'll understand if you can't wait."

"I love you, too, sweetheart. You know I'll be here." I throw my arms around her and hold her so close neither of us can breathe.

She whispers in my ear. "I have to go, love. Take care of Cassie and the foundation—start thinking of a good name for it. I love you." She has to push me away.

She turns to Agent Ballard and nods once. He protects her head as she climbs into the mini jail cell in the back of that Ford, makes sure she's in safely, and closes the door. He turns back to me, extends his hand again, and says, "If anything comes up, Matt, you have my card, right?"

I shake his hand. "Yes sir, I sure do."

"Don't hesitate to use it. You may still be in danger. We can't place you under protection, though please understand that to some degree there will be eyes watching over you."

Calmly I say, "More than you know, sir. More than you know." My eyes remain fixed on Wynne's gray-greens.

Ballard looks at me a moment, his head cocked just a little bit, and then turns away. He gets in, starts the mobile jail cell and drives down my gentle curving lane, away from Sleeping Bear Oasis.

Wynne turns, looking back through the rear window, and blows me a kiss as that gray Crown Victoria rounds the curve and winds out of sight.

Chapter Sixty-One: Waterfall

"It feels more like seven years than seven weeks."

"I know, right? Thank you so much, Matt, for being there for Mom—and for me. Mom and I always talked to each other or emailed at least every few days. It's awesome that I get to talk to you."

"Cassie, you and your mom sound so much alike—it's almost like having her to talk to. And you're keeping me on task here in the office, too—you tyrant."

She laughs with youthful exuberance. "You're so fun."

It was James' knock: a one, one-two-three, one-two beat. "Come on in, James."

"Sorry to disturb you, Matt, but there's some executive guy on the phone. He's insisting he talk to you right now, and says it's critical to the success of the foundation."

"Okay. Ask him to give me a minute."

He nods, and quietly clicks closed the solid wood door to my Manitou office. I was fortunate to find this suite. All of the original maple trim is that gorgeous, auburn, prosperity/fame *Feng Shui* shade. With its oak floors, wool area rugs radiating all the pure spectral colors, and southern and east-facing bay windows, sunny mornings in this antique space are especially warm, lush, and inspirational.

"I guess I should go, Cassie. It's another 'I'm here to save your butt, though we really just want to take your money' call. People from the dinosaur days of business annoy me. They still think that the economy will return to *normal*, and play the same old, tired, power games. Jeez. Well, I'm definitely not judgmental, am I?"

She giggles freely. "I grok that."

"Grok."

"Grok."

"Grok. How'd we start doing that, Cassie? We sound like alien frogs."

"Heinlein would be proud."

It's my turn to giggle freely. "I'll call back this afternoon—late tonight for you, eh?"

"You don't need to, Matt. You're doing great, right? Mom was totally on to ask you to run this operation. You don't need my input."

"Yes I do. Your thoughts are fresh, and your goals help direct the foundation's purpose—all in cosmic alignment."

She laughs. "Right. Dude, get to your dinosaur. Catch you later. Thanks, really, for being there. I love you."

"Love you too, girl."

I push one button to disconnect Cassie, and press the blinking one. "Hello, this is Matt."

"Mr. Hale, this is Charles Winsom, CEO of Particle Energy Corporation. How are you today, sir?"

"I'm well enough, I suppose, Mr. Winsom. How can I help you?"

"Call me Charlie. My Board has asked that I secure the rights to the foundation's products. We feel we can bring these technologies to market in a way that is acceptable to your organizational goals—and still enable enormous profits for all concerned."

"Mr. Winsom, thank you for your interest, but what this foundation is about...." I'm thinking. "...Is pretty much the exact opposite of what you propose. You see—"

He interrupts. "Mr. Hale, consider this: Grand ideas to create good never work out. Implementation of your product line will require a business organization with efficiencies and markets already in place. We can do that—we *will* do that. With Mrs. Worner in protective custody, you don't even have the head of the organization available to lead the charge, and make these kinds of critical decisions. You need us. And we will deliver."

"Mr. Winsom...."

"Call me Charlie."

"Charlie, let me just say this. You're welcome to send a proposal to my attention if you like, but I encourage you to not take the time. It's important for you to understand that your organization and this foundation are not on the same path. We have a plan, and we will successfully carry out that plan. Are there areas that we need help? Yes. Is there any room for the profit motive in anything this foundation is predicated upon? Absolutely not. So, while I thank you for your interest, I must get back to work."

"But Mr. Hale, we're offering...."

"Please Mr. Winsom, we simply are not interested. Thank you again. Goodbye now."

Flying fingers press the Find button after typing "Particle Energy Corporation" into Advanced Search. Up comes the website. "Knowledge Engaging Resources" says the motto, or slogan, or whatever it is. Locations: Headquarters and Corporate Offices, New Orleans; Leased refineries, Denningland, Texas and Zacapa, Guatemala. My heart nearly pounds its way right through my chest. There are hyperlinks for each location, and I click on Zacapa. Examining the website under a microscopic eye, intuition screaming, I find a staff directory subtly buried inside a site map—*Holy crap*!

I press the speed dial button for Donovan's personal phone.

"Hi Matt. What's up?"

"Donovan, how is it that anyone would know Wynne is in protective custody?"

"Only those in the loop know. The FBI knows. Gregg Kearney knows. You, Cassie and Clancy know, and my office knows. To the rest of the world, Wynne is in Spain attending family who are ill."

"Hm. Okay, I was just curious. Sorry to bother you for such a trivial question."

"There are no trivial questions, Matt. Are you and Cassie ready for us to establish a formal foundation name yet?"

"Not yet, Donovan. I really don't want to do that until we get Wynne back, and until then our 501-C-3 status is happy with the temporary name."

"You're right, Matt. Is there anything else?"

"That'll do it, Donovan. Thanks again. Talk to you soon."

"Have a good day, Matt. Bye."

I rifle through my desk-drawer cubby, filled with business cards, and punch in the cell number.

"Hello, Matt. This is a surprise. I haven't heard from you at all. Is there a problem?"

"No, sir. There's a solution."

~~~

Thump; thump-thump-thump; thump-thump.

"James, the door's wide open."

He's leaning on, and peering around the door jam. "I know. It's still polite to knock first, though."
~~~

"Fair enough. What's up?"

"Someone's here to see you."

I glance at the open appointment book in the lower right corner of my desk. "I don't have anything scheduled. Is it important?"

"I think so."

When I look up from my calendar, wavy golden hair is peeking over his shoulder. My eyes instantly flood with tears.

My voice chokes. "Wynne!" I shove my wheeled office chair behind me and run for the doorway. She moves to the middle of the opening, travel bag on her shoulder, arms wide open. I thump into her, my arms enfolding her with all the strength I can muster.

"Yuuuugh."

I squeeze even harder.

"Yuuuuuugh."

With my head in her hair, my nose inhaling her neck, and joyful water drips tapping onto her shoulder, I muster these words: "Wynne, oh Wynne—missed you—missed you so much. Oh my sweet Wynne...."

"Me, too, love. Me, too."

"Are you home to stay?"

"My hero—you freed me. *You* found the key. Clara told me she and Mark were separated—separated only by distance as it turns out. It was only a tiny subsidiary, hidden deep inside a corporate web that was trying in the most polite, innocuous ways to purchase the San Luis water, *and* take over the de Gracia trust's green energy plans."

I lean back to look in her gray-greens, and wipe moisture from my blues.

"That tactic was shrewd. If I were to sell out, they were the direction I was leaning. And it turns out the drug lord is real, but wasn't the man at the Puerto Barrios airport. He was instead a corporate executive—trying to set me up. The only flaw was that Clara, on the return flight, couldn't bring herself to tell me what our cargo really was—that was supposed to have sucked me in out of fear that anyone would find out, and let them blackmail me. I'm so thankful for Donovan's legal team, who were able to discover the mole in their practice; for Clara, who finally spilled truth onto the Denver Federal Center floor—and for you."

While I melt into her soul, she whispers in my ear.

"Yes, love, I'm home to stay."

<center>~~~</center>

"You had the lasagna."

"Yeah, I'm still relatively predictable."

"To some extent, that's a good thing. I don't think you're the type of guy to get into a rut too deep."

"Especially with you around to keep me growing."

She rolls onto her left side and slips a leg over me. With her voice low enough to be nearly a whisper, Wynne asks, "So are you ready to move to Aspen?"

"Are you serious? That's a giant leap for two lovers who've only just met."

"You really believe that?"

"What?"

"That we've only just met?"

"Well, sort of...."

"Matt, we've been together a long, long time. You know that. You feel it, too. Are you having second thoughts about us?"

I roll onto my right side, and shove down the edges of our pillows, so I can swim in her eyes. "No way! It's just—what are you saying? You want me to come live with you? Sweetheart, I'm there in a heartbeat. There's so much to consider. The foundation office is definitely not in a permanent location, but there's my house...all the stuff I've got in here...you haven't even seen inside the garage. That'll scare you away forever."

She laughs. "You don't scare me. We'll build an addition to the ranch house for you."

It's my turn to laugh—and then I roll over on top of my sweet lover and companion. "Now, *that* scares me."

"We have much to do, love, and so much is about to come our way together. We have an economic paradigm to transform—and our future to unfurl. I can't wait."

I whisper into that silky smooth crease in her neck, my face and nose nestled into that lavender scented sandy blonde hair, "Me too, Wynne—me too."

9 781946 736055